TIGER LILY

T STEDMAN

Tiger Lily

By
T Stedman

ISBN (print) 978-0-9933098-4-7

Website www.tstedman.com
Cover Art
by
Anna Dittmann

Print edition
Edited by
Helen Williams and Nicky Jeans

This edition published: March 2017

<u>*The Royal Families*</u>
<u>*Of Atlantis*</u>

Dubonnetti
Bonaci
Santalini
Florianna

<u>*Of Murrtaine*</u>
Borge

PROLOGUE

LONDON – EIGHT YEARS PREVIOUSLY

*I*t didn't take long for the nice act to wear off. Sid had brought her to this place. Lilian Gale thought her luck had changed at last after sleeping rough and wandering from one drug-infested place after another for the best part of a year.

He'd chatted to her over a period of time. Bought her cups of tea and doughnuts – she should have known. At only twelve years of age, life had already taught her that if something felt too good to be true, then it probably was. But she was sick of being cold. Sick of being hungry and in the company of drunks and druggies. And, most of all, sick of people who'd sell you down the river in a heartbeat. There had to be more to life than this, *didn't there?*

"Come meet some friends of mine," he said. "It's warm and dry, and if I ask them nicely, they might even let you stay. I've a few contacts, maybe you can earn some cash in hand, know what I mean," he finished, raising his eyebrows as if she followed his drift.

Slightly bewildered, and with the embers of hope still alive in her soul somewhere, she'd gone along.

It all happened so fast. After making her a cheese sandwich and several cups of tea, she was welcomed into the busy household. Any concern was quickly smoothed over with a promise that she could pay rent as soon as she'd earned it. Despite feeling uneasy, there didn't seem to be any logical reason to say no.

The place seemed to have loads of bedrooms with two girls to a room. Lily got to share a room with a girl called Holly. She couldn't believe her luck in landing a place.

Day by day, she began to relax. Not enough to let anyone see her weird striped skin, but enough that she smiled and went out and about with the other girls. The house was always full and noisy and never got dull. Everything seemed great and she began to think her first fears of a 'catch' were unfounded, and put it down to paranoia. Then, over time, as young as she was, it began to dawn on her what kind of place it was. And what the girls did to earn their money and their keep. But no one said anything to her and left her alone, so she settled into an easy life, with Sid coming around every now and then to check on her.

Conscious of not being a burden, she made herself useful by keeping the place tidy and by always being helpful to everyone. She was determined to carve out a role so she wouldn't be kicked out.

All was going well until Sid came one night, sat down in the kitchen and said he had a special job for her.

Her heart began to thump. She was mute, so thankfully, no one expected her to say anything. So she sat still and waited for him to explain.

"Don't worry, Lil, I won't let him hurt ya … he's proper posh. He'll look after ya." He winked and nudged her. "An' if you play your cards right, he'll see ya again … might even be a regular thing."

Prue, the mother figure of the house, and a couple of the

girls were standing around the room holding their breath, she was sure. With a heavy heart, Lily looked around at their regretful smiles. She wasn't so stupid that she didn't know what Sid was driving at. *What else could she do?* The alternative was the streets.

THAT NIGHT, Holly helped her dress. "Won't be too bad, love … you'll soon get used to it."

It was supposed to make her feel better, but her heart was filled with dread. She'd never had any illusions about love; the whole fairy-tale prince thing was so far out of her realm of experience, she wasn't sure she ever believed in him anyway. *Who would possibly want a freak like her? But still – this?* It was never on her list of things to do when she grew up.

Sid came for her at 8 p.m. and they rode in the back of a black cab together to a private address in Fulham. As they waited on the doorstep, Sid whispered, "Just go with the flow, girl. Okay? I'll just be waiting outside. Be back for you in an hour."

The door opened and a butler ushered them in. Lily thought it was the poshest place she'd ever seen. Walking slowly through the tiled hall with beautiful dark wood furniture everywhere, she felt self-conscious when the heels of her boots clip-clopped and echoed up to the ceiling. She wriggled the short skirt lower that Holly had lent her. She was supposed to look older, but her unruly curly hair stuck out in every direction like a doll's, making her look her age.

"Come in," a male voice said from the room in front of them.

The butler showed them in.

Even though she hadn't done anything like this before,

Lily felt ashamed. The butler, who never made eye contact with her once, swiftly left the room.

The man, simply referred to as sir, was fat, bald and sweating profusely. He was sitting next to an open fire, which made no sense. Her heart hammered, making her head swim for a second. The room was so hot.

"Wait there," Sid said under his breath, and approached the old gentleman.

Some hushed negotiations took place, and an envelope was passed between them. Have fun!" Sid said chirpily. "Be a good girl, Lil," he said as he passed her. "Be back in an hour."

Now left on her own, every part of her screamed for help. The man crooked a finger to indicate that she come closer. She swallowed hard and edged nearer. Her eyes widened in shock when he put his sweaty hands on her. She almost gagged. He didn't seem to notice and pulled her down into his lap, slobbering his mouth over hers. She retched, then choked, as if something were stuck in her throat. She was unsure what happened exactly. All she knew was the old git went the darkest shade of red she'd ever seen a person go – as if his head was about to explode. Lily jumped up and watched in horror as he grabbed his chest.

The old man began to sink and writhe in his chair, then slipped to the floor like a massive blob of quivering fat. But instead of hightailing it out of there, her feet were rooted to the spot. Her pulse was through the roof and she was paralyzed with fear. She knew she should run, but her breaths were coming out in shallow pants and she couldn't get any air.

Lily concentrated on getting a grip on her emotions before she lost it entirely. And when he hadn't moved for a whole minute, she inched forward and touched the side of his neck like she'd seen them do in the films. She couldn't feel anything. His eyes were open, staring ahead and unseeing.

Shit! He'd snuffed it. She began to shuffle her feet and edge towards the door. Opening it enough to peer her head out into the hallway, she sneaked out and crept slowly towards the front door. Then, snatching it open, she bolted down the steps.

Before she could disappear into the night, Sid stepped out from the shadows and caught her by the arm.

Gone was the chirpy cockney chancer; instead, his face snarled into a grimace while he spat through gritted teeth, "Get the fuck back in there and do your job, you little bitch!"

Having no voice, all she could do was shake her head maniacally and point back at the house in the hope he'd understand. She dragged a thumb across her neck to indicate the old bloke had died, but Sid was already pulling her back towards the house and the door, which had been left open.

They were halfway up the steps when the butler appeared in the doorway. "You there! ... Stop! Murderer ... Call the police!"

Sid stopped dead in his tracks. The mere mention of the police and he wanted as much space between them and him as possible. He turned on his heel and dragged Lily with him into the dark streets and away.

LILY WAS white with terror when Sid dragged her back into the house, where she stayed. The door slammed and he swung her around to face him. "What did you fucking do?" he shouted like a madman.

She shook her head, her eyes wide with terror.

"Whatever's up?" Prue's voice said from behind him. "Go easy, Sid ... What happened?"

"She killed him ... that's what she fucking done!"

Prue put her hand to her mouth in shock and Lily was still shaking her head like a maniac. The hallway began to fill with the others, all trying to see what the fuss was about.

Sid backhanded Lily across the face. "Tell me what happened!" he screamed.

Whispers and gasps came from the crowd that had gathered around them. Some tried to mention that she couldn't talk. Lily was so scared she felt a warm trickle down her leg.

"Yes, she fucking can," Sid shouted and swiped her face again.

"Sid, do they know who you are at that place?" Prue was saying in his ear. "Get a pencil and paper!" she ordered.

Everything was coming at Lily in a jumble and she felt faint from fear.

A couple of sheepish-looking male clients were slipping out of the door to escape.

"I'll make her fucking talk," Sid said, and began dragging her up the stairs by the hair.

They reached a bathroom and Sid held her while he screamed at a girl and a client to get out. They hurriedly wrapped towels around themselves and left. Sid yanked her in, slammed the door, and locked them inside.

"Oh my god, he's gonna kill her," Lily heard through the door.

Her knees shook, her eyes were wide and she was so scared she was numb. It was as though she were there but removed from the situation. Nothing was registering any more. She was standing stiff and powerless when he suddenly, roughly, turned her around and yanked her forward so she was bent over the filled bath. Then he plunged her head into the murky, warm water.

Sid held her under for one, two, three, four minutes, without letting her up for a breath. First of all she fought like a mad thing – bubbles sprouting from her nose and mouth.

All the while, his muffled voice was screaming, "Talk, you fucking bitch! I know you can talk … Whoring too good for ya? … I'll teach ya!" until he eventually yanked her head up out of the water. Then, when all she could do was gulp and gasp, he thrust her head back down and held it down for what felt like ages.

After a while, her head felt fuzzy; his shouting voice and the incessant banging on the door melded together into one thunderous drone. Lily allowed herself to relax. With her heart still beating like a train, she asked herself the question: why was she fighting at all? For Sid to find another punter for her? *No fucking way!* And so she allowed herself to go limp and the water to gradually enter her lungs.

At first she thought it would hurt, but as the water seeped in, she welcomed it.

WHEN THE LITTLE bitch hadn't moved for quite some time, Sid's temper abated. *Fuck! He'd killed her.* His mind whirred to find a way to get rid of her body without the others in the house knowing. Then he shrugged. The girls wouldn't say anything. It would serve as a good warning to anyone who would get any big ideas.

So he slowly let go of Lily's hair and stepped back. *Shit!* He wiped his sweaty brow on the back of his forearm. Drowning someone was harder work than he imagined.

A sudden twitch caught his eye. "FUCK!" he shouted, and bounced back, smacking himself against the bathroom wall.

The arms that had hung limply by her sides were moving to grip the edges of the bath. *She can't be?* He watched in horror as she pushed herself up so her face came up out of the water. What made it so terrifying was that, despite the fact that she should be dead, was the slow and deliberate way she was moving. It shocked him into inactivity. Then, when she slowly turned to face him and moved the sopping curls away from her face, all he could do was scream. Water spewed from her mouth as she coughed up her lungs and stood in front of him like some kind of monster. Like something out of a horror film. *The Ring*, perhaps, where the creature crawls out from the TV.

Her eyes were scary enough – they were the size of a two-pence piece. Huge black disks with jagged flecks of blue around the edge and no whites at all. But her face was like nothing he'd ever seen in his life before. Thick black stripes were slashed under each cheekbone, diagonally across her forehead and a V at her chin. They crisscrossed down her neck, covering her like some kind of snake.

She was slowly rising from her knees to stand up in front of him. By the time he realised that the awful wailing noise was coming from his own throat, she was moving towards him. His eyes darted left to the arm she used to reach out and slide the bolt on the door. Then she hissed at him like a vampire baring extended canines. She blinked slowly over her otherworldly eyes, opened the door and left the room.

He was left breathing hard, covering his eyes with his hands. Looking down, he realised he'd pissed himself.

Sid never saw Lily again.

CHAPTER 1

Southern California – Present day

It was already dark when Shona smacked the side of the van and it pulled away. It had been a while since she was last here. Unperturbed, she dumped her stuff off at a hostel she knew and went out to bump into old friends. She knew just the place to find somewhere more permanent to stay. It took her no more than half an hour to be out and in Blue Predators – a downtown San Diego club. Known for its live music, every surfer (particularly of the Atlantean persuasion) within a five-mile radius frequented it. Some joked that the club's name came from their tiger-like stripes that emerged on their skin, although it was probably one of those urban myths. Besides, most of the Atlanteans around here barely showed visible stripes even in the water, their blood was so watered down with Human DNA.

Shona went straight to the bar, ordered a beer, nodded at a few familiar faces, then wended her way through the crowds to the main room where the source of the funky music was. It was a surprise as this place usually played Alt or Trop rock. The sound would have been more at home in

Chicago, Philly, or Europe. It was cool though, and drew her closer. Looking around her, everyone was hooked into it, too. Three guys were playing their hearts out: lead guitar, vocals, keyboard, and a little South American guy was hammering away on percussion. *Sweet.*

Hello! ... There on the drums, partially hidden by a bank of impressive kit, was the most beautiful young ball of fury, pelting out rhythm with every muscle of her petite body. Even her head moved from left to right, swinging her shoulder-length dark corkscrew curls, making her look like a sea urchin.

Shona moved in closer to get a better look at her.

The girl was wearing battered, ripped jeans and a vest top, with red sweatbands around each wrist.

Shona's heart stopped. *She wouldn't ... would she be so stupid?*

Light grey but clearly visible, there were distinct stripes crisscrossing her arms and over her shoulders.

Shona looked around her nervously, hoping no one else had clocked the same thing. If the kid was some kind of tattooed wannabe Atlantean, she was taking a risk coming in here.

She breathed out uneasily. The place was buzzing, and everyone appeared hooked into the band's soul funk groove, but even here, where everyone was mainly Atlantean, no one came out of the water striped in public. It wasn't uncommon for people to come in off the street, oblivious to the club's orientation.

Shona edged towards the small raised stage to get a closer look. The girl was sweating, making stripes less likely to appear if she were a real Atlantean – a bit of a let-down. Stripes only usually put in an appearance when wet and cool. Wetsuits covered these, but if spotted at the beach, they always passed their markings off as tattoos. *And yet could she be?* They looked so authentic.

Shona was a common Atlantean from a family of all girls from Western Australia. Being common meant she was mixed-blooded and not royal. And being the eldest girl, the talisman for being a Protector – the ancient honour of being a body-guard to a Siren – had come down to her. A title she thought she'd never use. But today, looking around her at the sweating, dancing bodies, feeling the tingle that made her hairs stand on end, she had to begin to wonder. *Could it be that this ball of dyna-mite drumming everyone into a frenzy was one of the Sirens, the whole of the Atlantean, and much of the Human worlds were after?* It blew her mind when she got to thinking on it – children's bedtime stories of beautiful women luring men to the rocks with magical music and singing. *This was the twenty-first century, for Christ's sake. A drummer could totally be the updated version.*

Shit, even here, where she came on her quest for an endless summer, they'd all sat around the campfire at the end of a day's surfing and speculated. Comparing stories of old legends and whether or not they were true. Tales told to them by their families about their mysterious origins. And Sirens or, more accurately, Soul Breathers, imagined as objects of the supernatural and the stuff of dreams.

The more she thought, the more her heart began to hammer. *Just supposing she was one? What the fuck should she do with her?* She couldn't let her slip through her fingers, just in case. To her knowledge, she'd never come across one, nor had anyone she knew. *Should she tell someone? No, not yet ... she needed time to think – to make sure first.* There wasn't a list of dos or don'ts with her talisman, just an order to look out for one – *real helpful.*

Twenty-first century or not, Shona knew they were in constant danger, and were precious to the right people –

beyond price. The song was ending, forcing a quick decision – she would stick with her and try to get her to talk. For now, that was the best course of action before the girl shot through like a Bondi tram.

The band went on to play another two songs before they brought the house down with an old James Brown number. The rammed room was reluctant to let them finish, but Shelly – the resident DJ – quickly took over and the crowd soon simmered down to a hum of chatter and forgot about the band. The girl left her kit and soon got swallowed up by the hordes. Shona pushed through, elbowing people as she went so as not to lose her.

They came out to the bar, where the manager appeared to be congratulating them and shaking the lead singer's hand. He reached into his jacket pocket and handed over what looked like payment for their evening's work.

The girl was standing slightly apart, looking a little awkward and not talking to anyone. The band seemed to be ignoring her, unlike most of the men around her. The girl seemed oblivious to the effect she was having. Shona edged closer, trying to think of an icebreaker.

Then she wasn't sure what exactly started it. The band guys were laughing and fooling around and one of a group of drunken guys next to them seemed to get offended and pushed. Everything happened so fast.

Bloody Humans, drunk and spoiling for a fight, all started to get involved. A glass got smashed, a beer got knocked flying and fists began to fly as well. Bouncers soon homed in on the scene, surrounded them and began to herd the troublemakers outside.

The girl, now completely apart from the others, was shaking liquid off her arms and flicking it off the front of her vest quite anxiously. She must have copped the whole pint when it went airborne.

Shit. Shona knew instantly why the girl was so alarmed. The previously visible grey stripes crisscrossing her arms were now fast becoming darker and more prominent by the minute. She wasted no more time and pushed through a couple in conversation until she came up alongside her. "Put this on," she ordered.

The girl looked at her, bemused for a second. But necessity snapped her into action and she took Shona's denim jacket and quickly slipped it on.

"Let's get out of here," Shona said, grabbing her by the hand and leading her outside to the street.

The girl went along without saying a word.

When they were a safe distance away, Shona turned and faced her. "What are you doing, exposing yourself like that?"

The girl just glared at her like she didn't understand the big deal or what it was to do with her.

"What's the matter ... cat got your tongue?" Shona said, frowning.

The girl blinked and started to look even more pissed off.

Shona reined it in a bit. The last thing she wanted to do was send the girl running. "Look, I'm sorry I had a go at ya, but you can't go around like that – not here." She looked furtively around and indicated to the girl's now-covered forearms. The markings were now licking up the side of her neck and were amazing. There weren't that many people she had met in her life with stripes that dark.

"What's ya name? I'm Shona," she said, dragging her eyes away from them.

The girl bit her lip.

Shona shifted her weight impatiently. *Fuck's sake,* "Can't ya talk?"

The girl swallowed uncomfortably and shook her head.

Shona's heart stalled. *Shit!* Maybe she was foreign. "Can you understand me?"

The girl rolled her eyes and nodded.

After studying her for a beat, Shona came to a decision when more people began to empty out of the club and come their way. "Let's get outta here."

They walked away quickly, with the girl keeping step with her. Shona took out her phone and put it to her ear while she walked. "Lance? … yeah, it's me … no, I'm in town … yeah … I need a pick-up … I know, mate, but it's urgent. … No … I'll explain when I see ya." She clicked off the phone and put it back in her pocket.

The girl was walking silently next to her. *Who the fuck was she? Did she have somewhere to be? She wasn't acting like it. And why wouldn't she talk?* She looked like a little waif, but Shona instinctively knew she was tough underneath.

They came to a corner and Shona stopped. "We'll wait here. My friend'll pick us up in ten." She took a packet of mints from her pocket and offered them to the girl. She shook her head.

"Are you from here?" Shona said, pointing downwards. "America, I mean?"

The girl shook her head again.

"Me neither."

That must be the reason she was reluctant to talk. It was hard having a one-way convo when so many questions burned to be answered. "I'm here for the surf … you surf?" she said louder, as if the girl was deaf and making a waving motion with her hand like some kind of sign language.

The girl sighed loudly, shook her head and averted her eyes.

"What are ya here for then?

The girl shrugged.

"Where ya stayin'?"

The girl looked warily back towards the club.

"What … not with those fuckin' galahs?" Shona said, shaking her head. "Was the agro over money?"

The girl nodded as if embarrassed.

"They didn't want to pay your share," Shona said, filling in the blanks. A humourless smile confirmed what she suspected. "How long ya been here … in the States, I mean?"

The girl held up her hand.

"Five months?"

The girl nodded.

"Here in San Diego?"

She held up two fingers.

"Two months … no, two weeks?" Shona said after the girl quickly shook her head. "Shit …"

In the silence that followed, the girl looked around awkwardly, while Shona couldn't help studying her. Then, before she could launch into any more questions, Lance's van pulled up to the kerb.

He wound down his window and ran an appraising eye over the newbie, then Shona. "Get in," he said.

Shona quickly pulled the girl with her around the other side of the van. After glancing warily back towards the club, the girl got in alongside her.

"This had better be good, Shona, I was in bed," Lance said, with narrowed eyes.

Shona fell in instantly with what he meant and laughed, pulling him towards her roughly and kissing him on the cheek. "Ah, she'll forgive ya … I've got a surprise for everyone."

Lance pulled away and looked at her sideways, waiting for her to spill.

Shona wasn't giving anything away yet.

The girl stared out of her window, miles away.

. . .

LILY HAD NOTHING TO LOSE. The shits she'd tagged along with since leaving New York had refused to pay her, saying she owed rent for the shithole they were living in. They weren't even paying rent anyway.

That had been the story of her life; everyone taking their pound of flesh. She needed a place to stay, so these two would do for now.

She took a surreptitious glance left to check the bloke out and faced straight again ultra-quick. The Aussie bird was chatting away to him like she knew him really well. Not sure about her yet, she was guessing she was gay. Sharp as a tack, though.

She'd let her think she was thick or foreign a bit longer yet. Unable to speak, it was a convenient impression to give people till she could suss them out.

He looked like a typical surfy stoner. So many guys looked like that round here – a mess of blonde overlong hair and tanned skin – not that she took much notice of men.

Lily looked down at her arms. The black bands had receded to dull grey now. It was disturbing that the Aussie girl seemed to recognise them. Perhaps that was why she had allowed her to lead her out of the club and into this van. Since Sid, she had never been that foolish as to go off with anyone. However, always feeling a freak, the question of why and, more importantly, what she was, was something that had burned within her for longer than she could remember.

Shunning the care system, most of her teenage years had been spent on the streets of London. A life of trying to keep warm, ducking and diving, avoiding people traffickers, itching to put her into the sex industry. Hiding her differences until she managed to get into a hostel, a crap job and to play drums whenever she could.

Ever since she was small, rhythm had centred her soul. So it wasn't a giant leap to realise becoming a musician also offered her a way out of squalor. She had promised herself she would come to this sunny coast one day to play. Lured to it like some kind of Mecca. It had taken her a year to save, and here she was. *Whoop-di-fucking-do!* It had been a whole lot of same old, same old so far.

She chanced another quick peek next to her. Shona was rabbiting on and the guy was nodding and, for the briefest second, his eyes flicked to hers. It was only a glance, but a bolt of heat hit her chest and she put her hand to it quickly. A film of sweat then spread over her forehead and top lip. She breathed through it, hoping they wouldn't notice. *Maybe her blood sugar was low or something?*

As she fought to calm her breathing, he looked her way again. A moment of eye contact passed between them and warmth swirled all around her, settling in the pit of her stomach. *Shit!* Her pulse skyrocketed and she snatched her eyes away. She was completely unnerved. It made up her mind. Even though this place had acted like a beacon to her, when she'd had food, a warm bed, and a night's sleep, she was out of there. Something felt off with these people. Alarm bells were ringing all over the place.

CHAPTER 2

Cesaré Florianna stood on the sand and gazed out to sea, swigging his wine straight from the bottle. The one good thing about his hasty retreat from the king's court in Ireland to Southern California was that it was the fall, and the best time to surf. He thanked his lucky stars for that.

His head had been a mess since Isla Snow – the Siren he believed his that had turned out not to be at all. In fact, she had belonged to his first cousin and best friend since childhood – Prince Malleven Mancini, who had royally shafted him.

The two of them had been brought up and educated as brothers. One night, he had called him and told him he had a surprise. Then Malleven had taken him out, got him drunk, and done something to his divining ring.

Cesaré looked down and twisted the replacement he still wore on his left hand – the symbol of all of his hatred. The mystical piece of jewellery forged for each Atlantean prince at birth that could detect a Siren. Meant to be irrefutable proof of authenticity if the pearl-like stone changed to turquoise when one was near.

Cesaré laughed bitterly. *Or deepest purple if she was his destined mate.*

When this had happened for him and Isla, he'd been deliriously happy and felt so blessed. That he, a carefree, nomadic surfer, who never took anything seriously, could be favoured by the fates in such a way. He put his old frivolous life behind him and became Prince Cesaré Florianna, head of his family and member of the king's council, to rule and be revered by the Atlantean world.

Except the whole thing had turned out to be bullshit. Isla had felt so guilty that she wouldn't let him near her. She'd known all along she really belonged to Malleven, who'd got to her at every opportunity behind his back.

The sick truth of it was that not only did Malleven not care about Isla, his true mate, but he cared nothing for Cesaré. That's what got him the most. It had all been to get close enough to the king to try and take his throne.

It had failed, thankfully, but it was a poor consolation when he'd betrayed him so utterly with the woman he hoped to spend the rest of his life with. His ring had been discovered to be a forgery. He'd been disgraced. And, in an instant, his reputation was in tatters. With that, his family's seat on the council was gone, his many brothers and cousins couldn't bear to look at him, and he was laughed at by the whole of the Atlantean world.

Fuck! he was Cesaré Florianna, playboy and lover of women, and he'd been played well and truly by the two people he cared about the most.

He laughed bitterly.

Looking out at the sea and its crashing waves, he threw down the empty bottle of wine he'd been drinking. The ocean seemed to mirror his mood. It cared for nothing, but crashed and smashed itself into the rocks with one huge white roll after another. The noise, the smell, the sheer violence of it, felt like a balm to his simmering soul.

Two hours he'd been back. Even though it was late and dark, he'd dumped off his bag at his apartment and come straight down the many steps to the beach. This was his oasis of calm, a place he thought he'd have to give up for ever for a life of serious responsibility. Well never again. The rest of his life would be his now to do with what he wanted.

Armed with his board and in only his shorts, he paddled out to sea without his wetsuit. To hell with what anyone made of his stripes. *Fuck them all*. His pure royal blood had to count for something, even if it was just to endure the fucking cold. This was where he belonged. To be part of the ocean, where he felt at home, to ride its power and to feel free.

Catching the next wave, he was in the moment. Reading it perfectly, with his gravity low, he rode its energy like the back of a beast. It was the only place to be. Skimming, then flying and soaring, he prolonged the feeling as long as possible. Weightless and hungry for more, over and over, he paddled out, set after set. Focussed on one thing; to lose himself by seizing waves, harnessing momentum, revelling in the cold breeze stinging his exposed skin.

With every nerve ending buzzing with exhilaration, he was the closest to being happy in a very long time. It was the purest way of living that never failed to deliver. And that was where he wanted to stay – no going back. All the shit in his life – being an Atlantean in a Human world, a disgraced prince, was forgotten. Draining all the negative energy away until his limbs felt numb and vibrated with exhaustion. It was an intense cleansing of his soul that left him calm, straddling his board, bobbing and going wherever the undulating water took him.

However, he knew he couldn't stay there for ever. Soon it would be dawn and early surfers would be arriving to catch the dawn light. Life had to be faced sometime. Looking down at his body, he despised his damning Florianna stripes; his were the darkest and most defined of his small surfing crew. It was the reason they had to surf away from the crowds, as well as being the best places for excellent waves. All were Atlantean, to varying degrees depending on the strength of their bloodlines. Some wore wetsuits to cover them, but some were so minimal that they simply passed them off as tattoos. It had earned them the nickname of Tiger Crew around here. He could never escape entirely. The fucking destiny crap would single him out as a prince even if his vivid stripes didn't. He could never win. He sniffed and wiped the snot running from his nose on the back of his hand. Well, he didn't have to give in to it. He could fight.

The Florianna Siren was gone now anyway. Even his cousin Malleven, who'd screwed him over, had been rejected by her and left for dead. His blood boiled for a moment at not being able to have his day with him. Then he sighed deeply. *Poetic justice had won that day... argh, good riddance to bad rubbish!*

The irony of it all was, after all the back-stabbing, Isla Snow had been claimed by Prince Darres Borge from the Borge family of Murrtaine. So their Siren had not only rejected both princes, but the Florianna family as well. And was her prerogative. He chuckled to himself while he looked down again at his ring. The very thing that set him apart as a prince.

He cursed in his native Italian. That shit was never going to happen again. Lightning never strikes twice in the same place. Nor did he want any more of that kind of attention. No, he'd never settled down before Isla, and that was the way he liked it. Wine, women and song, and then fuck off before it was light, had been his motto. It had always made him happy. Only when he'd gone soft and sentimental and allowed his senses to leave him did his life go into a tailspin.

Cesaré worked the ring off his finger. It wasn't hard as he was cold. He held it up to his face, whispered, "*Arrivederci, amore mio*", kissed it and threw as hard and as far as he could. "Fuck all that shit!" he vowed to himself. He would live the rest of his life on his terms and fuck them all.

He caught a last wave into shore, somehow managed to cycle back to his apartment and collapsed into bed and comatose sleep.

CHAPTER 3

Dubonnetti Estate – West Coast of Ireland – a few months previously

Ruby Santalini didn't wait for her driver to walk around the car before she jumped out and slammed the door. "Wait here!" she ordered and turned around to face the imposing grey house that was the Dubonnetti residence. On a rugged coast on the west coast of Ireland, it belonged to a bygone age. The Dubonnettis, like her own family, could trace their roots back to the destruction of Atlantis.

Checking her face in a small compact, she snapped it shut and walked with a crunch over the gravel to the huge oak porch front doors. A loud clang sounded when she pulled the rope next to it. Her heart thumped while she waited. She wasn't sure what she'd do if they weren't in residence. She'd come on such a whim she hadn't thought it through as far as that. Her sources had told her Marco would be home – *the rat!* And she'd hightailed it over here from where she lived with her family in New York.

She'd been seeing Marco Dubonnetti for the last year, and when he'd asked for her to help him get information on her sister-in-law, the Siren Lacy Rain, she'd gone along with it because he was gorgeous and promised her she'd be his queen if he managed to take his brother Dante's crown. Now she was reduced to hammering on his front door when she'd heard he'd been seen with at least two other girls, making it really hard to ignore the little voice in the back of her mind telling her she'd been used. She'd been trying to get hold of him for ages, but he'd been totally elusive over the last few weeks. Well, she wasn't going to be made a fool of, and had come all the way here to have it out with him once and for all.

After what felt like a lifetime, the door creaked open. A maid answered and invited her into the dark, musty hallway. The wood-panelled room reminded her of something from the Addams Family.

"Mr Dubonnetti will see you in the study, Miss Santalini," the maid said, smiling.

Feeling justified in making the long journey, she marched past her into the study with her temper firing up and ready to go.

It deflated abruptly into irritation when she saw Christian Dubonnetti and not Marco sitting behind the old desk. "Where is Marco?" she demanded.

His father ignored her rudeness and smiled. "Please sit down, Ruby ... would you like some tea, dear?"

She huffed and plonked herself down into the chair opposite him.

Christian pulled a cord hanging from the ceiling next to him. The maid returned and Christian ordered the tea. She disappeared and left the two of them alone.

"I'm not leaving until I see him," Ruby said. "I can wait all day."

Christian smiled and leaned back in his chair, studying

her and steepling his fingers. "He's not home, I'm afraid, Ruby."

She huffed noisily again. "I know he's here, Christian."

"I assure you he is not," he said calmly.

The standoff was only interrupted when the maid returned carrying a tray. She placed it down and left quickly when Christian waved her away with a hand. "I'll pour," he said, smiling sweetly at Ruby.

She wanted to stamp her feet, but instead rolled her eyes.

He pushed her filled cup and saucer towards her. "What are you doing here, really, Ruby?" he asked, quirking an eyebrow.

His manner was really beginning to annoy her now. "I told you …"

Christian held up a hand, halting her mid-sentence. He nodded with a sigh. "Let me rephrase … why are you wasting your time on my son, who is clearly not interested in you?" he finished, blinking and smiling as if he was complimenting her and not stabbing her through the heart. Her lip quivered for a moment and she disguised it by taking a small sip of tea. "I don't know what you mean?" she said, more as a deflection to stop herself from bursting into tears.

Christian looked over the rims of his glasses at her sardonically. "Come now, Ruby, I know you are cleverer than that?"

She frowned slightly while she discerned the compliment hidden somewhere in there and set down her teacup. A lump had risen in her throat that she couldn't shift, making it very hard to speak without bawling like a baby. *What was she doing here, really?* She took a tissue hurriedly out of her bag and dabbed her eyes, trying desperately not to burst into tears.

Christian relented. "Come, come, please don't," he said, rising from his chair and walking around to her side of the desk, where he perched on the edge. He folded his arms. "I didn't mean to upset you. I just don't understand why a gorgeous girl like you allows someone to walk all over her like that."

For a second, her eyes darted to his in anger, but slunk away again when she knew he was right. It was a compliment, really, and he did seem genuinely concerned. She began to cry in earnest. It was as if all the waiting around for calls and hearing all the damning rumours all came to a head at that moment.

"There, there," he said, unperturbed, and patted her shoulder. "Surely you have men battering down your door to take you out?"

She pulled herself together slightly. "It's tough coming from my family, you know?" Her eyes went up to his.

Christian nodded sagely. "I can imagine … a family of soldiers would intimidate somewhat." He appeared to be studying her as if making up his mind about something. Then he shook his head as if he'd decided against it.

"What is it?" she said.

Christian sat back, pulled a face and frowned. "Well, I was thinking …"

"What?" she urged.

"What about if I helped you find a nice suitor?"

Ruby pulled a face and narrowed her eyes. The man was a crafty old reprobate – everyone knew it, and yet her life was miserable. And he was right about Marco; she had to admit to herself that he wasn't really interested in her, as much as it hurt her pride. Perhaps he could help her. "What do you mean, like set me up, or something?"

Christian put his head back and laughed heartily. "You youngsters, so forward these days," he said, still amused. "Nothing as vulgar as that, my dear. I was thinking of maybe putting someone in your path and letting you and your womanly wiles do the rest," he finished, letting his eyes roam over her suggestively.

She crossed her legs. Looking up into his enquiring, amused face, she forced herself to remember that the alternative was to go back to her previous existence, where any of the very few men she liked were too scared to date her for fear of her many cousins and brothers, all the size of houses.

Then she tried to think of suitable dates and came up with zero. None of the single royals she could think of were remotely interesting to her. She shook her head hopelessly and looked down at her hands. There was no one as beautiful and talented as her Marco. *He was a bloody film star, for god's sake.* No one could come remotely close to that.

Christian appeared to read her mind. "Marco is not for you, my dear … Even if he weren't selfish and disloyal, he has a destiny to fulfil."

Ruby sagged in her chair. He was right, it was hopeless. Whether she believed it was his destiny or not, Marco had designs on his brother's crown, and for that, he needed to marry a Siren.

A sob shuddered in her chest. How she hated the Sirens who ensnared everyone; she'd never get a look in. Then she took a deep breath of resignation. "Who did you have in mind?" she asked, hardly able to bring herself to look at him, she felt so wretched. Whoever it was wouldn't be a patch on Marco.

"I have another son …" he said quietly, waiting for her to cotton on.

Ruby looked at him intently, running through the names of all his sons. *Antonio was gay. Paulo … not her type at all. Stephan was too young and totally loved-up with the sea witch.* With no clue what he was driving at, she shrugged, shaking her head.

"My adopted son," Christian said finally, with a wicked smile.

It took her a full minute for her mind to catch up with who he meant. "Jason Gardiner!" she said loudly, her eyes wide. He had never even registered on her radar. He was Human and bound already to the king's Siren, Tia Storm, but her heart fluttered with hope. He was quiet and intense and utterly gorgeous. He was also bound to her race by adoption of both the Bonaci and Dubonnetti royal families, making him as eligible as any son. Her eyes glittered for the first time in a long while. This suitor would be very acceptable. "What do you want me to do?"

CHAPTER 4

allygowan Castle – West Coast of Ireland – Present day

A few weeks had passed, and it was now time for Jay Gardiner to come to Ballygowan Castle to visit his son, JJ. The few minutes it took to travel down in the lift below ground allowed him the time to prepare and get himself fully composed.

Visits were never easy as his son shared a mother with his best friend's two children, and his best friend happened to be king of the Atlantean nation. The mother, Tia Storm, was a royal Siren, and while she was trying at the best of times, the fact they were all tied together was none of their faults.

Jay had met her a long time ago, before any of them knew who she was or what she was to become. They'd got together only to discover that she had to marry a prince. What they didn't know, and was cruelly withheld from them, was that the prince was Dante – his best friend. As it turned out, he was her destined mate. That meant her most compatible partner in the whole world. It not only made Dante king, but the dynamics of their friendship and his relationship with

Tia strained – to say the least. In fact, she was the bane of his life. Despite this, she was like an addiction – even though he'd made the decision to leave her. Some prophecy from the dawn of fucking time singled him out as some malevolent influence, and he couldn't put her or his best friend in danger.

It was easier this way. Dante loved her with a passion, and could give her the kind of love she needed. And him, well, he didn't do relationships. He simply didn't know how. Love, romance, day-to-day life with someone, had never really been his thing. Even if it wasn't for the whole Dark Prophecy thing, letting someone in who got to him as much as Tia, well, it felt more like drowning than love. He closed down everything tightly, so he was as calm, cool and collected on the inside as he always was on the outside. Emotional distance had worked for him up until now.

So now Tia was with who she was meant to be with – all playing happy fucking families along with his little hybrid son. By his own logic, it shouldn't bother him, but it did. He immediately disregarded the thoughts as a futile waste of energy. Nothing else could be done. Running a hand through his immaculately cut hair, he walked out of the lift.

Jay jogged briskly down the marble steps and into the magnificent great hall just as Dante – the king – was leaving.

They embraced. Dante had no problem with shows of affection. In fact, he did everything with passion: love, rage, family and, these days, being a great ruler. Most Atlanteans viewed him as being tinged with more than a little bit of madness. They were right.

He was the only man alive that could have this much physical closeness with him. Mainly because Dante would ride roughshod over any reluctance, and hug him anyway. And so Jay succumbed to this force of nature as he had always done since they were boys. "You off?" Jay said, pulling apart.

"Yeah, heavy meeting I can't get out of," Dante said, grinning, holding his shoulders for a few seconds longer to study his face. The mischievous glint was never far from his eyes.

His old friend had come to take his duties seriously and was becoming a formidable king – one that could be respected and lead the quarrelsome nation. He'd come a long way and Jay was proud of him. But every now and then the old crazy Dante would make an appearance and he loved him for that too – along with wanting to kill him half the time.

Alfonzo and Sebastian, the elder statesmen and Jay's benefactors, came out of the corridor behind the staircase where their apartments were located. They stopped their conversation and greeted Jay. "Dante?" they said, prompting that it was time to go. Heads of the Bonaci royal family and uncle and father to the Sirens, they were Dante's closest advisors.

"Later, man," Dante said, touching Jay on the shoulder. Then he pointed behind Jay. "They're in the fountain."

"Later," Jay said, his mind already on the object of his visit.

Left alone, he made his way through the huge gothic hall to the large, ornate fountain decorating its centre. He smiled at the yelps of joy coming from JJ playing in the water. Tia was with him, already hooped in her Atlantean markings, in a one-piece black swimsuit – nothing overtly provocative, but failing miserably all the same.

Jay reined in his eyes and knelt down at the wall of the fountain's edge. "Hello, little guy." He smiled and his heart warmed at the sight of his son, cute as a lion cub, in his light grey stripes that were brought out by the cool water.

"Dada!" JJ squealed in delight when he realized he was there.

Tia smiled, staying at a distance. Things were still awkward since she'd released him as her Protector, but they couldn't go on as they were. It troubled him that she was deliberately staying out of reach. "He's having a whale of a time," he said to break the awkwardness.

"Yeah, I'm letting him have some playtime before I take him into the sea. I don't want him to be scared."

He nodded and smiled. "You like being a mum now?"

Tia's face fell. "I've always liked being a mum, Jay."

Jay held up his hands in surrender. She hadn't been that great in the past, swanning off anywhere she fancied, often leaving the kids for weeks. It was the main reason she'd released him as her Protector; when he and Dante had tried to clip her wings. But that was in the past and he didn't want to have words with her in front of JJ. Instead he turned his attention back to his son.

"I came to see him, Tia, that's all," he said, nodding and smiling at JJ, who was busy tipping water out from a plastic bottle.

Tia nodded, but the atmosphere was still charged.

Suddenly, JJ jumped out and flung his arms around her neck, biting her cheek while he jumped and sang, "Mum-mum-mum!"

"Agghh! JJ, stop," she said, half-laughing, half-whining. "It hurts."

Jay laughed. "I think he's trying to change the subject."

He let go and splashed over to Jay and patted his face. "Ah!" JJ said, as if something was lovely to him.

Jay smiled, not having a clue what the boy had discerned from the touch. The Murrs were the purest bloodline of all Atlanteans and could read thought patterns. JJ had inherited the ability from that side of the family, but had to touch skin to do it. "Do you want to show Daddy how you can swim now, in front of the big window?" Jay said, indicating with a bob of his head. The huge panoramic window ran the whole side of the vast room. It was the size of a cinema screen and revealed the sea behind it like an aquarium.

"Yes!" the boy said, delighted, clapping his hands and jumping up and down.

"I'll go sit over there and wait, okay?" Jay said and stood, shooting a look at Tia for confirmation.

Tia turned JJ to look at her and smoothed back the long blond hair from his face, obviously giving him instructions telepathically. Then she moved him with her to the edge of the deep water, put her arms around him and dropped down into the hole in the centre of the fountain.

Jay's heart was in his mouth. He still felt the worry of any parent when their child was in the water, especially when his was deep beneath the surface with no way to get air. He went over to the large window and waited anxiously for them to come out of the tunnel that led from the fountain to the sea.

When they emerged, he watched as spellbound as he always was when Tia transformed in the water. Zebra-like markings emerged all over her skin, her eyes closed and bubbles came from behind her ears and water filled her lungs. Then she looked into JJ's eyes and he squeezed his tightly shut and did the same.

Jay breathed a sigh of relief and wiped his brow with the back of his arm. Watching them was so intense.

Tia cuddled JJ close, rewarding him for being a clever boy and he responded by beaming back the cutest smile of pride.

Jay felt choked watching his boy achieve something as brave as this, even though he knew it was natural to him. As fantastic as it still seemed, his son had the blood of a whole other species in him. He marvelled as the stripes darkened all over JJ's body, mirroring Tia's, and his pupils enlarged to allow in more light.

He'd seen it in the Murrs. They were the purest of all Atlanteans and still lived in water. His son began to look just like them but a much softer, cuter version. Where their markings were thick and black, his were light grey. And where their lower legs grew at least a foot longer to make them more efficient swimmers, JJ's leg bones were set in human form. However it didn't seem to hinder him at all.

Tia let him go and he began zooming around her like a seal, shooting through the water so fast it made Jay chuckle and shake his head in amazement.

Jay's eyes rested on Tia, which they inevitably would. She was swimming as graceful as a mermaid in arcs and twirls while JJ swam around her at double her speed. It was a beautiful sight and he would have loved to swim with him like that. Then he rolled his head back on his shoulders, getting real. If he were really being honest with himself, he would have loved to be out there frolicking with the both of them.

He shook his head, dispersing the sappy, useless thoughts. *Never gonna happen.*

After around fifteen minutes, Tia steered JJ towards the tunnel and came back up through the fountain. Jay held out his arms to the boy when he coughed the water out of his lungs and began to cry with the pain. "Shh, little guy, be brave now," he said, soothing and holding him to his chest.

Tia hopped over the side of the fountain and grabbed a trainer cup that she'd left there earlier and passed it to Jay to give him. JJ took it hungrily and began gulping down the juice. "His throat hurts?"

She nodded. *He needs sleep now,* she projected telepathically.

Jay wrapped him up in a towel and walked and whispered

in his ear till he went off to sleep. He couldn't believe he could feel so much as he did for this little guy.

Tia walked with him when he took JJ to his bed in the nursery. "Where's Xav and Alex?" he whispered. He was surprised he hadn't seen Dante's children.

With my mum. She's showing them a Murr school … Dante hasn't made his mind up where he wants to send them yet.

Jay nodded and they left JJ to have his morning nap.

I need to get something to drink, Tia projected, pointing to her throat. *If you want one?* She turned towards the direction of the kitchens.

"Sure." Slightly bemused, he followed her down the subterranean corridor.

They came into the more brightly lit room. It was empty as it was mid morning, the staff elsewhere with other duties. Tia went straight to the fridge and took out two tins of soda and handed him one.

As she turned, Jay noticed a cut on her shoulder. For a second his head spun and his heart rate spiked. The blood was running down her shoulder in two small rivulets. Not sure what possessed him, he reached out and stopped it in its tracks with a finger.

Tia shrank away from him.

Frowning, he showed her the blood on his finger then put it to his mouth. His heart rate rose immediately to a thumping in his rib cage and he breathed through the sensation. He'd forgotten how good that was – a surge of energy like a shot of adrenalin.

For a second she looked like a frightened deer. Then appeared to compose herself. *Sorry, I must have knocked it in the tunnel. Some of the rocks are jagged.*

Jay was still breathing heavily after the rush and tried to get a grip on it. A bolt of longing stabbed his heart and made him dizzy. "Are you happy with Dante?" he asked, having to shake his head to get it straight.

Tia fidgeted uneasily. *Yes.*

Siren blood was so potent; his heart raced and it made him feel drunk and reckless. "But you still want me – I can feel it," he said, narrowing his eyes. "You're inside me, remember?" The fact they were physically bound through the Siren's kiss meant he would always know how she felt. The intimate act where her life's essence flowed into her chosen partner and bound them together for ever. It was the reason that he, Tia and Dante were tied together so tragically.

Her eyes darted about, trying to find a way out of the situation. He could see it – he could feel it. He almost laughed with the power it gave him.

Then she sagged, as if resigning her self to the inevitable confrontation. *But, fuck it,* Jay just didn't care at that moment. She was joined to him with the very fabric of their DNA, his life was miserable and they were both trapped on this merry-go-round. Whether it was the blood or the months of seeing her happy with Dante, he didn't know but, at that moment, he didn't give a fuck.

I don't want to be with you, Jay, she projected firmly. *It shouldn't mean anything to you anyway.*

Jay narrowed his eyes, normally able to stay calm in most situations. He should have put a stop to it there, but a switch in him had flipped. "You'd better elaborate."

"Okay," she said, gaining confidence, "You treat me like I'm some kind of idiot."

He looked away and shook his head, smiling bitterly at the non-answer.

She persevered anyway. *You were right ... I was ... because I thought you were quiet and damaged and just couldn't express your emotions. And that maybe in time you would open up, but what I came to realise is, you're just cold.*

Jay could feel his blood rising with every patronising word.

All you want is casual sex and nothing more.

Jay laughed aloud with his eyes wide. She had truly surprised him today, being so direct and yet getting everything so wrong.

I dismissed Dante initially because I thought he was superficial and incapable of a deep serious relationship ... and a cheater, she tacked on. *But when I got to know him ... really got to know him, he's the deepest of all.*

Jay really did laugh at that.

He watched her continue uncomfortably with her tirade and get angrier by the minute at him not taking her seriously. She just didn't get him at all – but why would she, he'd given away so little. Still, today it bothered him.

The night I was at the hotel, you came to me ... Dante sent you. You got into bed with me.

When her eyes lowered, he knew she was remembering the hot sex they'd had when she was still asleep. It had been the first time he'd tasted her blood, but the circumstances surrounding it made it a moment he wasn't particularly proud of.

Tia shook her head as if to snap her mind out of it. *After ... Dante came back and talked to me – really talked, and opened up about himself. I saw a new side to him.*

Jay sneered and looked around him. "You sure all this – singing Dante's praises – isn't just for his benefit?" he said, opening his arms as he spoke. He could just imagine Dante listening in through the mental link they shared. He'd be creasing up with laughter.

Fuck you, Jay! He's not listening. It doesn't work like that.

Jay adjusted his stance nonchalantly and smiled. "Alright, what did he open up to you about then?" Something had got a hold on him now and he couldn't let it go.

Tia frowned. *It's none of your business, Jay. It was a private moment.*

He laughed derisively. Dante's part in anything that had happened to her at that time seemed to have been conveniently forgotten.

She stamped her foot in annoyance. *It was something to do with when you were kids and became friends ... fighting the village kids ... stuff like that.*

Jay nodded, knowing exactly what she was referring to. Then he went for the jugular. "Did he tell you his father nearly killed him after?"

Tia visibly shrank as the air left her. *Why ...?* she asked in a small voice.

Jay cut her off spitefully. "Because he assumed he'd been fighting with me. His own father beat him within an inch of his life." When he'd finished speaking, Tia's face was grief-stricken. "No I didn't think so," he said a little more softly. "Some opening up." As his anger drained away, it was instantly replaced by guilt. Dante hadn't held back the truth from Tia which, judging by her face, he was sure was how she'd taken it. It would have been what was important to Dante: the beginning of his friendship with him.

It was too late, the words were out now.

With that she flew at him, crying, punching, biting and scratching. His blood pumped again and he made short work of grabbing her wrists and spinning her around so her back was against him. His cock strained through his jeans grinding into her backside, as he buried his lips in her hair and breathed deeply.

His arm was around her neck leaving his other hand free to travel down her body and into her swimsuit. He probed and delved into her slick, wet folds. "Now who's lying?" he whispered next to her ear – his fingers seeking deeper still while she writhed against him.

• • •

IN HER HEAD she was screaming "no" despite her body's reaction. The fact was she loved him, hated him and needed him. But she wouldn't allow herself to be used like this and renewed her struggles.

Then, as if she were a hot coal, he pushed her away and grabbed his head at the temples. "Okay, okay … Fuck!" he shouted.

Tia span around, perplexed, still breathing heavily. "I didn't do anything!" she said over and over, not knowing whether to touch him or keep her distance.

Jay slowly straightened up and let go of his head when the pain appeared to leave him. "Fuck!" he said, shaking his head.

"What was it?" Tia said anxiously, still searching her mind for something she could have done.

"Dante," he said simply. "Making his presence felt."

"But I didn't …" Tia tried.

But he shook his head before she could finish. "He's coming home and he wants me to wait for him."

Taking a moment to regain his composure, he winked at her and walked out of the room.

Tia's heart was hammering in her chest. *Oh fucking hell!*

CHAPTER 5

Jay was now feeling sober and cursed the behaviour that was so out of character for him. What troubled him was less about what he'd done and more about what it meant. The high-octane blood he'd tasted had merely acted as a catalyst for how he felt deep down inside. A pressure-release valve for the things he kept a tight lid on. He guessed he'd been a fool to think he could suppress it forever.

He took the lift to ground level, thinking it best to wait outside on the drive, near his car. If things got messy – well, it was better outside.

The day was sunny and he sat on a low wall and pulled a long piece of grass to chew. He mulled over just how fucked-up everything had gotten in such a short period of time. Then he heard the distinct whine of a car travelling too fast along the drive. *Here we go.*

A Range Rover roared into the shingle area in front of the house. Dante flew out of the passenger door before it even came to a halt. Dante's brother-in-law, Keenan, who was also one of his guards, followed straight after. Jay was glad to see him. They'd become close friends and things could get ugly.

"What the fuck did you do?" Dante shouted, pointing his finger as he came up to Jay, who remained seated, chewing casually on his blade of grass.

"You're the mind reader, you tell me?" Jay said, looking up at him. He knew he'd been out of order, but grovelling wasn't his style and, judging by the wildness in Dante's eyes, his temper was already past the point of no return.

Dante went to close the gap between them when Keenan blocked him. "Come on, guys," he said, looking from one to the other. Keenan had no idea what was going on, but it didn't take a mind reader to work it out. Trouble between the two of them was always down to one thing – Tia.

"That's not how it works," Dante seethed. "I felt it: her anxiety, her anger …" Then he narrowed his eyes, adjusted his stance and lowered his voice, " and your lust." The words were left hanging in the air.

Jay had nothing to add and didn't take his eyes off him for a second.

Realising he was wasting his time, Dante turned his attention to Keenan. "Stay here with him," he ordered, then strode off in the direction of the castle.

Jay sighed and nodded. The bond that linked them meant nothing was sacred between the three of them. "He's got every right to have the hump," he said quietly, as Keenan sat down on the wall next to him. "I was out of order." In the cool light of day, his behaviour had been deplorable. Inwardly cringing, he shook his head. He hated himself sometimes. "It was the blood … I just lost it for a while." He still couldn't believe what he'd done.

Keenan leant forward, resting his elbows on his knees, and considered what he said. "Yeah, it'll do that," he said.

Jay looked up with interest. Keenan was part of the

Santalini royal family. Respected as the Special Forces of the race, they were also vampiric. Although they didn't do it for food any longer, they were big, powerful and had distending fangs. They only used it as some right of passage into adulthood, now, and a way to bond with their chosen mate. It was a side to Keenan that fascinated him.

Keenan breathed out noisily. "Once you've tasted it, it calls you, you know? ... And a Siren's blood – very hard to resist." Then he seemed to shake himself out of his thoughts and slapped Jay on the back. "Welcome to my world."

Jay smiled a little when Keenan's big arm roughly shook him by the shoulders. "I don't think it's as simple as that, Keen ... it's fucking complicated, you know?" Keenan really didn't know the half of it. It was about so much more than blood.

"I get it," Keenan said, cutting the humour. "I don't know how you get through it?"

No one did. The terrible situation of being bound to a Siren who was married and with your best friend, the two people (apart from JJ) he loved most in the world. That was the operative word: love.

Jay was quiet for a while. His heart was heavy and dead and it had been that way for so long. It had felt like that his whole life – except for the short spells he had spent with Tia, together, as a true couple. Well, as true a couple as a Human and a royal Bonaci Siren could be. The burden he was carrying was like a lead weight. "She's chosen, you know," he said wearily, staring out unseeing ahead of him. "I never thought she would ... I'm a fucking idiot."

Keenan looked at him curiously for a second, then put his arm around his shoulder and shook him again. Even though he didn't fully understand what the fuck he was going on about, he was there. Or maybe he understood perfectly. The guy was fast becoming a firm friend.

His thoughts were interrupted when the front door opened and Tia came out holding JJ in her arms. *Shit*, he couldn't deal with another round and braced himself, ready to take the deserved lashing.

Tia stopped abruptly a few feet away from them – a safe distance.

Keenan went to stand immediately. "I'll give you two a minute."

Jay held him down by the arm. "Better stay where you are, mate." It pained him to say it, but it was safer that way.

Keenan relaxed back down onto the wall.

Unsure for a moment, Tia arranged JJ, who was whinging in her arms. "JJ woke crying for you. I thought I'd catch you quickly so he could see you before you go."

Momentarily stunned by Tia, as he always was, he held out his arms and took the little fellow from her. He dispelled the lump in his throat by blowing raspberries on his cheeks, making him giggle. When JJ sat in his arms happily, Jay looked up at Tia. "Thanks." As usual, she had totally thrown him off balance.

"Are you okay?" she asked, quietly.

"You haven't seen him yet?"

"No, I must go to him now."

There was an awkward pause where part of him wanted to comfort her and another part didn't dare. Instead, he turned his attention to the little boy in his arms. "I'll see you soon, little man." Then he passed him back to Tia.

Without looking him in the eye, she took him. "Bye then," she said quickly. Then, turning on her heel, she walked hurriedly back towards the house.

Jay watched her till she disappeared.

"She loves you," Keenan said.

Jay closed his eyes.

CHAPTER 6

California – Present day

The van pulled up onto a small parking space off the road in front of a pretty white house. All the lights were on and a throb of loud music was coming from inside.

Lily's heart thudded. It meant there were others in the house – perhaps a lot. Wary of strangers, she hoped he lived alone. The guy got out of the driver's side, and Lily felt rooted to the spot.

"You getting out or what?" Shona said, with a little shove for her to move. When Lily still hesitated, "It's okay … they're good people."

Lily had heard that before and searched Shona's eyes. She wasn't sure what felt different, but despite all her logic telling her to run the other way, an instinct told her Shona knew something about her – something she had waited her whole life to know. After what felt like a long moment, and a call from the bloke to hurry up, Lily slowly got out of the van.

Sticking close to Shona, she followed the two of them into the house, down a long hall lined with surfboards of varying heights and colours, to the back, where it led to a spacious living room. Her eyes widened with awe when she realised it was kitted out as a large rehearsal studio. There was a drum kit, keyboards and racks of guitars with every kind of pedal arranged in a semi-circle. Three huge floor-to-ceiling windows ran along one wall and looked out across a pool and the ocean just a couple of blocks away. The place was amazing.

Beautiful people looking like they were fresh from the beach reclined, smoked, drank and chatted on low sofas and beanbags. *Who were these people? They lived like rock stars.*

Three guys she spotted jamming together stopped what they were doing when they noticed her.

"Hey, did you remember the papers?" one of them said to the guy who drove them.

He threw a thin packet of what looked like cigarette papers at him, which he caught easily. The bloke grinned at her. "Shona, you gonna introduce us?" he said, pulling out a couple of thin papers, licking them and sprinkling tobacco along the centre.

The driver she gathered was called Lance. He took a couple of bottles of beer from a crate, opened them with his key ring, and gave one to Shona and one to her – all with minimal eye contact. "Yeah, Shona … let's hear it." He walked over to the rack of guitars, chose one and started strumming.

Lily found she couldn't take her eyes from him while his nimble fingers ran over the strings and his shoulder-length sun-bleached hair fell into his face.

"I dunno, mate. She don't seem to wanna talk," Shona said.

Everyone seemed to stop what they were doing and looked up. Even Lance looked over in question. Lily wanted the ground to open up.

"You mean you brought her here and you don't know her?" one of the guys from the band said.

Lily looked at Lance, then around the room, anxiously for a pencil and anything to write on. The vibe had suddenly shifted from chilled to hostile in a matter of seconds.

Shona was holding up her hands to keep everyone from moving. "Hang on … hang on," she repeated.

"What's she looking for?" the same bloke said.

Lily felt herself panicking – *For fuck's sake!* She mimed the universal "can I have the bill" sign.

"Pencil and paper … she wants something to write with," someone else shouted.

Lance quickly walked towards her with a pad and pencil. "Here … knock yourself out."

Lily took it from him and looked into his eyes deliberately for the first time. It wasn't just to convey her gratitude, but for a moment, she got lost in the warm feeling of recognition she saw there. It simply made no sense. Then her face blasted red and she swallowed, her throat suddenly dry and constricted. He just nodded once, a little awkwardly, and took a step back. It took her a moment to compose herself to concentrate, and then she scribbled quickly:

My name is Lily and I'm not an idiot!

Then she held it up so everyone could see.

A tense moment followed while people mouthed or spoke the words quietly.

"Welcome to our humble abode, Lilyandi'mnotanidiot!" Lance said, grinning and holding up his beer in salute. Everyone laughed and followed his lead and the joke.

Lily's heart pounded with relief.

Shona giggled. "Lily it is then … can she stay, Lance?"

Lance's face got serious for a minute, then he reached over and took the joint from one of the band and took a long drag as if thinking. "You don't even know her, Shona … no offence," he said directly to Lily, while holding the smoke in his lungs as long as possible.

"Ah come on, you guys," Shona whined, "She's been shafted by a bunch of assholes already tonight."

"Can't she stay with you?" Lance said on an exhale, the smoke lying heavy on the air in blanket-like lines.

"I was kinda hoping I could bunk here too?"

Lance sagged in exasperation. The other guys sniggered. "You kinda cramp my style, ya know?" But he was smiling as if he knew it was a battle he was going to lose and his eyes flickered over Lily.

Shona laughed, seizing the weakness. "Ah come on, Lance, people will all think you're some sort of stud with both of us here."

Lily watched as he sighed and took an obvious visual sweep of her. Her cheeks blasted red while he appeared to consider it, and she shuffled uncomfortably. Her inner voice reminded her that he wouldn't be looking at her like that when he realized what a freak she was. It was a place to sleep, that's all, even if it was the plushest she'd ever had.

"Oh yeah, I almost forgot," Shona added, "She's the sickest drummer I've ever heard."

A moment of stunned silence followed. Lily's eyes went straight to Lance's, which softened immediately. The guy who'd built the joint had lit another, stood and handed it to her. "Where are our manners?" he said, taking a dramatic bow. "I'm Nathan, guitar. This is Mike on bass ... River – his mum was a hippie," he said behind a cupped hand. "He's our drummer ... better watch it, man," he said, laughing.

All the guys nodded a hello and River beamed a huge smile. "Always a pleasure to meet a fellow drummer."

Then Nathan pointed at Lance. "And that's Lance ... he does a bit of everything."

Lance threw a football at him playfully. "Hey, I'm lead singer and lyricist."

In that brief intro, she wasn't surprised he was talented.

She had already committed to memory his streaky blond hair, and tawny brown eyes. As well as his toned and tanned body, beaten-up jeans that defied logic, staying put on his slim hips. In fact, it suddenly occurred to her that there had never been a man who had made such an initial impact on her.

"Well?" Shona was saying, dragging her mind back to the conversation. "Can we stay?"

Lance rolled his eyes, defeated. "Yeah, fuck it … you know where it is."

The others laughed.

Just as Shona was herding her out of the room, Lance added, "But I tell ya, if I need the privacy, you gotta make yourself scarce." But his eyes looked straight into Lily's when he said it, and up her temperature went again.

"Deal," Shona laughed, pulling her with her. "Come on, Lil."

Lily followed her, bewildered. They went down the hallway to a large room at the front of the house.

"This is Lance's room. The others are all upstairs."

Lily walked into the room and put her small bag down on the large rumpled bed and wondered where they would all sleep.

"Beggars can't be choosers," Shona said, echoing her thoughts. "We gotta share. Make yourself at home. I'll see if I can rustle us up a sanger and a couple of beers."

Lily raised her brows and nodded, guessing she meant some kind of food. Then she sank down on the edge of the bed to take off her boots. It had been a long day. Leaving them tidily at the edge of the room, along with her embroidered cloth bag, she decided not to go back to her old place to retrieve any stuff. Most of what she owned, she carried with her anyway. She peeled off her jeans, now smelling of stale beer, but kept her vest and underwear on to sleep in.

She yawned. It must be about two or three in the morning by now.

Several minutes had gone by and Shona hadn't returned. Unease crept over her. Staying alert had kept her alive until now. It also made any sleep impossible until she made sure everything was above board here. On the surface, they all seemed okay, but appearances could be deceptive, as she had found out to her detriment on more than one occasion. So she slipped out of bed and crept down the corridor and stopped just before the door to the kitchen. Shona and the four band members were in deep conversation. She ducked into an alcove and listened.

"So she's got a few stripes – no big deal."

"Yeah, I know, you wombat, but hers are like a hundred times darker than ours and they don't go." The Aussie voice was clearly Shona's.

"Wha'd'ya mean they don't go?"

Lily held her breath while her heart thumped so loud it almost drowned out the most important conversation of her life. Her mind was racing. *Should she run quickly while they were busy?* Stunned by what she'd heard, she just had to listen to the end.

Shona began to speak more quietly. "In the club she had her arms on show – like the whole fuckin' world could've seen, and they were as clear as day."

"Ah, she could've just got out the water."

"Or just tats."

Someone tutted. "Yeah, copycat."

"No," Shona said very definitely. "I thought exactly the same thing. It kicked off and a drink got chucked. She copped the lot and I'm tellin' ya', they went real vivid, like I've never seen before."

"More than Ches'?" Lily recognised Lance's voice.

Who was Ches ... was he like her? Running now seemed out

of the question. These people seemed to know more about her than she did and she had to get some answers.

"So what are you thinking?" Lance said.

The room appeared to go quiet.

"I think she's one of them," Shona said.

One of who? Lily was silently shouting.

The room remained so silent she thought they'd gone.

Then: "Can't be."

"Nah."

"Why here … what would be the point?" Nathan said.

"Why not? We've heard the kingdom has formed again. Come on, guys, we've all heard the rumours?" Shona said.

There were general mumbles of agreement.

"Yeah, Ches got called home on family business, remember? … There was talk he'd found one."

More mumbles.

"Do you think she knows what she is?"

"No I don't think so," Shona said. "I can't believe she would go around showing off her stripes like that all on her own if she did."

There were more murmurs of agreement.

"What shall we do then?"

"Should we tell someone?"

"I dunno," Shona said. "Got the necklace, but it didn't exactly come with instructions … What about you?"

There followed a few "Nothings" and "same".

"What now, then?"

"I reckon, keep an eye on her … put out some feelers," Shona said. "Someone must know what to do with a fuckin' Siren."

"Shhh!" everyone hissed. "She'll hear you."

"Don't you think we ought to tell her … you know, for her own safety?"

"Yeah, we don't know who might be after her," Shona said.

"Or how close they are."

They all mumbled a unanimous agreement.

Lily wasn't sure what she'd just heard, but it was monumental. She'd felt different her whole life and these people seemed to know what it was all about. She took some breaths to calm herself down. At least she was safe here for the time being. She turned and padded softly back down the corridor to the bedroom and got into bed. A nice soft bed that smelled completely of *him*. One night wouldn't hurt. She'd re-evaluate in the morning.

LILY WASN'T sure if she'd dozed off, but she lay in the darkness, buzzing with questions to be answered. She stopped breathing when she felt the bed dip on either side of her, and Shona got in one side, and Lance got in the other. *Fucking hell!* She'd shared many a bed for warmth over the years, but this man made her skin come alive just with his proximity to her. Surely they must know she was awake; she lay so stiffly.

After a few minutes, when no one spoke, Lily relaxed a little. The two strangers both faced away from her, their breaths now slow and even. Both had fallen asleep.

Lily turned as lightly as she could to take a peek at Shona, then shuffled back to look at Lance. This was the weirdest night of her life – and she'd had a few. Despite not knowing what the fuck she was doing there, she had a feeling deep down inside that she was the safest she'd been in a very long time. And for the first time in her life, she felt a small glimmer of hope.

CHAPTER 7

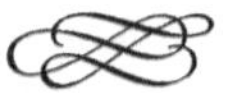

Ballygowan Castle – West Coast of Ireland

Tia walked into Dante's subterranean bedchamber after leaving JJ settled with the nanny. Dante was stripped to his shorts, leaning back on his arms on the beach, with his legs in the water.

The room was made from a natural catacomb with an outlet to the sea. The lagoon was lit from beneath, giving the room a subtle green glow. Torches burnt in roughly hewn alcoves, making it seductive and cosy. The only furniture was a wrought-iron four-poster bed at the water's edge, with transparent black gauze draped down its sides.

As Tia approached, she pulled her t-shirt over her head, then came around him into his eye-line and knelt in the water in front of him. His eyes rested on her without saying a word.

"Dante, I ..."

"I want you to project to me the whole thing," he said, cutting her off immediately. He was fuming and deadly serious.

"What?" she said, in a cracked voice.

"All of it – from the time I left, to the time I came back." His face was hard and implacable.

"Okay," she said, shuffling closer and putting her hand on his bare leg for the necessary skin contact. Then she projected the pictures of what happened straight into his mind, word for word, and nothing was left out. With that, he would feel her feelings and read her intentions. She had nothing to hide.

When she had finished, she remained quiet. He stood up and paced up and down in front of her while he thought.

"Dante, I'm sorry," she said eventually, when he still hadn't said anything.

"Stop!" he said, with his hand up to silence her. "You don't say sorry, you did nothing wrong."

Despite him not blaming her, she was afraid. Through the bond they shared, she could feel him fuming, and when Dante was angered, he could do anything.

"This is what you will do," he said, pointing at her with narrowed eyes. "You will never get near him if you are bleeding, however minor. You will never be with him alone."

Tia swallowed hard and nodded. Then he strode towards her and pulled her up into his arms, kissing the top of her head and breathing in her scent. "I love you," he said into her hair.

She hugged him more tightly.

"You don't understand ... no one's ever chosen me before – not over Jay."

Tia was stunned and pulled back to look into his eyes. They burned with emotion. "I chose you when we shared our first kiss. I chose you in the tank on our marriage. And I chose you at the wedding celebration when you stood up to your dad."

Dante squeezed her hands. "Yeah, you did, but it's not the

same. Today was different, babe. You chose me over him. It's the first time I've ever been in first place."

Her heart broke for him. She loved him and despised herself equally. Jay would always be their bone of contention. She pulled his face down and kissed him slowly and solemnly.

He pulled apart first. "Wait here … I'll be back."

She reluctantly let him go and he left the chamber.

JAY WAS BEGINNING to get impatient with the wait when Dante emerged from the house, having changed into jeans, his shirt left open and billowing behind him.

He stopped right in front of Jay and Keenan. "Right, I've seen the whole thing like a film … You!" he said, stabbing a finger at him, "took the fuckin' piss today."

"I know," Jay said simply.

"It was the blood, he couldn't help it," Keenan said in Jay's defence.

Dante just shot a dark look at Keenan to shut the fuck up and continued with what he was saying. "I've told her she's never to be around you like that again."

Jay nodded. "Yeah, I understand."

"You never see her unattended."

Jay looked up, frowning.

"You see JJ but not her," Dante continued.

Jay sighed and shook his head. He supposed it was always going to go this way one day. "What about the bond thing?" That was what had got them all into this nightmare in the first place. Not only did it splice their DNA together, but it also needed to be fed every so often by repeating the process. To ignore it would make both of them gravely ill.

"I'll know when she's getting weak. I'll call you then, but you'll be supervised … and handcuffed.

Keenan's eyes shot to his. "What ... don't you think that's a bit—?"

"Keenan ... shut the fuck up! I know he's your mate, but this goes way back and Jay knows it's been a long time coming."

Jay touched him on the arm. "It's okay, Keen, he's right."

"No fucking with her head ... your words!" Dante said, reminding him of when they'd almost lost her. "So you keep the fuck away." Then he turned and went to walk back towards the house.

"What if she comes to me of her own free will?" Jay shouted, throwing back at him their old pact, made right back at the beginning of their toxic triangle.

Dante halted in his tracks and turned and strode back towards them, his temper re-igniting. The two of them had to jump up, ready to defend themselves.

Dante bowled straight into Keenan's hands. "Oh no you fucking don't," Dante said, trying to get through Keenan to reach Jay. "You left her, remember? You got yourself deliberately released. I gave you plenty of chances to make it work with her and you didn't want it ... so no fucking way," Dante said, furious with him.

Despite having his hands full keeping Dante from him, Keenan looked at Jay in disbelief. "You got *yourself* released?" To be Protector to a Siren was a huge honour and one very few people got bestowed on them, especially a Human. It was a lifelong job, and the only way to be free was for the Siren herself to release you. In Jay's case, it was a hundred times more complicated because she'd bound him to her as well – and Keenan knew that.

"Yes he fucking did!" Dante said, going to push his way in closer again. "To make her hate him that much."

Jay looked at Keenan, who had stood still with amazement. "I couldn't be her servant ... just my stupid pride," he said, trying to explain, knowing it sounded lame and despising himself for the real reason all over again.

Dante laughed derisively. "Well ain't that the first bit of truth you've said in a long time."

Jay closed the gap between them. "But I'm not really released, man, am I … You pushed us back together. I tried to stay away. I thought if I could do that, then we'd all have half a chance." It was a little unfair and said in anger; Jay knew Dante had done it to save Tia's life and the stability of the kingdom.

Dante went to walk away in exasperation, then changed his mind and walked back again, pointing in Jay's face. "You just stay away, Jay." Cursing, he walked off back to the house.

Jay was left staring after him, with Keenan looking at him as if he'd lost his mind.

When Dante had completely disappeared, Jay looked up at the sky for the answer.

"She didn't deserve that," Keenan said quietly.

"I know and I've hated myself ever since … but it had to be done."

"No wonder she went to him … what were you thinking?" Keenan said, shaking his head.

Jay put his hands in his pockets and kicked a stone. "Fuck knows." He shook his head, not believing how his life could have gotten so out of control so quickly. Maybe it was his increasing preoccupation with blood, or the pressure of his Atlantean and business life taking its toll. He had to get his head in the game. It was time to get real before he lost it all. "The stupid thing is, it's not that I don't feel for her … it's that I don't *want* to."

CHAPTER 8

*S*outhern California

Lily slept lightly. It came from a long time being homeless and having to be aware if someone tried to pinch what little stuff you had – or, worse still, attempt to molest you. Most of the time, she managed to find a squat, and if she couldn't find one, she wouldn't let herself sleep unless she found a public loo with a lock. There she could allow herself to sleep – at least for a little while until the police moved her on.

Lily woke. It was morning, and the two strangers on either side of her still slept – Shona's light, purring snore to her left and Lance's deep, even breaths to her right. He was still facing away from her on his side with the sheet bunched around him, his ribs gently rising and falling. A beautiful blue-green pendant had worked its way around his neck while he slept and hung down his back.

Lily allowed herself to absorb the luxury of the soft, warm bed. The white blinds at the window with the early sun behind them bathed the room in a wonderful glow and made it easy to see. Her eyes meandered over what she could see of Lance's lean, muscled back. He had the most beautiful even tan, as if he'd been dipped in coffee. She had an almost overwhelming urge to touch the smooth skin. But as the thought occurred to her, he stirred and rolled onto his stomach with his hands under the pillow.

That was when she saw it. The sheet and the way he was lying had obscured it before. The most beautiful, intricate tattoo ran from his right hip to his right shoulder blade. It was a woman – but not just any woman. Emblazoned in thick black stripes reminiscent of a tiger, she was looking out over the ocean at the horizon. Her eyes were the deepest blue, her hair a mess of black curls that flowed behind her in ringlets. There was no doubt in her mind who the woman was.

Her breath caught in her chest and her heart skipped. She reached out a hand to tentatively touch the skin she knew would be warm and smooth and felt a mixture of terror and amazement. The stunning artwork was a depiction of her.

WHEN LANCE WOKE, he could sense she was awake. Easygoing by nature, he was always relaxed around women, but the moment he cast his eyes on this one, he knew she was different. It was a feeling he wasn't comfortable with. Like, right now, if he were lying next to any other girl, he would just roll over and kiss her good morning and try to convince her to make him breakfast – or be breakfast – whatever was easiest. The fact that Shona was in the bed probably wouldn't have come into it. She would have been grossed out, but he just found that amusing – not that he hadn't tried it on with Shona. It was years ago when he'd learnt, in no uncertain terms, that she was gay. He subconsciously touched his eye when he remembered the shiner she'd given him and chuckled to himself. *Well, you live and learn.*

He sighed. This one not only unnerved him, but she also reminded him of something he really didn't want to remember. He'd never met her, and yet when they were debating whether or not she could stay, he already knew he wouldn't throw her out into the street, which was what his instincts told him to do. Something about her made him think that Shona was right. That she was not only a Soul Breather, but the object of his recurring dream – and his nightmares.

Fuck! He needed to move; he couldn't lie there all day. He swung his legs over the edge of the bed and sat up without looking around. He reached for his board shorts and hurriedly put them on, only pausing when he realised he'd never been shy of his nudity before. *Fuck,* he needed to get out of there.

Lance stood and went to the bathroom and showered, but when he returned to grab his keys, Shona was lying like a starfish, and the girl had gone. *Fuck!*

Thoughts of letting her go quickly evaporated and he rushed through the house to the kitchen and stopped abruptly in relief. Bowling into the room so suddenly made her jump and she dropped a glass of juice she'd just poured herself. Her eyes went wide as if she'd been caught stealing and she quickly crouched to pick up the pieces.

Lance swore to himself, instantly feeling bad, and crouched to help her. "My fault … let me," he said, taking a large shard from her fingers. A warm tingle shot up his arm and he was drawn into her eyes again. They were deepest violet; large, soulful, beautiful and hypnotic and very definitely Atlantean. Something they held touched him so deeply, he had to shake himself out of it. Then she looked away and stood up. *Was she aware she just did that to him?*

He noticed her dirty cut-down jeans and her bag over her shoulder. She put up her hand. *Thank you* she mouthed as she went to go.

Suddenly it seemed imperative not to let her go – and not because of who they suspected she was, but because, *fuck …* *just because.* He wasn't willing to go down that route in his mind. A vision of Shona killing him was a much better pill to swallow. "Hey, where are you going? It's still early … I was gonna catch a few before everyone wakes up … wanna come?" was the best he could do off the top of his head – anything to delay her.

Her face remained blank, like she didn't have a clue what he was saying.

"Do you surf?"

A look of relief crossed her face when she fell in with what he meant, then she shook her head.

He paused for a beat and saw what Shona meant now: the light grey of her stripes crisscrossed her arms and went inwards to the centre of her chest from across her shoulders and neck. The vest she wore hid nothing. The only other person he had ever seen like this was his friend Cesaré. And even his went entirely when he was out of water. "Listen, you need to cover your skin in public."

She wrapped her arms about herself, suddenly self-conscious.

"Not from me, or the other guys, but strangers … okay?" He passed her a beach towel to wrap around her shoulders.

Lance followed her eyes when she looked down at her legs – bare from the knee down and as stripy as the top half of her. She looked back at him and frowned.

He laughed on a single blast of air. "Shit, girl." He rubbed his chin.

When she smiled back, the most adorable smile he had ever seen, he had to look away from the small mouth that completely distracted him. "We should be okay this early," he said softly, his eyes straying again to the curve of her mouth.

He shook his head. "Come on, tiger," he said, grabbing his towel.

And with the delighted look that lit up her face, he knew she had him.

LILY'S HEART fluttered all the way to the beach. The nickname meant he accepted her for who she was – the first time it had ever happened. He hadn't judged her as a freak or a tattooed weirdo, as the world usually saw her. She felt a curious sense of elation just being around him.

It was still early and few people were around the quiet stretch of coast where he pulled up his van. Lily followed his lead and got out. He slid the side panel open and passed her a board that was bigger than her, then took out another for himself. She frowned at the size difference – surely he should have the bigger board and she the smaller one.

He grinned, reading her mind. "Bigger is easier … believe me."

She tipped her head, bowing to his greater knowledge, and trudged after him down a rough path and a myriad of steps to the sea.

They came to an outcrop of rocks with a sheer drop into the ocean below. It was at least ten feet and she looked bewildered over to the sandy beach she could spy in the distance. *Shouldn't they be over there?* But he didn't see her confusion; his mind was already on the ocean, transfixed and studying it closely.

His face was captivating. She could watch it all day. His expression was one of concentration, but with it was awe – or was it adoration, she wasn't sure. But she decided she loved that look and wondered what it would feel like if he looked at her like that.

After what felt like hours, he bobbed his head for her to look where he was looking. She followed his line of vision.

The air was clean and fresh and smelt of the sea. The light was filled with the promise of a perfect day. It held just the right amount of breeze. Then he pointed. "See the lines? … See how they come at regular intervals?"

She did. The sea had a rhythm she'd never noticed before. She began to count. They were coming regular as clockwork. It delighted her. Rhythm was totally her thing. She grinned at him.

He'd been studying her, but his slow smile transformed his face. "You got it." He went on to explain the movements and swells of the sea and how important they were to surfers and how they followed them like some holy grail.

Her face turned to the ocean again, understanding perfectly when she saw the cresting waves curve and roll towards shore, making the perfect playground for surfers.

Then, as if to prove his point, someone paddled out over the waves in strong, powerful strokes until he cleared the powerful white water, then sat and waited for the next set to summon its energy and begin its roll to shore. When it came, he paddled with it and popped gracefully onto his feet.

Lily's hands flew to her mouth. It was the most graceful thing she'd ever seen. From the time he stood up, he moved with the board and the ocean like a dancer. Crouched low, he twisted and turned and rode the banks of the wave as if he were skateboarding. Launching into the air and grabbing the sides of the board, he twisted and landed perfectly on the water and continued his ride as if he'd never left it. He never once wobbled. It was as though the board were an extension of his body.

When his wave dissolved into the white water, he allowed himself to slowly sink, then paddled out and did it all over again.

Lily was transfixed. It wasn't just because his tanned, honed body moved like poetry, but that he was covered in black stripes, from head to toe, so similar to hers. Never in her whole life had she met another living soul who looked like her.

When she studied Lance to see if he saw what she did, he was as fixated on the surfer as she was. Then he laughed out loud, delighted. "He's back!" he said, looking at Lily. Then he put his fingers in his mouth and let out a shrill whistle.

The man in the sea, about to paddle out again, turned to look over his shoulder to see where the whistle had come from.

Lance waved his hand. "Come on … you should meet this guy."

EXCITEMENT AND TERROR took turns to clutch Lily's heart as she followed Lance across the rocks to reach the sandy beach a little way off. By the time they reached the keys and towel left in a heap, the striped man was wading out, carrying his board under his arm.

Her eyes skated over the many thick bands covering him completely and she realized they were intermingled with tattoos. His hair was long and bleached like Lance's, but curlier. As he came closer, she could see he was handsome, unshaven, and had eyes a brilliant sky blue.

Unsure as the man neared, she looked up at Lance next to her to gauge his reaction. He seemed completely unfazed by the guy's stripy appearance.

He walked up to them, stuck his board in the sand and clapped hands with Lance.

"Hey, when did you get back?" Lance asked, obviously delighted to see him.

Lily waited for his eyes to acknowledge her, but he didn't

look at her once. It kind of hurt. She didn't know him, but, for fuck's sake, she'd waited her whole life to meet another person like her, and now she had, and he wouldn't even acknowledge her. It was rude and obvious he was blatantly ignoring her.

"Ciao," he said, "just two nights ago."

"Why didn't you come find us?" Lance said.

He shrugged dramatically in a very Italian way, protruding his bottom lip. "I needed some time to get my head together."

Lance just nodded as if he understood. "We heard some rumours."

The guy sighed loudly, looking around him. "It sucked … what can I say … it is what it is."

Is what what is?

Lance nodded sombrely, then his face brightened. "Hey, listen … this is someone you should meet … this is Tiger Lily," Lance said, grinning at her as if the name had just come to him and he thought it awesome.

His playfulness snapped her out of her bad mood and she grinned at the nickname he'd christened her with. She kind of liked it.

"Lily, this is Cesaré, a real close friend of mine."

The guy glanced at her for the first time, then swept his eyes up and down in a way she could only describe as disgust. He couldn't have insulted her more if he had slapped her.

The towel was no longer around her shoulders, but instead of acknowledging their obvious similarities, he looked back at Lance, annoyed, pulled his board out of the sand and grumbled, "Don't let her walk about like that," as he walked past. Both she and Lance watched him walk all the way back to the road. She wanted to scream.

Lance looked as confused by the meeting as she was.

Then he looked down at her with an apologetic smile. "Sorry, Tiger, he's been back home and some major shit went down for him."

She would have loved to say that it wasn't an excuse to be a total dickhead to a stranger, but looking at Lance's expression, she didn't need to.

Instead, he asked, "How good a swimmer are you?"

She just shrugged and put her thumb and forefinger together to say she swam a bit.

"They didn't let you, I guess?"

She felt awkward, not really sure what he meant by that.

He passed her the big board and bobbed his head towards the crashing waves. "Do you wanna come get liquid with me?"

Her body ran molten for a second and her face blasted red. She didn't know what the hell he meant, but she sure as hell knew what those words did to her. How could she decline an offer like that? She swallowed hard and nodded.

He laughed as if he knew and jogged off towards the water. "Well come on then, Miss Tiger Lily, let's see what moves you got," he called over his shoulder.

Her heart skipped and she splashed through the shallows after him.

LANCE TOOK her out to where the water was waist-high. "Time to paddle out." Then he seemed to read her worried expression. "Don't worry, I got you," he said, laughing.

Everything he said seemed to make her blush, so she scrambled onto the board to hide it more than anything. He gave her a little push out to the deeper water. "Find your spot and you'll fly," he said.

She shuffled lower down her board so the nose was slightly out of the water.

"That's it," he said, climbing on his as fluid as a cat and coming alongside her.

Suddenly she remembered they were in the actual sea, a place she'd never been before – that meant creatures could be right below her. She froze for a second while Lance overtook her. "Come on, Tiger," he called.

She quelled her fear and pushed on. There was no way she was letting him see what a wimp she was.

He showed her how to paddle effectively and, before long, they reached the quieter water between the waves. She felt a curious sense of achievement.

Lance sat on his board, and she did the same, although not as gracefully. He pointed out to sea. "Watch how they come."

Lily wasn't sure; they looked so big and surely she would crash and burn on her first one. Her new confidence was evaporating quickly. Then she looked at the beach longingly and back to Lance.

"We're going to go under," he said, as if that was supposed to be a better option.

Bloody hell! The last time she'd had her head underwater, she'd been twelve years old. Not a period of history she wanted to revisit. Then she remembered what had kept her alive then and it calmed her a little. If she drowned, she'd know what to do. *Kind of.*

When she turned her attention back to Lance, he was explaining how to point the nose of the board down and duck under the wave so it didn't hammer them. "Get ready …" He counted them into it. "Now!" he shouted.

In a blind panic not to be left behind, she did as she was told. She pushed on her hands, holding the edge of the board with all her might, and bent her leg to push down the back and she was under cold water. Surprisingly, instead of feeling scared, she felt secure and safe. Everything was muted except for the bubbles and surges in the water. She felt a sense of freedom and weightlessness, even with the wave rolling over her head. It felt wonderful, like being safe in a car in a carwash while the brushes rotated over the roof.

She followed Lance's lead when he began to ascend and they came up in an arc on the other side.

He laughed again when she was right there with him and waiting for the next wave. "Hey, you're a natural."

Those few simple words made her feel brilliant. This was the best day of her life, for sure.

He went on to explain carefully how to face the beach when the wave was building and when she felt it pick her up, to pop up on the board as fast as she could and ride the wave into shore.

There followed the most fun she'd ever had. The first time, she was too far forward and nosedived straight into the water. Next, she let the wave pass underneath, so she was too far back and sank. Eventually, she felt it was right and scrambled up somehow and wobbled, but stayed up. It carried her all the way in. Over and over again, she did it till she could stay on for several seconds.

Eventually, her arms were dead weights sprouting from her shoulders, and she could no longer feel her toes. They both straddled their boards in the calmer water for a rest.

Lance pointed at the beach at the many surfers starting to pitch up. "We better get out before someone sees you."

When he looked at her body, his eyes were heavy-lidded. Her clothes were sopping and stuck to her, but his eyes skated over her with interest. Strangely, she didn't feel ashamed of her skin in front of him. Despite the full transformation of it – even her face – he seemed to accept her for the way she was, and that was a first. She looked over at the beach and nodded. This guy was fast beginning to be more than a pretty face to her – maybe she could even call him a friend.

"You don't know what you are?" his voice rasped after what felt like a long space of silence.

She sagged, knowing the question had to come sometime, and shook her head.

"I think I know."

Her heart pounded and she held her breath.

"I mean, I wasn't sure at first, but I am now."

She searched his face, looking for any hint of ridicule, but there was none.

"We'll sit down tonight," he said and flattened down and began to paddle away from her. "There's a way up through the rocks – away from everyone," he shouted.

After a moment's pause, she followed him in a daze. He climbed up through the push and pull of white water onto a low, smooth plateau of rocks, grabbed her hand, and hoisted her straight up off her board. The tingle of electricity that shot between them almost made her let go. Then, with their boards under their arms, they trudged up the steps in silence. At the top, he checked that the coast was clear and then signalled for her to make a break for the van.

Once inside, he didn't look at her again. She began to doubt whether the whole friendship thing was ever between them.

Stupid me, why would he ever want her as a friend?

He started the engine and pulled away.

CHAPTER 9

"You took her fuckin' surfin'," Shona screeched when they walked back into the busy kitchen.

Lily wasn't sure what to do. Her heart began to sink lower than it already was after Lance's apparent turn-around. She guessed this was it: the point she always got to when people were too weirded out by her. *Fucking hell.* She put up a hand to say goodbye and turned to walk out the way she came in.

Lance put out his arm and touched her gently. "Don't go … it's okay."

Warmth flooded through her, making her pause. Unable to help herself, she looked up into his beautiful hazel eyes, hoping hers conveyed all the "pissed off" she felt towards him. His look was soulful and honest. *What was with this guy?* He was turning her in cartwheels and she'd only known him for five minutes. She took a deep breath and bit her lower lip.

"Go take a shower … we'll talk, okay?" he said quietly while his eyes held hers with meaning.

After a moment of deliberation, she nodded and walked

out and down the hallway, not sure what to do. She paused at the bedroom door. Footfalls on the stairs made her dart into the room, but only leave the door ajar. With her ear to the gap, she held her breath and listened. *Shit,* they were too far away. She held her breath again when the voices came nearer.

"No one saw, we were early," Lance was saying. "Except Ches, he was already there."

"He's back?" another male voice said.

"What did he say when he saw her?" Shona said.

"He was weird."

"Was he excited to see her?"

"No … just the opposite," Lance said, sounding puzzled.

"Maybe he was just pissed … with everything that went down," another said.

"Maybe," Lance said, but he didn't sound convinced. "Listen, that's not important right now," Lance continued, "the thing is, *I'm* sure."

"Sure about what?" Shona said.

"Of what she is."

"Does she know?"

"I don't think so, but we need to tell her soon, for her own safety."

They all seemed to agree, which made Lily's heart race.

"Well, if we're convinced, then we need to get some advice and, whether Ches is in the mood or not, he's the best person to ask," Shona said.

"We'll get together tonight."

Lily silently closed the door. As badly as she wanted to find out what he knew, she wasn't sure she wanted to meet the grumpy sod again.

. . .

LILY MADE herself scarce for the rest of the day, feigning a headache. She went back to bed – not that she could sleep with all the "what-ifs" buzzing around her head. The others in the house seemed to leave her to it and she was grateful.

Shona came and found her in the early evening with a sandwich. Hunger forced Lily to sit up and accept. Then she was promptly told to get her ass out of bed and get dressed as they were going to the beach.

Lily looked at the blinds, now a blue grey with the dusk light.

"Don't worry, it'll be good, you'll see," Shona said, grabbing some things and stuffing them into her bag.

Lily reluctantly left the haven of the bed and began to dress. She was taking no chances this time and pulled on her holey jeans and a sweatshirt. There was no way she was going to let anyone look down on her again tonight.

They all piled into the van and went to a small, secluded beach in a cove. There was already a huge bonfire lighting the place, revealing at least fifteen people all playing ball, lounging and running in and out of the sea with surfboards.

Lily began to panic; meeting all these new people was her idea of a nightmare.

"It's okay," Lance said quietly.

She hadn't realised he'd been so close. Butterflies flipped in her stomach. She looked up into those honest-looking eyes of his. *Why was he making her trust him one minute, then ignoring her the next?* She dragged her eyes from his and jogged to catch up with Shona, who had walked on with the others.

When they reached the circle of revellers all seated around the campfire, Shona laughed and joked. The others from the band all grabbed hands and hugged people they obviously knew.

"This is Lily, everyone!" Shona announced loudly.

Lily stood, completely embarrassed with all eyes on her, and just nodded.

"Come on," Lance said, pulling her with him to a space around the fire where he opened two camping chairs and indicated for her to sit in one.

She spotted the miserable git from that morning and was glad he was occupied on the other side of the fire with two beach babes.

A guy came over, said hi to Lance, and offered her a beer. "Where you from?" he asked, smiling. He had a towel wrapped around his hips, but she could clearly see stripes on his torso. They were grey and only three or four of them on either side of his rib cage, but she couldn't help staring at them. The guy became self-conscious and looked at Lance for guidance.

"She's lost her voice, Sean … She's new to SoCal," Lance said, coming to her rescue.

The guy smiled at her and bumped his can of beer with hers. "Welcome, Lily."

She smiled. Then, when he moved off, she began to relax a little and people-watched. Realisation began to dawn on her that all those who had recently been in the sea were displaying stripes of varying shades and patterns. None had as many, or as dark, as the man she'd met on the beach today, but they were all undoubtedly similar to her.

LILY'S EYES FOUND LANCE. He'd been watching her the whole time and was obviously waiting for her to join the dots. That was the secret. Everyone here was just like her. It was a bolt to her heart. She relaxed back into her chair in a state of complete shock. She hadn't expected this, not in a million years.

No one seemed to bother about her after that. She

guessed that meant she wasn't that big a deal. Everyone appeared engrossed in their own conversations, sitting or leaning back in little huddles around the fire. Nathan began strumming an acoustic guitar.

After a while, a few people came and went, leaving only around eight.

"Ches?" Lance called.

Shit. Lance was beckoning him over. Lily sank into her chair, trying to be invisible.

Cesaré was lounging back against a rock with the two girls on either side of him. It didn't surprise her that he was a womaniser.

Cesaré just put up a hand in way of 'hello'. His eyes were low and he looked drunk. She couldn't see how anyone was going to get anything useful out of him tonight.

Shona went up to him and kicked his ankle. "Get up, you piss-head," she said with her usual Aussie charm. "We need some advice."

Lily heard a grumble, which sounded very much like swearing, while he extricated himself from the two girls to sit up. He leaned forward with his arms resting on his legs. "What?" he said, looking up at Shona with half-closed eyes.

She dreaded any further interaction with him; he only made her feel uncomfortable. The whole group went quiet. Nathan even stopped strumming.

Lance must have sensed her anxiety and touched her arm.

A warm current of security flowed from his touch and permeated her. It was the weirdest feeling.

"What's up?" someone else called out to Shona.

"We wanted to put something to the group. We need to know what you all think?" Shona said, looking at each one of the onlookers.

Cesaré just put his head in his hands like it was the last thing he needed, and knew exactly what was coming. When he looked up again, clearly wishing he was anywhere else but where he was, Lily knew he would be of no help to them whatsoever.

"So you know what she is," Lance said flatly.

"Yes, I know what she is," Cesaré said wearily.

His slow blink confirmed Lily's first impression that he was extremely drunk. Her initial interest in him was fast turning into annoyance – *the selfish bastard!*

Lance was beginning to mirror her thinking when he shot a look at Shona, which said it all. She looked just as bemused as he was and shrugged.

"Someone mind telling me?" one of the others said.

Lily nodded a thank-you to the first person to say something constructive around here.

Lance didn't appear to hear or ignored the question, his attention still on Cesaré. "What is wrong with you?" Lance said, shaking his head at a loss. "I thought you of all people …"

"Yeah, come on, Ches, we need a clue what to bloody do with her," Shona said.

Lily tutted and leaned forward to try to communicate to someone that they needed to let her know what was going on; otherwise, she was walking.

Lance didn't even notice; he was so absorbed with Cesaré. His patience was now gone. "The race needs her, doesn't it? Shouldn't you be attempting to keep her safe for your family or something?"

Shona pushed Lance back into his chair. "Calm down, mate." Then she turned back to Cesaré, got down on her haunches so she could speak to him at eye-level. "So the rumours we heard were true?" she said softly.

Cesaré nodded once, then pushed the girls on either side of him off, as if he'd only just become aware of them.

"And Malleven … he's dead?" Shona said.

Cesaré's face clouded over. "So it seems."

Lily watched the drama but kept an eye on Lance as her bullshit barometer. His face appeared to soften a little. "I'm sorry, Ches," he said more calmly. "I know you were close, but none of that has anything to do with her."

Cesaré threw his head back and laughed loudly as if to say, 'If only he knew'.

Lance ignored him and turned to her. "How old are you?"

She was taken aback for a second. Then held up both hands, then nine fingers.

"Nineteen," he repeated to himself. "Shit!" He faced the others again. "My knowledge of the legends is not great, but even I know she's of age and that puts her in danger, right?"

Lily looked around at all the rapt faces, all looking left and right to their peers for an answer to what was going on. Then they looked at Cesaré for his reply.

Instead of answering, he struggled clumsily to his feet. Then stumbled and swayed so badly that everyone stood as well.

Lily wasn't sure whether they stood because things were going to get ugly or just because Cesaré would fall over, maybe into the fire. He pushed Shona's hands off him when she attempted to steady him. Then held up his hands as if to say, "I'm okay".

"Look, I know you all mean well, and I know you think you're doing the right thing by her, but the best thing you can do for her sake is to keep her hidden."

Everyone seemed to speak at once as if it wasn't making any sense or wasn't what they expected to hear. Lance quietened them down and spoke for everyone again. "What about the kingdom, Ches ... shouldn't the king at least know about her?"

Cesaré reached down to retrieve the bottle of wine he'd been drinking from, took a big swig and staggered. He took it away from his mouth and wiped it with the back of his hand. "You think that is a good place for her? … You think she will be happy there? … You're fucking crazy if you think that."

The meeting was starting to crumble into some sort of farce; everyone began talking all at once, not knowing whether to take any notice of him as drunk as he was. Then he looked straight at Lily and pointed with the hand that held his bottle. His face was so contorted with hatred that she recoiled. Then he laughed at her. "If it's fame and fortune you're after, princess, then think again. Your sisters are all miserable trapped creatures … You want all this Atlantean crap?" And he slowly turned with his arms held wide. He laughed to himself again. "You can fucking keep it." He finished with a glare at Shona and Lance, who'd been watching him in a state of shock. "Do her a favour and never take her to court," he mumbled as he lurched between them and in the direction of the road. Everyone was left stunned.

Well that was as clear as mud. The guy was a raving lunatic. What a disappointment. To think that she had wasted time on all this, thinking she was going to have some life-changing revelation. The one person who resembled her physically turned out to be just another lush. She took a deep breath to gather herself. This was just another knock to take on the chin, like most things in her life. That was it. She'd had enough. She stood up and went to stomp off in the direction of the road. It had been nice having somewhere to stay, but quite frankly, it was outweighed by all the aggro.

Lance and Shona quickly caught up with her. "Wait!" they both said.

Lily stopped with a huff. Then gave them a look that told them her patience had well and truly gone.

"We want to explain," Shona said.

"We owe you that," said Lance. "Then, if you still want to go, we won't stop you. But at least you'll have all the facts."

She put her head down and went to keep walking.

"Don't you want to know who you are – what you are?" Shona asked, eyes wide with meaning.

Of course she did. It was the thing that had burned inside her since she was a small child. The freaky kid with weird stripy skin and no vocal cords. The kid you couldn't drown.

She put up one finger, telling them a minute was all they had, so they'd better talk fast.

Shona looked across her to Lance. "Should we tell her alone?"

Lance thought for a moment, then shook his head. "No ... everyone needs to know how important she is if we're all going to keep her safe."

Shona agreed.

That's if I'm stopping.

They led her back to the group and her seat by the bonfire.

CHAPTER 10

Once she was seated again, Lance nodded at Shona to do the talking. She took a deep breath and looked around her, searching for the right words.

Lily rolled her eyes; she wanted to scream in frustration.

"Look, you've seen everyone here has similar skin markings to you, right?"

Lily nodded.

"Well, it's because we're all …" She paused as if it was hard for her to say it. "We're all not from here."

Lily's frown deepened and she looked around her for clarification.

"This world, not SoCal," Nathan added.

Lily blinked, then looked at Lance. He was watching her closely and nodded. Staring into his eyes, she could see that this wasn't a joke and they were being deadly serious. She faced Shona again.

"A long time ago – like ten thousand years or something, our ancestors came from another world – a world covered in water." Shona paused, allowing it to sink in.

Lily could only stare at her, open-mouthed.

"Well, to cut a real long story short, they built a city under the sea called Murrtaine. It still exists – so people reckon – anyway, they went on land and started shagging humans until a city called Atlantis grew. You've probably heard of that one?"

Lily, still in a state of bewilderment, just bobbed her head to say "kind of".

"Well, the guys who left our ancestors here in the first place came back to check on them and got the right hump over some rule-breaking or something, and decided to teach every bugger a lesson. They destroyed Atlantis and cut off Murrtaine for ever.

"Now, right up to this day, there are five royal families." Shona held up her hand and counted off her fingers. "There's the Florianna – Ches' family, erm … the Dubonnettis – the king is from this one. The Santalinis – they're the badass soldiers of the race. Oh yeah – the Borge – they live in Murrtaine. I've never seen one." And she looked around at the others, who all shook their heads. "They are like the purest blood – you know, not tainted with humans," she explained. "Aaaand … blast, what's the fifth one?" she said, looking at Lance.

He just tipped his head in Lily's direction.

"Oh yeah, silly me. Yeah, your family, Lily … the Bonacis."

Lily found herself mouthing the name – her name.

"Well, anyway," Shona continued, "the bastards came back and, as a punishment, made them all give up a daughter from each royal family. They were right pissed off, as you can imagine, so they left a prophecy that the spirits of these daughters would appear every so often, hidden on the earth. But they warned they'd come back and check on us again one day and we'd better have our act together."

"Now I'm not totally sure on the exact wording of the prophecy, but it basically says that the princes must search for these princesses, and the first one to find one would be king. That's already happened," she said, pointing at Lily.

"They're all supposed to have freaky powers that the king needs," Nathan added.

"Yeah, he needs all five, though," another said.

Lily's head was turning to each one speaking, completely bewildered.

"Trouble is, it's kind of a free-for-all. All the princes want you for what you can bring them and also to take away some of the king's power."

"That makes for lots of in-fighting."

"Like what's just happened to Ches," Shona said.

Nothing was making a lot of sense to Lily, but she was kind of following the gist of it.

"We've heard the king already has three," Lance said. "That puts him in quite a strong position."

Lily absently looked the way Cesaré had gone.

"Yeah … he's a prince," Shona said, reading her thoughts. "The flaming galah is supposed to want to marry ya and keep you safe. You'd think he'd snatch you up after what's happened."

Ew! Lily recoiled at the thought. She didn't need protecting. She'd been fine on her own up until now. He didn't look like he could even look after himself right now.

Lance came and sat closer so she had to look him straight in the eyes, making everything go to jelly again. "The thing is, Tiger, you are what we call a Soul Breather." His voice was soft, lulling and completely hypnotic.

Lily dragged her eyes away to look around her. It had gone deathly quiet. Every person was watching with rapt faces – no grins, no sniggers, just serious and deadpan. She turned her attention back to Lance, feeling totally lost. *Was this it? Was this what she'd waited her whole life to learn?*

"Because of that, everyone is after you – not just the royal families but Humans, governments and shit like that. They all know of your existence. They know your age, they know your worth, so they'll all be coming for you," Lance said.

"It's serious shit, Lil, like world powers and everything," Shona said.

Lily looked back at the road again. *Cesaré didn't seem to think it was that urgent.*

Lance followed her eyes. "Something bad happened to Cesaré – to do with one of your sisters. He doesn't think the king's home is the best place for you right now."

She wasn't sure that Cesaré's judgment could be relied on at all at the moment. It all sounded so ridiculous to her, but everyone here was certainly taking it seriously. It was a lovely fantasy, and it intrigued her that she could have sisters, but when she thought of how she'd been brought up, she found it very hard to believe that she was some kind of princess.

"They reckon you've got powers, Lil," Shona said, crouching down so she was in her eye line and holding Lily's hands.

"Isn't she meant to breathe underwater?" someone said.

Lily felt heat burn in her cheeks and bit her lip, hoping that the firelight wouldn't show her obvious discomfort. She wasn't even sure whether she could trust these people yet.

Lance noticed. "You breathe the water?" Lance said softly – that coaxing tone that melted her insides.

She looked at him, still unsure. If they were feeding her a line, they were bloody brilliant actors. When she really thought about it, everything seemed to fit. All the differences these people seemed to know about—the stripes they all shared. And something in Lance's eyes and handsome face made her want to trust him. She nodded hesitantly.

They all seemed to let out a collective breath.

Lance grinned.

"Fuck! A genuine Soul Breather," someone said.

"Aren't we meant to test her or something?" another said.

"Simmer down," Shona said, taking charge.

Lily was grateful; it was all beginning to feel overwhelming. She needed time to process it all.

"I'm not a hundred per cent, but I think that's a royal's job – not ours. We're her Protectors," Shona said, turning her body so she could grin at them all.

"I don't have a talisman," someone said.

Shona pulled out a light blue-green pendant on a chain around her neck. "I do … I'll deputise ya."

"You're a girl," someone else said, making them all laugh.

"Shut it, ya drongo!" But Shona was laughing as she spoke.

Nathan came closer so Lily could see. "I've got one too," he said, grinning at her. It was almost identical to Shona's. "Show her yours, Lance."

Lily looked over, expecting to see the same.

"I'm not sure I qualify," he said, not looking at her.

She studied him carefully. It surprised her as he always seemed so confident. This was the first hint of vulnerability she'd seen in him.

His eyes went to hers. "I was adopted."

They held each other's gaze for a long moment. There was that elusive feeling again. Did he think he would be a lesser person to her if he were? If anything, he'd just become a whole lot more interesting.

Nathan swore loudly, forcing Lily to look over at him. "He's my brother and our mom had the pendant split between us. According to her, it meant that it covered us both."

Lily could see that the stone had been cut. It was circular on one side and flat on the other and set in gold – very beautiful.

Lance smiled indulgently at his brother. "Yeah, as some kind of good luck charm … I doubt she ever thought I would be a Protector?"

"I expect none of our parents did," someone said.

"What about your tattoo, Brah … what can you say about that?"

Lily's eyes flew to Lance's. He was uncomfortable again. Everyone else went quiet as if they all knew but hadn't spoken the obvious.

It had gone to the back of her mind, but she hoped it had some romantic meaning. However, looking at Lance's face, it quickly became dismissed with disappointment as one of life's spooky coincidences – especially now she'd learnt she had sisters. It could be any one of them.

"You gotta admit that it bears a pretty strong resemblance."

Lance tipped his head, but he wasn't just embarrassed; he looked upset – annoyed even. "I didn't do the actual inking," he said, trying to dismiss the comment.

It made her feel completely foolish for ever having hoped it meant anything.

"Well, you know how it works, Baby Bro – everything for a reason."

His eyes flicked to hers again and she could tell he was discomfited. For Lily, it was the last in a long line of extraordinary but profound disappointments. So for that reason, she didn't allow herself to think about it anymore. The whole evening had been bewildering.

Her life had been spent wandering, playing drums, trying to earn a quid here and there, and now they were telling her that, not only was she some kind of royal alien, but that she fit into some grand scheme of things from an ancient prophecy or something.

Some things had become clearer. Shona, despite her

bluntness, had always been straight with her, and she had to get real with herself about Lance. She had no experience at all with the opposite sex and he was stirring up feelings – feelings that clearly he didn't share.

FOLLOWING THAT EVENTFUL EVENING, Lily went back to the house. She moved in properly and was given her own room. It was the smallest in the house, but it was hers – the first she'd ever had. It gave her privacy and the necessary space she needed from Lance. It was very hard to share a bed with a man she found she wanted to be around more and more, who wanted to be around her less and less.

Life settled into a routine. Always surfing at dawn or dusk and sometimes both. She was even becoming a passable surfer, not getting in everyone's way, dropping in on their waves by accident and getting sworn at.

They were all protective of her. At first, it felt weird, but after a while, she grew to like it and felt like she belonged somewhere for the first time in her life. Accompanied everywhere and treated like everyone's kid sister, they were fast becoming the happiest days of her life.

Ballygowan Castle – West coast of Ireland

Tia had hidden it as long as she could, but she couldn't delay it any longer – she was ill.

Dante made the phone call she was dreading and Jay was to arrive the next day.

When the time came, Dante collected her to take her to the room where Jay was waiting. Everything had gotten so cloak-and-dagger, it was tragic. To think they had spent their whole lives as close as brothers.

When she refused to go, Dante went to pick her up. She tried to fight him, but it was no good. She was just too weak, and he lifted her easily. He carried her the whole way to the old library above ground in his arms and placed her down carefully onto her feet.

She was terrified to turn around and buried her face in Dante's chest.

You must do it, Tia, you're sick. He can't touch you this time. Dante projected lovingly while he stroked her hair.

That wasn't really what she was scared of. It had more to do with how she would feel about Jay after months of not seeing him. She took a deep breath and swallowed down the impossibly large lump in her throat and slowly turned. *Oh my god!* She couldn't believe her eyes.

Jay was sitting in the corner of the room with his hands behind the chair – clearly handcuffed to a pipe that ran from floor to ceiling behind him. His head was bent forward, looking into his lap, and he was thin – really thin.

"Jay?" came out as a husky whisper.

He raised his head slowly to look at her. Her hand grabbed her mouth to stifle a sob. His eyes were dark and hollow, and his cheekbones protruded. *Oh no!* She'd never realised that putting off replenishing the bond as long as she did would take this kind of toll on him. It couldn't be avoided. *Oh, why didn't she do it when she first needed to?* It didn't make sense that something meant to be a beautiful act of love was reduced to this?

How sick of all the Atlantean bullshit she was. The whole bond thing was meant for sharing the innermost soul of a person. In the form of breath in a kiss, her spirit had travelled from her heart into his, giving the most indescribable physical pleasure and complete understanding. However, this was the true cost.

The princes all wanted it, not for what it was intended – something pure and good, but for the power it gave them, and the psychic link that came along with it. And as much as she and Dante loved each other, with their bond being two-way, it was a strong factor for him too.

Jay was Human, and the bond could only be one-way. He could never breathe for her, but she'd assumed it meant he would escape its ill effects a lot more than her. Looking at him right now, he was an empty shadow of the man she knew, and far worse than she expected. Her heart bled out at the sight of him like this.

Dante, always attuned to how she felt, abruptly closed

his mind and his feelings off to her – a direct result of the bond they shared. The sight of Jay like this would be eating him up inside too. "I have to leave," he said, his own voice laden with emotion. "But Keenan will remain the whole time."

Her teary eyes met Keenan's, who nodded sombrely. The door clicked shut as he left and she faced Jay again. Their gaze was transfixed for what seemed a very long time. Weirdly, there was no hate or recrimination there. In Jay, she could see only longing or, dare she even think it, *love?* It was an emotion he seldom showed. And, as a Human, she couldn't sense it through the bond. Jay had always been an enigma when it came to feelings.

Slowly, she moved her stiff body towards him, swaying with dizziness and stopping right in front of him. He seemed too lethargic even to lift his head, so she knelt awkwardly in front of him and laid a hand gently on his knee. "I'm sorry, Jay."

His over-large eyes looked intensely into hers.

Her lip quivered in an effort not to cry. "I didn't know it was so bad for you."

He smiled and blinked slowly. "Shh … I'm tired, that's all." His head lowered as he appeared to drift off into sleep.

Tia anxiously looked at Keenan, who appeared to be wrestling with his own emotions. "Did you know he was like this? Why didn't you tell me?"

Keenan closed his eyes and shook his head. "He made me promise to keep quiet." Then he walked towards the door. "I'll give you some space … but five minutes is all I can give you, Dante will be back in ten."

"Thank you," Tia said, more grateful than he'd ever know.

When he disappeared, she turned to Jay and gently touched his face. Tears were now spilling onto her cheeks. She felt wretched. "What have I done to you?" she whispered.

His dark eyes looked intently into hers. "It's my own fault." A small smile played on his lips. "I'm an idiot."

Tia's heart was cracked open by the small glimmer of the old him – the Jay she'd fallen so utterly in love with in what felt like a lifetime ago. With great effort, she pulled herself to her feet and put her leg across to straddle his lap. Her face was now on a level with his. The handcuffs jangled behind him.

"You shouldn't sit like that," he warned in a small whisper, but he was smiling. Even like this, he was irresistible.

Holding either side of his face, she leaned closer and gently kissed the corner of his mouth. He remained impassive with his eyes barely open and waited, but his chest moved against hers with anticipation.

It had been a long time, and they both needed it so badly. Her breathing, already laboured, became harder the hotter she got. His lips slightly parted and his warm breaths tantalised her skin. "You better be fast before you get too hot," he said breathily.

Their lovemaking had always been in the shower or bath to keep her cool. They didn't have much time before she overheated. She nodded while she nipped at his lips and ventured with her tongue. Despite their physical weakness, their bodies were already moving together – slowly and deliberately undulating in purposeful circles.

Jay captured her tongue with his lips and drew it into his mouth and kissed her deeply. Deeper, hotter and with more longing than ever before. She became hopelessly lost in him. He was the partner, the lover, the soul mate she'd loved and hated and she'd forgotten how he felt – what he meant to her. At this realisation, her tears fell and feelings of love mixed with the hopeless sadness for their situation. Although with the rising of her building essence, she threw negative thoughts to the back of her mind as lust and need consumed her.

Tia knew Jay sensed how she felt in the way he moved beneath her, willing her to him.

When she went to pull away slightly, fearful of the sheer strength of her physical response, he bit her cheek, holding her where she was. "Give me as much as you can," he whispered. "Fuck the consequences."

In the past she had always been scared of hurting him, but today he was right. *What was she holding back for?* At that moment, nothing mattered more than filling his being with everything, marking him as hers, and revitalising him with her spirit. "Yes," she gasped, grinding herself into his lap. Feeling his hardness tantalising her core, she streamed herself into him in one agonisingly long stream, riding on the crest of her climax that reared up and overtook her astonishingly quickly.

Jay covered her mouth with the first breath and absorbed every particle of her. His head drifted back in ecstasy and his hips ground into her. But she stayed with him, giving him what he wanted—everything she usually held back. Showing no mercy until his orgasm hit with such ferocity, he was forced to break the seal of their lips with a sensual gasp. "Ah fuck, Tia."

Dragging her mouth away for fear of killing him, she bit his neck hard, allowing her own heart rate to slow down. She sat draped over him, boneless and replete. Her head rested on his shoulder, breathing in his scent as familiar as home. Briefly, she thought of Dante and wondered if he had closed himself off, knowing they would have this reaction to each other. It was just as well.

Their timing was impeccable. Keenan walked back into the room. "Sorry, guys, but I daren't give you any more time."

"Come and visit me in London," Jay whispered in her ear.

"When … the next time you need me?" she said, lifting her head slightly.

"No, anytime … I want to see you."

She straightened up a little more so she could look into his hot face and bloodshot eyes. He already looked better, with colour in his cheeks. The dark circles around his eyes were disappearing, and she was feeling better, too. It was miraculous.

"Please, Tia, come to London so we don't have to be like this."

The words and the longing in his voice were irresistible. She rested her forehead against his and smiled. It felt like a dream come true. She'd yearned for Jay so long. To hear the loving words from his lips, she couldn't believe it. "I quite like having control over you for a change," she said, grinning.

He beamed his gorgeous, heart-wrenching smile. His quiet confidence was returning by the minute. "If I let you chain me up, will you come?" he said so only she could hear. His eyes showed a small flicker of doubt despite his smile and she knew she could never shut him out of her life.

Instead of answering him, she stood up, straightened her clothes and walked towards the door. Before she disappeared, she turned and gave him a last look. His eyes were locked on her with an expression of awe and desire. She gazed at him for a full minute, wanting to etch that look on her memory for ever. Devastatingly beautiful, all roughed up and tied to a chair.

She giggled. "I'll try … I can't promise," she said with a wink.

He laughed loudly as she closed the door behind her.

CHAPTER 12

Southern California

After the night of the beach party, Cesaré remained around but never spoke a word to Lily. She often wondered what had happened to him to make him so bitter.

At first, she thought he hated all women, but the man was a babe magnet and seemed to be in their company all the time. It just seemed to be her he wanted nothing to do with, which kind of hurt.

Her eyes followed him while she and Shona bobbed around on their surfboards after he'd snubbed her yet again.

"Don't take it to heart, Lil … He'll calm down in time."

She looked at Shona sceptically. Not sure what she'd done to make the guy hate her so, but it obviously ran deep.

Then, as if she'd asked the question aloud, Shona began to answer it anyway. "I'm not completely sure," she said with a deep sigh. "The word is, his first cousin tricked him into thinking your sister was his. He's just still sore about it."

Lily listened with interest. She wanted to learn everything she could.

"It was a guy named Malleven – I've met him – a real

looker," Shona continued, "we all kinda knew him. Cesaré grew up with him and they were together a lot. I liked him. No surfer, though. They were chalk and cheese like that."

Lily frowned, not understanding.

"It was the whole compatible mate thing. Legend says there's a particular prince for each of the sisters. That means you'll have someone out there," Shona said, waggling her eyebrows suggestively.

There were still loads for Lily to learn, but she doubted that very much.

"Turns out she wasn't Ches' at all and Malleven had played a blinder to get a shot at the kingdom by using her against him."

Lily's eyes widened. She guessed that would piss a guy off.

"As it turned out, your sister rejected Malleven anyway. Everyone thinks he's dead and she went off with a Murr."

Bloody hell! Lily thought. *Quite an operator, this sister of hers.*

Shona nodded at Cesaré, climbing out of the water onto the rocks. "I think the guy is in mourning – plus Malleven and your sister made him look real bad in front of the whole Atlantean world."

Lily mouthed an O, then shook her head, absorbing the info. *Poor sod,* guess he did have a pretty good excuse to be upset. She watched as his striped back disappeared up the steps. He was ashamed and hurt – *little wonder he drinks.*

"This is a tough world, Lil. I feel for Ches, course I do, but it's all bets off when it comes to Sirens, you know? … Anyway, better go in. It's getting late and I got to be some-where," Shona said, snapping her out of her thoughts.

They caught their last wave into shore and Lily went back with some of the guys. Shona went off to wherever she had to be. She was doing it a lot lately. Lily wanted to ask where she got to, but never got around to it. She had more pressing worries. She had to start earning some money. She couldn't live off the guys for ever.

A FEW NIGHTS LATER, everyone came over to their house. It was the perfect party pad with large, spacious rooms and a patio and pool just outside. The big living room that served as the rehearsal space opened out onto it and people lounged and milled about, listening to music, eating barbeque and drinking cold beer. The longer she was there, the more she came to realise that the guys and this house were the centre for the Tiger Crew and the Atlanteans in these parts.

Looking around her, Lily felt strangely happy. Contentment was something new. It wasn't that she had become particularly close to any of these people, only counting Shona and Lance as her friends. The thing that was becoming alarmingly apparent was that she felt like she belonged. These people were her people. They all kept to themselves, letting few outsiders in, and she felt lucky to be included in that exclusive number. The feeling was a novelty. Usually, she never stayed anywhere long enough to form strong relationships.

As if to burst her happy bubble, Cesaré sauntered in with a very tanned leggy blonde hanging on his arm, with hair down to her waist and legs up to her armpits. It was as if the girls Cesaré kept company with were an attempt to deliberately rub in the contrast to Lily's zig-zaggy skin, dark, curly, unruly hair and petite frame. In fact, the only thing she liked about herself was her blue eyes that were so blue they didn't look real. The woman Cesaré currently paraded even seemed to trump that with eyes like headlights.

Perhaps she was being too hard on him. The story Shona had told her had played heavily on her mind. She decided to try hard tonight to bury the hatchet and perhaps then they could move forward – maybe not as friends, but at least acknowledging each other.

The guys were tuning up and playing scales to loosen up when she walked into the living room. The band was quite serious, she discovered, playing small gigs in and around the San Diego area, sometimes venturing to LA. They had one the next night and wanted to try out some of Lance's new material. They were an alternative rock band and called themselves Leviathan, named after some sea monster, which she thought was pretty cool. She really liked their stuff and thought they sounded really psychedelic.

"Where's River?" Lance shouted over the din to Nathan.

He shrugged. "Not seen him since the beach."

Lily found a beanbag and sprawled across it while she people-watched. The atmosphere was laid-back and chilled until Shona came blustering in, making Lily immediately alert. She never lost that "danger on the wind" instinct. "Hey, guys, weren't any of you with River today? He wiped out pretty bad. He's hurt."

The room fell silent when everyone cottoned on to the conversation and how serious it was. People started to stand up, ready to go.

"Is he okay?" Lance said, already grabbing his keys.

"Not sure, but he was in a lotta pain and couldn't move his arm."

Lance and a couple of the guys disappeared, she guessed, to the hospital. Shona went with them, making Lily feel at a loose end. Most of the closest people to her had gone, so she wandered outside to see who was out there. Scanning around, she realised they were people she hardly knew. She grabbed a beer from a crate and went to go back inside when Cesaré and the blonde caught her eye. The blonde kissed him and left. If she was ever going to build bridges with him, this was her opportunity. She picked up another beer and wandered over. He saw her approach and his expression remained closed. She passed him the beer.

"Grazie," he said, cracking it open and taking a gulp.

She waited for him to indicate the chair next to him for her to sit, but he didn't. After an awkward moment, she sat anyway. He was clearly determined not to make this easy for her. *Shit,* she wished she'd brought a pen and paper with her. The Grand Canyon of silence between them was becoming unbearable. He, on the other hand, seemed oblivious to the awkwardness.

In a white shirt and worn faded jeans, shades holding back his wavy shoulder-length hair, he looked effortlessly cool. Way more sophisticated than her. She was obviously wasting her time and went to get up.

"You like it here?" he said, surprising her.

Momentarily stunned, she relaxed back down into the seat and nodded.

"Don't get too comfortable, your presence here is getting around."

She frowned. *Was he being an asshole, or was he giving her a timely warning?* For politeness' sake, she decided to take it as the latter. She swallowed down her nerves and put out a hand for him to shake.

He flashed his eyes at her as if she were mad, swore in Italian, and got up, leaving her hanging. All she could do was blink. *What a dick!* Losing heart completely, she skulked off to bed, humiliation burning a hole right through her.

WHEN LILY REACHED HER ROOM, it no longer felt inviting and homely, but more like a lonely cupboard. She sat on her bed brooding. *Who was she kidding?* She didn't belong there. Even the ones who were nice to her saw her as a kind of mascot or pet, not the strong, independent woman she knew she was.

A tear ran down her cheek and she wiped it away with her fingers angrily. This was all her own fault for letting them get under her skin and allowing it to matter. There and then, she came to a decision. When everyone was asleep, she would slip away.

A knock at her door made her jump. *Fuck off!* She ignored it, hoping they'd go away.

"Lil, open up … it's me, Shona."

With a deep sigh, Lily went to the door and opened it. Shona pushed past her and into her room before she could stop her. She went to say something, then paused. "What's up?"

Lily shook her head and shrugged. Even if she had the power of speech, she just couldn't be arsed. The fight just seemed to have gone right out of her.

Shona was studying her with a weird, calculating look on her face. She pulled her down to sit on the bed next to her and stared at her for a long moment. "Are you happy here, Lil?"

It was an odd thing to ask right out of the blue, and Lily just looked back at her with lifeless, dead eyes to make of it what she would.

Shona pushed on anyway. "Only there's someone I want you to meet." She lowered her voice conspiratorially. "You gotta keep it under your hat for a while, okay? Not even Lance—especially Lance," she added. "He's a prince, Lil, and he can keep you safer than any of us can … a real powerful guy. I'm so hyped about it."

Lily didn't know what to think. Cesaré's warning came to her, quickly followed by his humiliation, and so she banished him from her mind.

Before she could sift through any of her jumbled

thoughts, the door knocked again. *For fuck's sake ... couldn't a girl get any fucking peace round here?*

"Come on, you two," Nathan's voice said. "Everyone's waiting."

Lily's mind was reeling when Shona took her by the hand and led her back into the party. She was so lost in her own thoughts that she wasn't conscious of anything or anyone until her eyes rested on River, sitting looking sorry for himself with his arm in a sling.

Lance promptly walked over to her and gave her some sticks. She looked up at him questioningly.

"River isn't playing any time soon."

Still not really understanding, she looked past Lance to River. "Dislocated shoulder," he said with an apologetic smile.

She looked at the sticks in her hand.

"We've got a gig tomorrow ... can you do it?" Lance said softly.

She felt as if she were in a bit of a dream with everything that had happened that evening. *Shit,* she'd practised on her own and stuff, but she didn't know their set. How would she learn it in a day?

"You can do it," Lance whispered next to her ear, sending shivers up her spine.

Her stomach fluttered as it always did around him. She sighed and walked over to the drum kit as if she were about to walk the plank. When she sat, the room erupted in whoops and cheers. *No pressure or anything. Bloody hell!*

The other guys picked up their instruments. Lance slipped his guitar over his head and gave her the list of six songs.

Lily felt the most on her own than she'd ever felt in her whole life.

· · ·

WATCHING Lily looking down at her hands, holding her sticks, sitting amongst the drum kit that dwarfed her, Lance was concerned. "Will she be okay?" he said quietly to Shona.

The room had filled and gone quiet as if they were all thinking the same thing. The last thing Lance wanted to do was embarrass her.

"She'll be fine," Shona said, with a wave of her hand. "She's heard the songs dozens of times.

Suddenly, it didn't feel like such a great idea as he watched her fidget and adjust her stool several times before dropping her sticks. *Shit.* The people in the room began to get restless watching.

Then she began studying the set list. He shook his head and strode over to her. "It's just us," he said, calmly. "Just play what you feel … it's no big deal, okay?"

"1,2,3," Nathan called loudly, and they all struck their first note, except Lily, who sat frozen in fear.

"Stop, stop, stop!" Lance called with his hand up.

He held her eyes, focusing her attention on him until he felt she had calmed down, then nodded.

"1,2,3!" Nathan shouted again, and the song began.

Lily was right on the button. The song progressed and she found her groove, losing herself in the rhythm. She listened to when the song was to break down, getting the feel of the groove changes and dynamic shifts and came down with heavy fills when it just felt right.

Lance grinned. She was a fucking awesome drummer, and he began to sing with confidence, knowing she could more than hold her own with the beat. But although he tried to sing out to those around the room watching, his body would turn and he would find himself watching her time and time again. He couldn't take his eyes off her.

He wiped the sweat from his brow. *Fuck! It had got hot.*

The perspiration dripped down his face persistently while they played song after song seamlessly as if Lily had played with them for years. She had fantastic feel for the music and his heart swelled with pride for her.

When, at last, she put everything into the final beats and crescendo of the song, he felt floored by her, as well as exhausted, overwhelmed and unbelievably hot. The only thing he could do was to walk out to find the cool and sanctuary of his own room, where he could think about what just happened. The room whistled and whooped in applause behind him.

LILY FELT ELATED at the end of the set. It hadn't taken long to settle down to the soothing sense of security that the rhythm always gave her. All her worries evaporated. She became lost in the music and in her own little world. Everyone in the room disappeared – everyone that is, except Lance. Her eyes had found his several times in the music, usually when his guitar riff was truly inspired, or his range and rasp in his voice were just too sublime for words. He was undoubtedly a star.

She'd found she wanted to play for him. To quieten to emphasize the quality in his voice, and then come in all guns blazing when he threw down and screamed when the song needed it. It felt as though they were musically made for each other. So when they finished triumphantly in a blaze of glory, she jumped up and wanted to run into his arms and thank him for showing her this side of herself she never knew. But as she left her stool, the world dropped away from her and she blasted red. Lance coldly turned his back and left the room as fast as he could. It was as though he couldn't wait to get out.

He couldn't have wounded her more if he'd kicked her in the gut. The other guys all came over and smacked her on the back and congratulated her.

River kissed her and pointed in mock anger. "Don't get too comfortable," he said and laughed.

"Smokin', babe!" Nathan said.

Not smokin' enough. Then, just when she thought her life couldn't get any worse, her eyes found Cesaré's – red and half closed. She thought he'd gone, but he'd been there the whole time. He sneered and walked out, too.

Lily swallowed down a lump in her throat. *Enough with kidding herself now. She had to get out.*

Shona pulled her into a hug. "Way to go, girl … that was awesome … I'm so stoked for you."

Lily nodded now, numb to emotion.

Shona held her at arm's length, sensing something was the matter. She frowned. "Let me get a pen and paper."

Finding nothing to write on, Shona led her back to the privacy of her little room. There, she saw a pad and a pen and put them in her hand.

Lily scribbled quickly: *When can we go?*

Shona read it then studied her face for a long moment. "You want to meet him … the prince?"

Lily cast her eyes downwards and nodded. There was nothing to keep her around there.

Shona was still thoughtful. "Righto," she said eventually. "You've made the right decision, Lil. As much as I love having you here, you should be with a prince … and Ches is as good as useless. I'll arrange it for as soon as."

Lily nodded sadly with her eyes cast down. She could tell Shona was dying to ask what was wrong, but knew her well enough by now to know that she'd be wasting her time. *What would she tell her anyway?* That the person most like her cruelly blanks her, and the person who affects her so deeply can't even bear to be in the same room as her when she plays —the only thing in her life she was totally confident with. *Get me out of here!* she silently screamed.

CHAPTER 13

*L*ance had to splash his face as soon as he was alone. He held the edges of the sink and looked at his face in the mirror. *What was the matter with him?* She was affecting him more and more over time. The recurring nightmares were getting worse, so he was barely sleeping.

He pulled his t-shirt forward over his head and turned sideways to study the inked Siren in the mirror. It was so like her, it was unbelievable. *What was going on?* Tonight, he'd resisted the most unbearable urge to run to her and snatch her from the drum kit and devour her whole like in his dreams – the ones where they had sex so hot it was off the scale. No one had ever had such a physical effect on him.

But she was a Siren – a Soul Breather, wasn't she? Didn't that explain it all? But she was not for him, and never would be. Besides, if the dreams were her—and he knew they were, then the nightmares were too. It was the biggest cold shower to his libido.

There was a loud knock at the door.

"Lance!"

He looked at it but couldn't answer. He just wanted to be left alone.

"Let me in, Lance … It's important. The Italian accent was unmistakably Cesaré. Given his recent unsociable attitude, it must be something important. The guy just didn't give a shit lately.

"Come in," Lance said wearily and grabbed a towel and sat on the bed.

Cesaré came in and quietly closed the door. He studied him for a few moments, then came and sat next to him on the bed.

Lance looked at him in a way that said, 'Be careful what you say right now.' He just wasn't in the mood. Cesaré grinned, showing him he got the message loud and clear. Instead of speaking, he felt inside his jeans jacket pocket and took out a vial of clear liquid and passed it to him.

Lance took it and looked at Cesaré enquiringly. "What is it?"

Cesaré sighed deeply. "Drink it … you're going to need it," he said, smiling ruefully.

Lance frowned, uncorked and sniffed it. Then, guessing it was some kind of alcohol, knocked it back and grimaced. It tasted disgusting. He shuddered, still pulling a face. "You gonna tell me what it is?"

Cesaré stood up and wandered to the door. "You're going to need another two doses … if you're going to avoid the reaction you just had," he said, all rolling Rs.

Lance was a little uncomfortable at the guy's knowledge of how he'd been feeling. *Had it been that obvious?*

Cesaré smiled knowingly and left the room.

Reaction to Lily? He'd posed more questions than he'd answered.

. . .

LILY WAS CONVINCED Lance was avoiding her now. The gig was cancelled and she didn't have a clue what she'd done wrong. Every morning when she woke early to surf, which had always been their regular routine, he'd already gone. And every time she tried to sit next to him when everyone was relaxing, he'd get up and say he had to be somewhere else.

She became furious with herself for letting it bother her, but it did. In fact, it hurt like hell. When she awoke that day, she decided to force him to tell her why he'd suddenly switched on her. She needed to know – especially now she'd made up her mind to leave.

The sun was a pink glow on the horizon when she jumped off the rocks with her board at their usual spot. His lone figure chopping through the waves was easy to pick out in the pastel light. Even if he didn't have her picture plastered over his beautifully tanned back, she'd know his effortlessly fluid style anywhere.

She paddled towards him confidently now. How far she'd come in such a relatively short time. Gone was any fear of creatures that shared the water with her. Right now, she was more scared of rejection from the man who skipped across the waves as if he were part of them.

She waited in the lull between sets, sitting on her board in the hope that he would notice her. He didn't stop, even though she was sure he knew she was there. In fact, he was surfing as if his life depended on it. Totally ignoring her.

All her anger and hurt began to rise inside her. She hadn't asked to live with them. *He* had convinced her to. She didn't want to play drums that night; she had done it for *him*. And now he seemed determined to humiliate her with his indifference. Well, she wasn't just going to skulk off to lick her wounds; she was going to have it out with him before she went.

She waited for him to catch his next wave, turned for

shore and did the same. As he took the wave, she made sure she dropped in right in front of him so he almost crashed into her. It was a dangerous manoeuvre and strictly against surfing etiquette, one she knew would piss him off. She heard his curse as they both wiped out in the white water.

"What the fuck?" he shouted as they both came up to gulp the air.

Lily glared at him, climbed back on her board and paddled back out.

He retrieved his board from the end of his leash and followed. His powerful strokes soon caught up with her in no time.

She went to turn away from him, but he grabbed her board and spun her round to face him. He looked furious with her, pulled her alongside him and sat up. "Sit up!" he ordered.

She did as she was told and they glared at each other for a long moment.

"Are you trying to hurt yourself with a stunt like that?" he said.

What do you care! she shouted in her head.

For a moment, Lance was stunned. His eyes widened and he moved his head back in surprise. "Did you just say something?" He knew what he was saying sounded ridiculous, as her lips never moved.

Oh yeah, course I did. I'm a great conversationalist. She continued to glare at him.

His eyes widened again. "There ... am I going mad?"

What?

"That's what!"

For a second, the pair of them frowned at each other in utter confusion.

Lance went to say something. Then changed his mind as if he was too flummoxed to phrase his words. "I think by some miracle …" He shook his head like he couldn't believe it. "I heard you … I'm sure I did."

He watched the frown evaporate from her face, replaced by a small smile. *You did?*

He laughed out loud. "I did." He pulled her in closer and touched the side of her face while his eyes searched it. "Fuck, Lily … what's happening?"

She moved into his touch. The familiar warm, tingly, safe feeling spread all over her. *I'm not sure … I'm just thinking.*

"But I can hear you – like some kind of telepathy," he said, staring at her in wonder.

The wonderful sound of her laughter bubbled up and he heard it.

Maybe we can all do it, but we just didn't know how. She smiled shyly.

As she thought the words she knew he could hear, he looked so beautiful – so handsome, like some kind of model with his long, wet hair tousled around his shoulders. However, when his expression changed to regret, the joy drained away from her.

"But we're not the same, Lily."

It doesn't matter that you're not royal … not to me.

His face looked stricken with regret. "It's not that, I'm not even Atlantean, Lily. I'm Human."

Her stomach felt like it fell away. *But … But … I thought.*

When he held out his beautiful, tanned arm next to hers, and it was covered in goose bumps, she looked down at it in confusion.

"No stripes," he said.

Of course. He'd worn a wetsuit more often than not, so the thought hadn't even occurred to her. She was forced to look down at her own body that never felt the cold, not even in the cold Pacific waters, covered entirely in thick dark stripes.

He never had any on his face, as many of the crew didn't; she'd merely thought his genes were really watered down.

Lance gave her his half smile as if to say, "You see", then lay down and turned to make his way back to the beach.

What ... wait ... is that it? You're giving up on me? she thought as loudly as she could.

"You are not meant for me," he called over his shoulder.

Please, Lance, she thought over and over. The tears streamed down her face as he got further and further away. He could either no longer hear or chose to ignore her. The subject was closed as far as he was concerned. He had given his definitive answer to anything between them, and it was a no.

LILY CAUGHT a lift back with one of the others. Lance had disappeared by the time she got to the road. He hadn't even waited to make sure. It was the final reality slap to her face that galvanized her decision. *How could she have missed something as simple as him being Human?* No wonder he wasn't interested.

So when Shona bowled straight into her as soon as she walked into the hallway, she nodded meekly to her whisper of, "There you are. It has to be today ... are you ready ... I mean, are you sure, Lil?"

A feeling of deep despondency swept over her. There was no reason to hang around now. Wasting no more time on sappy thoughts, she quickly showered and changed so they could be on their way before anyone else came home.

Shona borrowed a car from one of the guys and drove them all the way to LA. They travelled into the heart of the city to the mysterious prince's apartment. Lily wasn't sure it was a good idea at all the nearer they got. Despite what had happened that morning, she still felt guilty about sneaking off.

Then she got a hold of herself. This trip was just to check the guy out; nothing was going to get signed on a dotted line yet. Besides, she was a free agent. She didn't owe anyone anything – least of all Lance. Humans and Atlanteans didn't mix – not romantically anyway.

When they arrived, they parked in an underground car park, came up into a posh lobby and gave their names to the concierge. "You may go up," he said.

Lily was terrified of going up in the lift. The whole thing had the same feel as the time Sid had taken her to the old bloke in Fulham all those years ago.

"You alright?" Shona said.

She nodded, but totally gave herself away.

"Don't worry, I know him," she said, waggling her eyebrows playfully.

Lily looked at her sardonically. *Really?* Somehow, that wasn't cheering her up.

Shona smiled as if even she realised how silly that sounded, given the gravity of the situation. "Look, we'll just talk, you can suss him out, and if you're not happy about anything at all, we can just go."

It should have made her feel better, but it didn't. Old wounds ran deeper than she thought.

A man in Middle Eastern dress greeted them and ushered them in with a thick accent. *Shit, what was she getting herself into here?*

The apartment on the top floor was opulent but dark. The whole décor reminded her of a film set, done out like a sheik's palace or something. They walked on through a marble-tiled hallway into a spacious living room. The blinds were all drawn and the only light came from a real fire, making the air close and stifling. The old man in Fulham came to mind again, triggering her fight-or-flight response. It took all her willpower not to run out the way she came.

Two men stood as they came near to the large semi-circular sofa in the centre of the room. Both were tall, as she'd come to recognise in all Atlantean men. One was blonde with overlong hair and light grey eyes. He was good-looking in a boyish kind of way. The other was very dark with black hair and highly unusual, deep blue eyes. They struck her with a shrewd knowingness in them, as if there wasn't much in life they hadn't seen. Both men were impeccably dressed in suits in different shades of grey. Either could have been a fashion model and either could be a prince. Lily had no idea which one she had come to see.

"Enchanted," the dark one said in a strong accent, different from the servant who'd shown them in. He picked up her hand and kissed it. Then he nodded to Shona. "She doesn't disappoint … such a contrast to her sisters."

"Told ya!" Shona said.

Lily's heart sped up. This guy was obviously the one she was here for, and he knew her sisters. That meant he knew a lot about who she was and where she was from.

"Antonio, please take Shona for a stroll. I wish to discuss certain matters with …" and he paused for her to fill in the blank with her name.

"Lily!" Shona said for her. "Her name's Lillian Gale … she can't talk though."

His head tilted to the side slightly and he blinked as if he were considering the new information.

Lily just wanted the ground to swallow her up as she always did when she met new people who were made aware of her disability.

"Like our cousins the Murrs," he said, smiling. He seemed genuinely pleasantly surprised about it and not fazed in the slightest.

He seemed okay, but she wasn't sure about being left on her own with him. She pleaded with her eyes to Shona.

She understood and smiled weakly. "You'll be fine, Lil."

Lily anxiously watched Shona be led away at the elbow by the blond guy, still looking back over her shoulder at her with a face apologising without words. The blond guy flashed a wearied look at the dark one which didn't exactly fill her with much confidence either.

It took a minute until they were completely alone and by then her heart was hammering. Her eyes were already searching for an escape route or something to clobber him with should he get fruity with her.

"Sit, Lily," he said, indicating the sofa. Then he walked to a table and poured two glasses of what looked like wine. "Here," he said, offering her a glass. As her hand went round it, he allowed one of his fingers to linger and stroke along one of hers. It unnerved her when a tingle ran all the way up her arm, neck and face. It was the weirdest sensation and nothing like the comforting warmth of Lance's touch.

Don't be afraid of me.

Her eyes went wide. His voice came from so close it felt like it was inside her own skull. She hadn't even noticed that he now held her free hand. His thumb ran back and forth across the back of it and she went to pull it away in shock.

Don't be afraid, he said, gently again. *I'm just talking to you in the way of our ancestors.*

Her last conversation with Lance flashed into her mind – an ability she had stumbled upon by accident. Now she understood; it made perfect sense. She relaxed a little more and tried to control her breathing. She was learning a lot from this visit already.

Look at me, Lily. He was tilting his head again, reading her. She wasn't sure she liked it, but she stared into his eyes, the darkest blue she'd ever seen. His face was classically beautiful, with perfect lines and a chiselled jaw. He smiled as if he knew she was appraising him.

Have you ever projected speech before? he asked.

She concentrated on not blushing and shook her head.

Try ... I am almost there ... it will be easier for me, he said.

Her heart was beating. It felt as though he were in her head already.

He retreated slightly.

It gave her some space. She hadn't realised she was breathing like she'd been running. *Who are you?* she thought, eventually.

A stunning smile lit up his face and a shimmer like molten gold flickered through his eyes. It was both alarming and beautiful – he spellbound her.

My name is Malleven ... I am honoured to meet you, il mio fiore*!*

CHAPTER 14

Malleven glanced down at his divining ring. It was the ring given to all princes to detect a siren. It started white, turned turquoise when he came near one, then deepest purple if she was his destined mate by fate. His had already been purple once before, for Lily's sister, Isla. But she had rejected him in favour of Darres Borge – a Murr prince from Murrtaine.

His fist clenched at the memory. Not only had he been left for dead, but he had also been disgraced in front of the whole Atlantean world.

Now, when he studied his ring, it was blood red – a completely unprecedented colour. He had no doubt of Lily's authenticity as a siren, but it did mean his ring was either faulty – which was unlikely– or it meant something much darker. He suspected it meant he could never lay claim to a Siren again.

Malleven continued to hold the skin contact with Lily. She was powerful; he could feel it flowing through her. But she had no control or knowledge of it. This pleased him. She could be moulded and shaped to be whatever he wanted or needed her to be.

EVENTUALLY, Lily felt relaxed enough to sit down on the sofa. As he turned his body to face her in the seat, his eyes shimmered gold again. It was a startling contrast to his coffee-coloured skin. He unnerved her but fascinated her too. *What do you want from me?* she projected.

He bobbed his head as if it were a perfectly reasonable question. *I could ask the same of you, Lily ... after all, you must have chosen to come here for a reason.*

The question flipped back at her totally threw her. She frowned and thought about it for a moment. Shona had suggested it, saying there was someone to meet her, and that she should be with a prince to protect her. *To be safe!* she blurted, but she wasn't entirely sure that was the reason. He unbalanced her in a way she wasn't used to and seemed to turn everything she thought she knew on its head so she didn't know what was up any more.

His shrewd eyes were watching her closely while he took a sip of his drink and indicated for her to do the same. The fire was making her feel really hot, but the alcohol was beginning to relax her. *Or was it him?*

She found her eyes skating all over him. He was beautiful with a perfect physique. One that looked great in a suit – *an expensive one.*

Lance's lean surfer's body flashed into her head and she quickly swept it away.

Malleven's eyes seemed amused as if he knew exactly what she was thinking. Then, just when she thought he'd forgotten what she'd said, *Shall I tell you what I believe you came here for, Lily?*

Her eyes widened in surprise. She wasn't sure how he

could possibly know anything about her yet. Maybe he was just very arrogant. She shrugged. *Go on then.*

I think we are the same, you and I. He let his words sink in and continued to watch her reaction closely.

She looked him up and down again. It seemed impossible that someone who came from where she did could be anything like the dazzling prince who sat in front of her.

We both started with nothing, he said, eventually.

Her eyes went to his in surprise. There was a steely determination there, and his mind seemed to drift as he switched back to speech.

"I, too, grew up with no parents, no money, and no home to speak of, Lily. I know what it is to scrimp and save and claw your way out to have anything. To have to fight every single person you meet just to be considered equal. And to duck and dive to get anything you want for what you inevitably need." His words were strong and clear and his accent only made him sound more fervent. The intonation reminded her of Cesaré, but he certainly didn't act like him. What he said was filled with emotion and very definitely tinged with an undercurrent of bitterness.

His eyes bored into hers, shimmering gold, with intent so fierce she was glued to them. It was as if he echoed every thought or feeling she had ever gone through and articulated better than she ever could. As though he'd known her her whole life and knew the core of her. But her heart sank and her eyes travelled to her arm that showed the faint stripes she could never completely hide. It was the proof that she was very different from everybody, even a prince.

He was studying her again, like he didn't miss a thing. Then he looked over at the low table in front of them, where there was a pitcher of iced water, a remote control, and a pencil and paper. He startled her when he sat forward, removed his jacket, and began to unbutton the cuff on his shirt and roll it up to his elbow.

Just when Lily was preparing to run, not sure what he was doing, he reached over to the pitcher and tipped its contents over his forearm, without a care when the water splashed all over the polished floor. He set the jug down, then looked down at his arm and into her eyes again.

There in front of her was the living proof of his words. Thick black bands, similar to her own, had come to the surface of his brown skin. "You are most like the Murrs out of all your sisters, Lily, and you are beautiful—never forget that." His eyes were narrowed and meant every word.

Lily was choked with emotion, not because of their similarity, but simply because he found her beautiful and had explained more to her in five minutes than anyone had in a lifetime. She turned away before he could see the tears threatening to spill out of her eyes.

"Don't turn away," he said, putting his hand out gently and moving her chin back to face him. "I see everything … I can feel what you feel … remember that." There was no sentiment in his expression, just a cold, hard self-belief that he knew what he was talking about. But there was comfort in his confidence.

What was the matter with her? She hated that he was dragging this sappy, little-girl-lost side out of her. She was a tough cookie and she'd been one all her life. She huffed irritably and dragged the tears away from her eyes with her fingers. *What is it you want … what do I have to do?* she thought, getting them back on track.

He didn't rise to her anger but relaxed back into the chair and allowed her to calm down for a moment. His every action flummoxed her, so she never knew what to expect from him.

"I won't make you do anything, Lily. The whole point is that you should choose to stay with me."

She considered what he said for a moment and what it would mean to her life. *Then what?* He was going to have to spell out precisely what he wanted and what she was expected to do. She didn't want any nasty surprises down the line.

Lily felt him at the edges of her mind again. A slight pain made her touch her forehead and her eyes went to his.

He nodded slowly. "I want you to go home with Shona and think carefully. Tell no one that you have met me. And if you decide to take your chances in the life you have, you may go on your way. But if you decide to return to me, it will be to stay. You will be my mate and chosen partner and we will be together in all things. That means you will join with me in the way of Atlanteans. You will be tested as a Siren and we will be pledged, which in our world means an unbreakable marriage."

He allowed a few moments for his terms to sink in. What he was proposing was a massive step. It was, in effect, an arranged marriage with a man she hardly knew. But as he'd spoken the terms to her, she felt her heart flutter in a way she'd never felt before. "Partner", he'd said, "together in all things", all concepts she'd never dared to dream of expecting for herself in her miserable life.

"But I will expect total capitulation. I will love and care for you, Lily, but in exchange for you never having another care, you will allow me into your heart, your mind, and your soul." His eyes flickered again with the passion in his voice.

The strength of his words made her shudder. It touched her somewhere so deeply inside that she couldn't begin to work out why. She guessed it was because a man, and such a beautiful one, should want and need her to that extent. She wasn't sure if she was daft letting someone she hardly knew affect her like that. *How long do I have ... to decide, I mean?*

"I will be here another twenty-four hours, then I will be gone."

She was suddenly filled with panic. That wasn't enough time to make a decision like that. The other option was to stay from today, but the thought of not saying a proper goodbye to Lance cut her to the quick. It would be the last she would probably see of him. Sniffing back tears threatening to spill, she nodded. *Okay ... I will give you my answer tomorrow.*

"Very well," he said, smiling.

For a long moment, they looked intently into each other's eyes until noises in the hallway meant that Shona and Antonio had returned. It was so well-timed; she wondered if Malleven somehow knew they were coming.

Malleven stood and she followed his lead.

Shona walked in and looked at them cautiously. "Well?"

Malleven smiled benignly. "Lily has decided to go home and think about my proposition."

Shona's eyebrows went up like she had surprised her. "Great ... sounds like a plan!"

Goodbye, Lily thought quickly, and walked towards the door. For some reason, she needed air. The room had become unbearable.

"I hope to see you again. *Il mio fiore!*" He finished so only she could hear.

She closed her eyes and went out the door, leaving the oppressive darkness to come out into the light.

SHONA WENT to follow Lily out, relieved that the meeting had gone so well. She'd gone out on a limb with this ever since she'd been approached by one of Malleven's men. He'd insisted on secrecy to spare Cesaré's feelings and she'd gone along with it, but it hadn't sat well lying to her friends.

Shona!

Malleven's voice stopped her in her tracks as she was about to go out the door. She half turned, eager to catch up with Lily and get out of the place.

"You did the right thing."

It was spooky how the guy seemed to know everything. Didn't stop her from feeling guilty, though.

"I don't want any pressure put on Lily in coming to a decision. You should know that rumours of her being here are everywhere. Spies are flooding in as we speak, representing those not so intent on keeping the old ways."

Shona swallowed hard and nodded. His meaning was loud and clear and it scared the shit out of her. She could just imagine some of the types after Lily. *They were just a bunch of surfers, for fuck's sake.* It was all way out of their league. "So if you don't want me to pressure her, what do you want me to do?"

"Have faith, Shona … you must keep her safe."

Shona studied his face for a full minute; he was deadly serious. Then again, whenever she had seen him with Cesaré, he had always been that way. Working while Cesaré played, sober while Cesaré drank, single while Cesaré acted like some dog on heat. Cesaré was a friend and she knew he was in bits over what had happened with Malleven, but there were always two sides to a story. The guy standing here in front of her was a serious prince trying to do his duty. *Wasn't that what all the princes were doing – fighting each other to get what they needed for their families?*

Shona gave a slight nod and left.

CHAPTER 15

Malleven watched Lily and Shona go, satisfied with the outcome of the meeting. Then he whispered for one of his men to follow them. She would return, he was sure of it, but he couldn't trust her safety to a group of layabouts.

Lily reminded him of a bird with a broken wing, forced to trust while vulnerable, but with a little care and attention would flourish. Although in this little bird's case, she would not be released – ever. It had become very clear to him how she would be handled. The heavy-handed way he had treated her sister, Isla, had been a mistake, one he would not make again.

He looked down at his blood red ring, already returning to its opaque white, and snatched it off his finger. Swearing loudly, he threw it against the wall. "Get me another, Antonio, this one is fucking broken."

Antonio paused and blinked in shock at the sudden outburst, then he tipped his head slightly in acknowledgement. "I'll get onto it right away." Then he walked to the doorway and turned. "What if it's not … what if Isla's rejection means you can no longer make a bid for a Siren?"

Malleven narrowed his eyes at the one person who would dare ask him a question like that and live. "Have you learnt nothing about me yet?" Malleven growled ominously. "I am too strong … not the king, not fate, nor even the fucking Orb will ever stop me. Do you hear me, Antonio? … I will be making a bid for the kingdom." He enjoyed watching the fear creep into Antonio's features with every word, then threw his head back and laughed. *Poor Antonio*, their relationship had spanned several years and he expected to keep a man such as he all to himself. Sex was one thing, but marriage to a Siren was a whole other thing entirely.

He sighed, feeling a great sorrow for Antonio's delusion. The man simply loved him. "She will return to me, Antonio," he said more kindly. "And she will give herself to me." He knew this because he did see a little of himself in the girl – the one most like their ancestors. The power the girl held was an added aphrodisiac, but Antonio was also his. "She will be mine … and I never let go of what I decide is mine," he reminded him, looking into Antonio's eyes meaningfully. And they smouldered in reply.

Then he pointed an accusing finger. "And no fucking ring–whatever the colour can dictate otherwise."

LILY WAS SUBDUED when they set off for the long drive back to San Diego.

"Here!" Shona said, pulling a pad and a pen out of the door compartment, and passed them to her.

Lily looked at her questioningly.

"There must be stuff you want to ask?" Shona took her eyes from the road to glance at her briefly. "You don't have long, hun."

Why the cloak and dagger today? She scribbled and held up the pad for Shona to scan quickly. It had niggled her that they had sneaked her off and that Malleven had told her to keep quiet as well. If everything was above board, *shouldn't she be able to share it with the group?* After all, they were all supposed to be protecting her.

Shona tipped her head and sighed. "Well, it's kinda tricky," she said, scratching her head while she attempted to phrase her words. "Malleven approached me through somebody else on the sly. You see, he was the one fighting with Cesaré over your sister."

Lily widened her eyes.

Shona nodded without speaking. "Yeah, he was the guy who made Ches into the mess he is today."

Lily shook her head. *If Malleven was so bad, then why would she take her to him, of all people?*

"I know what you're thinking and, believe me, I had a real war with meself. The thing is, Lil, that these princes kind of have to fight to survive. There's only five of you and hundreds of princes … you know what I mean?"

She kind of did. There was no love lost between her and Cesaré, but still, she'd often wondered what could have happened to reduce a man to a state like that.

"You see, Cesaré has always been a playboy. He loves the surf, the girls and the easy life. Malleven, on the other hand, is the one who has always been serious. So when he got in touch, I kinda thought, well, Cesaré is out of the game. Malleven seemed like a good bet. And I think he didn't want to pitch up to all of us, given that all the guys are on Ches' side. I don't think he wanted to open old wounds with him, you know? A lot of people thought he was dead and he kinda liked it that way – at least for a while."

How did he even know about me? Lily wrote and held up on the pad.

"Well, that's the thing. He just told me that news about you is getting around. He reckons spies are everywhere."

Lily's heart thumped. Maybe Cesaré's warning was genuine after all.

"The Tiger Crew kinda knows everything going on south of LA, so it was a pretty safe bet that one of us would know something ... I think he was just fishing."

Lily stared out of the windshield. This was all so much bigger and more complicated than she thought. In the beginning, all she wanted to do was move on and get away from Lance.

"You alright?" Shona said cautiously. "He did behave himself, didn't he?"

Lily nodded, bewildered. She had to put personal squabbles between princes and politics aside. Most of it was over her head anyway. She had to break it down and look at it for what it was – a marriage proposal.

She calmed down her racing thoughts and replayed the weirdest conversation of her life – not that she'd had many. *But that was it, wasn't it?* Malleven was a beautiful and powerful prince, and he had communicated and really understood her more in about twenty minutes than anyone else ever had. That had to count for something. *Cesaré was a prince, but he made no effort with her.* Then her mind fluttered back to Lance as it always did. Sadly, she had to face the fact that Lance did not want a relationship with someone from another species. He had no intention of crossing the barrier. Malleven, on the other hand, had taken more care and made more effort to speak to her and get to know her than anyone else.

And yet ...

Her mind went back and forth the whole journey home. And Shona, who glanced at her repeatedly, had the good sense to leave her to her thoughts.

. . .

IT WAS late in the evening when they finally walked back into the hallway of the house. Lily chucked her things into a heap on the floor and went to get a drink from the kitchen to take to bed with her. She was dog-tired, emotionally worn-out, and had no intentions of socialising with any of the hangers-on the guys had around tonight. They always had a houseful.

The laughter and strumming guitars travelled from the living room. Shona was right behind her, probably worn out from all the driving too. It was a long round trip to do in a day.

"Shona, is that you?" Lance's shout came from the other room.

"Yeah, it's us," Shona said wearily.

Lance bounded into the kitchen and glared at them. "Where the fuck did you two get to all day?"

Lily turned in shock. She had never heard Lance raise his voice in anger before.

"Chill out, mate," Shona said. "We just had to nip some-where ... that's all ... ya know ... girl stuff!"

Oh bloody hell. The room was beginning to fill with the others, drawn towards the raised voices, including Cesaré. He was all she needed.

"Where did you have to go?" Lance continued in the same aggressive tone.

Lily watched, flabbergasted. She could see he was only just keeping a lid on his temper and beginning to get Shona's back up too.

"For fuck's sake, mate, I don't have to tell you where I go every minute of the blasted day!"

Despite her anger, Lily knew Shona's defensiveness came from guilt. They had sneaked around without telling anyone, but it was kind of justified, seeing Lance's reaction. Protectors or not, this was her decision, and they needed to give her the space to make it.

"We all have a responsibility to her,' Lance said, jabbing a finger towards Lily without looking at her. "You can't just take her off like that without letting any of us know."

Now he was beginning to piss her off; talking like she wasn't there, like she was a small child.

"Okay … okay," Shona said, with her hands up. "You're making a big fuckin' deal about nothing … point taken … won't do it again," she said with sarcasm dripping from her voice.

Shona was about to flounce off dramatically when Cesaré put out his arm and said calmly and quietly, "You still didn't say where you took her."

Fuck! Lily wanted to scream. *Since when was it any of Cesaré's business?* The very thing Malleven said before she left was not to tell anyone. *No!* she projected loudly.

The whole party turned their heads to look at her. Most were a little startled at hearing her and Lance blushed as if she'd embarrassed him *a-gain*. Shona looked at her with meaning, clearly saying they should own up.

Surprisingly, none of them seemed unduly perturbed at her speaking directly to their minds. *Guess they were accustomed to weird.* It was kind of an anti-climax. *For fuck's sake!* she projected more for her own benefit.

Their eyes widened.

Shit, it really worked. It had felt like a fluke when she'd spoken telepathically with Lance. Then, meeting with Malleven, she assumed it was mainly to do with him. It seems he was right; it did come to her naturally.

"It's okay, Lil," Shona said, exhaling loudly. "We should really let them know what's happening."

But he said I shouldn't tell anyone.

"Who … Who said that?" Lance said, getting more furious by the minute.

No! Lily pleaded.

"Look, I'll tell, then it wasn't you … okay?" Shona said.

Everyone began chiming in and demanding she talk and Lily knew she didn't have a hope in hell of keeping a lid on this and sagged in defeat. *Whatever.*

It felt wrong to tell. She wasn't sure why she felt so bad. Maybe it was breaking a first promise to Malleven. Or, more disturbing still, that she had betrayed a trust in Lance. It really made no sense, especially after the way he'd been treating her lately.

"I took her to a prince," Shona blurted out.

There was a moment of stunned silence where Lance looked directly into Lily's eyes. "You did what?" Lance said, still staring at her, while everyone else started speaking at the same time. "Who is it? Where?" came at them from all angles. The room was filling with even more people drawn to the drama unfolding.

Lily felt bombarded. She had absolutely no privacy. This was her life and nobody else's business. Tears of frustration began to fall down her cheeks.

Everyone was shouting and having a go at Shona. "Well, none of you bastards were gonna get off ya asses!" she shouted back.

Lily took a back seat and let Shona take all of the flak. It allowed her to notice Cesaré, standing apart with the blackest look of all. Lily's heart went into her mouth when he asked very low and deliberately, "Tell me which prince, Shona."

Lily had never seen Shona look shaken, but she did at that moment. She was completely shitting herself. Lily felt worried for her. *What was this bloke's problem?*

"Malleven," Shona said quietly.

After a stunned moment, the room erupted into questions and Cesaré just closed his eyes. It was as though someone had died. Lily felt anxious about what he would do next.

Shona began back-pedalling. "Well, you didn't want her," she shouted in defence.

"I can't believe you did that!"

"Without telling anyone," Lance added, shaking his head.

Cesaré held his forehead in his hand as if he were in pain, then stormed out of the room, barging between people without apology.

"She's still fucking here!" Shona shouted after him. "No harm's been done … bloody hell!"

After much swearing on Shona's part, people began to disperse, sensing the show was over, leaving them with just Lance and Nathan.

"I can't believe you," Lance said with disgust. "Cesaré thought … He hoped Malleven was dead."

Lily's head felt like it would burst. She didn't fully understand what was going on. Obviously, Cesaré had issues with this Malleven guy, but she couldn't take any more shit tonight. She pushed between them to go to her room. *I can think for my fucking self,* she projected as she went.

"We're meant to protect you!" Lance shouted after her.

She glared over her shoulder at his red and angry face. *I never asked for that,* she muttered and left him staring after her.

LANCE HELD Shona by the arm before she could disappear. She railed against him, but he knew it was borne out of guilt, knowing full well she'd been wrong to take Lily anywhere without telling someone.

Typically so laid-back, his own anger surprised him. It

was way off the scale and he held onto it, refusing to analyse it too deeply. After a shouting match, they stood and glared at each other.

In the end, Shona sagged wearily. "I had to do something, Lance. We can't keep her hidden just because Cesaré has a problem with his cousin. The place is filling up with all sorts after her. For fuck's sake, we have a responsibility."

Lance shook his head. "I'm not saying we should do nothing, but you shouldn't have decided on your own, Shona. We all agreed."

She fidgeted with annoyance, but she couldn't argue against that. There was no apology, instead she complained, "What difference does it make, anyway, Lance? It's not like she's your sole responsibility; you're not even blood."

Her words hit him like a punch and she visibly recoiled the minute the words left her mouth. "Look, I didn't mean …"

He raised his hand to stop her, then narrowed his eyes. "Thanks for the reminder, Shona … you rang me, remember? … The night you found her … *you* brought me into all this," he said, pointing a finger at her.

Suddenly, he felt weary with the whole thing, waved her away with his hand, and walked out, not able to bear the sight of her any longer.

Lance went to the quiet of his room and sat building a joint on his bed. Shona was right about one thing; his reaction was way over the top and completely out of character for him. It was because Lily affected him so deeply.

Of course, he'd heard the stories of how Humans reacted to Sirens, but he knew this was more than that. The erotic dreams leading to the tattoo on his back and the way he'd felt from the moment he saw her just proved he was meant to meet her in his life. *Fuck!* He'd even designed the tattoo and given it to the artist, despite what he said about not doing the inking. It *was* a representation of her, from the colour of her eyes to the design of the stripes he'd never laid eyes on. Coincidences didn't happen like that.

He let his head roll back on his shoulders. Even so, he couldn't escape the fact that Shona had so eloquently reminded him that he wasn't Atlantean, no matter how much his brother Nathan protested. They weren't blood and he would never have the standing to have a relationship with a Siren. Because that was where they were heading if he gave in to the chemistry that sizzled between them. *Fuck,* he couldn't even look her in the eye anymore without blushing like some inexperienced teenager.

And there was the thing that terrified him most of all; if he gave in to the pull between them, he couldn't get out of his mind how the dreams always ended: erotic pleasure morphing into blood. A lot of blood. And he was sure it was hers.

He had to face the harsh truth of what was really at the bottom of why he couldn't get close to her: he was petrified that the dreams were a vision of a future event – one where she dies, and he is the one who kills her.

CHAPTER 16

The joint was built. Lance put it in his mouth, lit it and took a deep pull – letting the smoke out slowly in one long stream. As he blew, he allowed himself to lie back slowly on the bed and stare at the ceiling. The smoke soothed and dulled the sharp edges of his mood.

Maybe Shona had done him a favour in the long run. If Lily went to Malleven, he could rest easy knowing he was a strong prince. Cesaré wouldn't like it, but at least he would protect her and take her to be part of his family. He hoped the politics within the Florianna didn't stop that. Lily needed stability. Even though she acted tough, he knew she was a lonely little girl underneath.

Lance had met Malleven only a handful of times, when he'd come there to meet up with Cesaré. He was no surfer, that's for sure. But Cesaré had loved him like a brother at that time and he'd been made welcome. Malleven seemed more at home in a boardroom than on a surfboard, so that was where Lance's interest in the guy had ended. If only he'd paid more attention.

Of course he'd heard the rumours of how he'd double-crossed Cesaré, but Shona was right; princes were supposed to fight over the Sirens like some kind of treasure hunt. And even though he'd bitten Shona's head off, putting his own feelings aside, now that he'd calmed down, he could understand why she did it. It would have been unpopular with the others and probably blocked because of Cesaré. He just wished she'd run it by him first.

He wasn't thinking objectively about Lily, and none of them really knew the whole story of what happened with Malleven.

And Lily, what would she do? Honestly, he couldn't make her out. Hopefully, she'd take her time, get to know him, and it'd all work out okay. Perhaps she'd like this Malleven, guy. Just because one of her sisters rejected him didn't mean she would. A dull ache hit his chest and he rubbed it absently.

Then he thought back to the beach that morning and how she'd spoken telepathically to him. *Kept that to herself.*

Lance needed to get real. The fact was, he didn't really know her at all. He sat up and pushed the end of the joint into an empty beer can and lay back down with his forearm across his eyes. He'd just rest for a couple of hours till daybreak, then he'd get the fuck out and surf.

Cesaré had crashed at the house and drank a whole bottle of scotch after learning that Malleven still lived. Although he wasn't surprised and suspected as much, it still reopened a festering wound to hear it spelled out like that. With no sleep and a temper ready to snap, he stumbled out the door at dawn and struggled to get the key in Lance's camper van.

"Need some help?" Lance's low voice said from behind him.

Cesaré swung round, steadying himself with an arm on

the van. He swore under his breath in Italian. "Go back to bed, Lance."

"I was just on my way out anyway. Why don't you let me drive?" He held out his hand for the keys.

Cesaré rolled his eyes, plonked the keys in Lance's hand and lurched around the van to the other side. "Suit yourself," he mumbled. Then he climbed in and sat in silence, holding his head, waiting for his brain to catch up with the rest of him.

After looking at him for a long moment, Lance turned the key and started the engine. They were about to pull away when there was a loud thump on the front of the van, which made Cesaré drop his hand from his forehead and look out through the windscreen. *Lily!* "Fucking hell." He turned in his seat to glare at Lance. *Was he trying to drive him to murder?*

Lance shrugged as if it was news to him.

"Well let her in, Bro, we'll have a fucking party," Cesaré said, turning his head to the side window, disinterested already.

The side panel opened and closed as Lily climbed in.

Lance pulled away and they rode the ten minutes to the isolated spot in brooding silence. Away from the crowds, it was a place frequented only by their crew, as its waves could be brutal near jagged rocks. It suited Cesaré's mood.

They came to a halt on the dusty road where the rocks opened to a natural gangway that could only be navigated down to the crashing waves below on foot. With the sun only a pink glow on the grey horizon, Cesaré wasted no time. He slid off his seat, out the door and pulled a short board from the rack on the roof. Without a word, and ignoring his muzzy head, he jogged off to the gap in the rocks and jumped, without hesitation, into the froth boiling up beneath.

. . .

CESARÉ'S hasty departure left Lily alone in the van with Lance. The awkward silence went on for so long that it was unbearable, until he opened his door and went to escape as well. *Wait!* she projected.

Lance froze, took his hand from the door and eased back into his seat. He waited like he dreaded what was coming. "You're telepathic," he stated flatly.

Yes.

"And you have been all along?"

I guess so ... I wasn't aware ... had no use for it. Pays to play dumb most times. Malleven spoke to me like it – said it is natural for us or something. It's been easy ever since.

Lance snorted, then smiled without it reaching his eyes.

Lily inched closer, so she was between the two front seats and could look him in the face. He moved away to look out the side window. She didn't miss his body language and climbed through, plonking herself into the front seat next to him with a huff. She was so angry and hurt with him that she wanted to cry, or hit him, or both. It didn't help that she'd lain awake all night tossing and turning over her decision about going to Malleven and, as much as she hated to admit it, leaving Lance. Then he treats her like this. *He was such an asshole.* His body language couldn't scream for her to get away from him any louder. He clearly couldn't stand to be this close.

"What do you want, Lily," he said wearily, turning to her with dead eyes.

The lump in her throat wouldn't go down, no matter how much she swallowed. A ragged breath escaped her. *Nothing much ... just wanted to see if you were okay ... you know, with the whole Malleven thing?*

When he looked at her his smile was mocking and his words were clipped. "Why not ... he's a prince ... and Cesaré?" He glanced to where Cesaré had disappeared. "He's no use to anyone right now." He sat for a long moment staring into the middle distance after speaking, as if there was a lot more he wanted to say but decided against it.

Lily waited and hoped he'd open up, but he didn't. He was closed off and out of bounds to her now – not that he was ever really available. She was wasting her time. She took a deep breath, nodded once in finality, and got out. Lance did the same without a word. He passed her a board from the roof in silence and together they walked between the rocks to the edge of the precipice.

Lily and Lance paused at the edge of the steep drop into the ocean. With the waves this powerful, crashing into the rocks, it was safer to jump in rather than climb down to get in at the water line.

They gazed out at the ocean to watch the lines of impatient waves queuing up to bombard the coast. The curls of water were molten bronze against the orange glow of dawn. It didn't take long to spot Cesaré skipping, soaring and doing reckless tricks as if his life depended on it.

Lily looked over at Lance to make sure he was seeing what she was. His eyes were fixed on Cesaré with a look of concern. *He's going to kill himself,* she projected.

Lance gave a slight nod. "Come on." Without preamble, he stepped over the edge, throwing his board out ahead of him. After a moment to gather herself, Lily did the same.

It was heavy swimming to get through the white water to the calmer sea further out. Cesaré could still be seen surfing like a man possessed, taking dare-devil risks in such shallow water so close to the rocks.

Then, no sooner had she had the thought, he disappeared from view. One minute he was there and the next he was gone. At first, she thought he was hidden by a trough in the waves, but it soon became obvious that he was gone. *Lance!*

As she turned around, anxious to alert him, he was

already paddling frantically to the area where Cesaré was last seen.

It was a mass of boiling white water churning the whole time. More water was crashing down onto the rocks, sending spray at least thirty feet up into the air.

Lily managed to catch up with Lance. He'd let go of his board and was putting his head beneath the water in an effort to see something, but it was a whirl of surging bubbles being sucked in and out with every wave.

Lily looked all around to see if she could spot his surfboard, but she couldn't see it anywhere. Her heart hammered. It meant the leash attached to his ankle was holding him under somewhere. She curled into a ball and released her own. It was the only way she could dive. The suck of the water quickly swept her board away.

Lance came up out of the water and gulped a lungful of air.

I'll go and check in the deeper water, she projected. His reply was lost in the din of the waves as she sank and allowed the water into her lungs. The salt stung for a minute. She hadn't breathed underwater for a very long time and never in the sea.

As soon as she was acclimatised, she dove down. It was a battle to swim below the strong current, trying to carry her out to sea. Eventually, she reached the rocky bottom that dropped off sharply into much deeper water.

The sea continued to surge above her, but below it felt like a strong sway that dragged her forward and back. The current was whooshing in an arc, depositing everything in its path down there like a dumping ground. It would be so easy to get pummelled against a rock and carried out with the undercurrent.

Her eyes cleared and she began to see through the debris of loose seaweed and small pieces of driftwood. It took no time at all to spot Cesaré's surfboard pointing upwards and swaying like a beacon. Gripping the leash, she pulled hand over hand down to Cesaré's unconscious body, hanging lifeless between a crevice in the rocks. His head had a huge gash on the side and blood was seeping out in a smoke-like swirl.

Lily followed the leash to its source and saw it was tightly snagged between the rocks. It was also wound several times around Cesaré's ankle, making it impossible to release even if he had been conscious.

She swam to his face hanging downwards in the water and felt his neck. He barely had a pulse. His eyes were open and his lips slightly apart; she was afraid she was too late. He'd drowned and his lungs were full of water, but it made no sense. She couldn't understand why he wasn't breathing the water like her if he was a prince.

Then she remembered the conversation she'd had with Malleven – the bit about the water and a Siren's power, but there was no time to think it through.

A hand gripped her shoulder and made her turn sharply in surprise. Lance had followed the same route of the current on a single lungful of air. Bewildered, she remembered that all the crew were experienced free divers for exactly this reason. He pointed his thumb upwards.

Cesaré didn't have long enough to get him out to work on him. She wasn't even sure how long Lance could hold his breath. *I need to work on him here,* she projected, hoping Lance would go back to the surface. Then she said, no more and put her mouth to Cesaré's.

It felt natural. Somehow she knew it was the right thing to do. Slowly and steadily, she began to blow.

Nothing appeared to be happening, so she smacked his chest. *Come on, you asshole. You're not going to hang this on me too.*

Lily summoned every ounce of strength from within her

with every puff of breath. Lance seemed to have disappeared, hopefully to take a lungful of air, so she continued her weird CPR over and over.

After what felt like an age, the whole top half of his body began to glow. It was the strangest sight – one that would have totally freaked her out had his eyelids not fluttered and a line of small bubbles escaped from behind his ears. A smile crept over his lips and his eyes closed again. *Shit!* He was still alive, but they needed to get him medical attention.

Lance came back with a knife. He cut the leash and they all rose to the surface with the added buoyancy of Cesaré's surfboard. They battled with Cesaré slumped across it through the white water and over the shallow rocks. Between the two of them, they managed to drag Cesaré up the steep incline to the parked van.

LANCE WATCHED in awe as Lily breathed life into Cesaré, because that was undoubtedly what she'd done. She was a Soul Breather, and he'd had the privilege to witness her power firsthand. He'd seen surfers die a couple of times. A bash to the head and then pulled into the grip of crashing waves for them to batter and squash what little air was left in a person.

Cesaré had escaped the weight of the waves only to get snagged in the rocks. With a head wound rendering him unconscious, without Lily, he would be dead for sure. What she had managed was nothing short of a miracle.

It quickly became apparent that getting Cesaré to the shallow water was the easy part. They almost lost him to the waves a couple of times. Every time the water retreated, they needed all their strength just to hold their position and not get dragged back out. Then, when it surged forward, they let it carry them in. It was slow progress with them only gaining a little distance each time.

Finally, after battling for several minutes, the water was shallow enough to stand up. Every muscle in Lance's body screamed with the exertion. He really got to see Lily's mettle because it was exhausting. At one point he thought they'd never make it up the incline. But it was Lily's sheer grit and determination that made him climb each tiny step one at a time – however small the advancement. They let go of the board, he pulled Cesaré from under the arms, and Lily took up the weight from under his knees. Somehow between them they made the climb. It took forever, but they managed to reach the top. Lance fell over backwards in one last, enormous heft to pull Cesaré over the ridge. Lily flopped down next to him onto her knees.

There was no time for taking a breather.

Lance pushed Cesaré's heavy weight off him onto his back. For a moment, Lily looked like she was being sick. But he quickly realised she was just expelling water from her lungs.

Help me turn him, she projected.

He roused himself to help her.

While Cesaré lay on his front, Lily rubbed his back hard until he coughed and his lungs emptied of water. Despite their efforts, he remained unconscious.

"Come on!" Lance said, sluggishly moving his dead legs. "We need to get him to a hospital.

With an exhausted nod of her head, Lily lurched to her feet too. Then, with the last of their joint strength, they partly carried, partly dragged Cesaré into the side door of the van.

Lance drove them as fast as he could to the nearest ER. After helping get Cesaré into the building, Lily hung back. He guessed because of her stripes, still prominent after being in the water. Thankfully, Cesaré's had faded. A nurse rushed over calling for a gurney, and his mind soon became focussed on what he would say.

He explained very little. Just that they'd pulled him out of the water after a surfing accident. He didn't want too many questions when they found temperature and blood oxygen anomalies. Things that Lance wasn't even sure of the answers to, anyway.

Cesaré had started to come round as soon as they got there, but he was in a lot of pain. He was quickly stitched and pumped with strong painkillers and kept for observation. He would sleep now for a good while and Lance felt confident enough to leave him. He rushed out to the waiting room to find Lily. He guessed she didn't like hospitals and hadn't argued when she said she'd wait outside. In all honesty, his attention had been totally taken up with Cesaré.

Now he'd had time to think, the guilt he'd felt earlier at treating her so badly had now turned into longing. He just wanted to tell her he was sorry and explain that the morning's events had clarified a few things. There was no excusing his behaviour; he was a stupid, jealous idiot. And although he didn't want her to go, he couldn't blame her. But before she went, she deserved to know the real reason he kept his distance.

When he reached the waiting room, it held just a few people and no Lily. With a horrible feeling creeping over him, he ran out to the car park to try the van. His heart sank. She wasn't there either. Lily had gone.

CHAPTER 17

*L*ily had taken the bus and cried the whole way back to the house. By the time she got there, she felt like a hollow shell with every emotion wrung right out of her. She'd done her best to fit in there and no one was willing to give her a break.

Cesaré would live, so he could carry on nursing his bitter hatred for the world, but without her to take it out on. And Lance, who was so friendly and easygoing with everyone else, could now totally relax. Today had helped her come to a decision. She'd be mad to turn down Malleven's offer. A girl like her was never going to get a better one. So when she walked in to find Shona in the kitchen after just waking up, she projected, *Get dressed, we're going.*

It took a minute for Shona's groggy brain to realise what she'd just said. When the light bulb finally went on, she brightened with a "Righto!" and rushed off to the shower. "Make us a strong coffee, hun … won't be two ticks."

Within fifteen minutes, they were driving Nathan's car to LA. Lily didn't have much to pack and she wanted to get out before she had to face Lance again. No doubt he and everyone else would blame her for Cesaré's accident.

Shona phoned ahead to warn Malleven Lily was coming.

What did he say? Her emotion tank was on empty and she wasn't sure she could take much more rejection. It had become like her middle name.

Shona looked at her with glistening eyes. "He said everything is ready for you."

Lily's heart began to beat fast. It was a mixture of nerves, excitement, and *dare she think it,* hope. After everything, it was what she needed.

His conditions ran through her head. Somewhere deep inside, she wondered if he was interested in her as a woman or merely as a Siren, but she dismissed it. She was nothing if not practical, and all out of options anyway.

"He also wanted me to tell you you won't regret it."

Her heart skipped and she looked out of her passenger window. She certainly hoped so. It couldn't be worse than the pain in the centre of her chest right now. One thing she was sure of: nothing would ever be the same again.

It was late in the evening when they arrived. Despite her early start and the drama of the day, Lily hadn't slept on the way. A mixture of nerves and excitement kept her brain turning everything over and over. It was better to think of her future than what – or rather who – she'd left behind. Not knowing what to expect made it really difficult.

Shona led the way into the swish apartment, but everything felt different. The day before, it had been quiet, oppressive, and dark. Tonight, even though it was late, every light was on and it was full of people rushing around. Bags and suitcases were all packed and piled up in the hallway.

Malleven breezed out of a doorway, smelling freshly

showered and looking like something out of a gentleman's magazine.

Nerves hit Lily immediately. He seemed so sophisticated; she couldn't for the life of her guess why he was interested in her.

Someone was gabbling in one ear in Italian, and he had his phone clamped to his shoulder while he listened. "Scusi!" he said when he caught sight of her and gave her the most beautiful smile. He was very handsome when he smiled like that. It was the first time she'd seen it. "You have everything?" he said in his beautiful accented English.

Lily just stood like a frightened animal. She was grateful when Shona spoke up for her. "Like what ... where you going? We just drove fuckin' miles, mate!" she said, indicating all the bags.

He held up a placating hand, then said a couple of "Ciaos" into his phone and ended the call. Then he slid it into the breast pocket of his beautiful steel grey suit. He ignored her question. "Passports ... you have them?" he asked.

Lily had forgotten just how Italian he sounded and nodded. She carried it everywhere with her in her cloth shoulder bag and hadn't packed it especially.

Shona became agitated. "No ... how was I ..." She shifted her weight and pointed a finger at him. "You didn't answer my question. I'm her bloody Protector, mate."

Lily hoped she didn't throw one of her hissy fits. It wasn't pretty when Shona lost her rag. Malleven seemed oblivious, came over, and stopped right in front of her. Riveted, she froze while he searched her eyes and picked up her limp hand hanging at her side.

His words rumbled quietly and reverently, all rolling Rs. "You honour me by choosing to return." Then he bowed over her hand and kissed it.

Bloody hell! She was left wide-eyed and amazed. A beautiful man – and a prince at that – seemed to give very much of a shit about her. It was new. Her heart skipped and she kind of liked it.

He straightened up and reluctantly let his eyes leave her to look at Shona as if she were an annoyance. "But we must leave this place. It is not safe for someone as important as a Siren. This part of the city is full of Atlantean and Human agents at the moment."

Lily's mind was still on the "important" part. It made her feel something she had never felt before.

"Where are we going then?" Shona was asking.

"You go nowhere," Malleven said, with a flick of his hand.

"You can't just take her," Shona said, beginning to raise her voice.

Two burly men came to either side of Shona and literally picked her up on each side and began to carry her towards the door.

Lily began to panic. She'd grown fond of Shona, and despite how nice he was being to her, she didn't like seeing her friend handled in this way.

Malleven glanced at her and must have seen the distress on her face. *Please, Malleven,* she projected.

He paused and seemed to consider something. *We need to leave. She has no passport ... I have no wish to separate you,* he projected back softly.

Shona was struggling and shouting obscenities from the doorway.

"Wait!" Malleven called to his bodyguards.

Shona pulled out of their grip and came running back inside and stood in front of Lily as if to protect her from him. "You can't just take her like that," she said through gritted teeth. Lily could feel her shaking in anger and fear.

Malleven conceded with a nod. "I understand that you are

unaware of the etiquette surrounding a Siren, you being of low birth."

Shona stiffened at the reference to her inferiority to him. Lily prayed she didn't do anything stupid. She didn't know this guy, but she instinctively knew he was very powerful.

"A prince about to pledge can dismiss a Siren's Protectors, as he then takes that place," his voice purred reasonably. "I am assuming that role by removing her from a dangerous place to another where our full pledging can take place safely."

"Where's that?" Shona said, not backing down.

"To my brotherhood, where a hundred powerful men would give their lives to protect her." He smiled benignly. "I am grateful to you, Shona … I promise you, should my mate request her own Protectors still, I will send for you … and you will have your passport by then," he finished with his eyebrows raised.

It all sounded so reasonable that Lily couldn't see how Shona could argue with that. He already sounded really protective of her. Shona turned to look at her face to see if she was okay with this turnaround in events. "What about you, mate … what do you think about all this. Cos you can come right back with me if you want?"

Lilly looked into her eyes for a long moment, then over at Malleven to see if that was true.

He tipped his head regally. "It must be your choice," he said with his eyes boring into hers with meaning. *Remember why you chose to return, il mio fiore,* he said privately in her head.

Malleven already had a pet name for her: his flower. She'd googled it yesterday. It was the final clincher and her eyes tracked back to Shona.

Shona rested her hands on Lily's shoulders. "Whatta *you* want?" she said.

Lily gave her a weak smile. The truth was, she didn't know what she wanted. On the one hand was what she knew back at the house: the music, surfing, and Lance – and with that came a sudden pain stabbing her heart. And on the other was a dark, mysterious prince who promised her things beyond her wildest dreams. Who made her feel good and beautiful and he'd spent less than an hour with her.

She shook her head. *I can't go back.* A tear tracked down her face and she looked down. It felt as though she had let Shona down.

"Right then," Shona said, removing her hands and taking a step back. She took a deep breath and nodded at Malleven. "I'll wait to hear from you then."

Malleven dipped his head, but his eyes washed over briefly in the gold shimmer that never ceased to fascinate Lily.

Shona walked hesitantly to the front door, rejected and indecisive. She gave Lily a last look over her shoulder. Lily swallowed hard. It felt wrong letting her go like this, but what else could she do? She had to remember it as the end of a chapter of her life and the start of another. Shona disappeared from sight, leaving Lily watching where she'd been.

Malleven picked up her hand. "Come, *il mio fiore* … the car is waiting."

Where are we going? she said, looking up into his strange, swirling gaze.

"I'm taking you where it is safe … to the temple of my brotherhood."

The words meant little to her, but she allowed him to lead her out to the waiting car.

At first, Malleven wanted to whisk Lily straight to his brotherhood's HQ on the borders of Syria and Jordan, but he changed his mind at the last minute. It wasn't that the political situation was a risk to them; the rebels lived in fear of the Brotherhood's fearsome reputation, and they were above the law. He decided to take her to one of his secluded Italian residences instead. There, he would work on her to win her confidence completely. He wasn't going to make the same mistakes he'd made with her sister, Isla.

When it came to the testing and marriage, he wanted to be absolutely certain that she would welcome him with open arms. The rejection and humiliation of being left for dead still burned like a canker on his soul. Isla would pay a heavy price for that when she fell into his hands again.

They boarded his small jet and settled into their seats. The reminder of Lily's sister prompted him to glance down at his divining ring, the symbol that had pointed Isla out to him on this very plane. Now it was blood red instead of the turquoise it should be in this close proximity to a Siren. Despite Antonio sourcing another, it still changed from the dormant opaque white to blood red. It seemed the Orb's decision was final. He knew what it meant. He had been rejected as a mate and as a prospective king, never to be allowed to enter the running again. He grit his teeth in anger to think that Fate should discount him purely on a silly girl's romantic whims.

Another reason he needed a detour before meeting with his high priest was that he needed to work on his ring before he saw it. It must be turquoise for them to back him if he were to make a claim again with a Siren. They treated their reputation as precious – especially in the powerful Atlantean world where they garnered respect and riches.

Malleven glanced sideways at his prize. Lily was staring out of the window even though it was a night sky. She wasn't his, and he knew she had a true mate out in the world somewhere – a prince who would cross their paths one day. Except it would be too late. If she accepted him willingly, the match would stand, and no one could do a thing about it. Being her first and only pledge, her power would transfer to him and secure an active seat on the king's council. The king had issued a mandate to all princes that the first pledge should go to him, building his power with each Siren, but there was no way he would give up that right to a king who was now an enemy.

The power-hungry Florianna family would get behind him for political reasons if nothing else. The mistakes he'd made in the past would be forgotten and the slate wiped clean. It was imperative he made no mistakes with this Siren.

Malleven reached for her small hand and gave it a squeeze. She turned her head from the window to look at him. Her eyes looked dazed and weary, but the beauty in them was undeniable. He smiled. "Why don't you sleep, *il mio fiore?* ... Please don't be nervous, I will take very good care of you."

After a moment of searching his face, *I'm not,* she projected back.

"I am glad," he said and his eyelids lowered with lust for her. All the Sirens had appalling upbringings, but this one held a vulnerability and fragility that he found irresistible. Everything became so clear to him in that moment while he battled not to ravish her in her seat. He decided he would make this one love him and trust him, so that she would hate to do anything to betray or hurt him. This delicate flower would open for him alone.

Lily was in a daze from the moment she said goodbye to Shona. To the private plane, all through the long journey to

Europe. Everything blurred into a hazy dream even when they reached the most beautiful house she'd ever seen, nestled in the countryside, just outside Milan.

It was like living in a fairy tale, where she was Cinderella, whose prince had finally come to take her away from everything that was bad in her life.

A flash of a memory of Lance pierced through her daydream. She refused to go there and squashed it immediately. Her life had been full of fresh starts and new people. It felt like she'd done it a million times. This was no different. And Lance and the surfers she'd come to know were in the past and would soon become a distant memory.

The car pulled up. Malleven walked around the chauffeur-driven limousine and held the door open for her. Cautiously, she took the hand offered and got out. For a moment, she couldn't move. All she wanted to do was take in the beauty of the place, and he seemed to understand and didn't rush her.

Tall trees and vivid pink flowering shrubs lined the yellow paved courtyard. More flowers climbed around the balconies and turrets, and the tinkle of running water was coming from nearby. It really was a slice of heaven.

"Come," Malleven said softly.

Lily took a deep breath and allowed him to lead her in through the large oak doors and into a huge vaulted hallway. She blushed as he introduced her to several members of staff, all lined up in a row. Then told her she could ask for anything and they would get it for her, whatever time of day or night. Apparently, the welcome was all for her benefit.

She was completely in a daze by the time he took her by the hand and they ascended the grand staircase to the huge bedroom.

Her bewilderment soon gave way to terror. Here she was,

all on her own in the middle of the Italian countryside with a man she hardly knew. A red-blooded, gorgeous man who would expect everything from her. Her throat threatened to close up, she was so frightened.

Lily put her small, tatty, embroidered cloth bag down on the bed and felt suddenly self-conscious. There was nothing to unpack. It was a poor show for her life.

"*Il mio fiore,*" he said softly, from right behind her.

Malleven was so close she could feel his breath on the back of her neck. After a moment's pause to gather herself, she slowly turned. He pulled her chin up with a finger so she was forced to meet his eyes.

"Please relax. Everything is new. It is bound to take a while to adjust."

Her eyes strayed to her paltry belongings on the bed.

He followed her gaze and understood immediately. "We will go out and get you many new things, *mio fiore.*" He pulled her chin back to him gently. "It will help me get to know you, even as you get to know yourself."

The man had amazed her again. Emotion threatened to bubble over into tears. He seemed so caring, so understanding, yet he hardly knew her at all.

The moment was so charged; she thought he was going to kiss her. She looked down at the bed quickly. *Will I sleep here?* It was both a deflection from the intense atmosphere and a need to know whether he intended to exercise his condition of her doing whatever he wanted.

His midnight blue eyes remained steady. "Yes."

Her eyes lowered. *And this is your room?* She swallowed with difficulty, which she was sure he noticed as he seemed to miss nothing.

Malleven nodded. "I won't take from you what you are not ready to give me, *mio fiore* ... but know this; we will never be separated." His molten eyes appeared to burn with his fervent words.

Her heart fluttered in her chest, but not out of fear as she would have expected, but with a strange exhilaration – an anticipation of a promise in those words. It seemed unreal to her that a man like him could appear to want her that much. *Okay,* she whispered.

CHAPTER 18

The further Shona drove, the more worried she became. Malleven had contacted her through a friend and met with her a few times. She'd felt as sorry for him as she had for Cesaré, after he told her the full story of what happened with Lily's sister. Then he'd plied her with drinks and gone on and on about how everyone knew the fourth Siren was on the west coast and how in danger she was if she got into the wrong hands—really hammered home the point that she needed a strong prince. That was when she'd admitted to him that she knew of her whereabouts. The rest was history.

Now she'd had the long drive to think about it, the rosy picture of Lily safely married off was eroding fast. By the time she got back to San Diego, she was convinced she had done the wrong thing in leaving Lily there. When she really thought about it, she wasn't sure what she expected. Probably for Lily to live somewhere where they could still see each other, but she was safe. Now it seemed a really naive notion. The thing was, she had no way of knowing whether Malleven was speaking the truth about dismissing Lily's

Protectors. She fumed. *How stupid could she have been!* But how was she supposed to know that Malleven would want to take her straight out of the country? *She should have taken her passport, just in case.* The more she thought about it, the more she believed Malleven had sweet-talked and used her in bringing Lily to him. *The slippery fucker!*

It was the early hours of the morning by the time she threw the car keys down onto the kitchen counter. She sat on a high stool and held her head in her hands. *How the fuck did she manage to lose a Siren?* One thing she was sure of, Malleven wouldn't get in touch, no matter what he said.

"You okay?"

Lance's voice from right behind her made her jump out of her skin.

"Yeah … no … ah, fuck!" She pulled at the roots of her hair and held her head again.

Lance was next to her, frowning now. "What's up?" He turned and brought out a carton of juice from the fridge. "Where's Lily?"

Shona felt wretched and just shrugged, hoping he'd drop it.

He was peering down at her through her fingers questioningly. "I wanted to let her know how Ches was."

She peeked at him through the side of her hands. "What happened to Ches?"

"He took quite a wipe-out this morning … he's in the hospital." Lance was frowning, as if he knew she was being evasive. "Lily saved his life."

Lily had kept that bit of info quiet. "Nasty," she said, keeping her answers to a minimum in the hope Lance would get bored, leave her alone, and go to bed. Emotionally drained, she was not in the mood for a row right now.

"So?"

"So what?" *Leave it, Lance.*

"Where is she?"

She closed her eyes and sat up, recognising she wasn't going to escape this.

"What is it?" Lance said, spinning her around on her stool to face him.

Shona sagged in her chair. "She's gone."

"Gone … gone where?" His expression changed from curious to alarmed.

With a deep sigh, she laid out the whole story this time. How Malleven had contacted her and soft-talked her into telling him about Lily. Promising Lance faithfully that she had done it with the best intentions. Reminding him that Cesaré had no interest in her and how Malleven kept scaring her with what could happen. And how he was offering the security Lily needed. "So she came home earlier today and said she wanted to go right away," she finished wearily.

Lance's expression slowly changed to horror as he listened and waited for her to finish. "Of all the stupid … why didn't she give it more time? … None of us really knows the guy," he said, beginning to lose his temper.

"Well, no … look, I didn't tell you everything before, but he only gave her twenty-four hours, and we've only heard a few rumours and Ches' side of things," she said, more to convince herself than anything. "Aren't all the princes meant to fight it out?"

Lance slammed his juice carton down on the counter, splashing it everywhere. "Ches is a man with a death wish, thanks to his so-called best friend!" He threw his hands up, turned and walked towards the doorway.

"Where are you going?" Shona called after him.

"We need to get back there."

"She's gone!" Shona shouted as he disappeared from view.

Lance came back, stood on the threshold and spoke low and ominously, "What do you mean, gone?"

Shona re-lived her stupidity all over again and took a ragged breath. "They were leaving as soon as I got there. He tricked me. I didn't have my passport."

Lance stood, stunned for a moment. "Did Lily?"

"Yeah … I guess. I think she carries it everywhere."

Lance rolled his head back on his shoulders in anguish. The stricken look on his face gave away more than concern of a Protector for his charge. Shona suddenly realized that Lance had real feelings for Lily. It made her feel even more terrible than she already did. "She chose to go, Lance," she said softly. "She wanted it … otherwise I'd never have …" Her voice trailed off. *Ah fuckin' hell!* Her eyes pleaded with him to understand the position she was in.

Instead, Lance began to pace in front of her. "We need to find out more about this guy." He walked to the counter and grabbed the keys to his van.

"Where ya goin'?" Shona asked, hopping off her stool to follow him.

"Back to the hospital. Ches is the only one who might know what to do."

"Wait up … I'd betta come."

The two of them rushed out to the van and drove as fast as they dared to the hospital.

Lance was focused on the road ahead of him, in deep thought. Shona glanced over at him, worried and guilty. "I know you're angry at me, Lance, but we'll get her back." She looked down at her hands in her lap. "Maybe if you'd told her how you felt?"

He shot her an angry look, then grit his teeth, and a muscle twitched in his jaw.

LANCE WAS JUST TOO angry for words. *How could she have been so fucking stupid?* It was so typical of Shona to take things upon herself and think she could handle them. But as angry as he was with Shona, he was more furious with himself. The way he'd continually pushed Lily away when she needed him to help make a decision like this. Maybe she had even tried to confide in him. Perhaps he never really thought she'd go. *What a fool.*

He gripped the steering wheel so hard it creaked. The real truth was that he was terrified of getting close to someone – scratch, not someone – *her.* Because he knew that he would fall so hard and then everything would be out of control. Keeping dispassionate was the only way he could deal with the possibility that his horrific premonitions could come true.

He dragged his brain back to the present. "It's deeper than competition between Ches and him," he said, breaking the long silence.

Shona was quiet, which was unlike her, just waiting for him to continue. She usually had a fucking opinion on everything. "The whole time he's been back ... you know what he's been like ... with all the rumours and all, but since you confirmed that Malleven was alive ..." He shook his head.

"So he's been a bit pissed off ... what's new?"

Lance shook his head again. "This morning, if Lily and me hadn't been there—"

"Yeah, he always was a lucky bastard."

Lance looked over at her in exasperation. "You don't get it, Shona. The way he was acting ... like he didn't give a shit. It was like he didn't care if he came out of the water or not." He gripped the steering wheel and felt terrible all over again. "If it weren't for Lily ..." He couldn't finish what he was saying as emotion suddenly rode him hard. He hadn't taken care of her, and she'd quietly slipped out of his life without saying goodbye – probably thought he wouldn't care either way. And the worst thing of all was that he knew instinctively that she wasn't coming back.

Cesaré was lying in his hospital bed, feeling doped up to the eyeballs, with a dull headache. He had fourteen stitches above his right eye, a cracked skull, and the hangover from the bottle of scotch he'd drunk before his accident. But the biggest and most troubling pain was in his chest. He rubbed it absently but knew it wasn't physical. It was an ache in his heart. And it wasn't the fact that his suspicions had been proved true – that Malleven still lived.

His love for his cousin had turned into a hatred so deep he couldn't even fathom it. The boy he'd grown up with, shared every memory, every secret and laughter with, had used and humiliated him like he meant nothing. No, as bad as all that was, the real object of his pain was Lily. The beautiful, damaged, foolish girl had no clue what she'd done.

He'd been unconscious when they brought him in, but when he had been treated, woken and left to his thoughts, he was plagued by snippets of memory of what had happened in the water that day. At first, he thought his euphoria was due to a dream or to delirium from the bump on his head. However, he felt strange and different, and he felt abnormally strong. He should feel as weak as paper, but he was bursting with energy.

He felt behind his ears and it confirmed what he suspected. What was once a thick line like a scar – an identifying mark on all royals – was now raised and pronounced. The girl, the Siren, the one he'd been unbelievably hostile to – Lillian Gale, had opened his gills and saved him.

Cesaré was sure she didn't know what she'd done, as she must dislike him intensely. He continued to rub his chest. She was right there inside him; he could feel her there – a living, breathing spirit. Instead of letting him die, which she undoubtedly should have done, the silly girl had – without a second thought – bound him to her for ever. It was the thing she should have reserved for her mate.

Oh no. He closed his eyes when the enormity hit him. There was one who should have been first – even before her mate. The living breath from one of the royal Bonaci Sirens should have gone to the king. No wonder he felt so good. The power that now surged around his veins should have been for him.

He groaned and turned onto his side. *What had she done?* Just when he thought he could escape the intrigues and all the shit of the Atlantean court, he found himself bound to a Siren, and taking her power from a king he liked and respected.

Cesaré sighed and turned onto his back. It was probably his death sentence. The very thing he'd sought earlier that day. It should be welcomed really, as now everything had got a whole lot worse. He was about to get dragged back in.

LANCE AND SHONA entered the hospital at a brisk walk and were challenged by a nurse. "Excuse me, sir … miss?" She was forced to run to stop them. "Visiting hours are over, sir. It's the middle of the night."

Lance huffed and was forced to stop. "It's real important, ma'am. I promise we'll only be a minute. It's kind of a family emergency."

The nurse quickly assessed him and looked around. "Who is it you want to see?"

Lance softened his tone in relief and she promised to turn a blind eye if they were really quick. "Five minutes," she called after them.

They got in the lift and hurried to Cesaré's room.

Cesaré was awake and propped up on pillows when they arrived. He had a patch above his eye, but his colour was remarkably good. He looked surprised to see them and tried to sit up. "What are you two doing here?"

Lance put out a hand to help him relax. "Sorry, man, we just had to come and see you as soon as we could. Something's happened with Lily and we need your help."

Cesaré pulled himself up anyway, putting a finger to his temple as if to ease a pain. "What about Lily?"

Lance paused for a second. Something with Cesaré had changed. He seemed more like his old self and didn't wear the usual scowl whenever Lily's name was mentioned. Then he looked scathingly at Shona. "Tell him what you told me."

Subdued, Shona outlined everything, from the time Malleven approached her a few weeks back to the events of that day. Cesaré listened to the whole story without interrupting, even when she kept stressing that it was what Lily wanted.

At the end, Cesaré lay back and closed his eyes. At first, Lance thought he was in pain and toyed with getting a nurse. Then he realised that it was the news that had affected him, like it was the worst thing he could have heard.

Lance was beginning to think they had done the wrong thing by coming there when Cesaré sat up, threw his legs over the side of the bed, and demanded his clothes.

"You can't get up," Shona said, trying to push his legs back in.

"Leave me alone, woman, you have no idea what you've done," Cesaré said, pushing her hands away from him.

Lance moved Shona away from the bed. "Where do you wanna go, dude?"

"We need to go to Ireland, now! There is no time to lose. I must see the king."

Lance and Shona looked at each other, not sure whether he'd totally lost it.

"He said if Lily wanted us, he would arrange for us to go to her … he seemed okay," Shona trailed off.

Cesaré fixed her with a hard glare. "You will never see her again, if he has his way."

Shona swallowed. "But he seemed okay … you were friends once," she tried half-heartedly.

Cesaré paused again, his patience now wearing thin. With a huff, he said, "He isn't what he appears. He will crush anyone or anything to get the crown."

It wasn't often someone shut Shona right up. Under different circumstances, Lance would have found it funny. Instead, he began to pass Cesaré the clothes they'd brought with them.

While Shona helped Cesaré dress, Lance pushed down his feelings. Lily was in danger, and if he allowed it, the worry would consume him. Even though he knew she wasn't for him and there was no way he could go there with her, hearing Malleven had taken her for the sole purpose of using her made him feel sick to his stomach. The L word was staring him in the face and yet he continued to refuse to acknowledge it.

It was a relief when Cesaré was ready. The two of them supported him on either side and the three of them crept out of the hospital without anyone seeing them.

Lance told himself that he was Lily's Protector and that he owed it to her to see that she was safe and happy and somehow his dream could be averted.

It had been a very long day with the flight and the time difference. Lily wasn't sure how late it was, but it was dark, and she felt exhausted.

She got into bed cautiously and lay facing Malleven. Despite her tiredness, she knew it would be hard to sleep. Her brain was on overdrive, turning over everything – what she'd left, what she'd come to – and what to make of the dark, mysterious man studying her now.

Her heart stopped when Malleven reached out a hand and gently touched her temple. "Sleep, *mio fiore*, I won't touch you, I promise."

She hadn't realised she'd held her breath and let it out with a smile of relief. *I want to sleep, but I think I'm just too wired*, she projected.

Instead of answering, he touched her temple again, drawing small circles with his finger. She began to relax, but he felt closer somehow, and he hadn't moved.

"Shh," he whispered. "I won't venture further than you want me to. I want to ease you so you can sleep."

Even though his voice was gentle and lulling, her eyes

were wide and her heart was beating wildly. The feeling was unsettling, like he was touching her consciousness.

"Trust me, Lily. We Atlanteans have capabilities that Humans do not. Don't be afraid. I am very skilled."

She tried to slow her heart a little while she studied his face for a clue whether she could relax her guard. It remained soft and earnest and the gold shimmer brimmed in his eyes again, making them hypnotic. The fact that she had come thousands of miles with him to a strange country to marry him meant she had accepted his terms. With a ragged breath, she nodded.

At once, she felt him enter her head. He was only at the very edge of her consciousness, but it made her hitch a breath in shock. It felt painful for a moment as if in the grip of his hand.

Shh! He began to move very slowly, gliding to and fro like a magician's pendulum. And his voice, no longer spoken, was right there in her mind. *Relax ...*

When she began to ease, his movement became stronger and a little faster.

Yes, mio fiore, *feel me ... feel the signature of my spirit, so you will forever recognise it.*

He sounded exultant, as if she'd given him something truly precious, but she was scared and overwhelmed by him. It began to feel like he was all over her, everywhere, so that she couldn't breathe. She began to hyperventilate and her head swam.

Lily felt him recede slightly. Then he gradually disappeared until he was gone completely. She found that she was breathing hard, as if she'd been running, and felt tearful.

He put a finger to her lips. "Shh, don't cry. You did very well. It can be overwhelming at first." He smiled slightly as if to put her at ease.

I'm sorry, I just panicked ... I couldn't ... what just happened?

His eyes were hooded. She didn't understand him at all. It dawned on her just how different Atlantean men were from Humans – and far more scary. Briefly, she wondered how he would react to her being a virgin. The thought of sex with him terrified her.

She flinched when his hand came out again. He noticed and held it away from her for a long moment as if to ask permission. She gave a slight nod. Then he moved it slowly around her neck to the nape. "Come closer, *mio fiore* ... just for a moment."

She shuffled a little closer to him on the pillow. With his hand still gently behind her neck, he pulled her in closer still so that his lips brushed hers. It was gentle and as soft as feathers. Her pulse rocketed along with her temperature, generating a film of perspiration all over her.

She went to pull back with embarrassment, but he moved his hand to her shoulder and gently stilled her. He smiled at her indulgently. "Don't be embarrassed, Lily. You heat up because you are attracted to me. You pay me a great compliment and shouldn't be ashamed."

Her eyes went wide that he'd read her so well.

"You see, love for us is meant to happen beneath the water," his beautiful voice purred.

Lily noticed, as he explained, that a flicker of something crossed his darkly intense face. It reminded her of a flash of fear or concern.

But I have never ... She stammered and lowered her eyes.

"Nor I," Malleven said with a small smile. "We will learn together."

She wasn't entirely sure if he meant he too hadn't had sex or whether he meant just underwater, but he did seem genuine and kind. Maybe she could trust this man.

A brief image of Lance flashed and she slammed it down

instantly. He was the past and must stay there. *You see, even on land, I have never ...*

His hand moved to stroke back the curls from her face. "You please me very much, Lily. You must not worry anymore. I will do all the thinking and all the worrying for us."

Her heart hammered as she stared into his unfathomable eyes. He was so handsome and seemed so loving, like he was too good to be true.

"Turn," he said quietly.

After a brief pause, she did as he asked.

His arm snaked around her waist and pulled her backwards to him so she sat snuggly in his lap. His breath was warm and even on the soft part of her shoulder. Her skin felt alive and her heart thumped more wildly at what he would do next. He felt wonderful and she felt a shift in her again, as if her body were accepting him even if her mind wasn't ready. Perhaps it was his unexpected patience and tenderness. Butterflies began to tickle her stomach and heat surged through her again. She recognized it as the stirrings of desire. She'd felt it before with Lance. But this was different. This beautiful man wanted her, and that was a first.

Tentatively, she laid her hand over his on her stomach, so softly she barely touched him. He groaned and pulled her in closer, and there they stayed for the rest of the night.

Malleven's breaths became deep and even in sleep, and Lily lay wide awake. Partly in terror and partly revelling at the closeness and the heat of this man's possessive embrace. *She could get used to this.*

CESARÉ BOOKED the three of them on the next commercial flight to London. There was no time and he didn't want to alert his family by requesting the use of the private Florianna jet. After receiving his hasty communication, Dante Dubon-netti, the king, offered to send his plane to meet them there and bring them to Ireland.

After a very long and tiring journey, the three of them swept up the drive in a chauffeur-driven limo to what could only be described as a castle.

"Where the bloody hell are we?" Shona muttered, more to herself than anything.

"Ballygowan Castle," Cesaré said. The very place he swore he would never set foot in again. He took a deep sigh. Nothing could be done now. The dice had been rolled. "It is the ancestral home of the Bonaci. And now the home of the king."

Lance whistled.

"The home of Lily's family." Cesaré didn't wait for the exchange of looks and hastily got out of the car as soon as it pulled up on the gravel directly in front of the dark oak doors.

"Do they know we're coming?" Shona said, looking around, no doubt thinking, as everyone always did, that it looked abandoned and unlived in.

Cesaré didn't bother to explain but merely nodded and pulled the rope to the side of the door. "The king has delayed leaving for Italy a day to make sure he meets us."

A deep feeling of foreboding crept over him at being back there again. Life was about to get very real. There was no predicting how the king would react to his being bonded to a Siren meant to be his first. "Come on … let's get this fucking over with," he muttered.

After what felt like an age, a male servant showed them through the wood-panelled hall to the lift that would take them down to meet the king.

"Down?" Lance said, frowning at Shona.

"The living quarters are below sea level," Cesaré said.

Thankfully, they read his black mood and asked nothing more about it.

The lift doors opened to reveal a black rock wall a few feet away. They stepped out and turned right and were on a marble staircase that swept down into the most amazing room. Even Cesaré, who had seen it many times, never failed to be amazed.

There was a vast window to the left of them, like the wall of an aquarium, with blue-lit water, swaying seaweeds, and fish swimming happily by. When you could drag your eyes away from that, a huge room lay before them, hewn out of solid black rock. Sumptuous sofas with upholstery in browns, russets and reds were tastefully arranged. The centrepiece was a huge ornate black fountain with what looked like hundreds of black chandeliers hanging from the ceiling, far above their heads.

They cautiously descended the stairs as if entering another world, feeling the room was spectacular and alien, like nothing any of them had ever seen.

Three men in deep conversation stood immediately when they realised they were there. Cesaré halted, not sure of his reception. He recognised the two older gentlemen and the dark, good-looking guy immediately. "Cesaré!" the younger one said, walking towards him and shaking his hand warmly. "Please sit, all of you, I'll arrange for some drinks," he said in his melodic Irish lilt. Cesaré relaxed a little. The king had his usual laid-back way about him and had been nothing but fair in his dealings with Cesaré and the sorry affair with Isla.

Shona and Lance both said, "Beer," and Cesaré shook his head. "Not for me." He pointed to his bandage over his eye. "Need a clear head."

The king smiled, obviously curious, but tactfully didn't ask how he came by the injury and faced the others.

"Please let me introduce my friends, Your Highness,"

Cesaré gestured to the two of them. "Shona Mathews ... Lance McCabe." And he watched as their eyes widened. They'd never met many royals and became suddenly aware they were in the presence of the king himself. Cesaré couldn't help smiling. Dante always had this reaction. They didn't know whether to bow, bob, or kiss his hand.

He merely laughed in his good-natured way, grabbing each of their hands and shaking them. "Call me Dante," he said, and put them instantly at ease.

Cesaré knew him well enough to know that, despite his easy-going exterior, he was a strong king, able to play hard-ball with the best of the world's leaders, as well as the back-stabbing, power-hungry Atlantean royals. He had proved he was a man to be reckoned with more than once, which didn't make Cesaré feel any better about what he had to tell him today.

Shona and Lance were then introduced to Sebastian and Alfonzo, who were his advisors and Lily's father and uncle.

A beautiful blonde girl approached. Cesaré immediately smiled. "Ches!" she said, bounding up to them and kissing him on the cheek. His eyes flashed over to Lance, who couldn't take his eyes off her. He was joining the dots. The same small, perfectly proportioned frame and face shape, but where Lily was dark, she was blonde, and where Lily's eyes were deepest blue, hers were green.

"And this is my wife, Tia," Dante said. Then he indicated for them to sit comfortably in a circle of soft seats around a low table.

Their drinks came and Dante studied Cesaré quizzically. Cesaré felt awkward. The king had been a good friend to him in the short time he'd gotten to know him, even after the time he'd been betrayed. And now it felt like he was about to tell him he'd repaid that kindness by stabbing him in the back. He had to say something, if only to break the weird atmosphere he was creating. "Forgive the intrusion, Your Highness, and I will be as brief as possible so you can get back to your business at hand."

Dante's eyes narrowed and he put up a hand to silence him. "Chill, Cesaré, you are always welcome here, you know that … It weighed heavily on me … if there were something I could have done to help you with what happened with Isla and your family, I would have done it."

Trust Dante to get right to the point. It was like a punch to the gut. Cesaré looked down, swallowing the hurt as if it happened only the day before.

"I still value you as a friend and a son of the Florianna family," Dante said.

Cesaré faltered for a second. With every word, the king's hand of friendship made what he had to say all the harder. "Your Highness is most kind," he said, bowing his head again."

"Now, what's on yer mind, Ches … or would you prefer some privacy?" Dante said, looking around at the party, eyes resting a little longer on Lance.

Cesaré shifted in his seat uncomfortably. Privacy wasn't going to make what he had to say any easier. "Thank you, but we can talk freely in front of my friends. They are involved in what I have to say."

Dante frowned quizzically, but before he could tell him to get on with it, the drinks came.

CHAPTER 20

*L*ance couldn't take his eyes off the girl who looked on silently. He wondered why she wasn't mute as well. She was totally stunning yet had an unmistakable otherworldliness that bowled you over. *Like Lily.* The difference was that her hair was blonde with large curls, and she didn't appear to have any permanent stripes that he could see. It made her look a lot girlier than Lily, who was a stripy tomboy with unruly dark corkscrew curls. He closed his eyes for a moment, then turned his attention back to the conversation.

The maid put down the beers, finished serving the others tea, and then left them alone.

"Spit it out, Ches," the king said, beginning to look a little exasperated.

At first, Lance couldn't believe anyone as young as this could be the king, but it soon became apparent that he was a respected statesman.

Cesaré put up his hands. "The first thing you need to know is Malleven is alive."

Dante stopped mid-sip and put his cup back down. Then he swore under his breath. "You've seen him?"

Cesaré shook his head.

"No, I have," Shona said, speaking up for the first time.

Dante looked over at her as if she had just spoken a profanity, then looked up and sighed deeply.

"Shit! We'd better warn Isla," Tia said, looking at Cesaré apologetically as soon as she said it.

Lance took note of her English accent.

Dante turned his attention back to Cesaré. "Thank you for coming here to let me know. I know it must have been hard for you."

Cesaré bowed his head slightly. "That's not everything, Your Highness."

His face looked so stricken that it surprised Lance. This was all way deeper than he thought.

"He has a Siren." Cesaré shook his head. "I'm such a fucking idiot."

Shona went to protest and Cesaré put up his hand to silence her.

Lance's confusion was quickly turning to alarm. He got it that the guy had double-crossed Cesaré or something, but there was something else, something he'd kept to himself.

All eyes were glued to Cesaré when the king asked, "Who?" in a low voice.

Lance and Shona were looking between the two men, willing Cesaré to just spit it out. Cesaré looked at the two of them with an apology in his eyes before he spoke. "Her name is Lily."

"Lillian Gale," Shona added.

Lance continued to study Cesaré. His body language alone told him he wasn't done yet and he wasn't going to like it.

Cesaré relayed the story they all knew. How Shona had

first found her and brought her into their close-knit circle and Lance and his group had sworn allegiance as her Protectors.

Hearing it all spelled out like that made Lance feel even worse. Each and every one of them, particularly him, had let her down.

"If I hadn't been such a drunken idiot, I could have brought her straight here," Cesaré continued.

Dante held up a hand, signalling he'd heard enough. Then turned his attention to Shona, who blasted red with surprise with the attention suddenly on her. "Malleven approached you?"

"Yeah, I kinda knew him from before, through Ches," Shona said, bobbing her head in Cesaré's direction. "I'm really sorry, I didn't know the full story of what went down between them."

Lance didn't think he'd ever seen Shona so shaken. He guessed she really was sorry.

Then Dante turned to Lance. "And you … where do you fit in to all this?"

For a moment, Lance was stumped. *Where did he fit into all this? Protector, friend, selfish idiot, who'd turned his back when she needed him the most?*

"He's Human – adopted into an Atlantean family," Cesaré explained for him. Although he didn't know what that had to do with anything.

Dante raised an eyebrow and then studied him for a long moment. Lance didn't need anyone judging him. He felt bad enough already. "Me? … I let her down," Lance said bitterly.

Dante narrowed his eyes and continued to weigh him up until Alfonzo whispered something to him quietly and he nodded in agreement. "We've been hearing rumours of a fourth siren on the west coast for quite some time," Dante said, breaking the awkwardness. "That means every family must be swarming the place." Then he pinched his nose as if it were another problem he had on top of a load of others. "Any other prince in the world would have been better than him." He let his hand fall and shook his head.

Tia touched Dante's arm to offer comfort. Lance wondered whether she was talking to him telepathically. Then both of them looked at Lance, giving him his answer. "You know her … you know my sister?" Tia said.

Lance immediately looked at Shona. She was far more qualified to answer questions about Lily. At that moment, he didn't feel worthy.

"No! I asked you," she said, drawing his eyes back to her.

Everybody then looked to him to answer. "Er, Shona knows her best," he said, shaking his head.

Dante gave Tia a meaningful look that went on a little too long. Their closeness only made him feel worse, and twisted something in the centre of his chest. It seemed everything always came back to Lily.

They both looked back at him knowingly and Tia spoke again. "I don't know why, but I get a feeling you were close."

Lance wasn't sure what freaky powers the pair of them had. Nothing would surprise him these days. The blush at getting busted probably gave him away, so he sighed and leaned forward with his elbows on his knees. "Well, she's dark, not blonde like you," he said, looking up through his eyebrows at Tia.

"And real curly hair," Shona chimed in.

"Blue eyes … the colour of the ocean," Lance said, wistfully.

"Really, what she like?" Tia asked, delighted.

Lance smiled. This was Lily's family. All the grounding and support she secretly craved – and they would love her, he just knew it. It was devastating. He laughed at the irony. "She's one of the best drummers I've ever heard."

Tia laughed, clapped her hands, threw her arms around Dante's neck and perched on his lap.

He smiled and circled his arms around her waist indulgently, proving Lance was right about their mutual love.

"Did you hear, Dante? … A drummer." She was clearly thrilled.

He nodded and kissed her on the lips. Then he grinned at Lance. "All the Sirens seem to have developed some kind of musical talent that links them together."

"I'm a DJ, my sister Lacy is a dancer." She looked Dante in the eyes with a frown. "And Isla?"

"The way she moves, babe."

Tia searched his face lovingly, then back at Lance. "She's a martial artist, but she can tune into the rhythm of the world around her like you wouldn't believe."

Lance was enraptured. It was the couple's closeness in front of him that he found most captivating. The wave of envy that followed was painful. This was the very thing he always knew could never happen between him and Lily. "She can't talk, though," he added quietly, waiting for the sadness sure to follow.

Tia's face fell, Dante frowned and Alfonzo whispered something again.

Dante nodded knowingly. "It sounds as though she has inherited the Murr characteristic from her mother."

That would explain a lot, including the way her stripes never really faded.

"Do Murrs talk in their heads?" Shona said.

Lance flashed a look at her as if to shut her up. He wasn't sure whether Lily would want them to know all this shit. It felt disloyal somehow. Then he felt Dante's eyes boring into him again. "I didn't know she could do that until right before she left," he added moodily.

"What I don't understand is, I know he's good-looking

and everything, but what made her go off with such an arse-hole?" Tia said.

In any other circumstances, Lance would have laughed. That was if he hadn't felt so damn guilt-ridden. Shona did too if the look on her face was anything to go by. "It was my fault … I was too hard on her."

Cesaré shook his head. "It was not your fault Lance, it was mine. I'm a prince and I failed in my responsibility to her."

Dante released Tia to sit in her own chair and sat back wearily. "If she were bound, we'd have a hope of finding her." He shook his head in frustration. "Now it's like looking for a needle in a haystack."

Lance's heart sank. He didn't know much about it, but he guessed it was like the whole marriage deal to Atlanteans.

"That is the main reason for my visit today, Your High-ness – and to offer my sincerest apologies. She *has* bound someone to her."

Every head looked up and everyone said, "Who?" at the same time.

Cesaré put his head in his hands. "Me."

CHAPTER 21

here was a moment of stunned silence. Lance frowned. *When did that happen?* He looked between Dante and Cesaré. No one seemed to know what the king would do. Cesaré obviously thought he'd committed some crime and looked gutted.

"Yesterday, I wiped out. Lance and Lily were there. I was unconscious … I swear I didn't know what she'd done until I woke up in the hospital. I'm sorry, Your Highness, I had no way of stopping her."

Lance continued to look between Cesaré and the king. *Would someone fucking mind telling me what's going on?* He glanced at Shona, who shrugged, as confused as he was.

Dante looked at Tia. They were communicating again.

"What's wrong?" Lance said. "Someone mind telling us?"

The king nodded and he and Tia looked in their direction again.

"I thought a prince was supposed to bond with her?"

Cesaré silenced him with a look, then put his hand over his heart. "I apologise, Your Highness. The Siren's first pledge should have come to you."

The two older gentlemen and Dante conferred quickly, then Dante faced Cesaré and smiled. In the end, he was grinning widely. Nothing was making any sense. Even Cesaré was looking confused. Dante's face dropped and he narrowed his eyes. "So *you* have the power, Ches," Dante said ominously, nodding slowly.

Cesaré cast down his eyes and nodded. "I felt it instantly, Your Highness."

Dante laughed aloud as if the news astounded him. Then he faced Lance. "Malleven didn't take your woman because he loves her or wants a wife." He laughed again as if the more he thought about it, the funnier it got.

"He took her for her power," Cesaré finished for him, realisation dawning on his face. Then he swore and looked away, ashamed all over again.

"For fuck's sake, Ches, in the circumstances, this is the best thing that could have happened," Dante said.

"Does someone wanna tell us?" Shona said.

"Ches has it," Dante and Tia both said together.

Lance locked eyes with Cesaré. In the moment that passed between them, Lance knew that Cesaré understood how he felt about Lily. *Wait ... your woman ... the king had said.* It seemed everyone had assumed she was his. He felt stunned for a moment and unworthy. After all, nothing had really been openly acknowledged or acted upon.

"Lily saved Ches' life by opening his gills. In Atlantean law, when a Siren breathes her soul into a prince to save him from death by drowning, she has accepted him as her husband," Dante explained.

So Ches was married to Lily. That part made sense. "Wait!" Lance said, with a hand up. "I don't get it ... if Ches is married to Lily, does that mean that even though Malleven has her, he can't marry her?"

"Yes, he can!" Both Dante and Cesaré said together.

Lance threw both his hands up in exasperation. Now he was lost again.

"He can marry her, but it's with the first prince that her power passes. By law, it should have come to me, freeing Lily to marry who she wanted, but she gave it to Cesaré," Dante explained.

"In order to be stronger than all other princes that seek to take the crown, the king needs the power of all five," Cesaré said quietly. "I stole this right."

Dante, suddenly serious, bobbed his head confirming he was right, and slowly stood. "Stand up, Cesaré."

Lance watched nervously as Cesaré followed and straightened up, not sure what was about to happen. Cesaré's head was bowed as if he were about to get the death sentence.

"Look at me, Cesaré."

Cesaré raised his eyes and, for a moment, they stared long and hard at each other. "You know the only way I can take that power from you is to kill you?"

"I do," Cesaré said.

Lance went to stand to protest, but Dante held up a hand for him to stay put. "There is another way."

CESARÉ WATCHED THE KING CLOSELY. There was no joking in him now. *Could it be, despite everything, that he was still offering him a lifeline?* He felt humbled. "It would be an honour to make amends and serve you in some way, Your Highness." He lowered his eyes again and waited for the penance.

"You must swear allegiance to me on the power of the Orb, then, when such a time comes where the bond can be completed and recognised publicly, you must take a seat on my council as my right hand."

To swear allegiance to the ancient power that governed

them all, he would have gladly done so anyway. He had already decided that when he first thought he would marry Lily's sister, Isla, but to be reinstated as the favoured son of the Florianna family and be the king's closest man on the council was just too much to take. A lump appeared in his throat and he went down on one knee to hide his emotion. When he got a grip on himself, he put his hand on his heart and looked up, with tears threatening to brim over his eyes. "As always, Your Highness's kindness astounds me. I do so swear my allegiance on the Orb and everything I hold dear. This I vow until I enter the ether in death."

When he looked down, he felt the king's hand on his shoulder. It was the last thing to tip him over the edge.

"Leave us, please … I need a few moments to discuss details privately," the king said above him.

Cesaré was grateful for the distraction and the time to wipe his miserable tears from his eyes. It was as though the betrayal by his best friend and cousin with the woman he thought he would marry, the disgrace in front of the whole Atlantean world at owning a false divining ring, the loss of the Siren that was due to his family and therefore their seat on the council, was all exorcised in those few moments. For what the king had given him in front of these few meagre witnesses was his self-esteem back. He was Cesaré Florianna, son of the royal house of Florianna, not only bonded to a Siren, but seated on the first-ever Atlantean council for over a thousand years and right hand of the king. The whole thing just overwhelmed him, and for a few minutes, he wept. And the king was magnanimous enough to allow it without saying a word.

When at last he had poured out every last emotion, he stood asking for a pardon in Italian, which the king dismissed as unrequired. Dante pressed a button to recall the others back as if they'd been discussing something that was now concluded. With every meeting with this new king, his respect for him grew. He had made his pledge and meant it.

The others trooped back in and sat back down. Cesaré did the same but was still bleary-eyed and slightly dazed.

"We still have to find her, though," Tia was saying. "Cesaré needs to complete the bond."

Dante nodded in deep thought.

"Hey, does that mean you still have to bond with her?" Tia asked.

Cesaré knew from his experience at court that Dante had a bond with each of Lily's sisters, not only to absorb their power to make him strong physically, but to maintain the psychic link between them. Through that, he could speak telepathically to them and, whomever they bonded with, sense their emotions and know when they are near. It was a stroke of genius on the king's part to set him above his competitors and keep the Sirens safe.

Dante looked at Alfonzo questioningly.

"There is the question of the link," Alfonzo said, mirroring Cesaré's thoughts.

Dante narrowed his eyes while he thought. Then he nodded and smiled and looked at Cesaré. "But the whole point of his tricking you with Isla was to get the link through you with all the sisters. He intended to bond with Isla and, through that, get access to all the sisters and, in turn, me. In a nutshell, he could have turned our greatest strength into our greatest weakness. We would have been wide open to attack," he said with a deep sigh. "We have to assume his plan has not changed."

Cesaré understood immediately. If the king didn't bond with Lily, then there would be no link with her sisters, and so Malleven's power would be severely inhibited. No power, and no link beyond Lily herself. He nodded at the shrewdness of it. "I understand," Cesaré said solemnly. In never bonding with Lily, the king trusted him with his life and the lives of all the sisters. Again, he was humbled as they locked eyes meaningfully. A moment of mutual respect passed between them.

"Her telepathy … can she do it at any distance?" Lance said, breaking the thick atmosphere.

The king averted his gaze and shook his head. "No, I've only known extremely strong Murrs be able to do that, but she can to Ches if she wants to. They can't have a two-way conversation until the bond is complete."

Dante stood again, signalling Cesaré to do the same.

His mind was in a whirl as he felt himself pulled into the king's embrace, where he clapped his back affectionately. "You got your Siren after all, Ches," he said quietly into his ear and drew away laughing. "But you might regret it once you realise what a pain in the arse they are."

Tia scowled at him playfully.

Cesaré stood, bewildered. This morning, he had come here expecting to be interrogated and, at the very least, imprisoned. The turnaround in his life in the last forty-eight hours made him question whether he was dreaming.

LANCE LOOKED on in a jumble of emotions. Of course he wanted Cesaré to get his old life back and be happy, but no one was thinking about Lily here, and how she was going to feel about all this. It seemed that these Sirens were just pawns to be used in a game between powerful princes.

His face relaxed from its scowl when Tia gently touched him on the shoulder. She studied him as if she knew exactly what he was thinking, then smiled kindly. "Don't give up on her, okay? … It'll be you that'll matter, I promise."

All he could do was frown. *Did she see right through him … did she know how he felt? How could she possibly understand what*

*it was like to love a Siren – someone far out of your reach ...
another species and know you could be a walking death sentence?*

She was right to some extent. He hated the way he had
left it with Lily the last time they'd been together, and if he
only ever got to do one thing, it would be to see her again to
say he was sorry.

As SOON AS he was left alone, Dante summoned his equerry,
Max. He was Human and an expert in ancient Atlantean
history and the writings carried out of Atlantis itself. Dante
had seen his worth as soon as he'd met him and employed
him on the spot. He conferred with him on most things –
especially those to do with prophecy and Atlantean law.
Dante was an avid student, but there was still much he didn't
know.

"Your Highness," Max said, with a tilt of his head when he
found Dante sitting in the great hall.

Dante brought him up to speed with the morning's revelations and Max agreed that there was nothing else that
could have been done. "Cesaré is a good man and deserves
the chance," Dante assured him. The Fates had spoken loud
and clear with Cesaré. He was destined to be with a Siren
and play a principal part in Atlantean history. Dante had long
given up questioning the Fates. It was never long before the
genius behind it was revealed. This brought him to the
reason he had summoned Max. "I want you to look into
something for me."

Max tilted his head again. "Of course, Your Highness."

"I want you to dig into everything you can find out about
Lance McCabe."

"The gentleman who just left, sir?"

Dante nodded, still lost in his thoughts. He told him what
he knew of him so far, which Max scribbled down quickly on

his notepad. "I want you to delve back into his past – who he is, from what family … go back as far as you need to. I want to know everything about this guy. Something is bugging me about him, and I can't put my finger on what it is."

"Would sir like me to consult the tomes?"

Dante tipped his head. "Why not … it couldn't hurt. Get onto it fast, though, will you?"

Max bowed his head. "Right away, sir."

CHAPTER 22

$\mathcal{M}$alleven didn't know how he kept his hands off Lily that first night, but he managed it. Her hunger for affection, so deliciously hidden beneath the surface, was just ripe for the taking. Although Malleven knew that wouldn't be in his best interest in the long run. Thankfully, he had Antonio nearby to take the edge off his frustration and so she continued to thaw to him little by little. She had no experience with relationships and thought Antonio was just a close friend, which endeared her to him and surprised him a little.

After the debacle of his own mate, Isla Snow, he was determined to bring this Siren totally into his power and to rely on him completely. It was the only balm for his injured pride and reputation, irrespective of the colour of his poxy ring.

That first morning, he awoke early and began taking samples of her blood. He told her to relax and take as long as she liked and the small blood tests were just a formality for proving her bloodline. *Partly true.*

He knew now, without doubt, that he could change the

colour of his divining ring to the turquoise it needed to be. Purple would be too obvious and would spark an enquiry into his ring's authenticity. No one would question the colour if it were turquoise, as all rings in her vicinity would be.

Never in all his experience and knowledge had a single prince's ring changed to the blood red that his was. It didn't matter how many new ones he obtained, they all went the same damning colour. He would need to consult the ancient tomes in his brotherhood's library.

For a moment, he smouldered with anger at the Fates for abandoning him. His whole life had been a continual struggle to change the hand he'd been dealt, and he wasn't about to alter that habit now.

Malleven left the house after reminding Lily the staff would get her anything she needed and promised he would return in a few hours and take her shopping.

Her eyes softened a little more.

Lily thought a blood sample was a strange request from a husband-to-be, but this was a new world with traditions and customs she knew nothing about.

She showered, then ate a large breakfast prepared for her by curious servants, then left the room and explored the palatial villa and strolled in the beautiful gardens. Her heart hitched at the beauty of everything so removed from her old life. It was the stuff of dreams or glossy magazines. At that moment, she decided that Italy was the most beautiful place on earth.

Then, around three in the afternoon, Malleven returned. He breezed in, tall, handsome, dressed casually, although expensively, like a catwalk model. Lily couldn't work out why a man as beautiful as him could want someone like her.

Malleven's eyes lit up when he saw her sitting in the garden in the shade. He approached and kissed her cheek. Then he pulled her up to stand in front of him by both wrists. He seemed in good spirits. *"Sei molta bella!"* he said while his eyes roamed all over her.

Her temperature rose immediately and she felt herself blush.

This seemed to amuse him and he pulled her close into the heat of his body and just held her for a few moments.

Lily allowed it somewhat stiffly, while her heart thudded in her chest.

"Don't be embarrassed, Lily, you please me greatly." He put his mouth tantalisingly close to her ear. "Let me shower you with beautiful things befitting a queen," his voice rumbled with an enticing breath of air next to her skin.

Her heart fluttered all over the place. *Queen?* She was bewildered. Such beautiful words, and he always acted like a perfect gentleman. *Wasn't one of her sisters a queen?*

He put her away from him. "Come, let me show you what I mean."

MALLEVEN INFORMED the servants that they were going out. They jumped into Malleven's waiting limo and he whisked her off to Quadrilatero d'Oro, to The Brera, exclusive shopping district of Milan.

There he took her from shop to expensive shop, kitting her out from head to foot, with shoes, boots, coats – basically anything any girl ever dreamt about. There were jewels, underwear and face creams that she didn't even know what they did.

Every garment he insisted she try on and parade in front of him, to which he nodded or shook his head. She never questioned his decision, trusting his taste implicitly. Even when something was strapless and she died a thousand deaths walking out and showing him her stripes, his eyes filled with appreciation. He stood and circled her, planting the gentlest of kisses on her shoulder. "Simply stunning!" he whispered. "*Mio fiore.*" He left the words floating in the air like a promise.

Everything she'd sought to hide all her life, he seemed to want to show or accentuate to the world. He left her speechless and wanting more.

With all the shopping, nightfall seemed to come really quickly and Malleven announced they would eat. Lily hadn't thought about food since breakfast, and her stomach growled, informing her it was time.

They ate at a beautiful open-air cafe. He knew exactly what she couldn't eat as it would upset her stomach, told her exactly what she should try, and ordered several dishes just for the purpose. The wine he chose tasted so sublime that she could only conclude she'd been drinking paint-stripper up to that point.

All Lily could do was sit there in a total state of bewilderment. It was simply too much for a girl like her to take in. Her life had changed many times and sometimes even for the better, but never had she experienced such a positive and seductive place as this. It was as though a spell was being woven around her to fall into, like a web of cocooning comfort.

Malleven sat back in his chair and eyed her shrewdly. "What is the matter, Lily? I know you can speak to me … I want you to feel you can tell me anything."

She pushed the remnants of a delicious dessert she couldn't remember the name of around her plate, then gave up and put down her spoon. *Malleven …* she faltered, not knowing how to explain. *Everything has been so wonderful … you've been …* She shook her head. Then she looked him straight in the eyes. *I can't think why?*

He continued to look into her eyes, considering what she'd said.

Why you would go to all this effort ... She held out her hands. *For me?* she finished, incredulously.

He frowned at that but remained silent.

She began to feel uncomfortable. *I mean, I said I would marry you, so it was a done deal anyway ...* Her eyes fell away from his and her voice trailed off with his frown that started to look a little angry.

The silence went on so long that she was forced to look at him again. He looked baffled. *I'm sorry, I didn't mean to upset you,* she projected.

"You have no idea just how beautiful you are, do you?" he said, astonished.

She sat there feeling small, shaking her head like an idiot. Emotion threatened to bubble up, making her swallow loudly. *Who was she kidding, she didn't belong here.*

All he did was smile at her as if he knew. The man was bewildering. *You said you're like me ... you're not,* she flashed at him angrily. Suddenly, she felt self-conscious and needed to get away from all these beautiful, successful people. She was a fraud to be among them. Just when she thought she would jump up and run, his hand closed over hers.

Relax, mio fiore ... he projected straight to her mind. She felt his presence very close to her, gentling and lulling. *It is a reasonable question, Lily ... please, hear me out.*

She relaxed a little, but her heart was still beating hard.

Malleven released her hand and sat back in his chair, taking a sip of his wine. "Life, Lily, is about taking what you've got, however little, and seizing opportunities when they come along. Work hard, focus on your goal and never tire until you achieve it." His words were clipped and very definite, while his face became hard. It was obvious that his mind had moved to a very dark place.

Lily had dark places like that and knew more than most how hard it was to drag yourself out of them. She leaned over and softly touched his hand as if to ground him. *Look at you,* she projected. *You've done it.* Her eyes swept over him to prove her point.

He looked baffled for a moment, as if he'd been a million miles away. Then he seemed to grasp what she'd said and smiled, bobbing his head slightly. Then he moved in closer so he was only inches away from her. "Almost, *mio fiore* ... there is one more thing to achieve." His eyes were searching her face intently.

And what is that, she thought. Even her mental voice sounded breathless. *Was he going to kiss her?*

Malleven paused and looked at her mouth. "I've never found the right person to share it with. The one who understands me and can share my journey." His voice purred seductively close to her lips in a vocal caress.

By the time he finished his sentence, she was sweating and breathing heavily. Then, when she thought he would kiss her for sure, he leaned back and asked for the bill.

Lily was left catching her breath.

It was late when they returned to the villa. Malleven dismissed all the servants. "Nightcap?" he said, holding up a decanter filled with a dark amber liquid.

Lily shrugged. *Guess so ... what is it?*

"This, my dear, is an excellent brandy." He put a small amount into a huge round glass, passed it to her and poured his own. "Come," he said, picking up her hand and leading her out onto the patio.

It was quiet, smelled of flowers, and had a warm glow

from discreet lanterns. There was a small fountain and beautiful sofas arranged to view the garden. Lights twinkled in the distance, mirroring the clear sky alive with stars. It was the end of a perfect day. Malleven indicated for her to join him on a red brocade daybed.

Lily sat propped up against the pillows, sipping the brandy. It warmed her throat, but by the time it hit her stomach, she pulled a face and shuddered.

"Do you like it?" he said, smiling next to her.

An uncharacteristic giggle escaped her. *Not sure yet.*

Malleven ran a finger gently down the side of her face, sobering her instantly with the tenderness of it. "I want you to trust me, Lily."

She nodded slightly. *I'm beginning to.*

"Good … And know that everything I do – even if you don't understand it, is for our good … Okay?"

She swallowed. He always had an effect that got straight to the heart of her, exposing her wide open. *Don't you ever get scared?*

He relaxed back into the pillows and took a minute to think about her question. She leaned on her side, waiting for him to answer. Then he reached for the decanter and topped up her glass. "Drink!" he ordered.

She sipped the drink, slightly disappointed that he wasn't going to answer her. With the wine at the meal and now the brandy, she was beginning to feel fuzzy and tired. It had been an exhilarating but exhausting day.

Malleven drained his glass, then eyed her shrewdly. "I will make a bargain with you," he said, mirroring her position, facing her. "I will tell you my deepest fear, *mio fiore*, if you do one small thing for me. But be aware, I have never admitted it to a single soul. I give it as a gift to you in respect of a mutual trust I hope we will build – and you grow to mean much already," he tacked on.

Her heart thundered and her face blasted red. The look in his eyes, now brimming with shimmering gold, shifted something deep within her. Emotion, she realised, was what triggered his eyes to do that. The rawness and vulnerability won her over. How could anyone rebuff a statement like that? She looked down, unable to meet his intense gaze. *Like what?* There were so many things that frightened her; he'd be spoiled for choice.

He shuffled a little closer and spoke in a voice like he was telling a story. "When we are bound in the way of Atlanteans, we will know each other completely, *mio fiore*." He paused until she was forced to look back into those swirling eyes. "Secrets will be pointless," he continued, "I carry a great blackness in my soul … you see, I was betrayed by one of your sisters."

Her eyes went wide. This must be the same sister who'd done a number on Cesaré.

"And I nearly lost my life."

She blinked in shock. He seemed so strong.

"The truth is … I loved her and I wanted to marry her." He laughed, ruefully, on an exhale. "She was mine." He looked down at his ring. "But she left me to drown in the water." His eyes met hers again, soulfully. "You see, only a Siren can enable an Atlantean to breathe the water."

For a second, an image of Cesaré drowning came to mind. *That was different,* she told herself immediately and squashed the thought. She turned her attention back to Malleven quickly with a frown. *And she could have saved you?*

He nodded slowly, but his face was pained. "It shamed me greatly." Then shook his head bitterly and looked away.

Lily reached out a tentative hand and touched his cheek. *You shouldn't feel ashamed,* she thought gently, *hey, but you survived.*

He nodded. "Thanks to my powers and my brotherhood."

Brotherhood ... who are they?

His eyes darted back to hers. "We are a society that dates back to the dawn of time." He softened a little. "Together, we are so powerful that we are revered even in the Atlantean world and by those truly enlightened Humans."

It was something he obviously felt very passionate about and also very protective of. *"What happened to her ... my sister, I mean,* she thought, steering him away from the touchy subject.

Malleven sighed dramatically and looked up to the bed canopy for answers. "I was left unconscious, for dead. I heard that she married a Borge prince moments later. I believe she now lives in Murrtaine."

The names and places meant little to her, but it appalled her to think that her own flesh and blood could have treated him like this. A handsome man who had only ever shown her kindness and consideration. She found herself hating that sister before she'd even met her. *My other sisters ... didn't they do anything?*

He shook his head. "They and the rest of the royal families looked on and did nothing." His eyes washed over with shimmering stars.

Lily couldn't believe her ears.

Malleven pulled her closer to him by the nape of her neck and softly brushed his lips against hers. "You will never treat me so, I know it in my heart." Then he licked the seam of her lips to part them, and kissed her hot, wet and open-mouthed.

Initially startled, she felt herself opening to him. The taste of him, the brandy and the beautiful surroundings were a heady mix. She found herself responding, allowing him to coax her with his tongue into passion.

When they pulled apart, some moments later, she felt a rush of cool air against her burning hot skin. She ran a finger across the sheen of sweat on his forehead in wonder at how alike they were. His hand caught hers and kissed the inside of her wrist. *What is it you want from me?*

His hand moved to cup the side of her face, while he ran a thumb across her cheek. His eyes were now awash in shimmering gold. Whatever he wanted meant a great deal. "I would enter your mind and you allow it – welcome it even. I promise I would not venture too deeply."

Lily continued to gaze into his strange, hypnotic eyes. The idea scared her a little. *Why ... why do you need to do that?*

A weary sigh escaped him. "You are no fool, as I suspected." His face hardened a little. "I have told you my deepest fear, *mio fiore*. Once betrayed, trust needs to be built again."

His eyes rested on her speculatively while she considered it. The idea frightened her; it was weird enough when she felt his psychic self at the very edges of her consciousness. *But I would never do anything bad to you.*

He tilted his head at an angle and moved his thumb across her cheek again. "I know you believe that, but I can never be betrayed like that again, Lily. Please understand."

Lily thought she did. It was as though it was more important to him for her to let him than what he would actually find. *Okay,* she thought eventually.

No sooner had she thought the words than he seemed to loom up over her like a huge shadow, making her flinch.

Without saying a word, he took the glass from her hand and put it on the small table next to the bed. Then he clutched either side of her head with his thumbs at her temples and began to circle them as he'd done on the previous night, except this time the pressure was harder. The darkly intense eyes that bored into hers churned with gold specs, then cleared to deepest blue, like the depths of space.

At first, she was scared, but then she found herself relaxing and falling hopelessly and completely into his eyes. Free-falling, twisting and turning, making her stomach go over and over. Her heart juddered and shook in her chest as she felt the fingers that held her face begin to venture inward through the tunnels of her mind. They crept and burrowed each passageway like tentacles.

The feeling in her chest began with a sensation like butterflies fluttering up towards her forehead, but then a dull ache extended in lines from her heart to her head, as if someone were pulling strings through her veins, growing more forceful until it began to hurt.

Lily moaned in pain.

Relax, my flower. Oh ... that's it, my beautiful one, let me in ... ah! .... Yes, let me in completely.

It felt like Malleven's voice echoed throughout her whole body. She was so disoriented and in pain that she couldn't tell if the voice was psychic or real.

Just when she thought she would panic, she felt his mouth on hers, forcing it open. In that moment, he stole her thoughts and invaded her with the most blistering of kisses. And when the tentacles of his mind reached the base of her skull, something happened that changed everything. It was like the world exploded from her, inside out. Her body lit her up like fireworks that rippled out from her heart to her fingers and toes.

Lily gasped Malleven's name. She'd never tasted anything like the dark heat of that demanding mouth. Then she kissed him hard, fervent and hungry, with everything she had.

CHAPTER 23

Malleven felt feverish as he held her face in his hands. He was rough and barely held back his excitement. Lust almost consumed him. He held himself at the periphery of her consciousness for as long as he could, while he kept her grounded by holding eye contact. However, something in her soul called to him, and his control snapped. He kissed her hard in a searing brand and let himself fly. His psychic feelers hurtled through her neural pathways as if the floodgates of a dam were opened, and he groaned at the jubilant freedom of it. Never had he felt so exultant or more euphoric – not even when he'd had sex for the first time with someone he'd had to pursue. This experience was on a whole other level. The complete surrender of a creature as powerful as a Siren – one who would now be his to control.

He roamed her mind purely because he could. Exploring areas he didn't even have any interest in, just for the hell of it. It was such a powerful buzz that he became rock hard. How he didn't fuck her, he had no idea. Despite himself, he curbed his roughness. He could feel her pain. So instead of pushing home his advantage and ravaging her both in mind and body, he continued with his plan to initiate her slowly to what he wanted.

Once he'd got a grip on himself, he navigated the pathway to that part of the brain where basic instinct stemmed. There, he wasted no time in giving her the orgasm of her life, without even physically touching her.

As she gasped in surprise, he covered her mouth with his and revelled in her response to him. Grinding his hips into hers, he exulted in his masterstroke of disguising his invasion with perfect pleasure. As she fractured in his hands, he knew this one was the one who'd be his. This one would help him fulfil his dreams.

LILY AWOKE ENTWINED in Malleven's limbs the morning after the night that changed everything, and it felt good.

Although the whole experience had been quite painful, it had given way to a feeling so exultant, so profoundly satisfying, that she couldn't stop replaying it in her head over and over. Butterflies fluttered in her stomach every time. And yet he still hadn't laid one finger on her to achieve it. This man was surely a master magician.

She shuffled around in his arms to study his still-sleeping face and traced a finger down the beautiful line of his dark temple and jaw.

He sleepily opened his eyes at her touch and smiled back at her. "Don't look like that, *mio fiore*," he said in a sexy, half-asleep rasp. "Not if you wish to keep your virtue a little longer."

Her heart hitched in her chest and her eyes went wide at what he meant. Then her butterflies somersaulted at the reminder that he was a very red-blooded male.

How did you ... was it that obvious? she thought, a little perplexed.

Malleven smiled a little and pulled her in closer. "You gave me a great gift last night, Lily, one that I will never forget."

She frowned, not really understanding what he meant or what enjoyment he had got out of the whole experience.

He ran a thumb across her lips as he cupped her jaw possessively. "Just as with a physical joining, it will never be as painful again."

Her chest tightened and her temperature shot up. She just couldn't help herself. Everything with him was so decadent and all about throat-clenching desire.

But instead of ravaging her, he closed the gap and kissed her reverently. His tongue ventured tentatively, bowling her over with the unexpected tenderness of it. This man continued to unbalance her at every turn.

The proud thickness of him pushed into her lower abdomen while he suspended his weight on his elbows. The darkness in his eyes held the promise that he wanted her.

SOMETHING STRANGE WAS SHIFTING in Malleven as he looked down into Lily's eyes. She wanted him and it was obvious to a man as experienced as him. Her eyes were dewy, her body pliant and giving, and her heart beat a mesmerizing pulse under her skin. It would have been so easy to lower himself and take her physically. Instead, he pushed back the wayward curls from her face and marvelled at how different she felt to her sister, Isla – his true mate. Isla was strong-willed and matched his fire blow for blow, but Lily seemed willing to trust him completely not to hurt her. And what amazed him was that he didn't want to. *Had he shot himself in the foot?* Perhaps this one was the cleverest witch of all. Then he shook away the thought as ridiculous. It was just that his plan to woo her slowly was working better than he imagined. In drawing her to him, he found himself drawn to her. He already had free access to her mind. There were dark shadows there, but ones that would be revealed to him in time.

So, despite the need to push into her beautiful, lush, waiting body and claim her physically, he came to an instant decision to wait until they were married in the way of Atlanteans. Then, together, they would conquer the world – he and his totally obedient Siren. Nothing could come against them and win.

He swore under his breath in Italian and kissed her chastely on the lips. "Soon, *mio fiore*. When we are married." Then he sprang off her body, leaving her blinking in surprise.

He stalked off to another part of the house to find Antonio. The lust and excitement that coursed through his veins needed instant and energetic gratification.

LILY COULD THINK of nothing else while she showered and dressed. For the first time in her life, she felt beautiful and wanted. Dressed in the stylish Italian clothes Malleven had bought her, she couldn't believe the difference he had made in her in just a short time. Smoothing down the fabric while she looked at herself in the full-length mirror, her heart leapt that such a desirable man could not only fancy her but want to marry her as well.

When he saw her a little later, he complimented her instantly and kissed her hand. "Stunning!" he said.

Lily blushed and butterflies tickled her stomach.

Lance had become a distant echo she shut down whenever he came to mind. She didn't need any negativity, not when she had a beautiful, adoring prince taking care of her every need.

Marriage was imminent, but he seemed to be taking the time and trouble to get to know her. He took her on endless shopping sprees, boating on the lake, horse-riding, the theatre and the opera. For each event, he bought her the perfect clothes and jewels, and showered her with praise to build her confidence – and it was working. It felt like she was living a delirious dream.

Each night, he would ask permission, then enter her mind. He asked politely and with little pressure and she found she couldn't deny him; in fact, she was growing accustomed to it. He always finished by giving her such pleasure that she longed for him to touch her physically and be a true husband, but he never did. It was beginning to dawn on her that she had found a rare gentleman – the stuff of fairy tales.

SEVERAL WEEKS HAD PASSED and Lily had completely settled into her new life. One evening, Malleven announced they were attending a nearby village fiesta where there would be good rustic food, local wine and fireworks.

She dressed casually in a short-sleeved top, cropped trousers and with her tight curls pulled back away from her face. After telling her how lovely she looked, she and Malleven set off.

They were joined at the table in the piazza by several of Malleven's friends – including Antonio. Lily didn't understand why Malleven liked him around so much, as he always seemed in a bad mood. Malleven seemed oblivious and introduced her to everyone and explained telepathically that all his friends were Atlantean and had varying degrees in strength of bloodline. Everything in her new world seemed exciting and interesting.

They all enjoyed a happy evening, with chatter and laughter and endless bottles of red wine. Lily was tired and just beginning to wonder when they would be going home when a group of men approached them. Lily couldn't help staring, as each man was so good-looking and seemed to know Malleven and all his friends.

Her eyes darted to Malleven in interest, mainly because he paused when they greeted him as if they had thrown him slightly – a rare occurrence. Then he begged a pardon and introduced two of them to her. "This is Dino and Luca Bonaci, Lily." Then he gestured towards her, "Lillian Gale."

The surname was familiar and she guessed they were probably royal. After being momentarily stunned by their beautiful coffee skin and light green eyes, she gave them her hand, which they both pulled close so they could kiss her cheeks.

Then a third came forward. He was blonde and beautiful with the lightest grey eyes. She hitched a breath when she made the connection. Her gaze shot to Antonio, who remained stony and silent.

"Forgive my brother's rudeness. I am Antonio's brother, Marco Dubonnetti."

CHAPTER 24

Marco picked up Lily's hand and kissed it flamboyantly. Her eyes flashed to Malleven, who was smiling benevolently, but she sensed an uneasiness in him.

"It has been so long, Malleven. I'm glad to find you in good health and the many rumours false. May we join you and your delightful friend?" Marco said.

Malleven smiled amiably, but there was a shrewdness in his eyes as he bobbed his head. "Of course." Even with all the good manners and pleasantries, Lily was getting the distinct impression that Malleven would prefer they didn't.

Waiters quickly brought extra chairs and the new arrivals sat. The initial awkwardness went quickly and Malleven's friends all chatted animatedly, but he seemed thoughtful and quiet. Lily observed the newcomers, fascinated as she always was by anyone from this new Atlantean world.

"Aren't you going to introduce us properly, Malleven?" Luca said loudly, making the table grow quiet.

Lily's heart thumped.

Malleven's eyes narrowed, but he was composed as always. "I have no secrets from my cousins."

Cousins? The men now took on a special interest for her.

"Come, come, Malleven, we can see she is of very pure blood," Luca reasoned.

Lily went to hide her exposed arms under the table. Malleven stopped her gently with his hand.

The table was now silent, and all were looking at her.

"What family are you from?" Luca said directly to her.

Lily looked at Malleven for guidance, who never missed a beat. "She is a cousin from my own family – another protégé of my Uncle Rodrigo, but, alas, she has lost her voice today."

The strangers all frowned and looked at each other.

"Oh … which branch?" Marco said.

Malleven appeared not to have heard the question and stood, holding out his hand for her to join him. "Come, Lily, let us dance. I need to whisk you away from these wolves," he said with amusement.

Everyone laughed and Lily allowed Malleven to lead her to the dance area lit with hanging lanterns. He pulled her into his body and she relaxed against him. His lips came close to her ear. "You are creating quite a stir, *mio fiore.*"

She looked into his face, alarmed. *I didn't mean to …*

He laughed and pulled her to him again, but didn't speak for a while.

Who are they? she projected eventually. *They say they are cousins and you never speak of your family.*

Now they were away from the table, Malleven seemed unaffected by them and continued to move effortlessly with her.

As they turned, she noticed that all eyes were on them from the table. Marco and Antonio looked as though they were arguing.

"They are just Atlantean royals … we have many cousins, Lily," he said as if they were of little consequence.

She nodded and snuggled into him. *But that meant they were her cousins, too.*

Her thoughts were interrupted with a tap on her shoulder.

"May I?" Marco said from behind her.

Malleven narrowed his eyes briefly, then smiled. "But of course." And he bowed his head slightly and left them.

Lily looked up at the tall, beautiful man now holding her. He was three or four inches taller than Malleven and had an almost boyish beauty, like a model or a dancer, and so opposite to Malleven in every way.

"You are incredibly beautiful, Lily," Marco said as they began to sway to the music.

She smiled, feeling embarrassed. She was only just getting used to being complimented by Malleven; from someone else, it was just too much. Suddenly, she became aware of his proximity to her and felt stiff and awkward trying to keep a gap between them.

"Where has Malleven been hiding you?" he said, smiling, then pulled her tighter to him.

She looked back at the table anxiously. Marco seemed friendly, but she didn't want to upset Malleven. It felt wrong, somehow, even though he appeared relaxed and in conversation with the other visitors. Still, she was sure he wouldn't want her to give too much of herself away and reveal that she could speak telepathically. She looked back at Marco and shrugged and touched her throat.

Marco swung her around playfully. "Never mind, my perfect Lily … I am an actor," he said, enunciating the "tor" dramatically. "I can speak enough for both of us." Then he whisked her around the dance floor as if they were ballroom dancing, making her giggle.

After her initial unease, she was really starting to enjoy herself with her charming dance partner. The song came to an end, and Malleven came back over to them, accompanied by Antonio.

"A little longer, Cousin," Marco protested. "We have barely had time to get to know each other."

Malleven bowed his head slightly. "Forgive us, but we must go. We have an early start in the morning."

It was news to Lily.

He was already holding her by the elbow to steer her away.

Marco held onto her waist and shifted quickly as if to bar his way. "Please, Malleven … let us have one more drink?"

Malleven halted and took a breath and blinked as if holding onto his patience. Lily's heart stopped. Malleven was always so calm and polite. For the first time, she sensed him coiled and ready to snap. He raised his eyes to Marco's, then stepped into his personal space despite his height advantage.

The mood had changed suddenly, making Lily's heart thump. Antonio looked as anxious as she was, but did nothing to intervene. Luca and Dino were there in an instant, along with several of the others from the table.

"It's okay, Malleven … they were just dancing," Dino said, trying to defuse the situation.

"Don't ever think you can fuck with me, Marco … or what is mine."

Marco appeared to crumple, then grab his throat, but Lily was sure Malleven hadn't touched him. While he was bent at the waist, Malleven loomed over him. "You are not even in my league," he said quietly. Then he turned, reached for her hand and led her away from the group with Antonio following along behind. All Lily could do was look over her shoulder at the three men watching them go.

"You're out of the game now, Malleven!" Marco shouted. "Disqualified!"

Lily was forced to run next to Malleven, he was walking so fast. The crowds quickly blocked out the scene behind them. She looked up anxiously at Malleven as she jogged. *What is it, Malleven?* She racked her brains to remember whether she had behaved inappropriately or missed something while she danced.

He glanced sideways at her sternly. "We must go!" was all he said, then hailed a cab.

MALLEVEN SILENTLY SEETHED ALL the way back to the villa. He sensed Lily anxiously glancing at him periodically, but he couldn't trust himself to speak to her in case he showed her his anger and fucked everything up.

The princes that happened upon them tonight were the worst possible people to bump into at that moment. Dino and Luca were Lily's half-brothers, and Marco, despite friendly appearances, was his enemy. They would have begun to suspect what she was the minute they met her, from her distinctive markings alone, and what they hadn't deduced, their divining rings would have confirmed. Soon, the whole province would be swarming. However, it wasn't the close shave of her discovery that had made him so angry; he usually thrived under pressure. Nor was it Marco's parting comments about him no longer qualifying for a Siren. No, what made him want to kill something was watching Lily dance with a handsome Dubonnetti prince and laughing and enjoying it. Such feelings of jealousy were unprecedented and unwanted. It made him want to enter her mind brutally to examine her feelings for him while he hurt and punished her small body to claim her completely.

Thankfully, his judgment was not clouded enough to

ignore the need to get her out of the country before the other families caught up with them.

As soon as they got back, he went through the house like a whirlwind, waking up the servants and issuing orders to pack.

Lily still ran along beside him with tears now running down her face. *Please talk to me, Malleven. Did I do something wrong?*

Malleven stopped and, after telling the last of the servants to hurry and load the car, he softened a little. "No, *mio fiore,* but those men tonight are princes from two of the other families, which means within hours, all of the families will know of you and your location. We must leave this place." He squeezed the top of her arm and looked earnestly into her eyes. "I do not want to lose you, Lily."

He was gratified at the look of relief that swamped Lily's face, but he spoke the truth; they couldn't afford to delay.

In less than an hour, Lily, Malleven and Antonio were in a car and on their way to the airport.

Where are we going? Lily projected.

"To my brotherhood."

Despite what he said, Lily could tell that Malleven was very angry, at who she wasn't sure. *Is it safe there?*

He nodded, but his teeth were clenched. Then he turned to her sharply, startling her for a second.

"I can delay it no longer ... it is time for the marriage."

She swallowed hard, not sure where his anger stemmed from, or what was really happening, but the ferocity behind the shimmering gold washing over his eyes frightened her. For the first time in a long while, Lance came to her mind. He had always made her feel safe.

She looked down at her hands. He was gone now and

Malleven was here. He'd been good and kind to her and she must learn to trust him.

Malleven relaxed back into his seat and stared out of the window with his mind churning. Lily studied his profile. He was a dark, dangerous prince and he wanted her. She must put childish crushes behind her now. She had chosen a new Protector.

CHAPTER 25

It had been weeks since Tia had renewed the bond with Jay and he'd been on her mind constantly since. A warring conscience of wanting to see him again and despising herself equally. Now, as she accompanied Dante to London on business, he was on her mind even more.

With the help of Keenan and Lacy, she had suggested renewing the bond while she was there. Dante would be busy with matters of state with his father, the Duke Ormond Delissi. Keenan would escort her to The Bluebell (Jay's hotel) as part of her guard and Lacy was coming for the ride, although she wasn't happy about it.

Tia had tried to justify it to her. "I have to breathe with him, Lace, there's no way out of it. And if I have to do it, I won't see him treated like an animal."

Lacy reluctantly agreed with her logic. "I've got a bad feeling about the whole thing," was all she said.

Tia had just shaken her head obstinately. "There's no way out." She brushed her tears away with her fingers.

When they arrived at the hotel where Dante would leave them to meet with the elder statesmen, he held Tia for a long moment – too long. *He knew.*

Tia despised herself for what she knew would happen when she met with Jay and, of course, Dante would pick up on that – anyone would, even without the deep connection they had. Nonetheless, she felt powerless to resist her compulsion, which was as strong as any drug. Every time she tried to talk herself out of it and abandon the idea, panic would surge through her at the thought of not seeing Jay. Followed swiftly by the realisation that the bond had to be replenished anyway. There was no way she'd ever allow Jay to get that sick again. The three of them were doomed to this merry-go-round, as long as it was necessary, and her heart and body would deliver her up to Jay gift-wrapped.

However, the way that Dante looked at her as he pulled apart broke her heart. She quickly sat back in her seat and averted her eyes. This was the hardest part of all; the knowing she was hurting a man as powerful, strong and dear to her as Dante was. He was as trapped as they all were.

After a long moment, he squeezed her hand. "Be safe," he said and turned. The door was opened for him and Tia watched him walk into the building with the two guards that accompanied him everywhere. Then the car quietly pulled away into the early evening traffic. Tia closed her mind to Dante and tried to quieten her rising butterflies.

It was almost dark when they arrived at The Bluebell. It held such strong memories for Tia—mostly of Jay. He was organising his staff next to the kitchens when they walked in and his beauty took her breath away as it always did. His eyes went to hers immediately. He issued a few last commands and walked purposely over to the three of them.

He hugged Keenan, kissed Lacy's cheek and pulled Tia with him to the lift without even saying a "hello". "You have the other penthouse suite … the key's at reception," he called back to Keenan over his shoulder.

Keenan was grinning back at him and Lacy smacked his chest in reprimand. Tia's butterflies somersaulted.

The lift doors opened and Jay pulled her in with him into a tight embrace. She was amazed when he buried his face into her neck and breathed. "Fuck, I've missed you."

Tia pulled away, slightly bewildered, to look into his eyes. "What have you done with the real Jay?" she said, with a nervous smile.

He held her face with his hand and rubbed her cheek with the pad of his thumb. "I know … I deserve that."

The doors to the lift opened and Jay was already taking off his jacket while he led her to his door. He put the card into the lock and loosened his tie, then pulled it from its knot. By the time they reached his bedroom, he was undoing his shirt buttons.

Tia watched him wide-eyed when he threw everything on the bed.

"I guess we don't have much time?" he said, going to one of his drawers and pulling out two pairs of handcuffs. He threw them at her and she caught them clumsily.

It was all a little bewildering and she looked back at him, puzzled.

He continued to undress. "Decide what you want to do with them," he said, pointing his finger. Then he walked to the bathroom where he turned the huge taps to fill the bath the size of a hot tub. He stood back up and indicated with playful eyebrows the two handholds on either side of the tub.

She couldn't help laughing at this frivolous side to him that was so new.

When the bath was full and frothing with bubbles and red rose petals, Jay, now naked, passed her a glass of champagne. "Can I trust you?" he said.

Tia just drank her glass in a single, unladylike gulp. "Get in!" she ordered.

Jay grinned and slid into the tepid water in a sitting position with just his head out of the bubbles.

Tia got in at the other end and quickly got into character. "Hold onto the handrail."

He did as she asked and his boyishly blue eyes didn't leave hers. She clamped the handcuffs around his wrist and the rail. She raised her eyebrows, unsure whether to continue. His eyelids lowered. "I feel very vulnerable," he said quietly.

Tia's temperature shot up and the familiar weight already pushed against the walls of her chest. This man could turn her on with the slightest look and a few words. Tentatively, she clamped the other hand to the other side so he was completely at her mercy. "I won't hurt you ... much," she finished on a whisper.

Jay groaned and relaxed back with his head on the padded cushion that ran around the edge of the bath.

Tia came closer and travelled up his taut, muscled chest, her hands meandering on the way up. "So Mr Control is giving up his power for one night."

He smiled and nodded, his hot breath tantalisingly close to her mouth. "Only to you."

As she was about to be lured into an all-consuming kiss, a thought occurred to her: "What's changed, Jay?" Then she teased him by biting in slow, sexy nips down the side of his neck.

"I've come to my senses," his voice tight with need.

She stopped what she was doing and straightened up to look at his flushed face. "What are you saying?"

He didn't answer; he was too preoccupied with her parted lips.

She narrowed her eyes, submerged beneath the water, and took him into her mouth.

When she rose out of the water some moments later, his face was hot and pained. She allowed her buoyancy to carry her face tantalisingly close to his. Although before she had time to think, his mouth stole her words, and the fire ignited between them. Her fingers clenched into the silk of his hair and she kissed him deeply. Jay groaned into it, his hips thrusting gently – his erection nudging and insistent at the softest part of her. "Tell me what you want?" she whispered, holding her arms around his neck, tempting and moving over him rhythmically.

"I want to be inside you when you breathe hard for me," his voice cracked with need.

Tia swallowed. The sensual invitation in his words would be so easy to give in to. "Is that all you want me for?" Her eyes followed her hand as it scratched down the warm skin of his chest, over the markings and swirls, connecting him to her race. It had been a common theme to their conversations since leaving him and going to Dante.

"It's never just been about that."

The unexpected tenderness of Jay's words was Tia's total undoing. Her hand found him and placed him right at the entrance of her possessive heat. Their eyes remained glued on each other. "Oh yeah, what's it been about then?" she said in a needy whisper, inching down on him, little by little, trying not to come apart.

His face became a picture of torment. His teeth clenched, and the chains jangled on either side of her when he tried to move his hands to hold her. She shook her head, tutted and teased him a little longer. Moisture beaded on his furrowed brow and he groaned in frustration.

Suddenly, she slid down the length of him, taking him fully, and he cried out in pleasure. She rose again and hovered while his hips gyrated and tried to get the necessary leverage and failed. She held onto him just at the tip, punishing him again.

"Come on, Tia, please … you're killing me."

Her heart was thudding double-time and she kissed him fiercely again. Branding him as hers. "I want to know what it is, Jay?" she said, pulling away roughly again.

He bit his lip and his heart beat hard against her hands, flat on his chest, keeping the distance between them.

She slid down onto him again, hard, twice.

"Fuck!" When he gasped, she captured his mouth, gripped him with her thighs and owned every part of him. With no mercy, she let him have a millisecond of her essence.

His head rolled back in ecstasy onto the cushion and it was beautiful to see him that way. It was so rare to get him at a disadvantage. "I can keep this up all night, Jay," she said, teasing him again. "But you don't trust me, do you?" She lowered herself onto him again and again, driving him wild, gripping him with her innermost muscles.

Then, when he'd given himself over to absolute pleasure, she slowed to let him breathe while she streamed her life's essence into his mouth over and over and repeated the process again and again.

"Babe!" he gasped like a plea, his teeth gripping onto her shoulder with a rush of air against her sensitive skin. His body tightened as his hips moved more slowly and deliberately. He was now close and she couldn't keep it up much longer without following him. So she let go with one final onslaught of her body, finally letting him have the strength and rhythm he craved. Then she plundered his mouth with her tongue and breathed into him from her toes. *Are you feeling me, Jay?*

Every part of him moved purposefully with her, straining for release. The water lapped over the edges of the bath all over the floor and they were way past the point of caring. *Tell me how you feel ... please, Jay,* she projected into his mind, desperately before her own need began to unfurl in her abdomen.

When at last his climax came, he groaned loudly, his hips circled and she clamped onto him with her arms and her legs. Her hands clenched him to her by his hair, and he finally uttered the words she'd waited a lifetime to hear. "I love you," he said in tormented pleasure and bit into her shoulder.

"Say it, please say it .... over and over."

"I love you," he groaned, completely lost.

Tears streamed down her cheeks, she exhaled loudly, then her own release overtook her in a backdraft of fire. "Jay!" she cried out, and they exploded together.

JAY BATHED in the euphoria for quite a few minutes after they came down to earth. They leaned their foreheads together. "Get the key," he said breathily.

Tia clambered out of the bath with difficulty – a little shaky and uncoordinated. She slid back in and grinned when she undid the cuffs with a click.

"What are you so happy about?" he said, half smiling while rubbing his wrists. Then he craftily pulled her towards him as if to kiss her and, before she could answer, he closed a handcuff around both wrists and clipped them to the left-hand bar in a flash. It happened so fast that all she could do was gasp with her eyes wide.

He raised his eyebrows, mimicking her surprise. "You don't think I'd let you escape without getting my own back?"

"No, Jay," she pleaded. "I'm not sure I like it."

He ignored her and got out of the water and returned with a sleep mask he'd kept from a recent flight.

She continued to panic, shaking her head. "Oh no, Jay, please."

He came up next to her in the bath. "Don't be scared." And he dropped beneath the water and came up between her arms, both clamped to the rail, so they were on either side of his neck. Before she could protest, he kissed her. "It's time for you to trust *me* … do you?"

Her eyes bored into his for a long moment, as if assessing him, until she eventually nodded. "Okay … I don't like being tied up though, Jay."

"Just five minutes, then I'll let you go, I promise … There's something I've got to do." He looked at her intently so she'd understand that it meant something to him. She nodded her head dubiously.

Jay bobbed out from under her arms and produced the eye mask. "I just want to put this on you for a minute so you can't see what I'm doing … just at first."

She looked really scared, but nodded hesitantly, giving him permission.

He slipped the mask over her eyes and waved his hand to test that she couldn't see. Then he reached under the cushion for the cutthroat razor he'd hidden there and gave his wrist a little nick. It stung and blood welled quickly on his wet skin until it streamed down his arm and diluted with the water.

Tia remained still but was nervous about what he was up to. "What are you doing, Jay?"

Jay caught some of the blood on his fingers. "It's okay, babe. I won't hurt you. Just open your mouth a little."

He needed to move quickly before she could smell the blood. Although she was still scared, she did as he asked and parted her lips.

Jay worked his way in small kisses from her shoulder to the side of her cheek like feathers, to get her to relax. Then he gently ran his bloody fingers across her mouth, softly pushing them inside, making sure the blood covered her tongue. Before her brain had a chance to work out what he'd done, he'd scored down the side of his neck and ducked under her arms again so she couldn't push him away.

The taste was beginning to register as she moved her tongue around in her mouth. "Jay, what have you done...?"

He pulled her close, making sure her legs were tightly around him. Then he positioned her mouth at his neck.

When the penny dropped, she recoiled and tried to pull back, but the handcuffs held her to the side and kept her hugged tightly to him. There was absolutely nothing she could do. She began to fight, but in doing that, his blood soon covered the whole of her face.

An animal instinct took over and he bit into her shoulder, sucking hard to let her know what he wanted.

"No, no, Jay," she pleaded.

"Yes," he said, holding her tightly, pushing her into the blood until she eventually gave in and did what he wanted and latched onto his neck.

"Yeah, babe," he gasped. He couldn't believe how it turned him on. He dragged the eye mask from her face as he'd promised, and positioned himself at her already swollen, sensitive sex. Then pushed inside her while she was gripped to his neck. Laughter rose inside him at the indescribable pleasure. With her breath already flooding his veins, never had he felt so utterly sexually connected to her. "Only you," he whispered into a kiss of raw sexual pleasure. All the while, he braced her and pushed ferociously into her.

As he neared his peak, and his heart almost beat right out of his chest, he bit her neck hard and whispered in her ear, "We've got a blood bond now, babe, no one can break it." On and on he pushed into her, until they both came apart in ecstasy.

CHAPTER 26

*D*ante had been in conference with his father and several elder statesmen well into the evening. The main topic had been the location of the remaining two sirens and what to tell the Human governments. He kept his cards close to his chest about the information Cesaré had given him. He didn't want to cause any possible panic and further infighting between the families. They still needed to get their house in order, should there be a visit from their ancestral planet of Atlas, as fantastic as it sounded.

Max had also contacted him to tell him he was turning up some fascinating facts about Lance McCabe – stuff that Dante needed to know. He told him to keep digging and they would discuss it when he came back to Ireland shortly. It was a discussion he wanted to have in private and give it his full attention.

The fact was that, even though it was an important meeting that evening, he had been completely preoccupied. It was true that Tia and Jay needed to meet to renew the bond, but he wasn't stupid in that he wasn't aware they had cooked something up between them. It still hurt; it always would.

Jay had angered him all those months ago, when it was clear that his advances were unwelcome. Dante and Tia usually had an open telepathic channel between them that either could close when needed – such as when renewing the bond. Today, Tia had closed her mind down from the instant he left her in the car. However, there was something even more disturbing about tonight; he could feel it like a strange vibration. The sneaking suspicion that he knew the reason was becoming harder to ignore as the evening wore on.

The conference call and meeting came to an end at last and Dante felt weary with it all. His father, the Duke Ormond Delissi, came to his side and spoke in hushed tones. "Please sit, Dante, I need to speak with you for a few moments."

Dante waited until the last of the men left, sat down and pinched the bridge of his nose. Then gave his father his attention when he became aware that he'd been silently studying him. "What is it?" he said wearily.

"Is your patience still being tried by your queen?"

Where to begin ... After a moment's pause, he decided not to lie. The duke always knew everything anyway. He was a master spy, which came in handy at times and was downright annoying at others.

He seemed to read his mind. "It wasn't difficult to find out, Dante. News of this nature spreads like wildfire between the families ... and Sirens are notoriously hard to handle ... being loving by nature," he added, smiling kindly.

Dante huffed. *That was one way of putting it.* He still didn't know his father that well, sometimes doubting even what side he was on, but he had absolutely no one to confide in on this matter. "So you know the predicament I am in ... we are all in?" he corrected, shaking his head in hopelessness. "And now I've learnt that Malleven still lives." He relayed to his father the outcome of the meeting with Cesaré.

His father looked thoughtful.

"You knew?"

"There had been sightings and rumours – nothing concrete. The fourth Siren … I didn't know."

Dante studied him and decided he was telling the truth.

The duke nodded. "This makes it all the more important how you handle your affairs, Dante." Then tilted his head to the side, puzzled. "The circumstances with your wife have gone on for some time now, my son … it has been my understanding that you have managed the situation. What has changed?"

Dante laughed mirthlessly. "She chose me, you know? We tried to separate – she even released him, but it has been impossible. It seems that to keep her power, which we all need, she has to keep him."

The duke nodded in understanding. "And now?"

"She was seeing him when I left her this afternoon … but…"

"What are you afraid of, Dante?"

As always, Delissi was direct and to the point, and saw right through him easily—perhaps because they were father and son. He shook his head and the sentimental thought away as a weakness. He took a deep breath and laid it on the line: "Some months ago, Jay accidentally ingested some of Tia's blood, and today … I felt … I'm not sure, but I'm afraid they may have completed the bond."

Ormond sat back in his chair as if he'd received a blow. "This is more serious than I thought, Dante."

Dante nodded, heart sick. "I know."

"You *are* aware of the strict laws on this matter?"

He was all too aware of the laws governing blood – that it was permitted only within the Santalini royal family because of their genetic make-up, and then only during their blooding at puberty and in bonding with their chosen mate. Especially as he knew his friend had developed a taste for Atlantean blood from an as-yet-unknown source long before tonight. He just looked his father in the eye wearily. "Of course."

"So you are fully aware that it is punishable by death?"

He sagged and nodded again. There were the words he'd been dreading for months. He'd warned Jay not to force his hand. Even turned a blind eye over and over, when he reeked of blood at times. The day had come that could no longer be dodged.

"You need to take charge now, Dante."

"I know."

"The families watch to see what you are made of – fail in this and you may as well give your crown up now, as no one will follow you … You must show you are a strong king."

His father was only voicing what he already knew – what he'd gone over in his mind a thousand times. Anger seared through him and he clenched his fists. *Why did Jay have to be so fuckin' stupid?* No matter which way he looked at it, there was no way out. His hands were tied. He turned to his father, resigned. "What do I need to do?"

"The most obvious option … the one that would send the strongest message. Then the bonds he has made with Tia would die with him."

Dante looked up at the ceiling as if in prayer. *Could he kill his dearest friend?* And yet he undermined him at every turn. He took a deep breath and became resolved. No matter how much he loved Jay or Tia, he couldn't let them continue to make him look weak. As gutted as he felt, he stood up and thanked his father.

"Remember, Dante, Jay Gardiner has dealings with many Atlanteans, friends and enemies alike. There are those who would seek to use this for their ends." Then he narrowed his eyes. "There are also those loyalists who would take this decision out of your hands."

Dante paused for a long moment to digest his meaning. Then smiled politely. "I will think on it and let you know how I plan to proceed."

His father bowed deeply. "Your Highness."

CHAPTER 27

_L_ily arrived with Malleven at a place that could only be described as a palace, on the border of Syria and Jordan. The whole building was built from sandstone the colour of buttermilk, ornately carved with deep pink and purple flowers growing from troughs beneath each window, and delightful little water fountains from every alcove. The grandeur even surpassed the beautiful Italian residences she had grown accustomed to.

After the long journey, many introductions, and walking along beautiful avenue after avenue, Lily felt exhausted. She meekly followed behind a beautiful, dark-skinned serving girl when Malleven took his leave to seek out his high priest on important matters. She was simply too tired to even wonder what that was. To bathe and to go to bed was all she could think about.

Nasr, the high priest of the ancient order of Magi, was lying on a high couch having his back massaged by a nubile girl barely out of her teens when Malleven breezed into the inner sanctum of the temple.

Instead of standing to greet him, Nasr put out a hand for

Malleven to kiss the sacred ring, as was the custom. Malleven bowed theatrically low as he did so. "High One … you received my message?"

Nasr sighed deeply as he sat up, resigned to his relaxation being interrupted. He shushed the girl away with a hand and she backed out of the room quickly. Then he arranged his towel strategically, drew his robe around his shoulders and eyed Malleven shrewdly. "Well, well, well … I must say the Fates have spoken loudly and emphatically in your case. There can't be many examples of having a second chance with a Siren – if at all."

Malleven gave nothing away. The old goat was reading him to see if he'd been up to anything where this Siren was concerned. Nasr also knew Atlantean law and tradition as well as any royal, despite being Human. He merely inclined his head as if accepting a compliment.

"Is she proven by ring?" Nasr said.

He bowed his head again. "She is not my most compatible mate, it is true." Then he frowned as the thought occurred to him, "But she has come to mean much."

Nasr laughed loudly as if he didn't believe him for a second and had to play along with Malleven's little game of prudence. "And of course you would marry her. … Tell me, is she in agreement knowing she is not yours?"

Malleven bit down the annoyance that this man evoked in him. *As if he would force her and invalidate his claim,* "We have an understanding," he said, coldly.

Nasr nodded and watched Malleven closely. "There will be uproar with your fellow royals, will there not?"

"She consents … there is nothing they can do when it is done."

"And you wish to do it here?"

Malleven looked him insolently in the eye. "My brother-hood stood with me once before."

"Yes," Nasr sneered. "You became a laughing stock and dragged us into that with you."

Malleven used every shred of willpower not to wring Nasr's neck. Instead, he spoke measured and evenly. "I haven't forgotten the pact we made."

Nasr sighed again as if it had slipped his mind. The charade was infuriatingly laughable. "Ah yes ... our little agreement. You are yet to deliver on that."

Malleven bowed again in a show of humility. "I cannot approach the Darkly Begotten without the power and standing marriage with a Siren brings. I am too low-born." His jaw was clenched and the strain was killing him, but he needed a refuge to do this if it was to work. Spies were everywhere. He was strong, but until he and Lily were married, she wasn't safely his. The magi brotherhood was powerful and respected in the Atlantean world. Even the Honourable Guard – the special forces of the race – would think twice before they stormed their headquarters. If he could pull it off, it was a great strategic move to marry here if his brotherhood were behind him.

"What of witnesses?" Nasr said. "Atlantean law requires representation as proof at the ceremony."

Malleven straightened, sensing Nasr bending to the idea. "I have just the contact. He has the right level of social standing and an unwavering loyalty to seeing the Fates observed without letting emotion get in the way."

Nasr sat forward, suddenly more interested.

"Of course, the invitation should come from you, Oh High One," Malleven said, allowing a small smile with his bow. Nasr was clever. However, he was vain and filled with his own self-importance. And above all, he wanted to get his hands on the power of the Darkly Begotten.

"Very well, Malleven. I will arrange it. The pool will be prepared, and a message will be sent to your contact with the utmost urgency. He had better be as highborn as you say," he finished with a raised eyebrow as if he doubted that very much.

Malleven smiled benignly. How he would enjoy gutting this pompous pig with a blunt knife one day. "Never fear, High One, he is of the highest lineage."

MALLEVEN FOUND Lily already asleep when he finally came to bed some time later. He decided to leave her; no point in her lying awake with nerves. He hated to admit it, but that would be him tonight. His witness had been called and agreed to leave right away. The ceremony was to take place as early as the following evening. A second chance was more than he could have dreamt of and it scared him half to death.

He stripped naked and went to the small shrine in the corner of his room. There, he mixed his usual concoction in a tumbler. It mattered little if he would need it. He'd long since become addicted to its power. Used for centuries by the Magi to levitate and dematerialise, it came with a heavy price of moments of delirium and madness.

Malleven held it in trembling fingers and watched as the real gold specs shimmered, alive with a million microorganisms. His hand shook violently as he brought the glass to his lips and knocked it back in one gulp.

His eyes washed over completely in gold and he doubled over in excruciating pain. Every muscle went into spasm one by one. He held his mouth so as not to make a sound and craned his neck around to see that Lily still slept soundly. Then he gradually breathed through the pain until he could straighten up. Clammy with sweat, he showered quickly, then pulled back the sheet and got into bed next to Lily. He nestled into her back, comforted by her usual sleeping position. Her fresh, tantalising scent filled his senses and calmed him.

Malleven's heart was still erratic. *This one was different*, he told himself. *This one was his* – even though she wasn't his most compatible. She had grown to trust him. And, little by little, he was beginning to trust her – surprisingly, more than any other female in his life, alive or dead. Despite this, he spent a sleepless night. Afraid to sleep in case he had his recurrent nightmare, he felt sure would come. It was the one he'd had since childhood, where he was trapped and couldn't breathe and he always woke before anyone could save him. And until he could sleep and see his dream through till the end, he would continue to have it. He was convinced it was prophetic.

Lily stirred and he pulled her tighter into his body. With his nose nestled into her shoulder, he resisted the almost unbearable urge to bury himself deeply into her sleeping mind and body. Tomorrow, she would be his completely— the first person ever to give themselves totally over to him.

His heart rate was gradually returning to normal. As his breathing slowed and deepened, he became strong and resolved again. After tomorrow, he would continue his search for the last Siren. Then he would beat Dante to her. And although Dante would have three Sirens to his two, he had some hidden surprises in Dante's own court. The battle would very definitely be on.

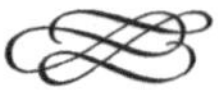

Tia daren't stay the whole night with Jay. She, Keenan and Lacy were whisked out of a private exit to their waiting SUV that pulled out unobtrusively into the night traffic.

Tia was looking out the side window at the blur of lights passing by when Keenan's phone rang. It was his cousin and fellow guard, Reeve. He was speaking in hushed tones, but it quickly became apparent that something was wrong.

She studied Keenan's face and the frown that was spreading across it. He ended the call and leaned forward to speak to the guard who was driving. "Turn around."

"What's the matter?" Tia said in alarm.

Keenan looked straight at her as if he didn't fully believe it himself. "We've got to go back … I've got to arrest Jay."

Tia sat back in her chair, feeling like the air had been punched out of her. *Dante knew, but why this, why now?* she thought over and over, while her world felt like it was crumbling around her ears.

The car pulled up at the front of the hotel. "Wait here," Keenan said, already getting out. Neither she nor Lacy took any notice. Keenan just swore under his breath and they ran along behind his long, purposeful strides.

When they reached the top floor, Jay was shutting the door of his suite, having redressed in a new crisp suit. A large plaster covered the side of his neck. He turned and paused, looking momentarily confused.

Keenan came to a halt right in front of him and pointed at his neck. "Fuck, Jay, what have you done?"

Jay half smiled, frowning. "What is this?"

"I'm sorry, mate … I've got to arrest you."

Jay closed his eyes, then looked at Tia wearily. She couldn't stand it any more and ran to him, flinging her arms around his neck.

"They can kill you for that," Keenan said.

Jay was still holding her tightly to him. "I don't get it … isn't it normal for you?"

"Only at a blooding, and only if you're a Santalini." Keenan appeared to freeze.

"What is it?" Lacy said in concern.

"I'm just thinking." He put up a finger for them all to wait a moment, then he took out his mobile phone. "Marius! … Yeah, it's Keenan … I need you to do a massive favour for me – and fast."

Syria

Lily woke late the next morning to find the bed next to her empty. She showered, dressed and ventured out of the room, not having a clue where she was going. Her stomach growled. Food was a good place to start, so she looked in both directions down the long corridor, picked left and began walking.

A little way along and a man emerged from one of the

rooms. It was Antonio. She felt a little relieved. Perhaps he would know his way around this huge place.

He smiled in recognition. "Lily … lost?"

She nodded.

"I know, monster of a place, isn't it? … Come with me, I'll see if I can find him for you."

Lily looked up into his smiling face. He hadn't been particularly friendly with her. She wondered what she'd done. Even now, as he led the way smiling, it was strained and didn't really reach his eyes.

"So today is the day," he said with an arched brow.

She shrugged. *I guess so*, she projected.

He bobbed his head. "So you can project already."

She nodded.

"And you're alright about the whole marriage thing?"

I wouldn't be here if I wasn't.

He laughed.

She frowned. *What's funny?*

He shrugged. "I dunno, I suppose I would feel second best – not being his mate and all." He held up his ring, which was the same colour turquoise as Malleven's.

I know about the rings. Malleven has one the same.

"Yes, but his is purple when he is near your sister, Isla."

Her face clouded. *Oh, her, didn't she leave him for dead?*

Antonio stopped, held her arm and looked left and right. "Let me give you some advice. Marry him by all means, but don't, whatever you do, give him everything."

Lily was stunned. Wasn't he supposed to be Malleven's friend? *I don't understand?*

"Look, he'll tire of you, okay."

But isn't "everything" what he wants – what he needs?

"Here's the thing … the reason he still hankers after your sister, is still in love with her, is purely because she didn't give in. Malleven didn't win." He stared into her stunned eyes for a long moment after speaking. Then he broke contact when a maid approached.

"Excuse me, I just realised I forgot something." Antonio backed up, turned and walked briskly back the way they came.

Still in a daze, Lily faced back to the middle-aged woman dressed in black. She bobbed a curtsey. "Let me take you to the terrace, Your Highness; their graces are there having coffee."

Bewildered and still looking over her shoulder, Lily followed.

She was taken to a shady terrace, covered by a canopy of vines, overlooking the most exquisite, manicured gardens. The tinkle of a fountain could be heard nearby.

"Ah, *mio fiore*," Malleven said, delighted to see her. He stood until she sat in a vacant chair next to him and introduced her to his high priest, Nasr. *It is okay to speak freely here,* Malleven said, switching to projected speech.

Nasr stood, took her hand, and bent over, putting his forehead on the back of it.

Good morning. I'm pleased to meet you, Nasr, she projected.

He straightened and looked over at Malleven. Then touched his forehead, which looked a little like a prayer. "Welcome to our brotherhood," he said, sitting back down.

Malleven clicked his fingers and spoke in rapid Arabic to a maid, who immediately scurried off. "I have ordered you some food, my love."

Lily was struck by the use of those words as a pet name, given what Antonio had just told her. It was the first time Malleven had referred to her like that. *Could it be that Antonio was wrong?*

Then, as if Nasr had read her mind, "I can see you are indeed a love match," he said, smiling broadly. "And why there is an urgency to this marriage," he joked, taking a sip of his coffee.

All Lily could do was look between the two of them like an idiot; a little paranoid there was a joke she wasn't included in.

Malleven picked up her hand and kissed it. "As soon as the representative from our people arrives, we will marry, Lily."

He was staring ardently into her eyes, with the now-familiar gold shimmering.

She nodded hesitantly, Antonio's words still buzzing around her head.

"You are positive this is what you want, Your Highness?" Nasr asked.

Lily dragged her eyes from Malleven's. *Why did it seem like everyone was trying to talk her out of it today?*

Malleven rubbed his thumb across her hand again to bring her attention back to him. "As I have said all along … you must go into this with open eyes, *mio fiore*. It has to be what you want."

All of a sudden, the enormity of what was going to happen hit her. This was massive. It was marriage and not in the normal Human sense – this was for life. An image of Lance, gorgeous, tanned, and smiling with that sexy, easy-going way of his, crept into her mind.

She closed her eyes for a second. *Who was she kidding?* These last few weeks had been the happiest of her life. *But did she love Malleven? Did he love her?* She wasn't even sure she knew what love was. *But she certainly loved the way he made her feel.* He took care of her, made her feel beautiful and safe.

Lily closed both her hands around his. *When will it be?* she projected with a small smile.

Malleven squeezed hers and, for a moment, looked

vulnerable. A look she realised no one ever saw. "In just a few hours."

"I'm ready." Despite what Antonio said, she somehow knew that she and Malleven had something.

A smile crept over his face, making him breathtakingly handsome.

Antonio, who'd been hovering in the shadows, turned and walked back the other way.

CHAPTER 29

Keenan led Jay into the Library at Ballygowan Castle in Ireland, where Dante sat at his desk, waiting for him, seething.

"Wait outside," Dante said. "Take a seat, Jay."

Dante waited for Jay to sit and the door to close before he spoke. "Do you know why I had to do this?"

"I've got a good idea."

"What were you fucking thinking?" Dante spat.

Jay looked down at his hands and shook his head wearily. "I love her."

Dante half-laughed and threw his hands up in exasperation. "What you were trying to do … what you did, Jay, is against Atlantean law. It carries a death penalty, for fuck's sake."

"So I've been told."

Dante bit down his anger that threatened to boil over. "I've given you every opportunity to be with that woman, only because you are like a brother and you met her first," he said, pointing his finger.

"I know."

"But ever since you got yourself released, you're like a fucking loose cannon, fucking with me at every turn."

Jay shifted uncomfortably in his chair. "That's not what I'm about."

"No?" Dante said, baffled. "You're jeopardising my throne, Jay. Everyone is looking at me now, asking themselves what I'm gonna do with you."

Jay looked him in the eyes with that steely stare he knew so well. "Do what you have to do."

Dante just stared back at him, lost for words. It was as if the guy had a death wish. There was more to this, but he was buggered if he knew what it was. He vowed to himself he would find out what was at the root of it.

His thoughts were interrupted by a knock at the door.

"Come in," Dante said, not breaking eye contact for a moment. "What, Keenan?"

Keenan walked quickly into the room carrying a brown envelope. "Sorry to interrupt, but this came, and it's relevant."

Dante finally broke his stare and looked up at Keenan with a frown. Then he took the envelope from him, turned it over and looked at the large Santalini seal. He narrowed his eyes at Keenan, broke the wax and drew out a parchment. His eyes skated over the ink lettering and he threw his head back and laughed. "Get out, Keenan!" he shouted.

Keenan widened his eyes at Jay as he left, who returned his to Dante cautiously.

"It seems you have friends in high places, Jay."

"What is it?" Jay asked.

"You don't know?" Dante said, leaning back in his chair, smiling in disbelief. "It's a proclamation."

Jay just shrugged nonchalantly and crossed his ankles out in front of him. "I've no idea."

Dante barked another laugh of astonishment. It amazed

him that he hadn't thought of it himself. "It seems you are the new son of Santalini." He shook his head. "I don't believe it. What is it about you, Jay? … Everyone falls in love with you." Dante was watching him closely. Despite the news, Jay still seemed uneasy.

"What are you going to do?" Jay asked.

"Don't you understand?" Dante said, narrowing his eyes. "Santalini are allowed a blooding. It's part of their nature. Your friend Keenan has been pulling strings for you to get you off the hook." Dante laughed again. "Quite brilliant!"

Jay took a deep breath and nodded once. "What now?"

JAY BREATHED A SIGH OF RELIEF, but he knew Dante well and he hadn't finished with him yet.

"Did you think I was gonna kill you, Jay?" Dante said with the look of the Devil in his eyes. "Stand up!" he shouted.

Jay stood up and began backing away from him, readying himself for the fight to come. He and Dante had been here hundreds of times.

"This is fuckin' priceless," Dante said, stalking towards him slowly, holding up the parchment like a lottery ticket.

Jay bumped into the bookcase behind him and couldn't back up any further. Then, as Dante neared, an invisible force gripped his neck like a vice and held him there. When he went to put up his hands to fight, his arms and feet were frozen to the shelves. "What the fuck?" Jay ground out, fighting for air.

Dante slowly came up in his face. "Don't struggle, Jay. This won't take a minute." It was said quietly, as if he was going to rip off a plaster, like when they were kids.

For a moment, Jay fought and swore, convinced Dante had finally lost his mind.

Dante looked him in the eye impassively, just a few inches

away, waiting for him to calm down and remain perfectly still.

Gradually, Jay managed to calm his breathing. There was nothing he could do but will him to get whatever it was over with.

Dante took out a penknife from his pocket and opened it slowly with the concentration of a surgeon, right in front of Jay's eyes that widened in horror. The penknife came closer and closer to his face, until Jay had to close his eyes to get a grip on his panic.

Even though Jay remained still, his mind was going haywire. Dante had finally totally lost it. This time, it wasn't just sex between him and Tia. After all, Dante had borne that before; it was the bond he refused to take – only he could have that with her.

His eyes flashed open when he felt the burn and then the sting of the knife cutting down the centre of his lip. *What the fuck?* Then he watched in horror as Dante turned the blade and brought it slowly towards his own mouth like some sick ceremony. Then made the same cut on himself.

The realisation of what Dante was about to do seeped into his consciousness. He tried to struggle, but it was futile. "Dante," he managed to grit out. "What the fuck?"

"Stay still," Dante said gently, like he was removing a splinter. "You left me no other choice." All the while, he was closing the distance between their mouths. "I must trump your blood bond."

Jay swore and tried with all his strength to move. All that came out was a loud groan. Dante was just too strong.

"I can't have you cutting across me with Tia ... shhh!" Dante whispered. His eyes closed, his mouth was almost there as if he were going in for a kiss.

Jay was going mad with anger and revulsion. He was a fighter by nature, a strong man, and couldn't do a damn thing about it. Except this kind of impotence was the lesson Dante wanted to teach him. It was the perfect punishment for the crime.

Jay groaned anew as Dante's lips gently covered his own. It was like a horror movie kiss that felt like it lasted an eternity. Dante only pulled away when it was evident that their blood had mingled both in their cuts and in their mouths.

Jay wanted to spit as soon as Dante pulled apart, but as it hit his nervous system, every muscle in his body convulsed, and his world went dark.

DANTE CALLED out to Keenan to come back into the room. He stopped in his tracks when he saw Jay's unconscious body on the floor with blood over his face, and Dante with a hand-kerchief to his mouth.

Keenan's face twisted with rage and he went to take a step towards Dante.

"Stop right there," Dante said, holding up a hand.

Keenan's progress was immediately halted. The same invisible force that held Jay was holding his legs frozen in place.

"He'll be fine … perhaps a headache."

Two guards came in with a stretcher.

"Take him to his room and have the doctor look him over."

Keenan looked at Dante with disgust. "He was Santalini. It was legal."

Dante let out a deep sigh and went and stood toe to toe with Keenan. He leaned in, spoke in low tones so no one else could hear him, but his meaning was clear. "I am not one with which you wanna fuck, Keenan. Think about your loyalty to your wife and family and less about my misguided

Human. So step off and think carefully about what you do in future."

"You broke the law as well," Keenan said.

It was true, he had, but Jay had left him no alternative. "A modern king has to do what he must when the equilibrium is threatened and everyone is out to fuck him. I'll take my chances with Atlas. You've had your last warning, Keenan."

Dante was still fuming when Keenan stormed from the room.

WHEN TIA WALKED into their subterranean bedchamber, Dante was standing fully clothed on the sand, facing the water. He didn't turn around, just stared out as if there was a horizon and not a huge cave wall.

A little scared, she approached him carefully. She wasn't sure what he would do.

As always, he sensed her feelings. "I won't hurt you." Then he turned his head to her and she saw the dry blood on the centre of his lower lip. His eyes were weird and bleary too – as if he was in shock.

She left him and immediately returned with a washcloth from the bathroom. Then she went to hold it to his cut lip, but he flinched away from her. "Let me help you."

He relaxed a little then, allowing her to dab it; his dilated eyes watched her the whole time.

"Did you fight?" she asked.

"No."

She frowned. That was more of a worry than a fight. *What had he done?* "I would have been satisfied with words. I didn't need a blood bond," she said, honestly.

His eyes remained cold, still following hers. "Tonight I voided it."

She paused, quickly added up what must have happened,

and continued to dab his lip cautiously. "Is he okay?" *God knows how strong Dante's blood must be with the power of three Sirens.*

"Unconscious."

She swallowed hard. "Am I next?" she said, pulling away and folding the flannel in her hands.

Dante nodded slowly, watching her closely for her reaction. He needn't worry, she felt bad enough as it was. She knew how she'd hurt him and would do anything to make it better. "Isn't it against the law, though … what you did?"

"It's all gone too far to be worried about that now."

"Do you really need to complete the bond with me, though? Think about it, Dante. You were righting a wrong with Jay … you know, for the state. But, with me, it's personal."

His smile was cruel when he grabbed her wrist fast.

"I don't care … really, I don't. Do it if you want … I mean it. I'm just afraid for you. If word got out … or you got judged in the future … we have the Sirens' bond, Dante. We don't need anything else."

Dante searched her face for a long moment before he let her go. "I need to be close to you," he said quietly, as if it were a test.

"Okay."

"Merge with me."

She nodded. The absolute connection of blending their spirits would be the only thing that would soothe him.

They both undressed and he led her by the hand into the water.

Tia knew that he would expect access to her memories now – the thing they'd said they would keep private from each other. He would demand it because of what had happened, but she would hurt him again and refuse. There was no way she would give him everything. They weren't his or Jay's, but hers alone.

CHAPTER 30

The hour came at last. The mysterious visitor had arrived, and the wedding was set for 7 p.m.

Lily had been pampered, plucked and preened by an assortment of women. Considering she was going into a pool, it all seemed ridiculous – especially all the scented oils rubbed into the whole of her body.

At last, she was finally dressed in a cobalt blue silk robe and led below ground to a magnificent rectangular pool. Mosaics in blues and greens festooned the walls and the pool itself, all depicting scenes of the ocean. At the shallow end of the pool was an area that stood out as if it didn't belong. It was an L-shaped screen of smoked glass in the corner.

Without time to wonder why it was there, she was led down some steps, still followed closely by six ladies who acted like handmaidens.

At the bottom, she could see a corridor that ran the length of the pool, with a large oval cut into the side so you could see into the pool room below the waterline. A huddle of men stood next to it.

For a moment, she hesitated and considered running until her eyes found Malleven's, and he smiled. He was dressed completely in black in a robe similar to hers. A black symbol was daubed on each of his cheekbones, giving him the look of a savage. He stood watching her, breathtakingly handsome. The others had stopped their conversation and were staring at her, too.

Come, Malleven projected softly. *It's okay.*

She resumed walking until she came face to face with him and he took her hand and squeezed it. She gave him a cautious smile.

Don't be afraid, mio fiore, *it will all be over soon.*

For the first time, she saw a flicker of doubt that troubled her. It was there just for an instant and then it was gone. Then he appeared to shake it off and was all business.

"May I introduce you to our esteemed guest, Lily. He is our official witness today. The Duke Ormond Delissi – a very important diplomat for our people.

Lily rested her eyes on the tall, greying man in front of her. He had long, wavy hair to his shoulders, a trim grey beard and dark grey eyes that appeared lively and mischievous. He reminded her of a princess's father from a fairy-tale film she'd once seen.

The duke took her hand and bowed over it, reminding her even more.

"It is my great pleasure to meet you at last, my dear," he said in his singsong accent, very similar to Malleven's.

Then he looked down at his old ring on his left hand and motioned for Malleven to do the same. Then he nodded once at Malleven in appreciation and gabbled something quickly to a man next to him, who wrote something very fast on a clipboard. "It is noted that you are the Siren; Aella Selene Parthenia Bonaci," he said, smiling kindly.

Lily frowned, not really understanding what was going on.

"Before we proceed, Malleven ... for the record, why didn't you go through the proper channels and present this Siren at the king's court so she can be with her family?"

Lily's heart hitched at the mention of the family she never knew. She had mixed emotions and a million questions. Then she remembered the sister who had left Malleven for dead and her heart hardened. She was glad she hadn't met them and didn't have to go through the pretence of liking them.

Malleven bowed his head slightly. "Given the circumstances of the last time I came to court, I didn't think I would get a fair hearing. I didn't ask you here to witness a wedding, but to bear witness that she chooses it for herself."

The duke appeared to mull over what Malleven had said. "Very well," he said, and turned his attention back to Lily.

"You understand that although this man is a prince, he is not your mate?"

Lily nodded and looked anxiously at Malleven, who was watching her closely.

"And you give yourself to him willingly? This is your last chance to speak up."

She swallowed and nodded. *I do,* she projected.

The duke raised his eyebrows in surprise and smiled. "Forgive me, you are so like your mother."

Malleven shifted impatiently.

"You understand that if you take this step, you are bound forever – both to Malleven and the Florianna royal family?"

She nodded again. *I do.* She got that it was a once-only deal. It was a whole lot better than anything life had dealt her before.

When his assistant had finished scribbling, the duke said, "Right! ... let us get on with the test and marriage."

Lily looked at Malleven fearfully.

Just breathe the water, that's all you have to do, Malleven projected quickly as they were led to the steps.

"Aella Selene Parthenia Bonaci and Malleven Rodrigo Mancini, I do hereby deem this test legitimate."

Lily looked up at Malleven's face; it looked hard with purpose.

The two of them were escorted to the pool by two huge, dark men, dressed similarly to Malleven and bearing the same markings on their faces. Lily guessed they were members of Malleven's brotherhood. They all began to take off their robes at the water's edge, so they stood in just their black shorts.

Lily quickly did the same and felt small and scared in her plain blue swimsuit, chosen to match her robe and her eyes.

The two men jumped into the water and Malleven reached out his hand to her. It surprised Lily to feel it shaking. His eyes had turned completely gold, making her even more worried. Now a complete bag of nerves, she allowed him to lead her down the steps and into the water.

They swam to the deep end and trod water. Malleven looked deeply into her eyes for a long moment and with the last words, "I trust you", he dove down. Lily had no time to respond and followed him, watching in horror as the two men attached a manacle to Malleven's ankle, which was bolted to the floor. They touched him on the shoulder and swam back up to the surface, leaving the two of them alone.

Lily circled her arms to stay close to the pool floor. There was no way Malleven could free himself to get to the surface to breathe. The significance of what her sister had done to Malleven was beginning to make sense. *But what was she supposed to do?*

"What do they want? she projected. *Just breathe the water,* she said more urgently.

Lily ... His pained voice projected. *Help me!*

She swam to him, distraught. *How ... What is the test, Malleven?*

I cannot help you further, or they will judge the test as illegal.

Lily let the water into her own lungs so she could think clearly. The tell-tale bubbles tickled in an upward stream from behind her ears.

Malleven shook his head as if it were fuzzy. *That's it ... now think, Lily. Think on the question ... do you accept me as your mate?* He grabbed his head and shook it again, pulling on the leg stuck fast in the manacle.

Oh my god, he's going to drown.

In her panic, Lily swam to the window and rapped on it with her knuckles for help. She projected *Help him* as loudly as she could. She looked up. No one was coming. Lily swam to the surface where the two men stood guard.

They didn't even speak, but shook their heads.

She was desperate. *Why wouldn't anyone help?*

Lily swam back down and frantically pulled on the chain, but it was no use. It was beginning to dawn on her that the whole point was to let him drown. His struggles were lessening and his limbs were clearly becoming very weak. He'd held his breath a very long time and was finally running out of air.

Moving up his body, she held his face in her hands. *It's all right, Malleven, just let the water in and your gills will work.*

He smiled slightly, but his eyes slowly closed.

Lily grabbed him to her and looked behind his ear. There was a raised ridge of skin, but no gills to speak of. *Think, think, think!* This was the point her sister must have got to and left him. She wouldn't betray him like that.

Lily shook him in frustration, but he'd lost consciousness. He couldn't breathe for himself now if he wanted to. At that realisation, she almost crumbled. Then she remembered Cesaré's accident, the day he'd been caught in the rocks. She'd helped save him by some miracle. Maybe she could do the same for Malleven?

She wasted no more time and covered his mouth with hers and slowly blew. *In one two, out one two.* She repeated it over and over. *Please, Malleven, wake up ... don't leave me alone again.*

Suddenly, he twitched.

She leaned back. The whole top half of him was glowing in a warm orange aura in the same way Cesaré's had. She blew once more and he jolted violently. Then the tiny stream of bubbles rose from behind his ears.

His eyes slowly opened, but they appeared vacant and dazed. She hugged him to her tightly in relief. *Thank god, you're okay ... you're alive.*

His arms came around her slowly and squeezed her so tightly she thought the life would go out of her. His words in her head were jumbled and made no sense – words of love, some Italian, and some English.

Then he put her away from him enough for his hand to grab the back of her head and pull her to his mouth, so quickly she didn't have time to think before his lips were on hers.

His tongue plundered her mouth and a blast of something hit her so hard her heart missed several beats. The coordination in her arms and legs floundered. Nothing seemed to work. Her heart kicked back into action, but so fast she thought she was dying. Her eyes widened in shock when everything inside her exploded, and she could barely open them as she floated in a sensation of bliss.

The two Brotherhood men appeared on either side of them and crouched to release Malleven's manacle. They smiled and congratulated him with pats on his back. Then they swam away again, leaving them alone.

Lily was still floating in the strange euphoria, but before she could project a word to him, he pulled her roughly with him to the corner of the pool in the shallows that had been cordoned off with the smoked glass. Very quickly, it became apparent what it was meant for.

DURING MALLEVEN'S last moments of consciousness, he had been overcome by a great sadness. It was the conviction that he would have to save himself yet again, and from that, there was no coming back. To be rejected twice was unforgivable as far as his world was concerned. So when a great heat entered his heart and surrounded him in such light and joy, he was sure it was the ether of the great beyond calling him.

However, the feeling exploded through him, igniting every nerve ending. In his dream, he shouted in triumph as it dawned on him that the only thing that could feel this good had to be the Siren's kiss. She had done it; Lily had saved him.

He was physically and mentally stunned. This Siren had chosen him. Not only had she saved his life, but she had unwittingly secured his position as a prince in the Atlantean world for ever. No one could ever discount him now or put him down because of his low birth.

After that brief, lucid moment, instinct took over like a feral animal. He kissed her with a fire and force of every-thing in him. There was no holding anything back to protect her. It came from the darkest depths of him and travelled into her like a bullet. Then wrapped itself around her heart and catapulted in every direction. Binding with every fibre, every cell, every molecule, like a possession.

Malleven didn't even know what to call it – his spirit, his heart, the root of him – whatever it was, it hit her hard. He was sure she passed out for a few moments. It intrigued the scientist part of him, but there was no analysing now. It was time to let his genetics work for the first time in his life. He was just along for the ride.

As soon as his leg was freed and his brothers congratulated him, his focus was on one thing: completing their bond physically. Just like the predator he undoubtedly was. The exchange of breath had unlocked something purely primal inside him. This would be no ordinary sex; finally, he could fuck his Siren like his ancestors. An honour even the most practised and liberated never got to experience.

With an erection like you read about and impossible to hide, he pulled her with him to the shallow end – to the private area prepared for them. At first, she seemed unsure and tried to pull back, but she went with him just the same.

The area had been lined with soft padding like a bed. Malleven pushed her beneath him as soon as they were alone and could no longer be spied on. Although knowing Nasr, he'd have something rigged so he could watch. *Well, let him,* he didn't give a fuck.

The water was shallow, but he wanted the whole experience of sex underwater and pushed Lily down forcefully. The look of fear in her eyes slowed him – *or did he feel it?* It astounded him for a moment. The reality and strength of the bond was a wondrous thing. It sobered him.

Now more in control and knowing she couldn't escape, he slowly lowered himself to look into her wide and frightened eyes. *Shh, mio fiore,* and he grinned when he felt her relax – so easily gentled.

Gaining confidence, she touched his lip tentatively with her finger. *Wow, you can breathe the water now.*

Malleven nodded slowly, kissing the finger that touched him. *You gave me a great gift today, Lily.* Then he laughed joyously in his mind. *You ended my nightmare ... do you know that? ... Because of you, I can never drown.*

She was smiling up at him now, completely at ease. *I would never have let you drown.*

Malleven felt sombre suddenly as he studied her face. *No, you wouldn't ... We are married now, Lily ... fully bonded,* he projected in awe. The psychic bond had been completed, and it was already a true marriage. However, he had no more of an idea how it happened than she did. He wanted to repeat the exchange, to know it and feel it and in some way to understand what was happening inside them.

He felt curiously vulnerable. It was one thing to take everything from her, but a whole other thing entirely to give her something of himself. It was a gift – something selfless which was way out of his comfort zone.

He put his lips on hers in a languid, lazy kiss. The first time it had happened had been more like an involuntary cough or sneeze – so fast it was gone before he realised. He wanted to go with the flow and see if it happened naturally. The kiss was slow and tender at first. Then he deepened it – building in passion until it seared through him. Pausing, he saw his lust mirrored in her eyes. *I must claim you, Lily Bonaci,* and he took her mouth in a blistering kiss again. Just the name turned him on. He wanted to shout it from the rooftops. He, Malleven Mancini, the poor boy from a small village in Italy, was one of the fortunate of all Atlanteans. He had met and bonded with a creature spoken about with awe for centuries. *Do you accept me, Lily?* he projected, grinding his hips into hers.

She nodded, her eyes barely open. *Yes, I do.*

Say it to me, he said, bending his head to nip the pulse at the side of her neck.

Yes, I want you.
Only me?
Yes, only you.
Then he took her mouth fiercely, his restraint now gone; he gave vent to his baser instincts.

CHAPTER 31

In Lily's mind, she had done no more for Malleven than she'd done for Cesaré. And if she had saved the sour-faced drunk, then she would never have abandoned such a good man as Malleven. What mattered was the joy she now saw in his face and the look of awe he gave her as he stared into her eyes. *She* had made him feel like that and it made her feel wonderful.

When he asked the question, did she accept him, it was a no-brainer – of course she did. He was the only person to make her feel like this in the whole world. Then he kissed her utterly and completely, and she knew it was time to give her body to him, too. It terrified her. She was a virgin, but she trusted him as she had grown to in all things.

The hair left longer on the top of his head swayed forward, blue-black in the water, and he looked feverish with the strange flecks of gold swirling in the midnight blue of his eyes. Then he kissed her hard and hungrily.

Their bodies aligned, moved and undulated together in the water. The straps on Lily's swimming costume were slowly moved down her arms until they were gone completely. His familiar hardness pushed against her lower abdomen and throbbed against her sensitive skin. His mouth travelled down her neck, biting gently as it went to lavish attention on the roundness of her breasts. He closed his lips on one stiff peak, gently sucking whilst rubbing the pad of his thumb over the other. The strength of sensation overwhelmed and drove her wild. Her temperature soared, and her heart fluttered erratically, but the cool water kept her comfortable. Her legs opened impatiently for more of him.

She jolted with sensitivity when his fingers sought her heat and parted her folds, easing into her to prepare her to receive him. Tantalising and teasing, he rubbed a thumb over the tight bundle of nerves. Quivering, she inwardly groaned to be put out of her misery. Her hips were now moving with his hand involuntarily, pushing up wantonly to meet him. *Please*, she projected, when she could stand it no more.

Malleven positioned himself above her, nudging hard at her core, his eyes glued to hers. *There is no easy way*, mio fiore *… there will be pain.*

Her legs clenched around the sensual intrusion of his big body, inviting him mindlessly. When his fathomless eyes held hers in the moments before, she knew she would accept whatever he wanted to do with her. There was no return. No going back.

MALLEVEN RELISHED every moment of having Lily like this. Even though he was a master hypnotist and could probably have had her do whatever he wanted from day one, having her in his hands with pleading eyes and a body in torment for him to ease it, touched something truly primitive within him. He wanted her completely – body and mind.

He slowly lowered his mouth to hers again. *Breathe for me again.*

Without question, she did as he asked, locking onto his lips like her life depended on it. The sensation that followed was indescribable – better than any drug known to man. Before the feeling subsided, he placed himself at her core, then paused while the tentacles of his psychic self moved to the edges of her mind.

Today was monumental. He would have everything.

The creeping feelers began their mental invasion as his pelvis pushed and retreated, a little at a time, in a steady rhythm. The now-familiar weight pressed on his chest – something he'd only felt a few times before Lily and only with her sister, Isla. Now he understood it was the bond waiting to be released.

The last traces of her breath made him feel euphoric, like he was floating, then a soaring of his spirit as his heart rushed. His lust inflamed as if he'd received rocket fuel, his leash slipped and any idea of him taking it easy with her on her first time evaporated. He snapped and plunged deeply within her on a single thrust.

Her mouth opened in a silent scream and, instead of slowing, he captured it with his. Mental sensors lit up and he ran amok in her head, exploring every neural pathway at breakneck speed. All the while, the weight in his chest felt heavier and more painful, until it bubbled up into his throat and flowed into her before he could do anything about it.

It was something so instinctual and so profoundly satisfying, one of those rare times in his life that he was out of control. His body took over and began to pump into her like a piston while he ravaged her mind at the same time. His essence entered her in one long, continuous stream, making his sense of dominance and ownership complete. He was so absorbed and delirious in his pleasure that he barely registered her screams.

. . .

THE FEELING that hit Lily the instant Malleven entered her was like being scalded from the inside out. Every sinew of her body, every pathway in her head, screamed in pain. Then, when he breathed his essence into her mouth, the sensation was so acute and overwhelming that she was sure she lost consciousness for a few minutes.

It was as though there wasn't a single part of her that he hadn't gone, seen and conquered. This undoubtedly was what he meant by total capitulation.

Thankfully, there was a tiny place, right at the back of her head, that she managed to safeguard. It was small, but it felt instinctual to save it. Perhaps it had been Antonio's warning that had prompted it. So when Malleven launched his assault on all her senses, all she could do was retreat there and guard it in any way she could. It contained the small memory of the day she saved Cesaré's life. She somehow knew that Malleven would hate that he wasn't the first to receive her breath. It also held the shame she felt at Lance's rejection of her that she somehow kept hold of despite how nice Malleven had been to her.

But Malleven's mind was so strong that even there wasn't safe for long. Cesaré felt so real in this corner of her mind, as if he were alive. It became like a nightmare where she grabbed Cesaré's ghost-like hand and began to run with him. They ran on and on with Malleven only a hair's breadth behind. When it seemed they'd run out of pathway, she shoved Cesaré out of Malleven's way and screamed. She braced herself for him to be discovered, but she found she was floating in blackness, and Cesaré was nowhere to be seen. It was respite.

Sex with Malleven had been overwhelming and painful, but he had warned her. At last, he slowed to a gentle rocking and came back to his senses. He was still inside her head, roaming her mind as if he were exploring. He wandered through it like a maze, reaching a dead end and going another way. It registered as a dull ache, but she was exhausted and allowed it.

Even his mind eventually tired of its search.

Will it always hurt like that?

He drew back from her and searched her face – his eyes still looked like the night sky with flecks of gold like stars. It was mesmerising. *You will grow used to it and it won't be as painful.* He ran a thumb across her lip. *You have pleased me much, Lily.*

It amazed her how much she seemed to understand about him now. Where the knowledge came from, she didn't know – perhaps through the bond they now shared. The strength and need in him was immense. Maybe that's what love felt like – a great weight that a person needed to hold up.

The bond is complete now ... we are married and you are mine, he projected and flipped her over onto her stomach. *All mine!*

Her eyes focused on the delicate stitching of the padded cushion under her face. As a naive girl, she had always hoped that when she met her husband, sex would be a wonderful thing that warmed her soul, but today, it only compounded her feeling of emptiness. This was what the reality of sex was – a hot crescendo of animal lust, followed by nothing – merely a vessel for a man to pound his body into. It was probably the reason she had never let anyone near her before – like a sixth sense. It was something that had to be borne and, as he said, she would get used to it.

An image of Lance was quickly squashed before Malleven could sense it. She was afraid of what could now be felt through the bond.

She was an Alien. That was what Lance had tried to tell her as kindly as he could. He was a normal, red-blooded Human and she was as cold as a fish.

Malleven renewed his thrusts, cupped her breasts and bit

her cheek playfully. *Don't be sad,* mio fiore, *let me make your melancholy go away.*

With a deep sigh that went to the centre of her bones, she decided he was right. She turned in Malleven's arms and he slipped effortlessly back inside her. Then she gripped her legs around his pumping pelvis and gave herself totally over to him.

CHAPTER 32

Ireland

Dante didn't need the new blood bond to know that the minute Jay had the chance, he would want to whoop his arse. *Fuck!* He'd be disappointed if he didn't. He could feel the simmering emotions of anger, frustration and injured pride and that was a recipe for a fight between them.

Dante stood facing the big window in the great hall with his hands in his pockets. He'd asked Tia to take the kids above ground with the nanny to play in the sunshine. Now he just waited. Keenan had been ordered to escort Jay to him as soon as he was up and about and ready to go back to London.

He felt him the minute he entered the room and allowed him to approach until he was about twelve feet away before he turned around.

Jay's face appeared calm and blank to the casual observer. Only Dante knew what boiled in him underneath. *Fuck!* He should have done this years ago. He could have prepared himself before many a beating.

"You think it's amusing?" Jay said.

Dante bobbed his head in acknowledgement. "So you feel my emotions too."

Jay's face remained implacable. "Where do you wanna do this?"

Dante just opened his arms wide. "Good a place as any."

Keenan and Reeve stepped forward quickly, realising what was about to happen and unsure of what they were meant to do.

"Stand back!" Dante ordered. "We won't take long. Then Jay will be on his way."

Jay pointed at him. "No Atlantean shit."

Dante nodded once. "Of course … it's enough you know what I can do."

Before he finished speaking, Jay ran at him like a bull. Dante dodged him quickly. They circled each other with their hands up. Jay threw a punch, followed up with a round kick that Dante blocked.

Keenan walked over and stood with Reeve and both of them just watched. The fact that it was a serious fight between the two friends made it all the more interesting. This was no sparring match. The two of them wanted to tear chunks off each other.

Every punch got faster and every kick landed harder. When one was unbalanced, the other seized the advantage and they rolled over and over on the hall floor, crashing into furniture.

Jay managed to get Dante on his back and he kicked him off. Jay grunted and fell backwards. They were both back on their feet in seconds. Jay came forward and kicked Dante twice in the stomach, knocking him backwards over an armchair.

The place was quickly looking like the set of a bar brawl, with chairs and tables flattened and smashed all around them. Their already cut lips were re-split and bleeding, and their eyes were beginning to swell.

Dante spat blood, but he felt alive and exhilarated despite the beating. It was real and it was physical. So much of his new life was in his head; he revelled in using his muscles, even in the pain. Plus, his friend's need to regain some of his pride was understandable.

Eventually, Jay had Dante on his back with his fist raised, ready to turn out his lights. They were both breathing heavily. Seeming to come back to his senses, he paused.

"Had enough?" Dante asked, spitting blood to the side.

Jay pushed off him roughly and shook out his bruised knuckles. Dante struggled to his feet, exhausted, but was smiling.

Keenan and Reeve looked at each other and shook their heads. They'd never seen anything like it.

Jay spat blood and pointed. "Don't ever do anything like that again."

"I'm not your enemy, Jay. We're on the same side," Dante said, coming closer and beckoning Keenan and Reeve to do the same.

Jay spat and chuffed a mirthless laugh.

"Look, unless we can work together, Jay, it ain't just our enemies we have to worry about. There are those close to me that would see you dead for the sake of stability, if nothing else."

Jay didn't say anything but heard what he said.

Dante turned to Keenan. "I want to give you a chance to redeem yourself. I'm gonna appoint you as bodyguard to Jay, instead of me."

"I don't need ..." Jay went to protest.

"You don't get a say in this," Dante said, holding up his hand to silence him. "Keenan's loyalties are split at the moment. This way should help, and besides, despite our differences, Jay, I don't want you dead." And he held out his bruised hand for Jay to shake.

"And Tia?" Jay said with narrowed eyes.

"As always, Tia has a mind of her own."

After a long pause, Jay put his hand cautiously in his.

"We've been through too much, Brother, to let this beat us."

Jay let out a resigned sigh and nodded. "Yeah, fuck 'em."

JAY AND KEENAN wasted no time in getting the hell out of the castle after the fight. They grabbed their stuff and, within ten minutes, were away. Poor Lacy was dragged along, asking what was up, and was ushered into the waiting Range Rover. Jay didn't look back as they wheelspan over the shingle and along the long drive with Reeve driving.

Keenan whistled in relief, buzzing to be out.

Jay was subdued, holding a cold compress to his lip.

"Fuck, Jay, that was intense. Dante's a fuckin' nutter."

"Dante's just Dante," Jay said quietly. He felt bad leaving the way he did. Tia and the kids were in the grounds and would have seen them speed away. He just couldn't bear for her or the kids to see him bloodied up like this. Dante could explain and he'd call her in a few days when the dust had settled. He needed to make sure his position in the company was okay first.

"Dante really surprised me though," Keenan said, interrupting his thoughts.

Jay looked across at him. "Why?"

"He hauls you in, arrests you, pulls some crazy-ass blood shit, has a proper row with you, then assigns me to guard you for your personal safety." A blast of laughter left him in disbelief. "To save my arse from messing up all the time." He shook his head.

Jay nodded absently and looked out of his window. Something was off. "He's the cleverest person I know; there's more to this."

Keenan bobbed his head. "Or he's lost it."

"Yeah, but when you know him, it's normal." Despite what he said, Jay continued to worry.

TIA STOOD with JJ on her hip and watched the revving Range Rover zoom away up the drive. They'd literally run away, and now she was worried about why. She called the nanny to take JJ and made an excuse to go back inside.

Dante was sitting deep in thought behind his desk in the study, with his face a bruised, bloody mess. His grazed knuckles wrapped around a glass of scotch.

She closed the door quietly and walked quickly over to him, pulling him around in his chair to look at her. He winced when she sat astride his lap to look into his eyes, already going a lovely shade of purple. Saying nothing, he searched her face as if he were putting it to memory. Fear crept over her, and her eyes brimmed with tears.

Tia touched his face gently. "My God, Dante, look at you. Let me clean you up."

He smiled and took her hand in his. "It's all you seem to do."

"Jay's gone," she said.

He nodded, still searching her face.

She leaned forward to kiss his bloody mouth gently.

He held up a hand to stop her. "Be careful of the blood."

Her heart broke for him. Ignoring his warning, she closed the gap between them, licked across his lip, and felt the coppery tang on her tongue. Then she sat back and closed her eyes.

It was such a minuscule amount, but the rush was like a

pot boiling over in her chest. Perspiration appeared on her brow and she opened her eyes again.

Dante had watched the whole thing, enraptured. He ran a finger down the side of her hot face. "Oh how I'm gonna miss you … you're such a bad girl."

Tia straightened up, frowning. "Why, where am I going?"

His face was filled with regret. "I'm gonna have to let you go, babe."

"Let me go? What have I done?" she said, not understanding at all.

Dante barked a single blast of laughter, but there was no bitterness. "Apart from shagging my best mate on a regular basis and disobeying me at every turn?"

She was left opening and closing her mouth, unable to argue.

Dante laughed. "It's okay, I don't blame you. It's a fact, is all." He ran his thumb across her cheek to catch a tear. "The pressure is on to kill Jay over this and I can't. He's my brother," he said, closing his eyes and sighing deeply. "Aaaand, now he's a Santalini makes it even more difficult … to protect stability …" He paused as if what he had to say was extremely difficult. "I have to give you up."

Tears welled and her heart constricted when she realised he meant what he said and there was no bending him. "But you cancelled it out," she sobbed.

Dante was saddened and filled with such regret. "To do nothing … Well, my enemies would have a field day."

Tia threw her arms around his neck. What she and Jay had done had been a step too far, and backed him into a corner. They'd done the very thing he'd warned them about – forced his hand. And now he had to act to avoid looking weak. "I'm sorry, Dante … so sorry. I really never wanted to be queen. I don't care about that."

He put her away from him to speak. "*You* will always be my queen, do you understand?"

She nodded with a sob.

"But as far as the Atlantean world is concerned, you are now a king's consort."

"I don't understand," she said, openly crying now. "Like I'm banished?"

He looked pained. "No, babe," he said, soothing and kneading her shoulders with his fingers. "Just going into what's called Retreat – like they did in the old days."

Tia sniffed. She didn't fully understand all of what he was saying to her, but she did get that he was expected to execute Jay. *God,* Dante was always so misunderstood. People always jumped to the conclusion he was an impulsive, slightly unbalanced, hothead – some figurehead just ruled by his advisors. And, to an extent, he allowed people to think that to get the advantage. But, in reality, he was a selfless, deep thinker, hardworking, and loyal to his duty – and a strategist, she was realizing.

"I want you to know that I've never loved, nor will ever love, anyone as I love you." He smiled the most gorgeous smile, despite his swollen, bruised face.

Tears were running down her cheeks and a sob escaped her. "What about the kids?" she hiccupped.

"We'll share them, shall we?" he said, pinching her chin. "Xav and Alexei will need to be at school soon, so it's only little JJ and he should see more of his dad anyway."

"When do you want me to go?"

"As soon as I can arrange your escort."

He looked devastated. It tore her heart to pieces to think her actions had caused all this. And yet she couldn't have done anything else; they were all so trapped. "What will you do?"

"I will spend some time with Cesaré. He believes your

sister is in Italy, and I need to build a strong alliance with him."

That was the saddest thing of all: that he and Jay grew further apart every day. She shook her head to try and pull herself together. "Can I have Cash and Sean?"

Dante nodded. "I'll arrange for them to come and take you to London."

It took her a minute to follow his train of thought. He was pushing her towards Jay again. Suddenly, the situation became intolerable. The idea of being passed between them like a favourite toy enraged her.

Jay hadn't even said goodbye, but caused all this trouble and left her to deal with the fallout. It felt like she'd been rejected twice today. Dante, she understood, but as usual, Jay had disappointed her. It was then that she decided she would go to Cash's.

She leaned forward and kissed Dante gently on the lips, careful not to hurt them. "I'll always love you, Dante.

"And I you."

CHAPTER 33

Filled with a new sense of purpose, Cesaré had gone straight to Italy when the king dismissed him. He knew Malleven better than everyone, and this was where he would come. It was home territory.

Dante had assigned him two members of the Santilini family for protection in keeping with his new status, and he dragged them, Shona and Lance up and down the country, to every place he could think of that Malleven might be. Mostly places they'd been to together growing up.

It was strange, Lily was a living thing inside him and he could feel her in his heart like a heavy ache. The feeling was stronger here and he rubbed his chest absently. The girl he was so determined to pretend didn't exist was part of him, and he was sure it meant she was in this country.

Then, just as he became sure they were on the right track, the feeling almost disappeared.

With eerie timing, his mobile phone rang. It was Dante. "She's gone … I know it," Cesaré said.

After a pause, "You must trust that instinct, Ches. It is the bond. It makes sense. I'm calling because I got a call from Dino a few hours ago. He was in Tuscany with his brother Luca and my brother Marco when they bumped into Malleven. He was bold as brass in the piazza of Montepulciano with a girl fitting Lily's description.

Cesaré's heart sank. He knew the place well. Malleven's Uncle Rodrigo had given him a small place there. "They were in the middle of town?"

"Yeah … Marco was all over her, and they left quickly."

"Did they check out the house?"

"Eventually, but by the time they could make it official with the Guard and an elder representative, the bastard had gone."

Cesaré's brain raced.

"What are you thinking?"

Cesaré didn't want to say it, but only one place came to mind: "Syria!"

"That's what I thought."

The only logical reason Malleven would take Lily there was to marry her and have protection while he did it – she was like a sacrificial lamb. "Can't we take some men and storm the place?" he said, grasping at straws.

Dante's voice was calm and authoritative when he said, "Stop, Cesaré."

It halted him spiralling down into a dark place where a man could lose his reason and get himself killed. But it didn't alter the facts. "He'll marry her there."

"We have to assume the worst, but the instant that happens, you will know."

This sobered him. Malleven would join with Lily and, in turn, that meant him. The three of them would be stuck together in a similar way to the king, Jay and their Siren, Tia Storm. Once inseparable friends, they would be mortal enemies who could never escape each other – that is, until one killed the other. He knew this would have to happen, for sure, for his life to be tolerable.

"What next?" Cesaré said, his voice rough with anger.

"Storming the Magi headquarters is not an option. It would spotlight us too much to the Human world, as well as seeming like we are interfering with the Fates in our own.

"What?" Cesaré said in exasperation. "How can it be Fated – with Malleven already rejected, and witnessed only by Humans – even if they are Magi?"

"I understand your frustration, Cesaré. I'd like nothing more than to crush him before he can do more harm. Think … where will he go next?"

Cesaré got his head back together and thought hard. He wouldn't risk going back to Italy after his close shave with Marco. He had to think like he did, planning every detail. Then it came to him. "It's my guess he'll go to New York. From there, he'll make a plea to the Guard for his safety and then request an audience."

Dante was quiet for a beat. "I'll meet you in New York."

WITH DANTE'S words still ringing in his ears, Cesaré went straight to bed, although he didn't expect to get much sleep. Over and over, he kept on turning things in his head. New York was definitely the place he would launch his next offensive; he felt sure of it.

He tossed and turned for what felt like hours and, when he did doze off, he was filled with the most disturbing, vivid dreams. It was as though he was drowning – no, suffocating was more accurate. Then he felt like his head would crack open in piercing pain that dissolved into a bone-deep ache that wracked through his whole body.

Screams echoed, asking, pleading and sobbing – a woman's voice – Lily. Lust overrode everything and throbbed through his nervous system. The feeling of suffocation returned with a vengeance, but it wasn't him; it was somebody else. It was so overwhelming it washed right over her, consuming every part of her – Malleven. Somehow, he knew Malleven sensed he was there, and Cesaré turned and began to run in the opposite direction. It seemed essential to Lily that he wasn't discovered. She ran with him closely behind.

They were holding hands, running as if through a maze, this way and that, zigzagging to outrun Malleven's all-consuming force of will. They were out of breath. Their legs wouldn't move fast enough, feeling heavier and heavier.

Then, suddenly, the world fell from under his feet, and he tumbled, free-falling into blackness. His stomach rolled over and Lily's words, "Hide, Cesaré!" echoed above him.

His shout woke him as he sat bolt upright in bed. Air hacked in and out of his lungs and sweat poured off him.

The door flew open.

"Shit, mate! You alright?" Shona said from the open doorway. Lance quickly came up behind her. "You were making one hell of a racket."

Cesaré tried to get his breath back and acclimatise to being back in his bedroom. Shona and Lance slowly approached, partially dressed as if they'd hurriedly got out of bed.

"That was the mother of nightmares by the sounds of it?" Shona said.

Cesaré continued to blink away his shock while he rationalised what had just happened. He dragged a shaking hand across his stubbled jaw. "Fuck! That was no nightmare. Malleven just bonded with Lily and I felt it all."

Shona and Lance stood in stunned silence. He didn't expect them to understand, and he didn't have the energy left to explain the bond, let alone with a megalomaniac like Malleven.

A glance at Lance's low-lidded eyes told him perhaps he didn't need to – and there was no time left for sympathy. The important thing was that it had taught him the strength of the bond he had with Lily already, even though it was only one-sided. He'd felt her anxiety to hide him. They'd been literally running from Malleven through her mind. Where he had ended up, he had no idea, but he was sure Malleven hadn't found him – yet.

Shona and Lance stood waiting expectantly for him to speak, but his feelings were just too intense to articulate – a jumble of hatred, frustration, guilt, and worry. "Get some sleep. We leave early," was all he managed. Still troubled, he lay back down and they left the room.

LANCE WENT BACK to the room he shared with Shona, quiet and subdued. He couldn't quantify how he felt; it was too irrational. The fact was, he had pushed Lily away and into this guy's arms, so why did he feel like he'd been gutted like a fish?

After witnessing Cesaré's reaction to the bond, all he could think of was Malleven all over her. The thought of anyone touching her physically repulsed him.

"You alright?" Shona said gently, closing the door.

He nodded, not trusting himself to speak.

"Cesaré will get her back, don't worry. He's got the king on his side; it's just a matter of time."

Then why did he have a hole in him, like it was too late? She'd married him.

He smiled weakly. There was no point in saying it had nothing to do with him, because it did, and everybody seemed to be cottoning on to this except him. But none of that mattered, because not only did his dream loom over him like a spectre, but he would always be her Protector and a lowborn weak Human who had no right to have any ideas where she was concerned.

It was all so out of control. He'd never felt like this about anyone, and it got stronger every day. He wasn't sure how much longer he could deny the pull between them. Married or not, if she came back tomorrow, he wasn't convinced he could keep away. That put them both on dangerous ground. He couldn't care less about Malleven, *but would she be any safer with him?* It would also put him in hot water with Cesaré – her real husband – and land him in serious trouble with the king.

Maybe he should head back to California for both their sakes. He didn't want to cause any trouble for her. He got into bed, resolved. He'd go with them as far as New York, then he'd make his excuses and head on back home. It was the best thing for everyone.

As SOON AS it was light, the three of them travelled to New York. Life for Lance was getting stranger by the day. One minute, he was a happy-go-lucky guy, smoking, playing in his band, living his life by the swell and the tides of the ocean; now, they were staying in the king's palatial apartment in Manhattan.

To compound that, when they were settled in that evening, Dante arrived looking like he'd done several rounds with a heavyweight boxer. Cesaré inquired after his health, and he batted the comment away with a hand, saying, "It's nothin'," and embraced Cesaré in a very Italian way. No more was mentioned about it. When Dante shook hands with him and Shona all they could do was exchange a look.

Food was ordered in as they had a lot to discuss, but

neither Dante nor Cesaré ate much over dinner. Instead, several bottles of expensive red wine were uncorked. They were a sombre bunch, feeling as though they had the weight of the world on their shoulders. When Lance thought about it, he guessed they really did.

Cesaré relayed his dream. Dante listened without interruption. Despite not wanting to hear, Lance listened with his stomach turning, riveted by Cesaré's vivid description of what was happening to Lily. It would have seemed bizarre to think it was real had he not been having his own visions since he was a boy. It just served to galvanise his fears – especially as Dante nodded and appeared to understand completely.

Lance was watching the king closely. Not only was he battered and bruised, but he also looked exhausted.

"The bond, Cesaré, is one of the most precious gifts bestowed on princes, but also one of the cruellest curses."

Cesaré sighed and nodded in agreement. "Is that what it feels like for you when …?"

The king was already shaking his head. "No … no, nothin' like that … Tia loves Jay, but he can't return the bond, so there is that small mercy," he said, smiling haplessly.

Lance's ears pricked up at that. He'd heard that the queen had a lover – that much made sense. But he didn't understand why the prince couldn't complete the bond.

His face must have betrayed his confusion as Cesaré turned to him to explain, "The king and his best friend, Jay Gardiner, are both bonded to his Siren."

"Yes, but why can't he return the bond – isn't he a prince?" It was a very personal question, but he just had to know.

"Only by adoption," Dante cut in. "And he is Human, and lucky to be alive." The king frowned as if something saddened him.

Lance blinked, and time seemed to stand still. He looked at Cesaré, who nodded once, then at Shona, who shrugged. Then his eyes found the king's again, who was watching him knowingly. "That's ... that's allowed," he stuttered, while his heart hammered in his chest.

"Well, it's not fuckin' ideal, you know?" the king joked with a blast of mirthless laughter. "The guy is like a brother to me ... Argh, it's a fuckin' mess," he said, not bothering to finish what he was saying.

Lance didn't really care about the whys and the wherefores. All that registered in his head was that this Jay had bonded with a Siren and been accepted into the Atlantean world. This was big news to him and held massive implications for how he felt about Lily.

Instead of feeling happy about it, he felt bitter. *What difference did it make?* He was still a commoner. One who'd had dreams for years of the hottest sex with the most gorgeous woman alive, which always ended in a pool of her blood. Even if they had a chance and he had ignored his premonition, this information would have been too late. He'd already pushed her away, so she thought he didn't care for her. *What an idiot he'd been.*

When his thoughts finally came back to the room, the king was studying him shrewdly. Then he looked across to Cesaré. "Am I right in thinking? ..."

Cesaré nodded slowly. "I fear you are."

Dante sighed deeply. "Tia was right then."

Lance shifted uneasily in his seat.

"My wife recognised something in you," Dante said.

Lance remembered the strange way she had spoken to him when they first met. "What?"

"Sirens have special intuition at times. She didn't know much for sure; all she said was that it felt like you had a bond with her sister already."

Lance was already shaking his head. *She'd never even met her.* "No … that's impossible. We've never …"

"There is something between you," Cesaré said. "I've seen it … we all did. And there was your reaction to her playing. I gave you Elixir, remember?"

"Look, I didn't think … I kept my distance, okay," Lance said, losing patience with them. He felt bad enough as it was.

"What about your tat, mate?" Shona said. "He got it way before they met."

Lance glared at her and didn't say anything – he couldn't.

The king looked at Cesaré.

"It's true … why don't you show Dante, then he will at least know what she looks like?"

Lance slowly stood and pulled his shirt over his head, letting his shoulder-length hair fall messily over his face. He moodily pushed his fingers through it, then pushed it back as he slowly turned around.

He felt their eyes burning into his back. He rarely looked at it; he knew it intimately, right down to the minutest detail. The beautiful striped profile staring out to sea with the wind blowing back her tight curls from her face. The sun was setting as she stood on the rocks at his favourite surf spot.

The room was silent for a long moment.

"How does she feel about you?" Dante said softly.

Lance turned, about to answer, when he realised Dante was asking the question to Cesaré. He frowned in confusion and began to pull his shirt back on over his head.

Cesaré laughed. "She hates me, and I can't blame her. Why she saved my miserable life, I have no idea."

Lance sat down again and the king looked straight at him with narrowed eyes. Then he grinned, confounding him further. "We are in a strong position," he said, nodding. "Even though Malleven has bonded with her, he is not her destined mate." Then he pointed at Cesaré. "You have her power and are loyal to me, and you ..." he said, narrowing his eyes on him again. "You are interesting."

Lance locked eyes with the king. He was beginning to annoy him the way he was assessing him without explaining. There was no way he wanted to come across as weak. Suddenly, going back to California didn't seem as urgent. It was the weirdest feeling. He could feel the sheer power emanating from the man, and all he could do was stand his ground. The standoff must have been obvious to the others as the atmosphere became electric. He had no idea why.

Then the king laughed and the spell was broken. "These Humans, coming over here and taking our women," he said, laughing loudly. Lance didn't understand the joke, but Cesaré grinned and nodded knowingly, then he and the king clinked glasses as if they agreed on something. Lance remained confused and irritated. A glance sideways at Shona proved she didn't have a clue either.

When they settled down again, Cesaré poured more wine. "You have a happy family now with Tia at last," he said.

"The king's good mood evaporated into fatigue. "There's no such thing as plain sailing with a Siren." He tilted his glass in Lance's direction in a way of warning. "I've had to send her away."

Cesaré was clearly shocked. "What do you mean ... surely not. Retreat?"

Dante looked at the ceiling, sighed, then recounted a very shortened, tidied-up version of events. It explained a lot. Although he didn't say exactly, it was apparent he'd fought with his best friend. "The upshot of it is, I couldn't do it – I couldn't kill him. I've assigned Keenan to him for his Protection. He was a pain in the arse anyway."

"So she's with Jay now?"

"Well, you would have thought so, wouldn't ya? After the fuckin' song and dance the pair of them made, when I gave her the chance to go to him," he laughed, shaking his head in disbelief. "She doesn't go to London, where I sent her; she goes to be with her Protectors in Montana. The girl will be the death of me."

Cesaré was studying him in all seriousness. "That must have taken strength to send her away like that."

Dante tilted his glass with a nod, acknowledging the compliment. "Sending away and keeping away is a whole other thing."

CHAPTER 34

*S*yria

When Lily opened her eyes the next morning, she was surprised to find herself in a soft bed with Malleven lying facing her, watching her closely. She went to move and winced slightly at her aches and pains. His appetite in the pool had been voracious.

"Good morning, *mio fiore*," he said, a little croaky from sleep.

She managed a small smile and shifted to a more comfortable position. *Good morning.*

"How do you feel?"

She looked around the magnificent bedroom. *How did I get here?* Memories of pain and fear suddenly swamped her.

Malleven frowned. "You were a little overwhelmed. I brought you here."

Oh my God! Could he now read her thoughts?

Confirming her fears, he bobbed his head slightly. "A little."

She stared at his shrewd face to try to gauge how little

that was. A slow smile began to creep over it. "You have nothing to fear, Lily … as long as I know everything, and now it is impossible for me not to."

Her heart thudded as he broke into a full smile that made him devastatingly handsome. The narrowed eyes that followed gave her the distinct feeling he was testing her. *Had he seen anything?*

She tried to squash any images of Cesaré and Lance the instant they threatened to surface. Her life had suddenly become precarious with Malleven. Despite him only ever showing her kindness, he had a vast darkness in him that she had only just glimpsed through the new bond. "How do you feel?" she asked.

He smiled beautifully again, as if she delighted him. His arm snaked around her waist and he pulled her closer to him. "I have my Siren at last, who shared herself completely and saved my life. What more could a male want?"

Again, those shrewd eyes toyed with her. She traced a finger down the side of his face. He was so attractive, but he was also terrifying. "Perhaps a kingdom?" she said with a small, uncertain smile.

Laughing loudly, he rolled on top of her. "My queen knows me well. A kingdom and maybe a little revenge …" He pushed the hair from her face.

She swallowed. He was a formidable male, but he seemed so devoted to her. And the feelings she felt sure emanated from him through the bond were genuine affection and possessiveness. Perhaps that's why she felt so disloyal. After all, he had given her everything.

Her hands came up to his cheeks and she kissed him thoroughly. When he pulled away slightly, she felt adoration with those flecks of gold dancing in his eyes. It was time to forget her misgivings. As he pulled her up and led her to the large bathroom, she decided to give herself over to the here and now.

SEVERAL HOURS LATER, Malleven emerged, satisfied, from his room to report to his High Priest, Nasr, and to say goodbye to the Duke Ormond Delissi. He found them having tea on the shady terrace.

He was congratulated on his marriage and new, important status, and coffee and breakfast were ordered for him.

"As soon as I leave, I will have word sent to Ireland informing them of these latest developments," the duke said.

"Will you inform the president?" Nasr asked.

The duke shook his head. He was permanently based in Washington and kept an eye on Human affairs for the race. "I fear it would make them too twitchy for the return. They believe Dante has four Sirens already. Plus, it could destabilise our alliance if they become aware that the power is now split between two princes."

Malleven inclined his head graciously, but his brain whirred, logging away the useful information. Besides, at this moment, he was too happy to think about politics. It was all music to his ears – a dream finally coming true. "I thank you for your impartiality in the matter. The Orb rests well in your keeping," he said magnanimously. He really did feel gratitude. If this statesman wasn't so determined on fairness, he could have helped Dante and his hopes would have been dashed. To Malleven, honour was to be admired even if it held no logic to ambition.

The duke just raised an eyebrow and inclined his head in return. No doubt he knew the shit was about to hit the fan with the new king. Malleven almost chuckled.

"What are your immediate plans?" the duke asked.

"We will honeymoon here and then my closest brothers will accompany us to my residence in New York. There, I will make my request to the Guard." He had no idea how that would be received by the Santalini royal family, who were already sworn to protect Dante. But he was now a prince married to a Siren and a member of the king's council, so that entitled him to their protection, despite what they might think of him.

Keenan Santalini would be a problem, one he would need to eliminate. He would never rest until Malleven was dead for abducting his Siren, and therefore, a constant risk. In the meantime, his brotherhood would ensure his safety.

"Good!" the duke said, satisfied. He stood, bowed, and shook both Malleven and Nasr's hands. "I will have word sent to you when I have spoken to the king." Then he left them.

Malleven sipped his drink contentedly. Never had he felt so close to his life's ambition.

Nasr didn't miss his smirk. "And so it begins ... a great day for you, my son."

Malleven turned his head to Nasr, whose eyes were full of meaning. Calling him a son was an honour coming from him. It meant he already recognised his rise in station. He felt exultant.

The magical feeling was shattered when Antonio walked out onto the terrace. Nasr knew of their relationship, made his excuses, and left them to it. In fact, everyone did except Lily. He frowned for a moment, not sure whether he cared if she knew or not. *Curious.*

Antonio sat down opposite him, a little petulantly.

"Curb your sulkiness, Antonio; you should be pleased."

Antonio huffed as if that was the last thing he was feeling and poured himself some tea. Breakfast quickly arrived for him.

Malleven watched him try to gather his emotions. It always amused him how openly Antonio wore his feelings on his sleeve.

"Well, how does it feel ... to finally have your Siren?"

Malleven continued to sip his orange juice despite Antonio's tone. "I feel very well, Antonio. It is how you would expect." He narrowed his eyes on him to let him know that if he continued in this vein, he was on dangerous ground. "Be careful," Malleven warned in a low voice.

Antonio's jealousy made him go on recklessly. "Oh, it's just that you surprised me, that's all."

"How so?" Malleven said, humouring him but beginning to lose patience.

"I never thought to see you go soft ... over a woman, anyway," he finished under his breath.

Malleven let the comment go and just smiled. *What the hell?* The girl did mean more to him than Antonio. She offers him the world, and Antonio offers him nothing. Instead, he went for the jugular. "She is a kindred spirit."

The visible flinch in Antonio was gratifying, but he appeared to harden under his glare.

"You still haven't told me how it feels," Antonio went on flippantly.

Malleven became irritated and was about to lash out.

Antonio sensed it in him. "The power ..." he blurted. "You've waited long enough."

Malleven relaxed down into his chair again. It was a good question and had been a slight niggle in his own mind. He had a Siren, could now breathe underwater, but in all honesty, he couldn't say that he felt any different. Perhaps it was because he was so powerful already and so one Siren was not enough to make any real difference. *No matter*, there was still one more Siren out there and she would be his.

He stood, walked around the table and placed his hands

on Antonio's shoulders. Then he bent down close to his ear. "Be careful, Antonio, you mean much …" He left the comment floating and let his finger gently drag along his cheek as he turned to leave. But the threat was very real.

Antonio's question did not leave him, though, but lingered on in the back of his mind.

CHAPTER 35

ontana

Tia breezed into the living room with Cash, without a care in the world, and stopped dead when she saw Jay sitting, one leg crossed over the other, tapping his fingers on the arm of his chair. "Jay!"

Shit! His face looked as bad as Dante's – well, it must have been, considering the amount of bruising still showing after several days. Now he looked like a boxer who hadn't lost his air of pissed off. "Shouldn't you be at work?" she said, trying to ignore his black look as if she hadn't noticed.

"I'm on compulsory leave for obvious reasons." His face remained stony and he continued to watch her.

"Oh, you got in trouble?" she said, as light and as "matter of fact" as she could.

"You could say I'm on a warning. What are you doing here, Tia?"

Cash said, "Hi," to Jay, who just nodded in acknowledgement. He was too irritated and his attention riveted on her to even make polite conversation. Cash was no stranger to their complex relationship and quickly made himself scarce.

"I decided to visit … I got dumped, you know."

Jay sighed and sagged in his chair. "I know, I spoke to him … after everything, I just couldn't believe it." He shook his head as if he still couldn't.

Tia plonked herself down in the leather sofa opposite him.

Jay narrowed his eyes on her. "Why didn't you come straight to me? Dante said that was where he sent you."

It was one of those rare occasions where Jay looked annoyed. Most of the time, he kept everything under wraps, but after the way he left, he had no right, and anger raged through her. "Oh yeah, like I'm going to turn up with JJ, cap in hand, 'please, Jay, let me stay with you,'" she said, in her best little girl's voice. "Even though you fucked off without so much as a goodbye," she ended up shouting.

Jay just raised his eyebrows in that infuriating way of his. "I went like that because I was a mess and I didn't want you or JJ to see it."

"But it's okay to see Dante like that? I cleaned his wounds, Jay. Like I always do, and as soon as JJ touched him, he knew what had happened. He cried and cried when he thought you were both hurt. Don't you think it would have been kinder if you'd have stayed and put his mind at rest?"

Jay visibly winced. "I'm sorry, I didn't realize."

"No, neither of you ever do."

They were silent for a few minutes.

He was still studying her like he was weighing something up.

"What?" she said angrily.

"I still can't believe he finished with you over it. I know Dante, it doesn't make sense."

"He didn't tell you?" Then she frowned. "No, I guess he wouldn't have," she said sadly.

Jay looked at her, confused. "You aren't angry with him?"

"God, no! He was in an impossible situation." She shook her head, feeling dreadful all over again. "I never realised the pressure he was under."

Jay frowned, trying to read between the lines. "Yeah, he was weird with me. He assigned Keenan for my own safety. I thought he'd finally lost it."

Tia nodded. It all made perfect sense, and her heart bled for Dante and what she continued to put him through.

"What?" Jay's face became hard. "What hadn't he told me, Tia?"

She swallowed hard, not sure how Jay would take it. "That he had to kill you."

Jay looked puzzled.

"Not publicly executed, but by his own hand. It was to do with showing everyone he was a strong king, or something." She sighed deeply. "When he realised he couldn't do it, the next best thing was to put me away from him." A tear rolled down her cheek.

Jay was shocked. When he thought about it, what else could Dante do now that he was a Santalini as well? "Some would say that made him look stronger."

The reference to how deep Dante's feelings ran for her made her burst into tears.

Jay stood and walked around the room to think. "I knew there was more to it. I said to Keenan, he was too pleased when the proclamation arrived."

Tia stopped crying, not following what he was saying.

He stopped pacing and gave her a wan smile. "I'm a son of the Santalini." A small blast of laughter escaped him. He continued to walk the room. "Then assigning me Keenan."

"He thinks someone else might do what he can't," Tia said.

Jay sat back down heavily, putting his weary head in his hands. "Are you coming back with me?" he asked, looking up eventually.

"No."

He threw his hands down and laughed in exasperation. "No," he mimicked.

"No, Jay. I'm not coming, I'm sick of it. "You're both married to your jobs. You fight all the time now, and I'm caught in the middle of it. I want my own life."

He looked dumbstruck, which was unusual for Jay.

"Don't worry, I'll see to both of your needs," she tacked on moodily. "I have my Protectors. Me and Dante are sharing custody."

He took a moment to absorb what she said, then got up and began pacing again. "Have you discussed this with Dante?" he said, glancing sideways at her.

"No, I haven't talked to Dante, but judging by the fact you're here, I'd say he knows." She'd had enough of this conversation. It was a mixture of guilt and anger. She felt guilty for betraying Dante with Jay, so that all this happened in the first place, and angry at not being able to help herself. Guilt that she had left Jay right when he'd finally come clean with how he felt about her, and anger at being passed between them like an old chattel. *Fuck!*

This yo-yo life had to stop. She couldn't do it anymore; it wasn't fair on any of them. She stomped out of the room, determined to distance herself from both of them.

LEFT ALONE, Jay walked up to the window and looked out onto the green pastures dotted with horses grazing. He laughed to himself. Trust Dante to go through all that fiasco over the blood thing and then finish with her anyway. It not only saved his life but also punished Tia as well.

He pulled a face. He didn't have to snog him, though; he couldn't help smiling. That would have purely been Dante's way of paying him back. He'd have known how much he hated it – *the fucker!*

Still, it felt good to know his old friend still had his back. *Fuck*, he'd even thrown Keenan a lifeline, who was definitely heading for some kind of court-martial, or whatever the Atlantean equivalent was. He'd thought of everything – so typical of him.

The one thing out of his control – as always, was Tia – *God*, the bane of their lives. She was his problem now. Dante would expect him to protect her as only he could. And she was going to make it as hard as possible to do it.

Well, he had three weeks off at the request of Alfonzo, so he'd stay here at Cash's. It was way past time for him to prove to Tia he wasn't going anywhere – even if she was pushing him away.

Jay shook his head, not helping the smile creep across his face. *God, did that mean he was committing?* He raised his eyebrows and supposed he was. He owed Dante that much after giving him his life and setting the love of it free.

And the Darkly Begotten thing? The conversation Christian Dubonnetti had had with him all that time ago and started all this shit off. He, Tia and the kids had been together and happy at the time. But Christian had made a point of telling him that he was more than just an adopted son. That because of some fortune-telling, hocus-pocus crap, he was born with a curse on his head to be the Darkly Begotten. A prophecy foretold in the old books or something. Christian had promised him that if he didn't get away from Dante, he would destroy his kingdom, and Tia would hate him for it. And so he'd set about putting some distance between them both.

He laughed and shook his head. In all honesty, he didn't know if there was any truth in it or not, but surely he couldn't fuck things up any more than he had already.

He poured himself a glass of Cash's best bourbon and sat back down in his chair. *Nope,* he wasn't going anywhere.

SYRIA

Despite his misgivings, Malleven threw himself into the role of besotted bridegroom. He attended to her every need, bringing her local delicacies to eat and feeding her from his hand. Delighting in the growing trust and adoration he sensed through the bond and saw in her eyes.

They swam often, and he made love to her fervently. Sharing each other physically and spiritually, their bond growing stronger every day. Lily was becoming so accustomed to him that she readily opened herself up to him every time.

Whenever he entered her mind, he mapped her neural pathways. They were something unique to each individual – like a signature, and he encouraged her to do the same. It would enable them to recognise each other instinctively at a distance.

The closeness he was developing with the girl quite surprised him. He never thought it possible for him actually to begin to trust her. He put it down to her complete lack of guile.

Occasionally, he thought of Isla, her sister. Her mental strength and the off-the-chart passion they'd shared. Then he would seethe at her betrayal. The day would come when he would crush the Borge prince who'd taken his true mate. Then he would spend the rest of Isla's miserable life making her pay in endless erotic torture. The thought always aroused him.

He shook himself out of it and brought his mind back to the pleasant evening he now shared with Lily, strolling through the beautiful gardens of the palace. She was a true treasure. She didn't exactly sparkle as much for him as her sister, but she allowed his star to burn brighter and that's what mattered. This truly endeared her to him.

Nonetheless, they couldn't stay in this paradise for ever.

He stopped walking and pulled her towards him. His hands gently held each side of her face while he looked deeply into her eyes, the colour of a lagoon. *"Mio fiore,* how beautiful you are," he sighed. "Tomorrow we must return to real life."

A flicker of fear crossed her face. It pleased him to think that she wanted to stay with him like this. "Don't be afraid, my love. We must fulfil our destiny."

A strange pain moved within his chest. *Was it the stirrings of love?* It overwhelmed him for a moment. "Together we will be strong, nothing will harm us," he said, his voice cracking with emotion. The feelings felt so unlike him that he had to clutch her to him so she couldn't see. It was foolish, he knew, as she would feel it.

LILY HAD FALLEN into a rhythm with Malleven after that first painful time. He was right; it wasn't ever as bad as that again. As long as she hid Cesaré in what she came to call her inner space, he seemed unaware of him.

Lance, Shona and the surfers were all part of her memories, but Malleven knew of them and where she'd lived when he first met her. There had never been anything other than infatuation between her and Lance, so there was nothing for him to see, and she hoped nothing to feel.

Lovemaking was as he had warned – his total dominance. His powerful psyche would loom up on her like a giant cobra that terrified her initially. Still, as long as she submitted unconditionally like a puppy on its back, he would soften immediately and dissolve into a loving, caring mist that permeated her soul, soothing, massaging and enticing—winning her over slowly.

Malleven was growing on her. It wasn't that he was devilishly handsome, powerful, or strong. Or even that he made her feel beautiful, wanted, and the most important thing in the world. It was more about the fact that, despite all those things being true, he had an immense darkness inside him, making him ruthless and full of vengeance, which should scare her half to death. However, deep down, at the root of him, was an unbelievable vulnerability. It was a need to be accepted as an equal in his world and it was that part of him that endeared him to her.

For two whole weeks, she had been in his magical world of hedonistic wonders, so far removed from anything she'd ever experienced, and now they must go back to real life. She couldn't hide her fear and he felt it straight away. "I want to stay here with you for ever." And, at that moment, she really did.

Malleven nodded solemnly and was silent for a few moments.

"What is it?" she said, picking up on his strange mood.

He shook his head. "When I first met your sister, my destined mate, I thought it was the reason why I had not been that interested in women before. Nothing could compare. But now ..." He touched her cheek tenderly and brushed her lips with his. "I find myself wanting to share everything with you."

It was as though his realisation was a revelation to him, and she felt a wave of affection hit her through the bond. "Take me to the pool," she whispered.

Malleven took her mouth fiercely so her temperature soared, then pulled apart suddenly. Perspiration beaded on his brow. He grabbed her hand. "Not tonight," he said, turning and pulling her with him towards the palace.

. . .

INSTEAD OF TAKING her to the pool – their preferred place for lovemaking – Malleven took her to the room they shared. He clapped his hands at the two maids, turning down the bed to leave them immediately. They scurried backwards, bowing their heads as they went.

As soon as they were alone, Lily went to turn towards the bathroom, assuming that was what Malleven intended. Their body temperature needed to be cooled if they were to make love out of water.

"Not there," he said, stopping her by her arm.

Instead, he turned her to face him. "Tonight I want to show you something few people have seen."

Lily studied his face. "Okay."

Malleven nodded and led her by the hand to the large dressing table that dominated a whole wall of the room, covered with different-coloured bottles. He chose two bottles and took out two heavy tumbler glasses and mixed the contents of the bottles in each glass. "Drink!" he ordered.

He drank his and then watched while she did the same, then winced at the disgusting taste.

"It is something I concocted so we won't need to be in water," he explained.

She understood, but something in his whole demeanour felt solemn. This didn't feel like a prelude to lovemaking. It seemed more than that – almost ceremonial.

Malleven pulled her in close. "You have married into the powerful Florianna royal family."

Lily nodded; her heart was beating wildly, waiting for him to go on.

"We are the mystics of the race, renowned for our magic ability."

To hear him speak was mesmerising.

"All of us are capable, but some of us go deeper. We seek a darker magic – the power of the elements – of the precious metals. Most of our knowledge came with us from our world thousands of years ago." He spoke passionately about a subject that was obviously dear to his heart. "Do you trust me, *mio fiore?*"

She swallowed while she studied his face. *I don't think you would hurt me?* After all, she'd followed him in all things this far.

"Good," he nodded. Then he turned back to the dressing table, letting go of her hands while he opened a drawer and took out a beautiful jewel-encrusted bottle that shimmered gold. With it he held a tiny ornate glass bevelled with intricate gold leaf. It was the most beautiful, dainty thing she'd ever seen.

He uncorked the bottle and held the glass up to his eyeline while he poured the liquid into the glass up to a precise level. It reminded her of a scientist in a lab. His actions were well practised and kept her riveted.

The contents of the glass seemed to be alive, swirling and moving like stirred glitter. It reminded her of something. When Malleven turned to face her squarely, she realised why. His eyes were glistening and shimmering exactly like the glass.

Her hand shot to her mouth. "Your eyes!"

"I am Florianna, but I am also Magi," he said softly. "An ancient, powerful sect. This place," he gestured with his arms wide, "is my brotherhood's palace."

He held the glass up to look at it. "Beautiful, isn't it? It lives, moves and breathes just like us?"

"What is it?"

He smiled at her, but his eyes looked wild and fervent. "Gold ... but in its purest elemental form. It contains its mass from the earth, particles of air, and a great heat, making it into a molten liquid. All my brothers take it, but for me, it is my passion. I have made it my life's work. It even saved my life when your sister left me for dead. It moves within me, it is a part of me as you are."

It all made perfect sense, the shimmering in his eyes was it shifting within him. "I see it," she said. "I'm glad it saved you."

He smiled and offered her the glass. "I want to share this gift with you. Then not only will you feel what I feel, but I can protect you like no one else. Together we will be untouchable."

As she watched him, his eyes washed over completely and she felt his emotion. How could she not get swept up in it, even though it terrified her?

"Don't be afraid, *mio fiore*. I will be with you through the whole transformation."

She reached hesitantly for the glass with shaking hands.

"That's it," he whispered. "Don't sip it, drink it all down. I will be with you."

She hitched a breath as his strong spirit entered the periphery of her mind.

Shh, he soothed, *I will bear some of your pain to begin with.*

Panic flashed through her at the thought of pain, but her arm was lifting of its own volition. Malleven was in control. The glass was coming closer to her lips. Her heart thumped.

Drink, my love. Join me.

She squeezed her eyes shut, counted to three and threw the glass's contents to the back of her throat.

The moment it hit her stomach she was blinded as if by the brightest sunlight, followed by a scalding pain ripping out her insides. Her feet appeared to leave the ground and a strobe light flashed in her head. White-hot tentacles began to seep through her veins, snaking their way, beginning to move faster and faster. They zoomed this way and that.

Excruciating pain radiated from everywhere they touched. Her internal scream was deafening. It felt as if she were being flayed alive.

She tried to roll over and over to escape it, but it was no use. Her arms and legs were paralyzed. The molten gold was burning and eating its way through her, and she wasn't alone. It wasn't just Malleven, Cesaré was screaming with her. He was dying too.

CHAPTER 36

*N*ew York

Plagued with disturbing dreams for two weeks, Cesaré hadn't slept much, but now he was burning up. He was aware of the many people around the bed while he shouted, "Fuck off, you madman! What have you done? What did you do? Lily! Lily!" over and over. His fever raged.

Despite his delirium, he was aware of what was happening around him. They packed him in ice and it sizzled on him like water on a hot coal. He saw the steam rising all around the bed.

"This is no ordinary fever," he heard someone say.

Cesaré knew it wasn't. "It's him, my enemy. He reaches out through her. Malleven, what have you done?"

He felt himself lifted and floated through the air, but was almost dropped several times until he was plunged into a cold bath.

"What do you need, Cesaré?" a familiar voice said.

"I don't know," he rambled over and over. "He seeks me. He's hunting his prey."

"Think, man," the voice said, shaking him by the arm. "It's killing you."

Someone tried to give him a drink, but he batted it away. "He's killing her," he continued to shout. "To get at me."

Then, two hands roughly grabbed the sides of his face to look at them. It took a moment to focus. A face blurred in and out of his vision. The hands were cool and soothing.

"Stop this!" the voice said calmly. It was the king.

It grounded him a little. "He's killing us," he gasped again.

Instead of thrashing, he felt the hand of the king waving to and fro at the front of his consciousness. It felt wonderfully cool, like a fan. "Shh," the voice soothed over and over. "Think, Cesaré, is this Florianna shit?"

He knew what he meant. This was magic. He tried to think. It was nothing he knew.

Water came to his lips again and he drank this time.

Cesaré was powerful, as all Florianna were, but Malleven had practised to a master's level. "Alchemy!" It came to him suddenly. "The Magi … brotherhood magic," he said.

"Good, can you push it back?" Dante spoke so closely, as if he were in his head. "Remember, you have Lily's power even though the bond is one-sided. I can help you with the power of three. Together we can push back and communicate with Lily, but to beat it must come from her."

"He will know," Cesaré said frantically.

"That cannot be helped, he's taking over. Time is running out. Soon I won't be able to help you."

LILY STRUGGLED through what felt like eternal torment in the fires of hell. She pleaded and screamed at Malleven to help her, but all he seemed to do was try to calm her and tell her it would pass. She was oblivious to everything except the burning pain. Until at last a voice reached out to her through the flames, almost engulfing her.

Lily. The voice said, sounding as agonised as her.

Cesaré! Help me, please! she screamed.

What is it, Lily? What has he done?

The golden drink, it's alive, Cesaré. It's burning us alive! It's in me ... all over me! She screamed and thrashed to get it out.

The more you struggle, the quicker it will work, like venom. Try to calm yourself and think. Use your mind. You are strong. I can help you, because the king is here. He will lend us his strength and that of your sisters, even though our bond isn't complete. Cesaré's psychic voice came and went with obvious pain and effort.

Even in her extreme agony, she recoiled at the mention of her sisters, and she hesitated.

Please, Lily, we haven't much time. Cesaré sounded very weak.

I'm not sure what to do. She thought desperately.

Let us combine our efforts in one place and push it back. Together, we can do it.

It was hard, but she stopped thrashing and straining. Then she concentrated on controlling her palpitating heart.

Good, Lily ... that's it.

She groaned with the effort and repelled the tsunami-like torrent back through her veins.

MALLEVEN WAS ready to catch her as soon as she fell. He knew what the pain felt like. Even after all these years, although he could breathe through it, he never really got used to it. On her first time, it would be unbearable.

After the first few moments, he'd had to retreat. If it became too bad, he would enter her mind again and calm her, but for now, he didn't want to risk absorbing some of its power and hindering its progress.

Sweat began to pour from every part of her. He carried her over to the bed, laid her down and stripped her naked. Then he switched on the large overhead fan. He placed a cool cloth over her forehead, but she still thrashed and gasped in pain. Her psychic voice was screaming out to him for help.

That he could not do. Nothing could be done; it just had to run its course, while the potent liquid navigated every part of her.

This did seem far worse than it had been for him, and for a moment, he became uncertain. Unease was quickly escalating into panic that it might seriously harm her – that her almost pure-bred Atlasian metabolism couldn't take the concoction of powerful elements. As she struggled and tore at her own skin in delirium, the only thing he could do was restrain her.

Quickly, he rummaged around until he found some neckties and a belt. He grabbed each arm and leg in turn and tied them to the nearest corner bedpost. When she could only arch and strain her body, he captured her red, burning face in his hands.

Fuck! To go into her now would be to enter her pain and torment. Nothing else could be done and he slowly crept inside her subconscious.

A tremendous force immediately hit him and took him by surprise. It threw him from the bed and knocked the wind out of him. It took him a long moment to compose himself enough to stand back up.

Gradually, he became filled with horror. She was not alone. It was as though she were possessed. He glanced at his bottles. *Had they become contaminated or, worse still, sabotaged?*

Malleven frowned. There was a familiarity about the presence inside her – something that couldn't have come from this place. It was the thing he had sensed within her many times, always out of reach. That was the real reason she'd reacted as badly as this. The gold was seeking out an intruder – a presence that shouldn't be there. A total disbelief and astonishment made him refuse to face the fact that he knew who it was.

Convulsions now racked her body, white froth bubbled from her mouth, and her eyes disappeared up into her head.

"Fuck!" He was going to lose her if he didn't do something. Everything that he had worked for would be gone in one stupid instant. In a split second, he pounced on the bed to try and enter her mind again and to hell with the consequences, but just as he gathered himself to begin, she stopped moving. Her eyes remained still and open, and she didn't so much as twitch a muscle. "No!" he groaned.

Malleven reached out a hand to feel her pulse at her neck, then stopped short in horror.

Her eyes washed over and shimmered gold, then became liquid and welled, tracking down her cheeks in golden rivulets. Her nose trickled the same. Gold flecks mingled with the froth at her mouth.

Malleven refused to be defeated and give up. He quickly untied her wrists and ankles. Then he almost dropped her in shock when he saw gold oozing from the beds of her toenails. Lifting her hand, her fingers were doing the same.

His brain raced frantically for an answer to this anomaly. It was simply unprecedented. The golden liquid was seeping from every orifice. Her body had totally repelled it.

After what felt like ages of immobility, he finally mustered the courage to touch her neck. He sagged in relief. It was as light as a feather and out of rhythm, but she had a pulse.

Malleven snatched her up from the bed and hugged her to him in relief. He could have lost her. It had all been to have her molecularly similar to him to make them strong and, he had to admit, his last way of conquering every part of her. The magic was simply too powerful for her.

He carried her, unconscious, into the luxurious bathroom and switched on the large showerhead over both of them. It didn't matter that he was fully clothed. He stood holding her in the fierce spray while the water pounded and washed all the gold particles away.

If he were honest, he was in shock. And things rarely affected him like that. There was only one person who had the psychic fingerprint of the one he sensed inside Lily, and it was a person he knew well. He tried to make sense of what had just happened and why on earth Cesaré was in her mind.

There was only one way that could be so.

When the answer hit him, he roared.

CHAPTER 37

ash's Ranch – Montana

It was a glorious day and Tia and Lacy decided to make the most of it and go out riding. They were soon in the rugged, beautiful countryside that went on for miles.

The two of them had become firm friends since they'd found each other again. It hadn't been easy as their lives as mated Sirens put a lot of demands on their time. Keenan, being one of Dante's guards, meant they were able to grab some time together. Now he'd been assigned to Jay – and he didn't seem to want to go home any time soon – the girls got to spend some precious sisterly time. It felt like a holiday.

They'd been out for a couple of hours when they decided to head for home. They rode in companionable silence for a while. "So do you think you'll get back with Jay now?" Lacy asked. "You know, now you and Dante ..."

Lacy didn't need to go on. Tia still didn't believe it herself. "Look, just coz Dante had to do that, doesn't mean he doesn't love me ..." She huffed. "Or that I'm gonna run straight to Jay." She looked out moodily onto the countryside. "He's got a lot of making up to do."

Lacy widened her eyes and held up her hands. "Okay, I'm sorry. You got to admit it looks like that's what he wants … I mean, he's here, you're here," she said, arching a brow.

Tia looked at her sister sideways, knowing precisely what she was getting at. "I haven't slept with him, not since … you know," she said, pointing to her neck.

Lacy looked a little surprised and thankfully dropped the subject. "What's Dante up to while you're here?"

Tia glanced wearily at her. "Nothing like that. He's helping Cesaré to find our sister."

Lacy nodded. "I wonder what she's like?"

"Do you think we'll like her?" Tia said, thinking it more to the point.

"I reckon we will."

"I couldn't stand Isla in the beginning."

"Yeah, but she was alright in the end."

Tia bobbed her head. "S'pose … She's a drummer … the new one, I mean."

"It's weird, isn't it … how we're kind of all good at something to do with music?"

"Mmm," Tia said, not convinced. "I reckon there's more to it … you know, than the luring Humans thing."

Lacy thought about it. "Well, everything's meant to happen for a reason. Maybe we were meant to start a band?"

Tia looked at her for a moment as if she were mad, and both girls dissolved into laughter. "What would we call ourselves?" Tia said in fits of giggles.

"Bass in Space …"

"Slippery Suckers …" Tia said.

"Erm, Balls in Chains!" Lacy barely managed to finish through her laughter.

"Blow Fish!" Tia added, almost crying – the horses' ears were flicking and turning, not sure if they should be scared at the racket coming from their backs.

Lacy was holding her stomach. "Yeah, we could have a little puffer fish as our logo."

"I was thinking more of a middle finger." And they doubled over the horns of their saddles again.

Eventually, when their stomachs hurt and they rubbed their tears away with their fingers, they stopped laughing. They had to turn their minds back to where they were going. The terrain was becoming rockier and had to be negotiated carefully in places. They rode in silence for a while longer until they came to an area of rocks that jutted out onto a plateau.

The girls looked at each other and frowned at the noises of splashing and laughing. They rode their horses to the edge of a precipice that fell away into a collection of smooth boulders forming a natural pool with a waterfall. The creek that ran the length of the ranch flowed into it.

Both girls grinned. There, playing like a pair of kids, were Jay and Keenan diving and bombing each other from a flattened rock that hung over the deep water.

The girls laughed. Lacy put two fingers in her mouth and wolf whistled.

Jay and Keenan both turned their heads and beamed. "Join us!" Keenan shouted.

Tia and Lacy looked at each other, eyebrows raised, with an unspoken question. Both thought the men could not be trusted.

"It is hot," Lacy said.

Tia squinted. "You want to go in there with them?" Her sister was such a sucker.

Lacy smiled and shrugged. *Hopeless.*

"Okay then, don't say I didn't warn you," Tia said. She dismounted her horse and led it away to a nice patch of grass. There, she dropped its bridle so it could eat and hung it on the saddle horn. Then she began to undress. Lacy copied her lead.

After stripping out of their boots and jeans, they both ran and executed perfect dives into the water.

The men looked at each other conspiratorially.

The girls came up out of the water opposite their men. Tia glanced across at her sister, who seemed very easy in Keenan's company now. They were a proper couple and seemed to have got over the terrible ordeal of her abduction and memory loss. Keenan wasted no time in pulling her into his body, and she wrapped her arms around his neck.

Satisfied all was well for Lacy, Tia rested her eyes back on Jay. He was watching her inquisitively. "What?" she said.

"Nothing."

"You think you've won something just cos you got me in here?" The memory of their last bathroom escapade quickly came to mind.

He grinned his "oh so innocent" smile.

"I would say it is you who are at a disadvantage with me in here."

"Oh yeah, why do you say that?" he said, closing the gap so he was tantalisingly close. His eyebrows were up in a silent dare.

"We'll see." She plunged under the water.

Jay took a deep breath and did the same.

The rocky-bottomed pool was crystal clear, so it didn't take him long to spot her. He wasn't far behind when she found a narrow channel between some rocks that came up into a small cave. Her feet found a ledge where the water reached her chest. Jay came up on the opposite side of her soon after. She was surprised. "You hold your breath well."

He narrowed his eyes. "Told ya. Don't forget I went to the Dante Dubonnetti School of Swimming."

She smirked. "Oh yeah, and what was that?"

"The one where Dante would hold me under so I learnt to hold my breath or drown."

She laughed loudly, not helping herself. "I can imagine. How did you put up with him?"

"There is always a method to his madness."

The smile quickly dropped from her face. The reality of those words hit her, pulling her hard back to their present situation.

Jay swam in closer so they were inches apart and frowned at her sudden sadness. When she said nothing, his eyes soon lowered and strayed to her lips.

"Shouldn't we find the others?" she said, barely a whisper, in a lame attempt to break the sexual tension.

"I should think we are the last people they'd want to see right now."

She frowned, then fell in with what he meant. "Oh, right," she said, averting her eyes.

He came in even closer and pulled her to him. "Why are you avoiding me, Tia?" He dragged her chin round to face him with a finger. "Now you know how I feel?"

It wasn't what she wanted. Every part of her was screaming out for her to leap on him right now and devour him whole. But she couldn't. "I won't keep hurting both of you. This is the only way." She ducked down and out of his arms and swam out to the main part of the pool. Jay was right behind her – or so she thought.

Tia surfaced in the centre of the pool and it was deathly quiet. There was no sound coming from anywhere. She twirled in the water. *Where was everyone?*

She dove down and swam right to the bottom. Then, as she reached the furthest point of the pool, a hand grabbed her ankle. Startled, she swung around to release the grip. *Jay.*

Instead of releasing her, he pulled her straight underneath him with a flick of his wrist. Shocked at the manoeuvre, she rolled with him so he was now under her, but his arms were tight around her back and held her fast.

She held herself away from him by leaning up on her arms. His eyes looked straight into hers, waiting for what she would do next. It felt suddenly odd to be underwater with him like this. This was strictly Dante's domain. The whole thing felt confusing. Except Jay was always her weakness, and a bolt of physical need pulsed through her. He wasn't being fair. No sooner had she had the thought than her lips were on his, and she kissed him under the water for the first time.

Squashing the life out of her, he kissed her hard.

They were almost lost to each other when a whooshing noise pierced through the water. It was shrill enough to make them stop what they were doing. They just froze and looked into each other's eyes. *What was that?* she projected.

He shook his head.

Then it happened again.

She scrambled off him, but he signalled for her to stay down. They swam back towards the channel that led to the cave.

"What was that?" she said as soon as they surfaced.

"Gunshot."

Her heart thudded.

"Stay put!" he ordered, then disappeared under the water.

Several minutes passed and Tia became frantic. She was just about to follow him when he surfaced again with Keenan and Lacy. Except something was gravely wrong.

It was unclear at first because it was Keenan who appeared to be in agony. Within seconds, it became apparent that Lacy was the one who was hurt. Blood was oozing from her shoulder. Then there was pandemonium.

CHAPTER 38

"Quick! We need some sort of tourniquet," Jay ordered.

Tia wasted no time and removed her bra, not caring about her nakedness. She wrapped it around the top of Lacy's arm – making sure the padding was over the wound. Then she pulled it tight. "Is Keenan okay?" she asked, while she knotted it in place.

He looked in so much pain that she had to look him over for injuries, too, but couldn't see anything.

"It's the blood. He's trying to get a grip," Jay said.

"It's no good," Keenan said, his voice barely recognisable.

Tia caught a glimpse of his face and was shocked at the transformation. His canines were extended to twice their size and his eyes were the colour of blood, churning like a tempest. He looked in agony.

"I'm so sorry, I'm going to be useless."

Tia looked back at Lacy, who was being held upright by Jay as she was drifting in and out of consciousness.

"You need to keep her warm, Jay. I'll see if I can contact

Dante to get him to ring Cash, but what can we do? We need to get her out of here." Tia asked.

"It's not safe to go out yet. Keenan, go and see what's out there?" Jay said, rearranging Lacy in his arms.

Keenan nodded, pleased to have something useful to do; he submerged and disappeared.

Tia concentrated and reached out to Dante in seconds.

What is it, love? He immediately knew through the bond that something was wrong. She flashed him the mental pictures of what happened. Their thinking had become more Murr-like every day, and today she thanked god for it. He ordered her to be careful and keep close to Jay, and then said he would contact Cash and Sean to pick them up. They would check the area for a sniper so they could make a break for it.

Be quick, Dante, I'm not sure how bad Lacy is.

He promised he would, whispered he loved her, and was gone.

When Tia became conscious of her surroundings, Jay had hugged Lacy into the heat of his body. He was the warmest and the strongest out of the two of them, and Keenan was of no use at all.

Tia reached out and touched Lacy's face. She was still deathly cold. The thought that she could actually lose her gripped her heart. On impulse, she leaned towards her and put her mouth to her sister's blue lips. She blew a little of her essence, hoping it would fortify her and warm her, if nothing else.

Jay was eying her closely.

"Are you okay?" she asked, noticing he was covered in Lacy's blood.

"Yeah," he said. "It's just yours that affects me ... and nothing like Keenan." His eyelids went low, followed by an awkward silence.

She swallowed and nodded, ignoring the stab she felt in the chest. She couldn't deal with guilt as well right now.

Thankfully, Keenan surfaced, breaking the atmosphere. "I've circled the whole perimeter and all seems clear. It must have been long range and could have only come from one direction because of the rocks."

It made sense. "I've contacted Dante. He's sending Cash with a pick-up."

Keenan breathed deeply in gratitude, but had to turn again when the scent of blood hit his nostrils.

Tia touched his tense back. He flinched slightly, furious at his weakness. "It'll be okay," she said quietly.

They waited for what felt like hours. Tia breathed into Lacy every so often and checked the makeshift tourniquet. Eventually, the toot of a car horn made them all look up.

"Go and check," Jay said.

Keenan disappeared beneath the water, then, after about ten minutes, returned and gave them the all-clear. "Cash is waiting to take us back. A helicopter is coming in to take us to a private clinic to patch Lacy up, then on to the airport for a plane to New York."

They all followed Keenan out of the cave, taking special care with Lacy, who was now unconscious. Everything went according to plan after that. The clinic did their patch job and they boarded the Bonaci plane that flew them to New York to the private airstrip used by the Santalini family. There, a car whisked them off to Santalini HQ, where a medical team waited for their arrival.

As soon as they arrived, they were ushered in through the majestic marble hallway to the back of the mansion, where the sick bay was situated. There, a team of doctors quickly took over and took Lacy from Jay, exhausted and blood-spattered.

Tia leant against the wall outside the room, so tired she could hardly stand. She'd used every ounce of her energy breathing for Lacy all the way, and her tank was nearing empty.

Keenan was beside himself with worry and frustration at not being able to help. He was banished from the room for obvious reasons and cursed the genetic weakness that made him like this. Every time he tried to get near her and fight it, his fangs descended and his eyes filled with blood. The urge to drink from her was simply unbearable.

His eldest brother, Marius, tried to calm him and reminded him that it would do Lacy no good if the doctors had to fight him off if he lost control. Keenan reluctantly agreed and stood with the rest of them.

Dante was already in New York – a real stroke of luck – and had been contacted. He would be there any moment. As soon as the doctors had done their work, he could breathe for her and boost her system with his great power. It was one of those times that everyone saw the genius in the bond they hated that held them all together.

They were all a rag-bag bunch. Tia looked at Jay. He'd washed off most of Lacy's blood, but he was shirtless and still in his cut-down jeans, long since dried. Smears and spatters of blood still covered his face, upper chest and forearms. Tia stood in her old t-shirt and the jeans she'd managed to grab from the pile of stuff they'd left near their horses at the creek.

Keenan walked over to them, his eyes still swirling and feral. "Thank you – both of you. I don't know what I would have done if ..." He couldn't finish his sentence as emotion overtook him. His hand went to his head as he fought it back.

Tia had never seen him so near breaking point.

Jay put his hand on his shoulder. "No problem. We're just glad we were there to help."

"It's the second time I couldn't help her," Keenan said bitterly.

Before any of them could protest, a commotion of voices and footsteps caught their attention. Tia smiled as Dante strode towards them, all business, surrounded by a group of advisors and guards.

He squeezed Tia's arm and touched Jay on the shoulder as he passed. Keenan quickly showed him to the room.

A feeling of love and Dante's warmth washed over her and was gone as he concentrated on the job at hand. With the close of the door, it was as if he'd let go of her, and she fell against the wall. She grabbed onto a large plant pot to stop herself from falling. Her head swam and she felt faint. Nausea threatened to overwhelm her.

"Hey, you okay?" Jay said, quickly steadying her.

"Yeah, just a bit light-headed. Probably need to eat." It had been almost a day since they'd all eaten.

Jay swooped her up in his arms and walked over to a couple of guards standing in conversation in the hall. He asked if they could get her something to eat and drink, then asked if they could use the pool.

They were pointed in the direction of a corridor and told to follow it until they reached the gym. Jay walked with her quickly and pushed open the door. The smell of chlorine hit her nose, rousing her from her stupor.

Inside, there was a round, sunken whirlpool and a large, rectangular swimming pool with a few sun loungers and garden chairs at one end. He stepped down into the spa with her in his arms and arranged her in the warm water with her head back on the padding that went all around it.

The bubbles surrounded her and it felt wonderful. She almost went straight off to sleep, if it weren't for the voices of several guards. They came in, shook Jay's hand, and introduced themselves. She didn't catch every word, but understood they were thanking him for helping Keenan and their Siren. Another welcomed him to the family. She'd forgotten he was the newly adopted son of Santalini. She drifted in and out after that. Her fuel tank was now empty. Everything she had had gone into keeping Lacy going on the way home, and now she had nothing left.

Jay's voice was the last thing she heard. "Can you do me a favour, mate?"

"Sure, anything."

"Could you get a message to Keenan in the sick bay to send Dante here as soon as he's finished helping Lacy?"

Syria

When Lily awoke the next morning, she felt as though she'd run a marathon the day before. She was listless, bruised and ached all over. Her eyelids could barely open. Then the memory of what had happened before she slept hit her. She inwardly groaned. Her knees came up to her chest and she hoped the whole world would disappear. She forced her eyes open, only to see if Malleven was there.

He was lying on his back next to her, awake and staring at the ceiling. She wondered how long he'd been like that.

"You are awake," he stated quietly.

It was uncanny how he seemed to know everything. *Yes,* she projected.

"Are you well?" he said, without looking at her.

Her heart was thumping. "Okay. A bit achy." His demeanour had completely changed. He was cold and made no effort to turn towards her and caress her, as she'd grown used to.

The more she remembered about what had happened, the

more her unease intensified. Cesaré and the king she'd never met helped her last night. Was Malleven seeing it as a betrayal? They had undoubtedly saved her life, but in doing so, Cesaré had warned her he would be revealed. Surely Malleven would understand?

Lily wanted to broach the subject, but she was terrified. She didn't want Malleven to reject her, and she desperately didn't want to hurt him after all the kindness he'd shown her. She suddenly despised herself. *Are you okay?*

He just nodded and put his forearm across his eyes. A wave of unhappiness seeped from him. She could feel it so clearly through the bond. It was grief, as if someone had died.

The gold didn't work, she projected lamely.

"No," he said, after a while. "*You* rejected it."

It was said like an accusation. As if it was a rejection of him, just the same as with her sister. He was devastated. She couldn't bear that he thought of her like that. *I'm so sorry, Malleven.* It felt so unfair; after all, she'd been fighting for her life. If she'd known what it signified to him, then maybe she would have accepted it. But then Cesaré would have died. It was a hopeless situation.

"Go back to sleep, Lily. You need it," was all Malleven said, and she knew the discussion was closed.

With a heavy heart, she closed her eyes.

MALLEVEN HAD BARELY SLEPT all night. Partly because he wanted to make sure all the gold was out of Lily's system and she survived, and partly because he kept on going over and over what he'd discovered.

He'd come to the conclusion that although Cesaré was inside her, the bond wasn't complete, which explained why he hadn't detected him. That was something at least.

Malleven was annoyed with himself as he'd been aware of an elusive force inside her, but ignored it because he'd been wrapped up in his own ego. He simply never even entertained the idea that he might not have been the first. Cesaré has her power, was all that kept going round and round in his head. It all made perfect sense now – how he could conceal himself.

His blood boiled at the thought of her participation in it. And yet there was no love in her for him. It was the only thought that stopped him from torturing her till she begged for mercy, and condemning her to a life as nothing more than a minion.

After several hours of ruminating on such deep thoughts, things began to solidify in his mind. When he was calmer, he would insist on access to her memories – to hell with what she thought about that. All was not lost as long as he came up with a plan. It was disappointing, yes, but she was still his legally witnessed wife. He knew she cared for him – she couldn't hide that. So in that respect, she was still under his influence.

The ancient powers of the gold he worshipped never ceased to amaze him. It had spoken and would never occupy her. He began to piece together a puzzle that started to fit. Cesaré now hated him, so he must have aligned himself with the king, but without a complete bond, their influence remained stunted. This made him feel better. All he had to do was make some minor adjustments to his overall plan. It just made finding the last remaining Siren more urgent.

With a deep sigh, he decided to stop wallowing and get up. He needed to get away from her for a while to think. He showered quickly, slipped on his silk robe, and walked out through the large glass doors onto the shaded patio area outside. He pulled out a chair and sat brooding with a heavy heart.

Malleven shook his head. He was still in a state of shock that *he* – a master magician – just didn't see this coming. He'd been totally broadsided. The girl had actually started to get to him and get under his skin. In some ways, it was far worse than her sister. At least that was only a case of lust and hurt pride. With Lily, he had allowed himself to be vulnerable. *Perhaps it was because she was honest and naive? Did he still believe that?*

Briefly, it occurred to him that it was a master plot by the king, but he shook his head. He knew, deep down, that Lily couldn't be that deceitful; it simply wasn't in her nature.

A rustle in the bushes brought his head round. Antonio stood there, unsure whether to approach. "What do you want, Antonio?" he said wearily.

"I haven't seen you in ages. I just came to see if you were okay?"

Malleven's eyes misted over for a moment, and he smiled regretfully. "Come here," he said softly.

Antonio walked to him quickly and sank to his knees in front of him. His faithful eyes were filled with adoration for him.

Malleven reached out a hand and pushed his fingers through the mess of blond hair. He sighed and caressed the side of his face. "Always you are here for me …"

Antonio leaned into his hand and closed his eyes.

Lily woke with a start and found Malleven gone. She sat up too quickly and grabbed her head. Gradually, the feeling passed and she scanned the room. Malleven wasn't there. Low voices were coming from outside on the terrace.

She grabbed a glass of water left on the nightstand and glugged it down. Then padded over to the glass doors to the gardens. For some reason, the sight of Antonio on his knees looking up at Malleven while he held his cheek made her pause. The sight was captivating. It was a very private moment and she felt like an intruder. Instead of turning and leaving them to it, waves of emotion emanating from Malleven made her stay riveted to the spot. It felt like hurt tinged with sadness, followed by a great affection.

It was the first time she'd seen Malleven take much notice of Antonio, other than necessary conversation. She had no idea that this level of friendship existed between them. She was fascinated.

Malleven was such a strong man; probably the strongest she'd ever known. Such displays of intimacy were rare – especially with anyone else.

"I am yours for ever, you know that," Antonio said, and rose slightly to crawl up Malleven's body like a cat. He didn't stop until their lips were almost touching.

Malleven continued to lounge back in his chair, allowing it with not so much as a twitch of a muscle. He remained perfectly relaxed, as if waiting for Antonio's next move.

Mesmerised, Lily held her breath. Surely Malleven would push him away to a comfortable distance any moment? Instead, he said something so quietly that she couldn't make out the words. Her hands went up to her throat. The feelings coming through the bond were loud and clear.

Antonio covered Malleven's lips with his own and kissed him long and deeply. Malleven remained passive, allowing it, only moving his lips in response. The erotic kiss was nothing about friendship and all about raw sex.

Lily's eyes widened with realization.

Antonio began a slow trail of kisses down Malleven's bare chest, now exposed by his open robe.

Lily grabbed her mouth as she hitched a breath and turned away. Her eyes darted without seeing. *What had she just seen? They were friends ... weren't they? Was this a thing with Atlantean men?*

Her mind raced, juggling the information with thought after thought. However she twisted and turned it in her head. It was all starting to make sense now – the way Antonio always seemed a little off with her. *How stupid could she have been?*

The memory of Antonio's warning not to give in to Malleven completely came to her like a bolt of lightning. Then Malleven's own confession about not being interested in women.

Her hand held her mouth as her heart thumped.

He was gay.

They were lovers.

Oh my God!

Lily began to pace the room. An erotic moan from outside pulled her up short. She put her hands over her ears and ran to the bathroom. She switched on the shower and stepped in, her mind going a hundred miles an hour.

She'd promised him complete obedience, but this was a game changer, *wasn't it?*

There had to be a catch with this bloke; there always was. Maybe this was why her sister rejected him?

No matter how much she went over it, and how much she reminded herself that she was married and bonded to him, all she could think of doing was running away, getting time to think, going to Lance.

CHAPTER 39

It had been a turbulent last few days for Dante. He'd breathed his power into Lacy to aid her recovery and now she slept peacefully. A guard showed him to the poolroom. He frowned at the sorry sight of Jay, exhausted, holding Tia asleep in his arms. Then, he quickly shed his clothes when he felt no response from her through the bond.

Jay roused himself when he saw him.

"What's the matter?" Dante asked, stepping into the pool with them.

"Not sure exactly. She kept Lacy going by breathing for her all the way here. I think she's just run out of steam."

Dante gingerly reached under her, relieving Jay of her weight. "I'm going to take her into the pool, okay?"

Jay hesitated for a moment, nodded and helped him out of the spa with her. "I'll go and chase up the food." Things were still strained.

This wasn't the time to address any issues between them. Dante was filled with concern as he slipped into the main pool with Tia. He supported her head out in front of him, waist deep in the water. Then he moved her around, letting her know he was there, but she didn't respond. His concern grew when he leaned over her to breathe a little for her, but she wasn't conscious enough to take it in – her breaths were too shallow.

He felt her neck. She had a pulse, but it was very weak.

He brought her with him to the edge, rested his back on the tiles and hugged her to him. He needed to rouse her and decided the only way to do that was from her mind's eye space – the private place in her head – where only he had access.

He closed his eyes and concentrated. Within moments, he walked into the dark room with the leopard-print bed in the centre. There she was, lying listless and exhausted. His stripy form approached the bed and stroked her face. "Tia, baby, it's me, Dante. Please, can you wake up for me?"

Her eyes cracked a tiny bit. "Dante?" she croaked.

He scooped her into his arms and sat with her on the bed. "Hey, what you been up to, eh?" He grinned at her, but his eyes were misty with tears, seeing her like that.

She smiled a little. "I'm a bit tired, Dante. Is Lacy okay?"

"She's grand, thanks to you. But look, darlin', I need you to do something for me?"

"Mmm?" She began to drift off. He needed to be quick.

"I need you to wake your conscious mind just enough to let me breathe for you, okay?" He was trying desperately to keep the panic out of his voice. The truth was, he was terrified she'd depleted herself too much. This was a whole other thing entirely to a Siren breathing life into a prince when tested. He was a healthy male brought to the point of drowning and just needed his gills started. Tia couldn't drown, but the spirit had literally been syphoned out of her. She'd given all of herself to save her sister.

"Okay," she whispered.

Dante kissed her and quickly left her mind.

When he opened his eyes, she was blinking up at him. He laughed up at the ceiling and crushed her to him. "Hey, sleepy!" he said and wasted no time, but leaned forward and breathed a steady flow of his spirit into her lips. All the while, he walked her gently out into the deeper water. He repeated over and over until he was satisfied she'd had enough to fortify her, then carried her up the steps and placed her gently down onto a sun lounger. He pushed another next to it and lay down beside her.

Tia rested with her head to the side, just watching him.

Dante leant on an elbow, gazing down into her expanded eyes. They were so wrapped up in each other that neither of them noticed Jay walk in until he was right there with a tray of food.

"She okay?" he said.

"She'll be fine." But his eyes stayed glued to hers.

Jay put down the tray, paused, and quietly left.

"Are you going to stay with me?" Tia asked, trailing a finger down the side of Dante's cheek.

He laughed, grabbing the finger and kissing it. "I'm supposed to have put you away from me," he said, sadly.

"I'm supposed to be finished with both of you."

Dante laughed out loud. "Is that what you decided?"

She nodded in all seriousness.

"So that's why you went to Cash's instead of London, where I told you to go?"

She nodded again with a small smile.

He narrowed his eyes. "And you're telling me because my pride will have to see if you weaken for me?"

She grinned. "I'm not that clever."

He snatched her to him and rolled on top of her. "Yes you are, you little devil."

"Couldn't you say it took a while to revive me?"

"Mmm," he pretended to think about it, but she'd delighted him. "I think I need to punish you for disobeying me." He picked her up and walked back towards the pool.

IT WAS some time later when he walked out of the pool with Tia in his arms, both covered in thick stripes and unable to speak. He placed her down on the makeshift bed he'd made earlier and wrapped her in dry, fluffy, white towels. He kissed her one last time and projected that he loved her.

It was morning and he needed to go. It had already been late when he'd arrived. He'd left Cesaré when it looked like he was out of danger, but there was a whole other mess there that needed to be sorted. He didn't want their cover blown and the Santalinis to assume they were still very much a couple. Jay's place in their world was still shaky, even if the Santalinis had adopted him. The conversation he wanted to have with Jay would have to wait.

He dressed and perched on the side of Tia's bed, pushing back the matted hair from her face. *Please stay safe, Tia. That means close to Jay, okay?*

She sighed. *I have Cash and Sean.*

I know, but for me, please promise?

She nodded reluctantly.

And eat! he added.

She smiled up at him. *I love you.*

He kissed her forehead and walked towards the door. His heart was heavy; he hated being apart from her, but it was necessary for the time being. Besides, Lily needed to be found fast now that Malleven knew about Cesaré; there was no telling what he'd do.

Before he left, he made sure sentries were on the door and told that the queen was sleeping. No one was to enter until she awoke.

It struck him as strange that they'd been left to it. Then he shrugged. A lot was going on with Lacy, and they were probably giving them space.

CESARÉ WOKE late in the day feeling like he'd had a bad bout of flu. He groaned as he shifted slightly in the bed. A glass appeared in his face.

"Drink!" Shona said.

When he focused on his surroundings, Lance and Shona were sitting on either side of him, looking almost as worn and washed out as he was. "Have you been here all the time?" he said, after taking a few gulps of water.

Lance nodded.

"Yeah, you've been out for like twelve hours straight," Shona said.

He sat up and frowned. Everything was coming back to him. It hadn't been delirium; Malleven had pulled some stunt last night and almost killed the pair of them.

He tried his best to sense Lily, but there was nothing. He cursed the one-way bond. Without the king's power, he had no way of reaching out to her. "Dante … is he here?"

They both nodded. "He got back a few hours ago. There was some major agro with Lily's sister or something. Lucky he was here, he reckoned."

"Go and get him!" Cesaré said more sharply than he intended. Now that everything was solidifying in his memory, he knew there would be repercussions. They needed to come up with an action plan.

"Dante seemed to think that Lily was okay when you passed out?" Lance said, like he really needed him to say yes.

Cesaré could see the fear in his eyes, but he couldn't fool him. Malleven would know about him now, and he knew his cousin well. This was a devastating setback for him – not only as a prince but also as a man. He'd been outwitted by someone he viewed as inconsequential and would hate it.

Cesaré laughed mirthlessly to himself. *Ain't payback a bitch.* It was he who now led the Florianna family and had the seat on the king's council.

Dante walked in before he could answer Lance, with his phone to his ear. Shona resumed her place next to the bed.

He ended the call in Italian and grinned at Cesaré. "Still in the land of the livin', I see."

Cesaré swore. "I can't sense her."

Dante became serious. "That's not necessarily a bad thing. She could still be out like you were, or her emotions are even."

That didn't ease Cesaré's worry. "There will be some kind of confrontation. He will want to know what happened." He shook his head. "What if he tortures her?"

Dante touched his leg through the blankets, understanding completely. "One thing I know is that if anything goes on, you will feel it. I know it's hard, but we have to leave her alone; it will only make matters worse for her if we interfere again. I still think his next move will be to come here to New York. Then you'll sense her and we can start to search."

Cesaré exhaled loudly. He was right.

The king turned and walked back towards the door. "I'm gonna get some rest. I had a fuckin' hell of a night. You best get some too."

"What happened?"

"When it fuckin' rains, it pours. I'll fill yer in later. Wake me if you sense anything." He turned and left the room.

Only another Florianna understood what Malleven was capable of.

CHAPTER 40

Malleven left Lily alone for a full twenty-four hours. Antonio's open adoration was a welcome distraction to his simmering anger. It had been a good test to see how she reacted to abandonment. First, he felt shock and hurt, then, as the evening wore on, insecurity and anxiety. She'd reached out to him psychically a couple of times and he'd slammed her down, but he couldn't ignore her for ever. Satisfied that he had her at a disadvantage, he returned to his apartments.

He found her sitting huddled on the bed, with her knees up to her chest. She'd been crying, but swiped her forearm across her eyes in a vain attempt to hide it. He walked into the room silently, emptied the contents of his pockets onto a low table and unbuttoned his shirt. Then went to the sideboard where he poured them both a drink. He passed her one and sank heavily into an armchair opposite her.

Her eyes hadn't left him, waiting for him to speak. He sipped his drink, his eyes on hers, not giving anything away. He wanted to make her sweat. The truth was, he was fighting the urge not to crush her for answers. That wasn't in his best interest here. His brain whirred on how to turn this catastrophe around to work to his advantage; after all, it had been his expertise his whole life.

I'm sorry! she projected suddenly.

After a long pause while he scrutinized her, he finally said, "What are you saying sorry for?" Her upset did smooth over his anger slightly.

She battled back her tears and shook her head. "For whatever that thing was, not working ... for upsetting you."

Anger surged through him. He gripped the arms of the chair and clenched his teeth. Instead of pouncing on her, he counted until he had his temper under control. "I will ask you this question once and you will answer me fully and honestly. Do you understand?"

She nodded manically and he felt her terror.

"How did you come to bond with Cesaré Florianna?"

LILY WAS MOMENTARILY STUNNED. Cesaré was hidden in her mind, but a bond? *Did he think they had history? No, no, no, it was nothing like that.*

Malleven leapt to his feet in one lightning-fast move. "Do not try to lie to me, girl. I can access your mind and take your memories, should I so wish."

In reflex, her arms went up to defend her face, and she was shaking her head. *No, please, Malleven, it wasn't like that at all.* Her eyes were squeezed shut, waiting for his mental or physical onslaught. When it didn't happen, she took a peek.

His eyes were narrowed on her, and he slowly lowered himself back into his chair. "Then what was it?" he said, quietly.

"I saved his life one day, that's all. He was drowning." She went on to recount the events of that day.

He listened quietly and gave nothing away. It all seemed

so unfair that she should be on trial like this, when he had spent the last day with his lover. But he was a prince and they didn't exactly have a conventional marriage. Didn't kings and princes always have mistresses? *Fuck,* she didn't even know what to call the male version of it.

It all crystallised the feeling that she wasn't sure she was okay with it. In fact, she wasn't sure she wanted to be with him any longer.

MALLEVEN LISTENED to the whole explanation without butting in. It did make sense. It tallied with what Shona had told him initially, and Cesaré being a drunken fool with a death wish fitted his profile perfectly.

It still didn't alter the fact that Cesaré had her power even if she'd given it without realising what she was doing. "You have no feelings for him," he said as a statement. It was a fact that astounded and curiously mattered to him.

No, she projected, looking him dead in the eye.

"You understand that it is impossible for secrets between us?"

She nodded.

He watched her closely. He knew she was telling the truth, but it still bothered him that she'd sought to hide Cesaré from him. There was also guilt in her somewhere; he just couldn't put his finger on why.

Malleven sighed deeply. There was no point in questioning her further. The priority was where they went from here. The situation had to be salvaged somehow. The question was how. "Tomorrow we leave for America," he said, standing up.

Where?

There was a quickening of her heart that made him pause.

Was it excitement or fear? "New York," he said, watching her closely.

Okay, I'll pack. She pulled out her case and began throwing things into it.

He frowned. *Fuck it,* something else was really bothering him. "Who are your Protectors?"

LILY STOPPED what she was doing, but didn't look up. *Shona,* she answered, and resumed packing. Everything in her was on high alert and she did her damnedest not to let on.

"Just Shona?"

Briefly, she considered lying, but she sensed his eyes burning into her as if that was what he expected. *Well ... all the surfers adopted me as a pet project.*

"No one particularly swore themselves to you?"

Shit, he knew ... he just had to.

Suddenly, Antonio's warning not to give Malleven everything came to mind, and she felt anger. It became clear that maybe he hadn't had her best interests at heart that day. There she was, getting the third degree, and it felt fucking rich coming from Malleven. She huffed. *Okay, while we're having a heart-to-heart, honesty-type thing, what is Antonio to you?* She turned her head to look daggers at Malleven with her hands on her hips.

A flicker of amusement played on his lips and brow, but he schooled it fast. He wasn't even taking it seriously – *the bastard.* Then he looked at her quizzically as if he wasn't sure what she knew.

She decided not to play all her cards. *Well?*

He sat back down, openly amused now. "You don't like my friendship with Antonio?"

She thought carefully about how to put what she said

next. *I am your partner in everything – we have no secrets. Is that right?*

He inclined his head.

Then, just as I have no Protectors, you should send away your friends. Her adrenaline was pumping and she began to shake.

His eyebrows popped in surprise. Then he laughed loudly and became serious again. "As you wish, *mio fiore.*"

Relieved she had salvaged a tricky situation, she averted her eyes, as his had taken on a more amorous look.

Santalini Mansion – New York

The following afternoon, the house was in a state of consternation. Marius, Keenan's older brother, was organising a ceremony to give thanks to the Orb for Lacy's survival after her close shave with death, and to welcome Jay into the family. It was a morale-booster for the Santalinis to distract them from taking matters into their own hands.

Tia understood the motives behind it perfectly, but thought it was strange that she had only heard what was going on through Cash and Sean, who came to find her in the pool house.

"They're treating Jay as a hero," Cash said.

"What I don't get is why there has been no mention of you?" said Sean.

Tia frowned. She didn't mind not being in the spotlight, but everything did feel weird. Maybe it was to do with her new position with the king. She wasn't really sure. "Where's Jay?"

"I looked for him this morning. Someone said they were tattooing him with the Santalini crest and fitting him with his red and black uniform." Sean said.

Tia nodded with a wan smile. That explained why he hadn't been to see her yet. She was beginning to feel uneasy, though. No one had been to see her. Everyone in the household would be expected to attend the ceremony, but neither she nor her Protectors had a thing to wear other than what they stood up in.

She looked down at herself. Tatty jeans, an oversized t-shirt, and no shoes were all she had.

Sean shook his head and tutted, reading her mind.

"They've probably just overlooked it with Lacy and everything," Tia said.

"You're still a queen, Tia. This isn't right," Cash said. "I'm gonna say something." And he went to make for the door.

Tia caught his arm. "No, leave it, Cash. The family heads may not know I'm here. I'll just creep in at the back and then sneak out." She laughed. "You know me, I don't care if they don't."

The Protectors smiled at her. Sean put a hand on her shoulder, but they weren't happy at all.

THE ROOM WAS plush and red with ornate gold fixtures and fittings. There were grand paintings on the walls and huge chandeliers on the ceiling. It seemed like every member of the Santalini family was there, making it really easy for Tia, Cash and Sean to slip in the back of the room unnoticed. Tia sat on a sofa with Cash and Sean on either side of her, guarding her like a pair of Dobermans.

"Why didn't you let us get you out of here?" Cash said, looking pissed off at the dirty looks from the women she was getting.

Tia was starting to wish she had when yet another Santalini woman tutted and shook her head. "We can't go back to yours yet, Cash, and I made Dante a promise that I'd stick with Jay."

He sighed, not convinced it was the right thing at all.

Keenan's brother, Marius, was delivering a long, boring speech about duty and honour, then handed over to his Uncle Andreas – the head of the Santalini family.

Tia could just about make out Jay right at the front, next to Keenan, when Andreas pinned some kind of medal to his lapel. Then everyone clapped. *God, he was breathtakingly beautiful.* Uniform really suited him. Despite being much smaller in stature than most of the Santalini men, he was in great shape. She found herself imagining peeling that uniform off.

It was quite nice to be separate from the proceedings – able to watch him interact with the alpha males, smiling and completely at home.

The ceremony was soon over and people began to mill about. It was then she noticed a particularly beautiful raven-haired woman in a scarlet dress sidle up to Jay and congratulate him. Everything about the woman matched what the men were wearing. It was quickly apparent that Jay knew her when he kissed her on the cheek and they laughed together. They were a perfect, beautiful couple.

A huge lump appeared in Tia's throat, and she fought to keep the hurt down.

Sean touched her on the arm.

"Who is she?" she whispered.

"I'm not sure. I think it might be Keenan's sister, Ruby."

Her heart plummeted. *Fuck.* The girl hadn't registered on her radar before. She was all over him, twirling her hair in her fingers and giggling like a schoolgirl. A tear escaped the corner of Tia's eye, which she caught before anyone could notice.

Then a male voice shouting brought her out of her emotional tailspin. It was coming from right down the front of the hall. She sniffed and wiped the remnants of her tears, welcoming the distraction. At least the entertainment was about to start livening up.

The crowd began to part in front of her and some bloke started to stride towards her. She quickly recognised him as Andreas and he was pointing in her direction.

Confused, she looked about her, but they were at the back. Gobsmacked, she realised that he was shouting at her.

Cash and Sean were slowly rising, getting ready to protect her, while she actually registered what the man was shouting.

"You! ... Yes, you! You're nothing but a tramp. Look at the state of you. Call yourself a queen. You are a guttersnipe and have no business being here."

Tia stood up, but Cash and Sean made sure she kept behind them. She forced herself between their arms. "How fucking dare you call me that." Then she flew at him to scratch his eyes out, and everything exploded like an assassination attempt on the president.

The guards leapt in between her and Andreas. Cash and Sean were in the fray to protect Tia, who was kicking and flailing like a mad thing. Somewhere in the middle, Jay had jumped in to try to calm down the factions, who, after much shouting and pushing, managed to shout at Cash, "Get her out ... quickly."

Cash held out an arm in bewilderment.

"Pool, I'll meet you there."

Cash and Sean bundled her out through the crowd that had gathered around them.

By the time they reached the poolroom, Tia was shaking violently with adrenaline. "Fuck, what was that? What did I do?" she said, her eyes wide with fright.

Cash couldn't answer; she could tell he was too angry. "I'll guard outside. If anyone else has something to say, they can say it to me."

Sean looked into her face, about to crumble, and pulled her to him. His hand gently rubbed her back while she cried into his chest. "This whole thing has been out of order. I've never seen anyone treated so badly, let alone a queen." It was then that it began to sink in. Now that Dante had put her away from him, she wasn't. She was a nobody. No longer anyone of standing, and she wasn't allowed to be Human either.

WHEN TIA'S shakes finally subsided, she was left feeling a bone-deep weariness. Jay still hadn't come to find her. As always, Cash and Sean were her rocks. She pulled away from Sean's chest to look up into his strong, handsome face. "Thank you."

A muscle ticced in his jaw. He was angry. "No need to thank me. I'm always here for you."

She smiled. "I'm gonna rest for a bit till Jay gets here."

After a pause, he nodded. "Okay. I'll wait outside with Cash. Speak to Dante," he said, pointing to his temple.

"Yep!" she said as cheerfully as she could. She wouldn't, though. She had to get used to being on her own. After all, she'd brought it on herself.

Sean walked away, but he was fuming.

Tia went and sat on the makeshift bed that Dante had made her only a few hours earlier. A ragged sob escaped her. Never in her whole sorry life had she been made to feel like scum before. Not until tonight.

How did everything get so messed up?

She looked over at the tray Jay had brought in while she'd been with Dante. *God, she missed him.* She couldn't remember the last time she ate, but she couldn't. Instead, she reached out for the glass of water. Her hand fumbled and she dropped the glass. Tears were streaming down her face when she reached down and picked up the largest shard.

She sat back and closed her eyes and took a deep breath.

In, one, two, out, one, two. She repeated over and over. It was a well-practised routine. Slowly, she raised the shard and put it to the inside of her left wrist and scored down from her hand towards her elbow. It was weird; although the cuts were superficial, they always brought relief. It was real and it somehow helped the ache trapped so deeply within her. It was that part of her that could never be expressed. The pain grounded her. It was hers to control – the only thing that was hers.

IT WAS A DELICATE SITUATION, but Jay managed to smooth things over for the time being. He left the Santalinis with a promise he'd get Tia out of there. Now it was time to see how the other side were doing.

His phone rang. He took it out of his pocket and saw that it was Dante. *Fuck, he didn't need this.* "Dante," he said, walking briskly to the poolroom.

"What the fuck's going on? You haven't been answering your phone. Tia's emotions are like the national grid; she's locked me out, and Cash and Sean's phones are off."

Jay allowed Dante to finish, then calmly explained what happened. "Everything went tits up. I've no idea what started it. But Tia, in her usual spectacular style, managed to insult the whole family by assaulting Andreas."

Dante went quiet for a bit. "Fucking hell, Jay. You gotta help her out."

Jay was still pissed off at Dante anyway. This whole thing was kind of the cherry on the cake after Ireland. "I'll deal with it, but I'll deal with it my way. I'm not pussyfooting around."

"Just do it and ring me back."

Jay clicked off his phone, nodded at Cash and Sean, and walked into the poolroom.

. . .

A DOOR SLAMMED BEHIND HER.

Tia's wrist was throbbing, but she felt calm and remarkably serene.

The next thing she knew, the side of her wrist was hit hard, causing the shard to fly out of her hand and smash against the wall.

She opened her eyes with a scowl to see who it was, but there was no time. She was roughly hauled across a lap, both her hands held in one hand and her jeans ripped down to her thighs.

She screamed first in surprise and then in pain as she was slapped hard across the behind – really hard.

It took only a millisecond to work out who it was. The tattooed arm holding her hands and the fuming voice, such as she'd never heard it. "You. Selfish. Fucking. Bitch." It was slap, word, slap, just like when she was a child.

"You want to get all of us fucking killed, bleeding in a house full of fucking vampires?"

With those words, she stopped crying out. She took the beating quietly, as she'd learnt to do.

Cash had come in, not sure what to do. "Hey, hey!" he shouted.

Jay just barked at him to get some dressings. "She's cut her fucking wrists."

Sean joined him. "What the fuck?" And took a lunge towards them.

Jay stood suddenly, still holding her wrists and pointing at Sean, bringing him up short. "Get Keenan," Jay continued, "get him to guard, let no one else know about this and let no one else in."

Sean hesitated, then, after Cash touched his arm, they hurriedly left; Jay threw her away from him in disgust. Tia fell on the floor in a heap and looked up at him through her sweaty, matted hair. His face was so red and angry, she barely recognized him.

His hand flew to his mouth as if he was about to be sick.

All she could do was stare up into his wild eyes, dilated and as much in shock as she was, while he appeared to fight to get some sort of control. It was a side of him she'd never seen. *The blood.*

Cash came back in, pushed past Jay, and gently picked her up. "You better go and calm down," he said ominously.

Jay spat and took a few calming breaths. "I'll be outside in case any of them smell the fresh blood."

Cash didn't answer, but held her tight against his body.

Tia watched Jay walk away, silent in shock.

JAY LURCHED AGAINST THE WALL, relieved to be out of there, then leaned down with his hands on his knees and spat. *Fuck!*

His head raged in a storm he didn't understand. Partly in irritation by the fact that his actions had been wrong. The reason far out of reach because of this overwhelming sickness – *no, more than that* – it was a hunger or a thirst. One like he'd never had in his life before.

A hand landed on his back, making him look up with a start. It took him a full minute to focus and recognise the serious face looking down on him. *Keenan.*

"I heard. Go and sort yourself out. I'm here, okay?"

Jay still couldn't speak and gawped bleary-eyed at him through his frown. Gradually, his meaning seeped through to him. It was in his expression, in his body language alone. *Pity.* The thing he could never stand.

Before his anger began to rise up in him again, Keenan just nodded and spoke reassuringly. "It's the blood, mate. Just breathe."

Feeling completely left-fielded, he swallowed, took a deep breath and straightened up. Then, without saying a word, walked away slowly, utterly confused.

This wasn't the extreme lust he'd experienced when Tia bled before. It was a jumble of anger at Dante and at Tia for hurting herself. That his loving her wasn't enough – could never be enough. He was dark – that was what Christian had called him. *Perhaps he was the Darkly Begotten.*

His hand went out to steady himself on the corridor wall. The clouds in his mind were gradually thinning, but the thirst didn't budge. It dawned on him how powerless he'd become. He was beyond even helping himself. Instead of going to his room, he went to the only person who could.

CHAPTER 41

A few uncomfortable hours followed while arrangements were made. Then they boarded the Bonaci jet to Ireland. Dante had already left New York to attend to urgent business there. No one was speaking.

Tia walked in gingerly, refused to sit in the seat next to Jay, and went straight through to the little bedroom at the back of the plane. She closed the door and flopped face down on the bare mattress. No rose petals and ice cubes on this trip. Her hands went to her eyes and she curled into a ball as her hurt and humiliation flooded back to her.

The door was snatched open.

Jay spoke in a low voice. "Get the fuck back out here and strap in for takeoff."

She leaned up on her arms to turn to look at him. "I can't sit down. Please ... I don't care about crashing ... I don't care." And she flopped back down to sob into her hands.

If he tried to force her, he'd have to carry her, because she had no fight left in her.

He stood there for a moment, as if unsure what to do, then went back out to the main area of the plane.

. . .

A FEW HOURS later and Malleven and Lily arrived at his huge apartment in New York. Much to Lily's frustration, Antonio was still part of their entourage. It was as though Malleven had totally disregarded her feelings. They were surrounded constantly by Magi warriors, which only served to make her feel increasingly stifled. She just had to get away. She needed space to think.

MALLEVEN CONTINUED TO BE PREOCCUPIED. Marrying Lily was only the first step on his journey to gaining the kingdom. He had a long way to go yet. To be recognised as her husband, he had to be acknowledged not only by the Atlantean world but also by the king himself, who despised him. It would be no mean feat. To do that, he had to meet with the Santalinis, and they hated him as well.

In his haste to bag himself a Siren, he'd kidnapped theirs – Lacy Rain, and attempted to have her mate, Keenan Santalini, killed. It had all been for nothing when Isla Snow turned out to be his legitimate Siren anyway. But it was too late by then, and, unfortunately, the Santalinis had long memories.

The fact was, he *was* legally married now, and that was irrefutable. It was just a small matter of staying alive long enough for it to be public. As promised, the Duke Ormond Delissi had set the wheels in motion and arranged a meeting. It was to be on neutral ground between him and the heads of the Santalini royal family.

"Let me come with you?" Antonio begged.

Malleven touched him gently on the cheek. "There can be nothing personal in this meeting. It is business," he smiled. "I want you to stay here and make a friend of Lily. She will become wearisome when she realises I haven't dismissed you."

Antonio scowled. "So she finally knows about us?"

Malleven shrugged slightly. "She suspects. You must get her to like you."

Antonio laughed derisively. "She's gone up in my estimations. I was beginning to think she was a bit dense."

Malleven nodded, his face serious. "Do it … Don't make me have to sort it out." Then he nodded to the Magi brothers who would accompany him, and left to attend the meeting at the hired conference room in a nearby hotel.

MALLEVEN HAD to go along with every stipulation suggested by the duke. He'd been lucky they'd agreed to meet with him at all. It crossed his mind that he could be walking into a trap, but he had his brothers with him, and the duke would officiate. The only condition he had insisted upon was that Keenan was not present. His reason was one of bias, but the truth was, Keenan would not rest until one of them was dead. It was the nature of the Santalinis.

Malleven arrived with eight of his strongest Magi warriors in full black regalia. The four Santalini brothers looked majestic in their scarlet-and-black uniforms. Andreas, the family head, was noticeably absent. The duke was as regal as ever as chairman. Each faction sat on either side of a huge oval boardroom table with the duke at its head. They eyed each other with suspicion.

The duke started proceedings with a cough and passed a parchment along the line of the Santalini brothers.

"What is this?" the eldest, Marius, said.

"It is the decree showing Malleven Mancini as bonded Prince to the Siren, Aella Selene Parthenia Bonaci."

"How can this be?" one said.

"The fourth Siren?"

"But he was rejected!"

Malleven shifted in his chair, but remained silent. He wasn't expecting them to like it.

"You know as well as I do that as long as the Siren accepts the prince, it is legal – even if she isn't his destined mate," the duke said.

Marius smashed his hand down on the table in temper.

Malleven felt the brother next to him tense in readiness.

"And what of our Siren? She lies recovering from a gunshot wound. Are you saying you have nothing to do with that?" Marius spat.

Malleven's cool detachment fell away and he was genuinely shocked. "How is she? Will she live?" When he received no explanation, he looked to the Duke.

The Santalinis all rose to their feet.

The Magi did the same.

Marius pointed a finger at Malleven. "You were responsible for our Siren's disappearance. If our brother were here, you would be dead."

Malleven narrowed his eyes. "Whatever you think of me, know this: I am also an Atlantean and a prince. I am bound to a royal Bonaci Siren and, by law, I would be recognised as such. My sole mission in life has always been the advancement and prosperity of the Florianna family and to see the Atlantean nation united under one king. That can only happen if all five Sirens live."

"You are a low-born liar!" another Santalini shouted.

Malleven was running out of patience and looked to the duke to bring order.

"How do you answer these charges?" the duke said directly to him.

Malleven bit down his rising temper and answered low and deliberately. "I made no attempt on the Siren's life."

"What if it was an attempt to kill Keenan and she was caught in the crossfire?" one of the Santalinis said.

Malleven bobbed his head. That would make more sense, but he was done pissing around. He wanted to get this meeting over and get the hell out of there. "I made no attempt on Keenan's life." He turned to face the duke. "We can sling insults all day, but you yourself can attest to me enjoying my recent nuptials."

The duke nodded, having heard enough. "It is true."

"He wouldn't do his own dirty work!" another Santalini said.

"Enough!" the duke said. "Everyone, sit."

The Santalinis sat begrudgingly and grumbled. The Magi sat in silence but remained alert.

"What do you want of us?" Marius said eventually.

"It is an appeal to you as the Honourable Guard for recognition as a bound prince and safe passage to the king. He would claim his place on the council," the duke explained.

The Santalinis all muttered and shook their heads. "That's it?" Marius said.

Malleven inclined his head. It had been unsettling; his advancement could only be made through them. Everything hinged on the success of this meeting and their commitment to honour tradition being stronger than their hatred of him and his family.

"We will need time to discuss this. We need to decide for ourselves whether the Siren in question was coerced into marriage."

The duke sighed. "Very well, I give you twenty-four hours."

Marius nodded and marched out of the room with his brothers.

The duke gathered his papers and put them back in his briefcase. "If they agree, it will be a shaky truce."

"Can they say no?" Malleven said.

The duke shook his head. "They won't like it, but their hands are tied. You were wise to call me as a witness."

Malleven inclined his head. The duke was an influential and respected man.

"You would also be wise not to further piss them off."

It would be hard, but the duke was right. He needed his marriage proclaimed and accepted as soon as possible, before Cesaré could cause him any damage. It was a race against time. Cesaré may have her power, but his bond was not reciprocated. All the while that was the case, Malleven had a chance to contest his position on the council and head of the Florianna family.

Malleven said a farewell to the duke and they filed from the room. He felt quietly confident. He knew Cesaré of old. His strengths were drinking, surfing and bedding women. He was no statesman.

And he held Lily's affection; of that he was sure. The thought ignited a need to reaffirm it and he hurried back to his apartment.

CHAPTER 42

*L*ily waited until everything was quiet and tiptoed through the marble hallway to the door to the apartment. Holding her breath, she clicked the latch and slipped out.

"May I be of service, Your Highness?" a heavily accented voice said, making her jump out of her skin. The Magi brother bowed his head.

After she gathered herself together, *It's okay, I'm just nipping out to the shops. No need to bother.*

"It is no trouble, your highness. It is a dangerous city."

She smiled weakly. *Don't worry, I just remembered something I have to do.* She turned around and went back in the apartment, bumping straight into Antonio. *Bloody hell!*

"Going somewhere?"

I just wanted some air, she huffed. *I don't seem to be allowed to do anything.*

"You are an important person now, Lily. Allow me to escort you?"

Lily tutted, pushed past him and went into the large

lounge area. *You don't have to pretend to be friendly with me any longer, Antonio. I know who you are.*

Antonio stepped closer so he loomed over her. "Not as daft as you look, then."

She narrowed her eyes at his smug face. *You told me to hold back from Malleven; now I know why.*

His smile morphed into spite. "You're not his real mate. I was doing you a favour. You won't hold his attention for long."

And you hold his attention, do you, Antonio? It was a catty thing to say, but she couldn't help herself.

"He always comes to me. You girls come and go, but in the end, it's always me. And do you know what? You're not a patch on your sister."

The real Antonio showed himself at last, but she was still shocked at the hatred etched all over his spiteful face. It would have been easy to fall into a slanging match with him. She had to remember that her objective was to get away. *What if I went away? You could have him all to yourself then.*

Antonio hesitated slightly and narrowed his eyes. "Is this some kind of trick? Where would you go?"

Just back to my Protectors, no harm would be done.

"But you and he are bonded," he said, frowning.

He was wavering and actually considering what she said. Her heart quickened.

Antonio shook his head. "No, he'd kill me if he found out."

If he loves you like you say he does … All I need is some space for a while. She touched him gently on the arm. *Please, Antonio, I care about Malleven, I really do, I just need some time, that's all.*

He went quiet while he considered what she said. "How could we do it without him knowing I helped you?"

Voices in the hallway stopped her from answering. He

pulled her with him out onto the roof terrace and studied her face until he was sure they were alone. "If you have feelings for him, why do you want to leave him?"

If you love him like you say, why do you think my sister's so great when she betrayed him like that?

His frown turned into exasperation. "Look, it's complicated between destined mates. And Malleven ... well, he can be somewhat demanding."

She raised her eyebrows, unsure what he was driving at. *She left him to die, didn't she?*

"Yes, but ... she had a choice whether to accept him ... You had that choice. She just loved somebody else."

A picture of Lance came to mind. Even if Lance had returned her feelings, she was sure she wouldn't have consciously hurt Malleven like that. The whole thing was confusing. *Will you help me or not?*

Antonio still looked unsure, as if he were weighing things up. "Where would you go?"

To my Protectors.

"Where you were before?"

She nodded manically.

"Then he'll find you straight away."

You see ... this is why I need your help.

He was studying her face while he racked his brains. Her stomach fluttered. It appeared like he was actually considering it.

"If I do help you, you must be completely honest with me. You are extremely valuable to him and he'll kill to keep you."

Malleven's power was obvious to her, but despite his infidelity with Antonio, she believed he cared for her. *I promise. What do you want to know?*

"You have genuine feelings for him?"

Yes I do.

He shifted his feet in exasperation. "Then why on earth would you want to leave him?"

Lily sighed and looked out over New York. *Everything has been fine between us. He's been the kindest, most generous man I've ever met.*

Antonio quirked a brow.

What?

He shook his head and waved a regal hand. "Continue."

I didn't realise what I'd done at the time, but apparently, when I saved Cesaré's life after a surfing accident, I'd done something terrible. Her eyes warily tracked up to Antonio's and he looked horrified.

"My God ... you breathed for him."

She nodded slowly.

"Did he return it?"

No ... I didn't know what I was doing, I swear.

It explained a lot – why Malleven had been so upset and why, after weeks of neglect, he was seeking him out again. Elation bubbled in the pit of his stomach. He wanted to punch the air and kiss this stupid girl on the mouth. He sobered himself. "So Cesaré has your power," he said, beginning to pace before he got too excited.

Guilt did prick his conscience as this was catastrophic for Malleven, but it was oh so fortuitous for him. *Thank god she'd told him.* He stopped pacing and faced her. "Are you trying to get back to Cesaré?" It would be impossible to help her do that. Malleven would surely kill him. "Are you aware the king is in New York and Cesaré is undoubtedly with him?"

Lily was shaking her head, looking wide-eyed and manic. *No, we haven't spoken. I'm aware of him – I feel him, but that's it.*

Antonio tutted. It was too risky. "I can't help you go to him, I'm sorry." Despite how it would bring him closer to Malleven, he couldn't help destroy him like that.

Lily looked uncomfortable, like she was looking for the

right way to put something. "What if I said I had no interest in Cesaré or the king? What if I said I wanted to go to my Protectors because there was someone else – a Human?"

Antonio narrowed his eyes and studied her for any hint of a lie. Her other sister had left Malleven for love, clearing the way for him. It could work. "It would need some planning. We'd need to get you out and create some kind of diversion. Otherwise, he'll catch up with you within minutes."

She nodded, her eyes shining with hope.

"You're absolutely sure you want to do this?"

Yes!

"Because I will not defend you after. I will deny all knowledge."

I understand.

"Okay ... this is what we will do ...

MALLEVEN RETURNED TO THE APARTMENT, tense and annoyed. Antonio was gratified that he was the first person he sought out. It definitely marked a shift in Malleven's affections.

"What happened?" Antonio said, massaging Malleven's shoulders.

"Argh, the usual. Fucking posturing show of strength from the Santalinis."

"Will they acknowledge you?"

"They don't like it, but they have to. Delissi will insist upon it."

All was not well. "So all is well then?" Antonio said, trying to sound upbeat. Malleven was irked. His body radiated pent-up aggression. "What is it?"

"There was an attempt on their Siren's life. They actually thought it was me – as if I had no honour." He swore under his breath and a muscle ticced in his jaw. "Then they accused me of hitting her by mistake in attempting to kill Keenan." He shook his head in disbelief. "To put a valuable Siren in danger like that – of course, the death of Keenan would be desirable, but still…"

Antonio's hands slowed with his preoccupation with what Malleven was saying. He was a clever man. Very often using less-than-honourable tactics to get what he wanted. He would have to tread extremely carefully from now on. Plus the fact that he was so affronted by all this meant he still very much had his eye on the crown. His heart thumped in his chest at what he and Lily had planned for the next day.

A foolhardy craziness came over him and he pushed Malleven face down on the bed. Pulling off his shirt, he disposed of it over the side. Then worked his tight muscles to disguise the tremor in his hands. There was no going back now. He wanted Malleven to himself. "I had quite a chat with wifey today."

Malleven let out a lazy blast of air in amusement. "Ah, yes … how did you get on?"

"Well, you were right, she isn't keen on me being so close to you."

Malleven smiled and crossed his arms under his face. "She will learn."

Antonio swallowed. "And she told me something else."

Malleven's eyes opened and he was quiet for a beat. "Go on."

"Why didn't you tell me about Cesaré?"

Malleven's enjoyment of the massage stopped immediately and he sat up. He rolled his head to free some tension and sighed deeply. "I only found out myself two days ago."

Antonio understood. The timing would have corresponded perfectly with their passion on the terrace. It explained why Malleven had seemed so heartsick. He'd been bitterly disappointed.

Antonio felt a pang of guilt at being glad, but Malleven would rally quickly; he always did. "What do you propose to do about it?"

"I don't know," Malleven said wearily, rubbing his jaw. "I'm still working out where I go from here. I will commune with my brothers tonight."

Antonio knelt on the floor in front of him and touched his cheek. "Know that *I* am always here for you."

Malleven looked so deeply into his eyes that they shimmered.

"I'll make some arrangements. I have some major sucking up to do with that Siren of yours. I've managed to get her to agree to come sightseeing with us tomorrow."

Malleven looked away as the laughter bubbled up in him. Then sighed as if he'd be the death of him. "Very well, *migliore amico*, as you wish."

The laughter subsided and his eyelids lowered. "Come here," he whispered.

CHAPTER 43

That night, Malleven assembled eight of his closest Magi brothers. Candles were lit and the room made dark. Everyone was given strict instructions not to disturb them.

Then, at precisely the right time, they sat on the floor around a crucible with a flickering yellow flame in its centre. A chalice of gold liquid was passed around and each took a small sip and passed it on to the brother on his right. Then, with closed eyes, they began to chant.

Malleven led the ceremony, opened his eyes and began to raise his hands. The chanting gradually increased in volume and the gold they'd just drunk shimmered in their chests like tiny fireflies. The lights dissolved and new ones appeared in their place until it funnelled out of their hearts in a stream towards the crucible. The shafts of light met in the middle, where it pulsed and glittered, changing the yellow flame to a fierce blue.

At the moment they were joined, the chanting suddenly stopped. The particles separated and circled like the Milky Way above their heads. Orbs and spheres resembling the planets appeared. Spears of light zoomed from one side to the other like shooting stars. It was the cosmos in miniature.

The brothers began their chant again, more quietly this time. Malleven watched the apparition silently, taking it all in to interpret its meaning.

Each of the spheres represented someone significant in his life. He could see himself clearly as the dark star. Lily was a bright moon right next to him. Cesaré, the blue planet, covered in an ocean, was nearby. All were moving, swirling and colliding, happening so rapidly it was hard to take it all in.

Then, slowly from the centre of the blue flame, the earth rose up. It was clearly identified by the shape of the continents and seas. It began a slow, steady orbit of the crucible, joining the other planets, but the bright moon left the dark star and followed. The nearer to it it got, the brighter it shone, until they were almost touching. The moon orbited the Earth as surely as they both revolved around the crucible. They became completely dependent and inseparable in some spellbinding dance.

Malleven's heart was pounding. The mini universe was moving faster and faster. He searched frantically for the blue planet of Cesaré, but it was on the far side of the galaxy, as was his own dark star.

The blue flame became so ferocious that it turned white, and a giant orange molten ball rose. It was the sun. All the planets sought it and circled, and four more moons joined them. The chanting grew louder. The planets and stars moved faster, and Malleven became so hot that he was feverish.

It was clear that the sun was the king and the four moons were Lily's sisters. Everything was building to some huge crescendo. Malleven could no longer stand the heat and the erratic beating of his heart. Suddenly, he could take it no more, dropped his hands, and shouted, "Cease!"

The chanting stopped. The gold particles separated and returned to the body they had sprung from, and the cosmos projection disappeared.

Malleven was left breathing hard and dripping with sweat. Each brother slowly opened his eyes and looked at him for direction. He took a handkerchief from his pocket and dabbed his forehead. He could hardly believe what he'd just seen, but there could be no other interpretation. He couldn't understand how, and he certainly didn't know why, but the gold he worshipped never failed him.

The Siren depicted was meant for the earth. He racked his brains for an alternative meaning, but kept coming back to the same thing. Not only would this Siren – his Siren – join the king and her sisters, but she was meant for a Human. This time, and for the first time in Atlantean history, a Human was a destined mate.

Unsure yet what he should do with this information, he was convinced of one thing: no one must know what he'd just seen.

LILY TRIED her best to tamp down her excitement and nerves to get a decent night's sleep, but it was impossible. Malleven had come to bed really late and hardly noticed her; he was so subdued.

After initial panic that he'd found something out, she gradually calmed herself when he turned away from her and pretended to sleep. It was probably just a problem with his brotherhood or something.

The next day, Antonio was annoyingly chirpy. If it wouldn't have given something away, she would have told him to rein it in a bit. Instead, she stayed very quiet and went along, a bundle of nerves, while they visited the Empire State Building and Bloomingdale's.

The nearer it got to lunchtime, the more anxious she became. She was sure Malleven must be picking up on it, but he'd said very little all morning. Whatever was on his mind last night was still eating away at him.

Eventually, Antonio suggested they break for lunch at a nearby restaurant. Malleven agreed and, with a thumping heart, Lily smiled sweetly and went along.

The three of them sat at a circular table. The Magi brothers seemed to accompany Malleven everywhere he went now. Lily wondered why, but guessed it was to do with them being married and more important. It made her uneasy and struck her as a little ridiculous as they sat at the tables around them, looking so conspicuous in all their black clothes and swarthy good looks.

The restaurant was part of a hotel and looked very expensive. The tables were all covered in white linen, gold cutlery and good glassware. The gold theme continued in the frames around huge mirrors and oil paintings on the walls and the ornate light fittings above each table.

Lily studied Malleven's profile, puzzling over why he seemed so distant today. It almost made her abort her plans. He hadn't given her more than the briefest of glances all day. But as she looked around her, the place seemed to symbolise her relationship with Malleven – all flashy show and no real substance. She wouldn't miss it.

Antonio snapped them out of it by ordering for them all and raising his glass. "To my two favourite people."

Lily frowned, but tipped her head and raised her glass just the same.

"Grazie," Malleven said, clinking his glass with Antonio and smiling a little.

"Yes, it has been a pleasure to finally get to know you a little, Lily," Antonio said.

She felt sure that Antonio was noticing Malleven's lack of interest, too. She just smiled back at him.

"Tell me, my dear, what was it like living in California with a bunch of scruffy surfers? You've told me so little." Malleven said, smiling.

The question was so out of the blue that she dropped the knife she was holding to butter a piece of bread. It took all her concentration not to let her eyes fly to Antonio's. Instead, her face blasted red. *Shit!*

Er ... not much to tell really. You pretty much know it all. Learnt to surf ... She pulled a face as if thinking hard. *You know, that kind of thing.* She knew she was rambling.

"Come now," he said, smiling. "You are a beautiful woman. Was there no one – a particular admirer – one of your Protectors, maybe?"

His eyes were boring into hers, although he was still smiling. Her heart rate was through the roof and she was perspiring. He must know. *How could he know?*

In panic, she looked at her watch.

Malleven looked at her quizzically. "Do you have an urgent engagement?"

No, silly. She smiled awkwardly. *I'm just starving. Where's that food?* Then she swore inwardly at the twenty minutes remaining until the appointed time.

Malleven continued to study her, but his eyelids were low. Suddenly, he reminded her of a predator just biding its time – a Komodo Dragon, following its prey, waiting for it to weaken or slip up. "Are you feeling well, *mio fiore*? You didn't answer my question.'

Despite trying her hardest not to, she glanced at Antonio, who was watching the situation closely. *Have you double-crossed me?* she projected so only he could hear. He picked up his knife and, almost imperceptibly, shook his head.

Lily camouflaged her anger by directing it back to Malleven. "No, there was no one. You know everything. "I …" And she put emphasis on the "I". "… Have no one else," she finished with a glare.

Malleven laughed then, as if he'd merely been toying with her.

MALLEVEN LAUGHED at her veiled scolding. It was gratifying to think she was jealous and wanted him all to herself.

It was quite possible she was telling the truth and hadn't met her Human mate yet. The vision he had seen could have been a glimpse of the future.

He believed her explanation of what happened between her and Cesaré. There definitely was no love between them, and she'd never lied to him up till this point.

It didn't hurt to put a few security measures in place. One would be to limit her contact with Humans, and the other to get his High Priest to look closely at the ancient tomes for any prophecy relating to a wildcard destined mate.

In the meantime, all he could do was keep her sweet and watch her closely.

LILY ATE her first course in silence after that. Not only could she not think of a single thing to say, but every mouthful had to be forced down as if she were eating sawdust. Time had stood still since she'd become convinced Malleven knew something and was fishing for answers.

Something nudged her foot under the table. Her eyes slowly tracked from her plate across to Antonio, who flicked his in the direction they'd come in.

Shit! It's time?

He *gave a small nod.*

Excuse me for a moment, she projected, standing up. *I'm just going to the ladies' room.*

Her heart stopped when Malleven grabbed her wrist and gabbled something in Arabic. One of his brothers at the next table dabbed his mouth on his napkin and stood up. "Hassan will accompany you," Malleven said, releasing her arm.

It was a rough gesture, and she rubbed where his grip had been and shot Antonio a look.

"He won't go into the actual toilet with you," Antonio said, laughing a little too loudly.

After a moment's pause, and realising she could do nothing else, she turned in the direction of the toilets. When she got there, she looked over her shoulder at Hassan. He inclined his head, and she took it that it was as far as he went. She breathed a sigh of relief and went inside.

There were two women next to the basins, so she went into a cubicle and used the loo. When she came out, they were still there. She washed her shaking hands and began to dry them under the dryer on the wall for way too long. Her heart was beating frantically, so hard and so fast she thought Malleven would come and find her for sure. It seemed an age until the women eventually finished chatting and left.

As soon as she was on her own, she went to the end of the line of cubicles to the fire escape and pushed down the bar. She held her breath. As promised, it was not locked or alarmed.

Outside, she could breathe at last. The sunlight made her squint as she quickly scanned the Tarmacked area. Just past the large dumpsters, there was a taxi with an engine running. *That must be it.*

She jogged over to it and the window wound down.

"Lily?" the foreign voice said.

She nodded.

"Get in. We have to hurry."

She jumped in. Soon, they were zipping through the traffic on their way to the airport, where a commercial flight would take her back to California.

When she was at a safe distance, she would project to Cesaré that she'd run away, to warn him. It was very possible he would be the first place Malleven would look. Since being in New York, she'd sensed him closer than ever.

Then she allowed herself to relax back into her seat. She could hardly contain her elation. She'd done it; she'd actually got away.

Her jubilation was short-lived. She knew the moment Malleven was aware she'd gone. Her head began to pound with the sheer force of his mental energy, trying to batter his way into her mind. It almost made her collapse at the airport, and it took every ounce of her strength to lock him out.

She projected a simple, *Leave me alone. I need some time to think,* and clamped down all her mental barriers hard. It was almost impossible to keep him out.

By the time she got into her plane seat, she was holding her head.

"Are you okay, miss?" A stewardess said.

Lily nodded, but the pain was excruciating. She wasn't sure if she was strong enough to hold out, and prayed to god it would ease the further away she got.

Then the ultimate terror hit her: that Malleven would come straight to California and get her.

She wasn't sure what scared her more: getting to California and Lance not being there or, worse still, him not willing to accept her. Or, if he did, Malleven finding her with him and Lance facing his wrath. *Oh no, what have I done?*

CHAPTER 44

It was the spike of excitement that came through the bond that first alerted Malleven. His eyes shot to Antonio, who was busy pouring more wine. "Where is she?" Malleven said.

Antonio frowned. "Give her a break, Malleven. Probably powdering her nose, I should imagine."

Malleven jumped to his feet and almost ran into someone in his haste to get out to the toilets. Hassan was still stationed outside, looking surprised to see him. Malleven halted and glared at him.

"She hasn't come out yet," Hassan said.

Malleven pushed past him and into the toilet, where he smacked open every cubicle with a loud bang as each door bashed against the wall. They were all empty.

He stood with his hands on his hips while he carefully surveyed the room. *There.* The fire exit door. He strode over to it and pushed it wide open. She'd gone.

Wasting no time, he reached out with his mind and found her quickly, but she shut him down. He raced back to the restaurant.

Antonio stood up as he approached. "What's the matter?"

"She's gone ... come!"

They rushed out to the front exit, oblivious to the waiter running after them for payment. One of Malleven's men stopped and put a wad of cash in his hand. The cars were already waiting and they all bundled inside.

Malleven's mind was racing for the most likely place for her to go.

"Do you think she was kidnapped?" Antonio said from next to him.

Malleven looked sideways at him. "No!" He didn't explain what he'd felt, which made her a willing party.

"Then where would she go?"

"She doesn't know anyone." He narrowed his eyes. "Do you have something to do with this?'

Antonio blanched. "What would I have done with her?"

Malleven studied him for a long moment. It was true; Antonio had no designs on the crown. He put the thought on the back burner and took out his phone. "Delissi? Lily has disappeared." It was prudent at this stage for Delissi to assume she'd been kidnapped. The last thing he wanted him to think was that she was in any way unhappy and, possibly, coerced into marriage. "Who else is in the city?"

When the answer came, he almost crushed the phone in his hands.

"Who ... who else is here?" Antonio said.

"Cesaré ... and just a few blocks away."

Cesaré was aware the minute Lily was nearby, but daren't contact her. It was not only safer for her, but Malleven would be after his blood now to eliminate his bond. The war between them was very definitely on.

Unfortunately, the king had returned to Ireland, so he

phoned him and said he was sure Lily was close. "I have felt her for a full twenty-four hours now."

"Shit! I was hoping you'd be able to complete the bond before I notified the duke and family heads of your position, but Malleven will be contacting the Santalinis, if he hasn't already. Be on high alert, Cesaré. There's no telling what he'll do," and the king ended the call.

Cesaré sighed and put away his phone. Now all he could do was wait for the news of his new standing to reach all the families in the Atlantean world. It still hadn't fully sunk in that he was now head of the mighty Florianna. Where only a little while ago he was treated as a disgraced fraud – an embarrassment to his family. Being first bonded to a Siren and acknowledged by the king not only earned him a place for his family on the king's council but also raised him higher than any other prince. To be the king's right hand was a truly exalted position. And for what his family would rejoice, Malleven would kill for.

Gradually, cousins began contacting him to pledge their support for his cause. The process had begun. Instead of feeling elated, he was twitchy, waiting for the inevitable fight to begin.

It wasn't long before members of the Florianna family began to assemble in the king's apartments where he was staying.

Shona was jubilant. "This is it, Ches … you're getting it all back."

He gave her a half-hearted smile. He wasn't home and dry, not by a long shot.

His telephone rang in his pocket – an unknown number. He put it gingerly to his ear. "Who is this?"

"Cesaré, this is the duke. I have just spoken with the king and have been notified of your situation. This is important as a grave incident has occurred."

"What is it … Lily, is she okay?"

There was a pause. "She is not with you?"

"No, she is not. I have not approached her in respect of her recent marriage. She is not with Malleven?"

There was silence again on the line for a beat. "She has disappeared, feared kidnapped. Be vigilant, Cesaré, in case she contacts you. And, be warned, Malleven is on his way to you as we speak."

Cesaré thanked him and ended the call.

"What is it?" Shona asked.

Lance was at her elbow, waiting silently, but his body was wrought with tension for any possible news of Lily. He reminded him of a coiled spring.

"Lily has disappeared. I think she may have run away."

Shona whooped, but Lance looked at the ceiling in anguish and made no attempt to hide his anxiety. "Where will she go … does she know anyone?"

"She came to New York for a couple of months before she came to us," Shona said. "But I don't think she had any real friends exactly."

Cesaré shook his head in frustration. "If only the bond was complete, I could speak to her."

Knowing he only had a few minutes to centre himself, Cesaré asked to be alone. Then he concentrated deeply and sent his emotions outward in a blast. It was a meditation technique learnt years ago. Many Florianna practised the throwback from their Atlasian heritage. He prayed that it would register enough with Lily that she would contact him. Worry and anxiety were the principal emotions he eradiated. Then he waited as the minutes ticked by.

The loud buzzer from the concierge downstairs sounded. His full consciousness came back to the room as his time had run out.

A servant passed him the phone. All he could hear was a

commotion. "Sir … Sir, you can't go up!" the concierge was shouting.

Cesaré called to his cousins. "They are here!"

Thankfully, Dante had left two Santalini Guards with him, who were calling for backup from their New York HQ.

He ran to the kitchen and grabbed knives and anything that could be used as a weapon. It was while he was searching the drawers that her voice filtered through. He held his temples and concentrated as hard as he could on what she was saying.

"Cesaré … Cesaré. I'm not sure if you can hear me, or where you are … but I'm on my way. I'm getting on the plane now. Better not say any more, as Malleven will hear. Bye!"

Lily … Lily! he shouted in his head, but she'd gone. He cursed the one-way bond for the millionth time. *Wait a minute … plane?* His mind raced at where she could be going.

There was only one place he could think of; *San Diego!* She was going home. "Lance!" he shouted.

Lance was busy with Shona and the other men, helping to barricade the large doors to the apartment. Huge bangs were rattling it already as Malleven and his men tried to smash their way inside. Lance looked over and he beckoned him quickly.

"Vincenzo!" he called. A member of his family jogged over to them. "Take Shona, Lance. Vincenzo will take you to my family's plane. Get back to San Diego. I think Lily is heading back there."

The door was being bashed and making progress all the time, pushing the furniture away. The Florianna cousins were holding it in place but were gradually losing ground.

"Open the fucking door, Cesaré!" Malleven shouted.

Cesaré pointed at the window. "Take the fire escape. Go now!"

The furniture was moving, inch by inch.

Lance, Shona and Vincenzo took the escape route and left Cesaré to face his cousin.

CHAPTER 45

*I*reland

Eventually, Tia, Jay, Sean and Cash all trooped into the main hall of Ballygowan Castle. Dante was waiting for them, already pissed off. It changed immediately to concern when he read the serious faces on them all.

Dante opened his arms wide to greet Tia, but his eyes were on Jay. "This had better be fucking good, Jay. I've got a major situation happening in the States and I need to be on it." Then he frowned when he realised Tia hadn't run into his arms as she always did when she saw him. Instead, she walked over slowly, as if treading on broken glass.

He hugged her as soon as she was close enough and did a sweep of her body and her emotions. It was shocking to register pain. He looked over at Jay angrily and was met by his usual unreadable, unrepentant expression. "Make yourselves at home. I'll be back in a minute." He eyed Jay suspiciously and led Tia away in the direction of his subterranean bedchamber. There he could speak to her more freely and get to the bottom of what was wrong.

Dante led her to the shallows lapping under his wrought-iron bed and looked deeply into her eyes. His fingers pushed back her matted hair from her face. In fact, she looked terrible.

Anger was building in him, and he wanted to shake her to tell him, but she leaned into his hand and welcomed the affection as if she was starved of it. Something was very wrong. "Sit down, babe. Please tell me what happened?" And he gestured with his hand to the bed.

"I'd rather stand."

Dante frowned, trying to get a handle on his frustration, to read her. "Can you project to me what happened if it's too hard to tell me?" A lump was forming in his throat as tears started to well up in her eyes.

"No, I can't."

Concern was quickly turning into fear. "You can't?"

She shook her head and swallowed hard.

"Tia, you're scaring me. Now what the fuck happened?" He stepped into her and used his body weight to force her to sit down on the bed.

She yelped and bounced back up as if she'd sat on hot coals.

Shocked, he grabbed the tops of her arms and looked into her face, contorted with pain. "Take off your jeans."

Dante watched, horrified, as she carefully eased her jeans down her legs and stepped out of them. "Turn around!" he ordered. He lifted her t-shirt. The first thing that bothered him was that she had no knickers on, probably because she'd been in the same clothes for days, which brought up its own questions. Then, what he saw shot him through to the marrow, and ignited a slow burn of his temper. There, in every colour of the rainbow, was handprint over handprint, on the perfect rounds of her backside. "Who did this?"

At first, she didn't want to answer.

"Tell me!" he shouted right in her face.

She closed her eyes and whispered one word: "Jay."

Dante immediately let her go and marched across the sand towards the cave entrance.

"Dante. Please. Stop!"

His fuse had blown and his temper was now in charge. He barely heard what she was saying.

"I did something stupid," she was pleading.

"Stay here, Tia, and do as you're told," he said, turning on her fiercely.

Realising that she was half naked, she nodded and let him go.

Dante took a minute to get a grip on himself before he entered the great hall. He wanted to know the whole story before he exploded. Tia was a mess.

Everyone stood up as he walked into the room. They all looked bedraggled and exhausted – well, all except for Jay. He looked pristine and well-groomed with an obvious square plaster stuck on the side of his neck.

He studied them all one by one. They looked uncomfortable under his scrutiny. "Before I speak to Jay, I want to know what happened. Is anyone going to tell me? Tia doesn't lash out for no reason."

Sean and Cash looked at each other awkwardly. Jay looked straight at Dante. The two Santalinis, with them, looked at the floor.

Dante's eyes fell on Cash, who sighed and stepped forward. "I wasn't happy with the way Tia was treated at the Santalini place." He looked around him as if to say he wasn't able to keep quiet any longer.

It was a relief that someone was willing to speak up and he nodded for Cash to continue.

"Yes, sir. Well, after you left, it was as though we were ignored – especially Tia. She wasn't given anything – not even a room of her own."

Dante looked immediately at Jay, who looked at the two Santalinis with him as if it was news to him. They shrugged.

"Then, when we heard there was to be a ceremony for Jay, we were told everyone was expected to attend, but we only had the clothes we stood up in."

Dante was feeling more and more furious with every word.

"Poor Tia didn't even have shoes. But, typical of the gal, she went anyway, figuring it was their problem."

"So none of you were given anything?" Dante asked, making sure he had it all straight.

"Except food, which we got from the kitchen ourselves, nothin', sir. We crept into the ceremony and sat at the back, hoping no one would notice us."

"Then what?"

"Then that asshole, Andreas, starts shouting at her in front of everyone. He came at her. Me and Sean stood up to force him back. Then he starts goading her with abuse and she flew at him. That's when it all blew up."

Dante closed his eyes, letting the catalogue of events sink in. "Thanks, Cash." Then he looked at the floor while he said, "Would you mind giving me a minute alone with Jay? Go to the kitchens. They'll sort you something to eat."

When the Santalinis went to follow, "Not you … wait over there. I'll deal with you in a minute."

He gave Cash and Sean enough time to disappear down the corridor, and the Guards to stand out of earshot. Then he walked over to Jay and stood right in his face. Cool as ever, Jay waited without moving so much as a muscle. Although he was tense, he could feel it.

Dante didn't hit him as he was expecting, but flashed him a mental picture straight to his mind of the black and blue handprints all over Tia's backside.

Jay doubled over, holding his temples as if he'd been

struck. When the mental blast disappeared, he straightened up, obviously shocked. "She cut her wrists ... I just lost it," Jay said, unnerved for the first time in living memory. "She was bleeding ... in a house full of vampires. She'd just attacked Andreas." He shook his head, lost for anything else to say.

Dante stepped forward, nose to nose. "You are a liar, Jay. You flipped out of spite."

Jay was shaking his head, getting angry as well. "No, that wasn't it."

Dante was incensed with rage. To think the lengths he'd gone to save this man's life and he did something like this. He grit his teeth. "I'll tell you this for nothin', if you ever touch her like that again, I will kill you meself." And he meant every word. His mouth was millimetres from Jay's cheek to emphasize the promise.

Jay's composure returned. "So it's okay to fuck her but not hit her?" he said with a blast of mirthless laughter.

"No, Jay ... It's never been okay to do that." Dante turned away from him. "The last few days have clarified a few things."

Jay's eyes followed him as he began to pace slowly in front of him.

"I'm taking Tia to Murrtaine – personally, this time. And, while I'm there, I will insist on them looking into a new medication for you," he said, pausing in front of him. "Tia will be away for a while, and in that time you will marry." Dante stared Jay in the eyes and was gratified at his sudden frown of shock and confusion. "You have standing, she can be royal ..." Then he tilted his head slightly at an angle, indicating the plaster on Jay's neck. "And, by all accounts, you're cosying up to someone already."

Jay went to open his mouth, but was utterly gobsmacked.

Dante continued to look into his face. It would solve a lot. It would appease the families who saw Jay as a threat to the stability of the crown, and would allow him to have Tia with him, which, after this debacle, he was determined to do. "Besides, it might keep you alive a bit longer," he added. And he wasn't talking about assassins. Jay was driving them slowly but surely to that end if he didn't do something.

Satisfied he'd made his point with Jay, he signalled for the two Santalini Guards to come back over. They stood to attention in front of him. "You can return to that piece of shit uncle and tell him I want to see him immediately for his explanation of his treatment of the queen."

"But he is elderly, Your Highness," one of the guards said.

"He wasn't too old to threaten a woman. He can get his fuckin' arse here."

Dante was done, sick to the high teeth of the Santalini family, and he went to walk away.

"There must have been some sort of misunderstanding," the other Guard said.

Dante turned back to him sharply. "No! The only misunderstanding was that your fucking uncle assumed that the queen had passed out of favour because I'd left her in the hands of her Protectors." He finished looking daggers at Jay. The fact he'd been released was just a technicality.

Jay looked away as if his face had been slapped. "Look," he began wearily. "I did what I thought at the time. You're too soft on her. She gets away with murder." He rubbed his hand over his head, messing up his usually impeccable hair. "I had no idea she had all that to deal with."

Dante's eyelids went low with contempt. "No, Jay, you were too busy with your new family instead of bothering with your old one."

CHAPTER 46

Cesaré's heart sank when he saw three men climb in the way he'd just sent Lance, Shona and Vincenzo. All was lost before it had begun. Then he smiled with recognition and relief. Two out of the three were his brothers.

They came straight to him and shook his hand and embraced him.

"We secured the fire escape. Men are stationed at the bottom."

"Vincenzo and the other two?" Cesaré asked.

"Safely away."

Cesaré breathed. "Thank God."

Any further conversation was halted when fighting broke out in the large hallway to the apartment. Before he could join in the fray, his eldest brother held each side of his face in his hands. "Forgive us, Brother, for ever doubting you?"

Cesaré closed his eyes. "It is forgotten."

An ornament used as a missile hit him in the back, bringing them both back to the commotion now surrounding them. "Keep them fighting for as long as you can," Cesaré said quickly.

His brother frowned, but nodded, then spun someone around and hit them squarely in the jaw.

Cesaré just wanted to give Lily enough time for a head start and Lance time to get away on his jet. He scanned the heads of the fighting men to find Malleven. Their eyes found each other at exactly the same time. They both continued to fight, but were doing their best to move towards each other.

It was no easy battle. Both sides had extraordinary abilities and they were forced to give their full attention to their opponents. Objects were being levitated and crashed on people's heads. Sharp pieces were propelled like arrows. Mirrors flew off walls, splintering on impact and creating more deadly weapons.

Eventually, the two of them fought side by side, so they were close enough to link their minds. At that moment, everything disappeared around them. The loud crashes and bangs were relegated to distant echoes, and their psychic selves stood still and regarded each other with hatred.

Where is she? Malleven projected with venom. Gone was any pretence of pleasantness. No one else could hear them— just two men, once like brothers, who now hated each other's guts.

Safe! It didn't hurt to let Malleven believe that he and Lily shared a closer relationship than they really had.

She is my wife, Malleven spat.

She is my chosen mate. Cesaré let a vindictive smile spread across his face.

Malleven flinched with the blow he was not used to receiving from Cesaré. The easy-going boy Malleven once knew had gone for ever. He had seen to that.

One-sided only, Malleven drooled.

Cesaré would not let him rile him and bobbed his head. *A technicality that will soon be remedied.*

Malleven's face contorted with rage. The tentacles of his

mind began to travel quickly into Cesaré's body until they began to wind themselves around his heart and squeezed.

Cesaré gripped his heart with the sudden, excruciating pain and began to choke for breath.

Malleven stood over him as he attempted to stop his heart and kill him. *Farewell, Cousin.*

Cesaré's first instinct was to flail and lash out madly, but he knew the barbs of Malleven's mind would only embed themselves more tightly. Panic almost overwhelmed him as his heart floundered. Malleven was a powerful Florianna prince with many years of training with the Magi. For a Human, or regular Atlantean, it was certain death. Except he was Florianna too, with the power of a Siren.

He managed to centre himself and stop his paralysing terror. Then he sent out a single mental blast so strong that not only did his body heat repel Malleven's mental hold, but it shot Malleven's physical body clear across the room.

Everyone around them felt the energy. When Cesaré became conscious of his surroundings, he realised that everyone had been knocked off their feet.

Malleven stood first and shook his head as if to sharpen his mind again. Then he frowned in confusion. His eyes went wide with understanding and he nodded slowly. "The power of one," he stated simply.

Cesaré nodded back.

Everyone from both sides went quiet and openly stared at them.

Despite the show of Cesaré's new power, Malleven walked right up into his face. "She doesn't love you."

It was a puzzling thing for Malleven to say. Love was not a word he often used. Life for him was always about power, especially over those who cared about him. Then it hit Cesaré like a bolt out of the blue. "You care for her," he said, amazed.

Malleven's face darkened, but he didn't deny it. "Where is she?"

"She is not here."

Malleven turned to one of his men. "Search the place."

One of Cesaré's men went to step forward, but Cesaré held up a hand. "I have nothing to hide."

At that point, it was clear there would be no more fighting today. Santalini Guards began to pour through the battered front doors and step through the debris.

Keenan's brother, Marius, marched over to the two of them. "I have a message from the duke."

Cesaré's heart quickened at what it might be.

"It is to be proclaimed to all Royal Atlanteans that the marriage of Malleven Mancini to the Siren known as Lillian Gale is recognized and should be accepted by all."

Malleven sneered at Cesaré.

"Also," Marius continued, "The Prince Cesaré Florianna has claimed first right of the same said Siren, and recognized by the king as such, and should be accepted by all."

Cesaré began to smile.

Malleven frowned, a little confused at first. Then his face darkened.

"Cesaré Florianna is now head of the Florianna family and, by request of the king, will sit at his right hand on his council."

Malleven's eyes narrowed on him with pure hatred. An emotion he very rarely showed openly. Losing the exalted position in the council was the lowest blow. Cesaré had won the round. Both of them now had the protection of the Santalini family, so neither could openly kill each other without good reason, which didn't include being bonded to the same woman.

"Where has she gone?" Malleven barked furiously. "I demand to know as her husband."

"The king left and went back to Ireland," Cesaré said, allowing Malleven to jump to conclusions. "She projected a farewell to me only moments ago from the plane."

Malleven's anger was clouding his judgment, as he didn't see the deception. He felt him scan him for any hint of a lie, but of course there was none. Both things were true.

A muscle ticced in Malleven's jaw when he moved in closely to Cesaré's face. "I will not rest until you are dead."

Cesaré turned his face into his and didn't miss a beat. "And I you," he whispered.

Malleven pulled away, shouting his orders in Arabic to his men. They picked up their injured and left the apartment.

Cesaré quickly put his phone to his ear and dialled the king.

Dante sat impatiently, steepling his fingers, behind the desk in the study at Ballygowan Castle. "Come in," he said.

Max walked briskly into the room and bowed in front of him.

"It had better be urgent." Dante relayed the recent events in New York as just reported to him by Cesaré and Marius Santalini.

Max kept his eyes down and listened attentively.

He paused when he noticed Max's troubled expression. "What is it, Max?"

"After my last report on Lance McCabe, relating to his ancestry, I wanted to report my findings in the ancient tomes."

Dante became slightly impatient. "Did you hear what I just told you, Max? Can't this wait?"

"I'm afraid not, sir. It could have a huge bearing on what you've just told me?"

"How can this have anything to do with Lance McCabe?" Dante said, becoming a little exasperated with him.

"And Lance has been sent to California to retrieve the Siren, you say?"

"Yes, Cesaré sent him while he still could."

Max shifted uncomfortably. "I fear Cesaré's trust could be misplaced."

"For fuck's sake, Max, what are you saying?"

"That Lance finding her could have grave implications for her, and for you."

*N*ow safely on the Florianna private jet, Lance was anxious to get there. He felt as if he finally had his head together where Lily was concerned. Learning about the king's best friend and his Siren proved Humans mixed in high circles. It was just a bitter twist of fate that they couldn't be together. The new knowledge made him more confident as her Protector. There was no way he could turn his back on her if she needed him. He just had to make sure he didn't weaken and get too close. That was all he had to do. She was married, but from what he'd heard, Malleven didn't deserve her. It was time to admit there wasn't a woman alive who made him feel this way, and he'd do anything to make sure she was safe.

"We'd better warn them at the house," Shona said, interrupting his thoughts. "Make sure someone's home when she gets there."

Lance nodded and put his phone to his ear. "Nathan?"

"Hey, man, how ya doin'?"

"Good man, Lily's on her way there. When you see her, hold on to her till I get there."

"Gotcha … what's going on?"

"I'll explain everything when I see you."

"You should know there's been some suspicious-looking dudes scoping out the place. I'm sure they're watching the house."

"Fuck!" Lance's brain raced. "Look, she's coming in on a commercial flight, go and meet her. Don't take her home, and make sure you're not followed."

"I'm on it." Then Nathan was gone.

Lance was worried as he put his phone away.

"What?" Shona said.

"They're watching the house already."

"Malleven's men?"

Lance shrugged.

Vincenzo had been listening to the whole conversation. "It could be anybody. Agents of one of the royal families, the Guard, or the government, she will never be safe on her own. A Siren is an extremely valuable possession."

Lance sat back and looked up while a ragged breath escaped him. He prayed that he wouldn't get there too late.

LILY CLEARED the airport without incident, but she daren't go to the house. What had at first filled her with excitement now felt foolhardy and dumb.

With just the clothes on her back, she headed to the only place she could think of. There, maybe she could spot him or someone she knew. With just enough money to get to the beach, she found her way to the private surf spot she'd come to think of as their place.

It was just as she remembered it. A jumble of huge rocks with waves crashing in, making pools, smooth platforms and caves. The sandy beach was a couple of hundred metres away to the right. In the lazy late afternoon sunlight, a few surfers remained. She watched them skip across the waves, but they were no one she knew well.

The sea was beautiful this time of day, with the sunlight making the surface glitter like diamonds. The lines of waves queuing up to come in reminded her of all the lessons she'd learnt from Lance about the sea. How ironic that she, an Atlantean, should learn all that from a Human.

A wave of desolation crashed over her. If only he had felt the same as she did about him, life could have been so different. Back then, she'd been so naive. Now she knew that she loved him. It had always been him.

She closed her eyes and remembered every line of his beautiful face. The honesty in those tawny hazel eyes, the scraggy mop of sun-bleached hair that always looked like it needed a good brush, and his smell. She'd never get enough of that. It was just him – no perfumes or colognes, it would never stay on him in the sea.

A tear tracked down her cheek.

"Why are you crying?" a quiet voice said next to her.

WHEN LANCE LANDED, he was partly relieved and partly bewildered when Nathan reported there had been no sign of Lily. If she weren't in California, no one would have a clue where she was. She was extremely vulnerable now that everybody knew about her.

In a snap decision, he did the only thing he would do if it were him returning to SoCal after a long spell away. He'd go straight to the ocean.

Nathan drove him out to the spot he loved to surf. He got out and banged the side of the van in thanks. Then he jogged to the rocky path, down the natural steps, to the flat rocks that led to the sea.

The smell of ozone exhilarated him as it always did –

that, and the sight of the object of his search. He stopped dead.

There she was.

So still.

Searching the horizon like she was hoping for something. It was the expression on her face that spellbound him. The wet spray and wind had brought out her vivid markings, reminding him of a snapshot in time – the very one an artist had captured and inked onto his back.

Her hair was blowing behind her, revealing the longing on her beautiful, striped face. Her arms were bare and striped too. And she was tense, as if she was waiting for something.

Lance realized she was crying. He just had to know why. At the sound of his voice, her head suddenly turned. She was beautiful but so sad. *You're here ...* she projected.

He approached her until he was close enough to touch her face. His finger ran along her cheek and glided through her tears. His heart thundered in his chest as it always did when he was near her. Like he had just come alive. "Why are you here, Lily?"

She shuddered and a sob escaped her. *I came to find you.*

His eyes took in her lovely face – so striking and Alien. She was a married royal and he'd promised to keep her safe. And even though he registered her eyes straying to his mouth over and over, he had to remember that. *Who was he kidding?* What was going on between them was stronger than a mere two people held together by some contract. Despite it being wrong on so many levels, his mouth came closer to hers.

IT WAS JUST the lightest of brushes, but when their lips finally touched, it ignited something in Lily she never thought possible. Electricity shot through every vein and tingled through every nerve pathway. Her arms came up around his neck into the long strands of hair and pulled him to her tightly. She stepped in closer to feel every single part of his lithe, lean surfer's body.

Even though she knew he was holding back, and their mouths remained closed, he swamped her senses. He filled her with something so uniquely him it took her breath away.

Lance groaned and crushed her to him, as if he needed her to be as close as she did. Her heart soared, beating a drum next to his. It was the closest thing to a response she had ever had from him.

The embrace was so sweet and so honest that she could have stood there for ever. It was Lance who pulled away to look into her eyes. "I'm sorry," he said.

What for?

"For not being kinder to you and explaining myself before you went and married him." He looked so sad and soulful.

However, it wasn't the declaration of love she'd hoped for.

Her fingers ran across his lips that still tempted her. *Please don't push me away again, Lance, it's you ... it's always been you.*

He stiffened under her hands and her heart went into her mouth. She couldn't bear it if he rejected her now.

Instead, he snatched her to him, almost crushing her. With his mouth in her hair and a cracked voice, he said, "We need to talk."

Lance took her hand and led her through the rocks to a jagged alcove. The waves had carved it from continual washing in and out and made a pool in its centre. They both sat down and stared into the surging water in silence.

"Malleven ... has he been good to you?" He didn't want to

come crashing in with the fact that he knew he'd nearly killed her a few nights before.

Yes ... no one has ever been as kind to me.

It felt like a slap to his face – a painful reminder she'd gone to Malleven because he'd rejected her. *But kind?* That was very hard to believe. "Why did you need to leave him then? ... Cesaré was really sick a few nights ago because of something Malleven did to you." He raised his eyebrows in a question. "Be honest."

She looked right into his eyes then. *I don't think he meant to hurt me. In a strange way, he did it to try to get closer to me,* she projected, looking back into the pool. *Lance, I tried to forget ... everything here, but in the end, when I found out about his lover, I needed to get away. I needed to think things through away from him.*

Lanced nodded. *A lover ... that more fit the profile.* Then he looked into the pool, straight into three pairs of black soulless eyes.

CHAPTER 48

"What the fuck?" Lance shouted, springing to his feet and dragging Lily with him.

There, submerged in the water, and looking straight up at them, were three huge men – except they weren't, they were something else. They had white blond hair, their skin was grey and covered in stripes; except theirs were the thickest, darkest stripes he'd ever seen. Even their faces looked tribal.

Lily was clinging to him, as fixated on them as he was. They must be Atlantean, but they looked so Alien. There was only one thing they could be.

"I've never seen one, but I think they're Murrs." He gripped Lily more tightly as they breached the water and began to crawl out.

Don't be afraid, a male voice said in his head.

"Did you hear that?" Lance said, slowly backing up with her.

Yes, she said, nodding manically.

You know what we are. We are Murrs. We mean you no harm, the more senior one said, straightening up to his huge height.

Lance and Lily were now flat against the rock wall and there was nowhere else for them to go. They were totally hidden and cut off. "What do you want?" Lance said, with his hand up in front of him. He'd heard the legends of the Murrs. They were a royal family named after the city of Murrtaine where they lived. He hadn't really believed they existed until today.

All three of them now stood out of the water and were incredibly tall – more than six and a half feet. Their black eyes were unblinking and large in their striped faces and they were naked apart from a shimmering material covering them from the waist to their knees and reminded him of scales. Their tribal-like markings went the full length of their bodies like an intricate tattoo. "What do you want?" Lance said again, holding Lily to him more tightly.

The leader stepped forward, but he looked awkward, as if he couldn't move that well. Lance weighed up his options to run.

We mean you no harm, he repeated, as if he'd read his thoughts. His mouth didn't move. Lance touched his forehead. They were using telepathy, just like Lily. It dawned on him then how like them she was.

My name is Vionne. Prince of Murrtaine. And these are my brothers, Dax and Caan. His hand gestured slowly to the others on either side of him. *We are messengers of the king, sent to bring Lily safely back to Ireland.*

Lance frowned. He didn't want to let go of her that easy. There was no proof they were who they said they were. They could be spinning him a line.

It is not safe here. The area is swarming with government agents. Several factions have been watching your house for weeks.

Shit. Lance wasn't sure what to do. Up until then, all he'd worried about was Malleven.

At that moment, a picture of the king flashed in his head. *It's okay, Lance ... You can trust them.* Then the image went as quickly as it came.

Lance winced and shook his head. *What the fuck?*

I projected to you a memory the king intended for you to see, Vionne explained.

Suddenly, life was even more complicated for Lily than he thought. He knew they spoke the truth about the house being watched, as Nathan had warned him. Any one of those could be an even worse option than Malleven. *But could he trust these people?*

I won't go anywhere without Lance, Lily projected, stepping forward out of the protection of his body.

I am sorry, but the journey would kill him, and Vionne indicated the water behind him. Then some kind of mental exchange went on between him and his brother, Dax. He nodded. *Do you have somewhere safe to go until dark?*

Lance thought quickly. It had to be close to there. "A friend of mine has a beach hut not too far up the coast from here." He explained where it was, and Vionne nodded.

Very well, we will come for Lily at midnight when we can bring our marine craft closer to shore. Then he pointed at Lance. *We are taking her to safety. Please do not put her in danger by taking her anywhere else.*

What about Lance? Lily projected.

He can meet you there. The king is expecting him.

Lance turned over the options. He hadn't thought beyond finding her. Now it seemed there wasn't much choice. The house was no longer safe.

He took out his phone to try Cesaré, but there was no signal because of the rocks.

You can trust us, Vionne said in a calm, authoritative voice.

Lance looked down into Lily's eyes and she gave him a

small nod. "Okay," he said eventually, still not sure he was doing the right thing. "Is there any news of Cesaré?"

He has fought ... with your husband, Vionne said, letting his eyes fall on Lily.

Oh no ... are they both okay?

Vionne nodded once. *You will see* Cesaré *in Ireland.*

Lance saw how desolate Lily looked. She was blaming herself for the whole thing. "It's not your fault," he whispered. He turned his attention back to the three Murrs. "Okay ... midnight." He held his arm around her tightly and led her past them and out of the cave.

He took one last look over his shoulder at the three strange men who watched them walk away. Then led her along the rocky coastline and phoned Nathan as soon as he had a signal. He spoke cryptically to avoid giving away their location and asked him to bring them food without being followed.

IRELAND

Dante showered Tia with attention over the next couple of days, making sure she healed and spent time with JJ.

Andreas made the journey and presented himself, and Dante made sure Sebastian and Alfonzo were there in an official capacity to put the fear of God up him.

He threatened to remove the 'Honourable' prefix from his family's title and informed him that the queen no longer trusted the Santalinis as her Guards.

This was not only a major headache for him, but a huge insult. They only held their privileged position because of their connection with the crown and the Bonaci, who had overseen the Atlanteans for the last five hundred years.

Dante hammered home what a big mistake it had been to

fuck with the woman of his heart. Whether she was with him or not, it would always be her position.

When the necessary reprimands were out of the way, Dante made preparations for Tia to leave for Murrtaine.

The night before she was due to go, the shit had hit the fan in New York. Cesaré had arrived, and the Murrs had been sent to bring her sister Lily to Ireland. The chance to spend some time with her in Murrtaine soon evaporated, and he felt the heavy burden of being king.

Dante went to his bedchamber and found Tia in his bed, now looking rejuvenated and beautiful. He looked down at her gorgeous face with regret.

"What's with the look?" she said.

"It's our last night."

"I know … you can't help it." She reached out for his hand. "I'm going to miss you. These last couple of days have been … amazing."

He sat down on the edge of the bed and produced a small box from his pocket.

"What's that?" she asked.

He smiled. "Well, when we got married, it was all a bit rushed, and I wasn't exactly prepared.

Tia giggled.

Dante dropped down off the edge of the bed onto one knee.

"Dante! What are you doing?" she said, grabbing her mouth in shock.

"Tia Thingomybob Whatshername Bonaci, will you take me properly this time, as your husband, for ever, until we join the ether together?"

She laughed. He could never remember her full name.

Then he opened the box to reveal the most exquisite antique ring. It looked like a pearl that was so perfect it glowed in its gold setting.

His fingers shook as he took it out of the box and slid it gently onto her ring finger. She wore no other rings and it looked made for her delicate hand.

Tia held it out to see how it looked and gasped. "Dante, it's so beautiful."

"Don't leave me hangin', babe."

Laughing, she flung her arms around his neck and kissed him over and over. "Yes … yes … I will, for ever."

He pulled her down onto the sand with him and kissed her as softly and as lovingly as if they'd just met. It made the pair of them hot and breathless. He broke away first and pushed a stray lock of hair out of her eye. "It's an extremely rare stone from Atlas. It was in my mother's private letters. My real father gave it to her as a love token before she married Dubonnetti. There is no other gem like it in the whole world." His eyes bore into hers with meaning. "Like you."

Her eyes filled with tears. "Aren't we meant to swap rings? What can I give you?"

"I don't need a ring." He held up his hand with the purple divining ring. This reminds me of you every day of my life. All I need is for you to come into the water with me, and seal it like we did the first time."

She said nothing further, pulled her t-shirt straight over her head, and stood in front of him completely naked.

Tia laughed when he grinned and stripped in seconds. Then he held out his hand and led her to the water's edge.

This was her gift to him, so she let him determine what he wanted. He headed for the deep water.

They both sank beneath the surface, and she let the water into her lungs quickly. Intrigued, she waited for him to do the same, but he surprised her by simply beckoning her to him with his arms. Then she got it. He wanted her to breathe for him just as they did on their wedding day.

She swam right to him and locked lips with him immediately. Wrapping her legs behind his hips, she happily breathed herself into him. He did the same right back and, after the euphoria passed, he trod water as he watched her—such a beautiful sight, decorated entirely in his Atlantean stripes.

He seemed to be waiting for something. *What is it you want, Dante?* she projected.

I want us to have another child.

She stilled in shock. It was the last thing she expected him to say. She swam over to him slowly and wrapped herself around him again. This man never failed to amaze her. A huge lump had appeared in her throat with a wave of emotion. *Let's merge as we make love. I can think of no better way to make a baby.* She began a trail of kisses down his neck to his chest, skimming her hands over his muscles taut with anticipation.

Yes, he said simply, and pushed her beneath him.

They went right down to the sandy bottom of the lagoon and he kissed her passionately, igniting the fire between them. They were so in tune now that arousal was instinctual and immediate. Just the feel of him close, needing her like this did it totally for her. After cupping her heat between her legs, caressing her desire-swollen folds, he placed himself and thrust straight into her. Beginning a torturous pace while her hands bit into the muscled flesh of his shoulders.

Their mouths quickly found each other and formed the seal needed to merge. They began to breathe for each other, over and over in a continuous loop. It required extreme focus to cope with the overpowering ecstasy, but it was necessary to take them to the level for what they had planned. It was a tall order not to dissolve too quickly.

When, eventually, they found their rhythm, Dante walked confidently into her mind's eye, where she was waiting for him on the usual leopard-print bed. Both were smothered in stripes and completely naked as their psychic selves. She pulled him down, straddling and dominating him on the bed. Without preamble, she put her lips over his and began to breathe into him, mirroring what they were doing in their physical bodies. Welcoming and holding her to him, he did the same.

The feeling was indescribable. Doubling in strength, it quickly grew exponentially, sending them soaring higher than they'd ever been. The white light engulfed them, warm and all-consuming. Their bodies blended into each other and their senses fused into one. Until they reached the point where they felt each other's urges, pleasures and innermost thoughts – Tia only just managing to safeguard the tiny corner of her mind that contained her private memories of Jay. It was the one thing she kept for herself.

When Dante climaxed, and his seed, with his life's spirit, entered her, it was astounding on both a physical and psychic level. They both instinctively knew that she had conceived, and the exact moment it happened. Neither of them had any doubt. It was awe-inspiring and terrifying. The power and togetherness it brought with it was over-whelming.

It took a long while for them to float in the bliss that followed. It resembled floating down to earth on a feather, going gently this way and that. Drifting back to the psychic room, where he kissed her a slow, fond farewell, then back to their physical bodies, where they lay tangled together on the lagoon floor.

Both felt serene and contented. Love didn't cover how they now felt; there simply were no words.

What's the ether? she asked eventually.

He studied her face for a moment, not mocking, just surprised. Then he kissed her delicately on her lips. *It's the cosmos – never-ending space, I suppose you could call it. It's the place where all life came.*

And we'd go there together?

Yes. We'd not survive without the other.

Good, she said with a lump in her throat.

Don't you know yet, Tia, there is nothing I wouldn't do to keep you?

She did. Where feelings were concerned, there were no secrets between them. It was his deepest truth.

CHAPTER 49

*S*outhern California

The beach hut Lance had mentioned was really just that; it was literally a shack that stored surfing equipment.

Lily laughed. *You really know how to show a girl a good time.*

"Hey!" he said, pulling her close. "I'm not a prince."

She hitched a breath. *I didn't mean ...*

"Shh!" he said, smiling. "No one will think of looking for you here. I'll build a fire; get us some food ... it'll be like we're camping."

She looked around and wondered how exactly he would do that. *I've never been camping.* Living rough on the streets of London didn't exactly count.

"Well, you don't know what you're missing." He shoved a lump of driftwood into her arms. "Come on." Then he set about collecting any dry combustible material he could find on the beach.

It was almost dark when Lance lit the fire with the help of some flammable liquid and matches he found in the shed.

Then he disappeared for no more than a few minutes and returned with a blanket, beers, and a perfect picnic.

Where did you get all this? There weren't any shops that she could see.

He laughed. "Nathan … he delivered it close to the road up there. There's nowhere close. That's what makes it such a great place to hide out."

She nodded and smiled, sat down on the blanket and took a bite out of a sandwich as big as her arm. Everything was tumbling out of the sides. Lance watched her, smiling. *What? I'm starving*, she projected, chewing a huge mouthful.

He laughed and then took a bite of his own.

They ate in silence after that. It felt awkward. There was so much to say, so much had happened, she didn't know where to start.

When they'd finished, Lance cleared away and sat next to her on the blanket. It was a perfect night, and they both stared out at the sea. The fire made a cosy glow around them, and the moon cut a shimmering path into the water.

The silence was heavy between them. Lily wasn't sure what to do now she'd found him, and she felt sure Lance felt the same. The familiar attraction was still there. It crackled like electricity between them. *When I leave with the Murrs, what will you do? I mean … will you come to Ireland,* she asked eventually.

Lance didn't look at her, but continued to look out to sea. "Do you want me to?"

Her heart beat hard against her chest. She'd had so many chances to tell him how she felt and chickened out every time. It was time to let go of any pretence or pride before her chance went for ever. She swallowed hard.

Lance looked at her when she took so long to answer. Then frowned and let out a long sigh.

I need to tell you something, Lance, something I should have said a long time ago, but I was too chicken. I don't think I under-stood it myself at the time.

When she turned to face him, he was leaning back on his arms, waiting for her to continue, his eyes on hers.

Lily swallowed hard. *Look, I know I'm married, and I do care about Malleven, I really do, but I know something for sure now that I didn't before.* She shifted uncomfortably and let out a ragged breath. *I know now,* she repeated. *That I'm in love with you.*

LILY HAD FINALLY TOLD HIM. She'd laid herself wide open for the first time in her life and he continued to stare at her. In fact, he looked stunned as if she'd hit him.

Oh God, he didn't feel the same way. Blurting it out like that was a mistake. It was like she'd learnt nothing from their time together. If her memory served her right, he'd always acted like this. *Sorry, I shouldn't have said anything.* She swallowed down the lump in her throat and sat back and faced the sea again. *It was my last chance.* Her face blasted red and humiliation washed over her in a tsunami.

When he slowly stood up, Lily assumed he would walk off. *Fuck! He was embarrassed.*

"Lily," he said quietly.

When she looked up at him, he was reaching down to her with his hand. His eyes were moist and soulful in the orange glow of the fire.

"Wanna get liquid with me?"

Her stomach flipped. That accent, and the way he said something so simple and surfy, was so amazingly sexy. She'd never wanted to get so liquid in her life. Her hand nestled in his and he pulled her up.

They stripped like a flash down to their underwear. Lance

held up a finger for her to wait, then disappeared into the shack and came back with a couple of boards.

The waves are small, she projected, unsure about surfing in the dark.

"They're always small here … great place for the groms." He passed her a board. "There's enough for us to play."

Again, he gave her that smouldering look that sent her butterflies haywire. Her eyes raked over his perfect, tanned physique. His wide surfer's shoulders, ribbed torso that tapered into narrow hips that just about held up his shorts, made her completely melt. No one ever did this much to her without so much as a touch.

Well, if it's good enough for kids … she thought, dragging her eyes up to his from his hot body. *Come on then!* And she ran laughing towards the sea.

His wonderful laughter came from behind her.

There followed the best couple of hours of her life. They played in the little waves over and over, paddling out and riding them in. Lance showed off his talented aerial tricks and laughed when she tried them and took tumble after tumble.

Eventually, they flopped down in the shallow water together. Lily's pulse jacked at the familiar warm tingle when his hand circled around and held hers. Her heart thundered and she lay stiffly while they looked up at the sky. Gradually, she relaxed. The evening would end soon and it was sobering.

"I felt it too," he said quietly.

She turned her head sideways to look at him.

"The pull between us, I mean." He continued to gaze up at the sky, avoiding eye contact.

She said nothing, holding her breath, afraid he'd clam up now that he was finally talking.

"I was too dumb or scared to do anything about it." He

turned on his side, leaned up on an elbow, and traced a finger down her cheek.

His hand was so cold and she realized he was shivering. They seemed to arrive at the same thought at the same time.

"I'm Human in an Atlantean world," he said. "You're a princess. It was all so hopeless."

It still seemed odd to be thought of as royal. She understood completely, but refused to accept that there was no hope. *Do you still feel that?*

He pulled her closer to him and neatly rolled on top of her. The heat she radiated at his skin contact was enough for the two of them.

"You're so warm," he smiled, as a wave lapped over them.

Do you still think it's hopeless? She repeated, staring up into his beautiful, intense eyes and running her hands gently over the smooth, honey skin of his back.

"I've learnt a lot while you were away … I'm not the only Human … and I got to thinking about fate, and all that stuff."

Instinctively, her hand traced over the tattoo on his back.

He nodded, understanding without her saying a word. "There's a lot about me you don't know, Lily."

He looked pained. "There's something I've never told you."

Lily waited with her heart beating so frantically that he must feel it.

"I had a clear vision of you before we'd ever met."

Her eyes couldn't help straying to his lips. It felt like she already knew that. *Maybe we … maybe this was meant to happen?* Totally distracted, she touched his lips with her finger, which he kissed heartbreakingly softly.

Pain was still etched on his face as if he battled with something inside him. But his lips slowly came down to hers anyway, and it was all she cared about. It was as if his soft kiss ignited sensations so alive, so acute, that she'd never felt anything like it. A drugging taste that inflamed a million little lights so brightly, it stole her breath away.

Every time they'd accidentally come into close contact from the moment they'd met, she'd had a glimpse of this – as if they were both somehow electrically charged. This superseded everything that came before.

When his tongue entered her mouth for the first time, swamping her senses, the already high voltage sparked and almost consumed her. It was a white heat only he could dowse, and she needed him to so badly.

A brief image of Malleven came to mind. He was a beautiful man and a skilled lover, but this was something on a whole other level. It defied explanation, so she didn't over-think it.

Lily rolled with him, pushing him beneath her in the surf. The cold no longer had an effect on him, beautiful in the bubbling water surrounding him. She moved away his sexy strands of hair from his honey-tanned face and kissed him again, fiercely and deeply this time. Any restraint she felt at the beginning was now gone. He accepted and received the kiss reserved just for him—one she'd never given another soul.

The dull weight of numbness she felt during sex lifted in her heart. This was different. It felt perfect and right. Every fervent kiss, every gentle touch of his hands, massaging her back and moving down her body, had a direct link to the centre of her, and it ran molten. *Please, Lance.*

He stilled and studied her for a moment, as if deciding something. Then he blinked slowly and pushed her over onto her back.

Lance gazed down into her beautiful stripy face, so savage, and yet her eyes were pleading. The most unusual shade of blue he'd ever seen. They were the colour of deep ocean water. He pushed the sexy wayward wet curls from her face, and his mind still warred with what was the sensible thing to do, and what he wanted – what he needed. This thing between them – whatever it was – was soul deep. He couldn't ignore it.

The fact that she was married seemed an irrelevant issue. She'd run away to find *him*. And even though she'd have to go back, and knowing it was emotional suicide, there wasn't a damn thing he could do about it. The vision, the blood, and hurting her was the furthest thing from his mind at that moment. It seemed ridiculous. He'd only be putting off the inevitable.

Before he knew what was happening, his hand reached behind her back, unclipped her bra and removed it. He took a moment, stroking his eyes down her perfectly formed body to appreciate her skin. The stripes went everywhere, and intrigued and delighted him. The beautiful, pert roundness of her small breasts enticed him, and he lowered his head to take the pebble of her nipple into his mouth. Swirling his tongue, gently teasing with his teeth, the salt of the ocean and something so inherently her overwhelmed his senses.

Lily groaned in his head every time he played with his tongue and lavished the hard peak with attention. *Please, Lance*, she repeated, now writhing underneath him. Her legs had opened, bent, and gripped him on either side of his thighs like a vice. She wasn't letting him go anywhere. *Fuck!* He rested his forehead against her collarbone to gather himself and watch as his cock now nudged impatiently against the softest part of her. His shorts and her panties were now the only barrier.

God, he was so turned on. His body had already aligned itself and started to move with her with a mind of its own. He looked around them, conscious of how open it was, but there was no one else around. "What, right here?" he said, breathless, and lowered his head to nibble down her neck, pulsing under his lips, while his pelvis pushed hard against her core.

She nodded. *Yes ... I need the water, or I'll overheat.*

He rested on his hands to gaze down at her beautiful, suddenly self-conscious face, and it really hit him then: what she was and what he was doing. *Of course she needed the water.* It blew his mind. His hand smoothed its way down her writhing, hot skin and pulled her panties out of the way. Lily was way ahead of him and managed to get her toes into the waistband of his shorts and pushed them down. He grinned into a kiss at the cheeky manoeuvre. "Easy, Tiger."

Lily giggled, and he realized it was the first time he'd truly heard her laugh.

Sombre suddenly and, realising all barriers were gone, his hand dipped beneath the waistband of her panties and made her jump. It glided through her silk and found the hard nub and felt her tighten. He placed himself where he needed to be and teased her clitoris, smoothing through her slick wetness. Then his hardness nestled where he'd always wanted to be and the need to tease suddenly dissolved. He gasped. *This was actually happening.* It was now completely out of his control.

As if she sensed it too, Lily stilled and waited for him to move. Then, as if to give him the confidence he needed, she held the sides of his face and brought his mouth to hers, moving her softness up against him. And he was so there, so powerless, nudging and rotating his hips, restrained and holding back. Until her nails scored down his back and lust got a hold on him and he plunged deeply on a gasp.

Their mouths found each other again, except this time it was frantic with no restraint. The salt in their mouths and the water washing all over them drove him on. He held her leg over his hip and pistonned madly into her over and over, as if he'd die if he stopped. There were moments when they were completely submerged and he wasn't sure when he last breathed.

His mouth left hers and travelled down the column of her neck, his face under water where he could bite and mark the soft part of her shoulder. Still, he kept up his punishing rhythm. He couldn't stop or slow down even if he wanted to – like a programme that had to finish its cycle.

Even when her nails scored into his back again and again, which he usually hated, he welcomed it like a brand. Groaning, he buried himself deeper still.

She'd found her rhythm with him, and they moved together. Her pelvis was coming up and rotating with his, her innermost muscles gripping him. He leaned up on his arms to get a look at her face in ecstasy. The only place he'd seen anything as sexy as this was in his dreams, and it was her – always her. But it was a fleeting memory – a poor imitation. This undoubtedly was the real thing. Not even his inner voice of doom could dissuade him from this moment that seemed to make sense more than anything else in his life.

Her face, framed by the bubbling water, created a picture of pleasure and agony. Her eyes changed in front of him into huge dark disks, the pupils into the deep ocean lagoons he loved to swim in. She was literally a creature from a whole other world. Everything then became clear, and it wasn't that she was a different species; it was that it was the first time he'd made love – truly, mad, love.

In that moment, she was his – even if it was just for a short while.

His mood suddenly became solemn and he slowed his hips to take down the pace a notch. Aware that their time was running out, he wanted to prolong this feeling for as long as possible. Staring into those fathomless eyes, he wanted to commit everything about her to memory.

"I love you," came out all on its own. "I shouldn't, but I do." *Why fight the truth.*

Her eyes went wide and softened with understanding. He captured her mouth, kissed her hard, and renewed his thrusts. Holding her tight to him, it became imperative to push them on, to really feel her, savouring every nerve-tingling moment, until she had to leave him.

LILY'S whole life suddenly made sense – even all the shit and hard times. Because without all that, she wouldn't have arrived at this point in time, with the man she felt like this about. How could anyone regret something that brought her to this indescribable joy?

When she felt the heavy weight loom up in her chest, she knew exactly what it meant. But she'd already bound two men to her. Cesaré was an accident, but without that bond, she'd never have been able to escape. And Malleven. He was still a living, breathing thing in her life, still trying to reach out to her, even now. His affection reminded her of a savage, demanding beast.

She sighed into the raw pleasure of Lance – his smooth, muscled shoulder moving tantalisingly close to her mouth, muscles cording under her hands. No less masculine, but this was love, and the one that ran deep. It felt as though a part of him already flowed through her veins. And with every inti-mate touch, and even the way his body moved so beautifully with hers, it longed to find its way back to him like an eternal cycle. Sex with Malleven was like mating a wolf; with Lance, they moved like they were dancing.

With this comparison, the need rose higher in her chest. It had to come out and she wanted it so badly. She rolled with Lance until he was on his back and she straddled him like she would her board. His eyes were half closed with yearning, waiting for her to make her move. Her inner muscles clenched around him and her abdomen coiled in readiness.

Lily moved forward, taking his hands from her thighs to either side of his head. Part of her still battled with what she was about to do.

Lance sensed her distraction and undulated his hips to bring her mind back to him.

"What is it?" he said, pausing.

The weight in her chest was so close to coming out, it was painful. She grimaced with pain. *I'm sorry, Lance, I have to stop, otherwise I'm going to go all Alien on you. I might hurt you.* But her hands refused to move and she still had his arms pinned.

He circled his hips underneath her. "Are you talking about the bond?"

She leaned up a little in surprise. *You know about the bond?*

"I've learnt a lot in the last few weeks." He undulated his hips under her again and looked preoccupied with her mouth.

The thought of it didn't appear to scare him – if anything, it seemed to turn him on. His hard cock twitched inside her.

Once it's made, I don't think it can ever be broken. Her face creased in pain. Time was running out.

LANCE WAS on the brink already, gazing up at this outrageously sexy, vividly striped woman, moving erotically on top of him. He guessed he felt all in with her emotionally anyway, whatever happened next. He wouldn't have searched halfway around the world for her otherwise. "You're asking me … if I mind being bound to you for keeps?" he said breathily. It was a huge deal.

She gasped. *That's it … for ever.* She let go of his hands and threw her head back in her fight to contain it.

That did it. He gripped her hips tightly and ground her into him to snap her reserve. "Go, babe … just do it," he whispered. "We're tied up anyway." And that was how he felt. There wasn't another woman alive he could be into as much as this.

Her face creased in pain and she lowered her mouth hesitantly and came close to his. His chest hammered like a drum and he parted his lips for her.

At first, it felt like hot steam. It tingled over his tongue, travelled down through his oesophagus, and wrapped itself around his heart like a warm glow. *It wasn't so bad?* Then, no sooner than he had the thought, the heat spread outwards like a shockwave, and the true explosion followed. It mushroomed out through every neural pathway, vein and pleasure receptor in his body.

He lost all sense of time. Of where or who he was. Spasms racked and bowed his body. All he was aware of were the extreme sensations flowing through him one after another. It was a barrage of thoughts, pictures, concepts and deep emotions and all of them Lily's. It was a total download of the inner *her* in superfast time.

When his mind finally became responsive again, he realized that Lily still held him fast behind his neck and shoulders to keep him clasped to her mouth. She was still breathing into him, and he was still soaring; he was just controlling the buzz. It seemed to go on so long; he wondered why neither of them needed to breathe air.

At last, she released him. He expected the feelings to subside, but that was when the orgasm hit him. It consumed him like a hungry fire sweeping through a dried-up forest. His heart beat so fast he thought he'd burst an artery if it went on any longer. He wished he could say she was right there with him, but, in all honesty, he had no clue. He only realized she'd come when she flopped her weight down, exhausted, on top of him and his head felt like it was orbited by stars on his slow descent back to earth.

He didn't move. He couldn't – not for ages. They both lay breathing like they'd just run for their lives – Lily flaked out right on top of him as boneless as he was. He could still feel the delicate tremor of her internal muscles every now and then. He remained immobile as his body continued to shudder for several minutes.

Lance eventually managed to open his eyes into thin slits when he felt Lily lean up. He smiled to see her worried expression. "'tsup?" he said.

She breathed with relief and hugged him to her.

LILY WAS SO relieved that Lance seemed okay. She wasn't sure if the Human body was even able to tolerate her essence in the way an Atlantean could. He was obviously stronger than she thought. In reality, the urge to bind him to her had been so strong that she couldn't help herself.

When at last his breathing returned to normal, he looked up at her. "What did you do to me?" But there was amusement in his very bloodshot eyes.

She grinned. *Do you feel okay?*

He nodded, taking in her whole face as if for the first time. "I'm not cold any more."

As if reminded, her eyes went to the fire that was almost out. She clambered off him and pulled him up with her to stand – although a bit wobbly at first.

"Come on, surfer girl, we'll build up the fire if my legs will work … Better find some of your clothes before the Murr dudes come back."

He led her out of the water and she couldn't stop smiling as he staggered and tripped. They were soon sitting with the blanket wrapped around them in front of a much livelier fire.

Lance still looked red and flushed. *I hope you are okay. It was selfish of me to do that to you.*

He squeezed her to him and leaned his head into hers. "Don't regret it." He laughed. "It was the best sex I ever had."

She grinned and nudged him playfully with her shoulder.

He got more serious. "You know I can feel everything about you now. It's awesome." He was looking at her as if he still couldn't believe it.

Her heart sank a little, and she gave him a small, regretful smile. *You have to be more careful of Malleven now, Lance. If you're bound to me, I think he'll know, and he may even be able to get to you mentally.*

He hugged her to him again. "Don't worry about me, I'll be fine. I'll contact Cesaré and make sure we're both in Ireland."

Relief flooded her. *You will?* Suddenly, she felt like crying. A mixture of tiredness and raw emotion, she guessed. It had taken her all this time to get close to Lance and now she was going to have to leave him to go into the unknown again.

He kissed her lovingly on the lips, as if he knew. "Don't be sad. I didn't get you stamped on my back for nothing," he said, with a grin.

Her amazement at his accurate reading of her feelings gave way to laughter. Even though it was silent, he'd hear it in his head. But he was right. Somehow, they were meant to be together; she just knew it.

She hitched a breath when she caught sight of the three shapes coming slowly towards them out of the water.

Lance followed her line of vision. "I guess your ride's

here," he said quietly and pulled her slowly up with him to stand.

Suddenly, she felt terrified. She didn't know these people and they were so strange and alien-looking.

She'd gripped onto Lance without realising. His arms came around her to steady her and his mouth was next to her ear. "It's okay. It's just safer this way. And I'll meet you in Ireland, I promise."

When she looked up into his eyes and saw that he meant it, she felt so grounded and safe. If only she could have had this before she'd met Malleven. Running to Ireland wasn't going to alter that. She kissed him softly.

It is time, Vionne said softly. *We have a small vessel out in the deeper water. It's just a short swim.*

Lily nodded but still clung to Lance.

"It's okay," he said again and kissed the top of her head.

The time had come to let him go. She reluctantly released him and walked towards the Murrs.

CHAPTER 50

Lance watched the four of them wade out until they dove down and disappeared. He was left with mixed feelings of elation and trepidation. One thing he was now certain of: there was no going back.

He rummaged through his things, found his phone, and tapped in Cesaré's number.

"Lance?"

"Yeah."

"Lily's okay?"

"Yeah, she just left … Ches?" He wasn't sure exactly how to say it, but Cesaré needed to know. "Lily and me …"

"You don't have to spell it out, Lance."

"You know?"

Cesaré laughed. "I felt something; it was only a matter of time."

Lance smiled, as it seemed so obvious to everyone else but him.

"But listen, Lance. Malleven has a two-way bond with Lily, which means he will definitely know. And it means that through Lily, he can gain access to your mind. Be careful."

It was a sobering thought. Malleven wasn't going to take it well, him muscling in on his girl. "What now?"

"Go back to the airport and head for Ireland. I'm on my way there now. We'll talk more when I see you."

"You beat him?" Lance said, smiling.

"I won the round, shall we say. He'll come at us now with everything he's got."

AFTER LILY ESCAPED, Antonio had slipped back to Malleven's apartment, a bag of nerves. Malleven was spitting blood and he didn't want to be in range when he unleashed his temper. Thankfully, Malleven was with several members of his brotherhood and he'd just be in the way.

He paced up and down, running over and over what he would say. Now that their plan was successful, he realized the folly of it. Jealousy had clouded his judgment. How stupid to think he could pull the wool over Malleven's eyes. As soon as he'd finished with Cesaré, he would come at him.

For a moment, he thought of running. *But where would he go?*

The noise of the large apartment doors opening and voices made that option impossible. His heart plummeted. He shakily poured himself a whiskey, sat down and tried to look relaxed.

"You're here," Malleven said. "Get me a drink."

Antonio was shocked at how ruffled Malleven looked. He poured the drink, walked over and put it straight into Malleven's hands. He looked worn-out and dishevelled. A state few people ever saw.

Malleven shook his head as if with disgust and knocked back his drink in one. Then held out his glass for another.

Antonio refilled it. "What happened?"

"I went to Cesaré. She's gone to Ireland."

"Can't you contact her?" Antonio said, pointing at his own temple.

Malleven shook his head. "She shuts me out."

"I don't understand it," Antonio said, flopping down into a chair. "I thought the two of you were lovebirds."

Malleven stilled and narrowed his eyes.

Antonio tried to hide his discomfort as Malleven scrutinized him and his mind whirred.

"She found out about you."

Antonio shifted in his seat moodily. "She seemed fine yesterday."

Malleven tilted his head on an angle. "She couldn't have done this on her own." Then he walked slowly over to where Antonio was sitting until he loomed over him.

Antonio's heart was thumping with fear. "Cesaré must have helped her … or the king."

Malleven was really studying him now. He hoped to God he wasn't picking up on his increased heart rate and sweat.

"She didn't know they were here. How did you know?"

Antonio sidestepped the question. "Can't she reach him in her head?" he said, pointing at his head nervously. The more he spoke, the guiltier he sounded.

Malleven frowned while he thought about it, then shook his head. "No, Cesaré can't reply … You didn't answer my question."

"I still speak to my brother, Paulo," he said, flashing a furtive glance at Malleven.

Malleven raised his eyebrows. "Again, you surprise me, Antonio. How are Dad and the Dubonnetti clan?"

Antonio let out a ragged breath. He was by no means out of the woods yet. "Hatching schemes as usual."

"I see," Malleven said, looking mildly amused.

Antonio allowed himself to relax a little, but he was all

too aware how Malleven's mood could switch on him in an instant.

"What is the latest?"

"Marco is becoming a loose cannon. My father no longer trusts him."

"So what will he do?"

Antonio paused for effect. He wanted Malleven to see where his loyalties lay with the information he would tell him. "He is putting all his eggs in one basket."

"Stop the dramatics, Antonio, and tell me."

"My father has taken Ruby Santalini under his wing to matchmake her with Jay Gardiner."

Malleven looked ahead of him and smiled. "The king's best friend – the cunning old goat. Very interesting."

"There are rumours that the king and Jay are not as close as they once were. My father seeks to drive a wedge between them."

Malleven held up his glass in salute. "I'll drink to that." Then he swallowed its contents and put the glass down on the low table and came at Antonio so fast, he barely saw him move.

His hands were around his throat and squeezing in a vice-like grip. "I warned you, Antonio, never to betray me."

Antonio clawed at his hands to loosen his grip – desperately trying to speak or shake his head to deny it.

MALLEVEN WAS incandescent with rage as his hands tightened around Antonio's throat. His face was changing from red to purple and his eyes threatened to pop out of his head. His arms and legs flailed and kicked. "Shall I rape your mind for the answers, Antonio, to see the exquisite pain?"

Antonio's struggles began to diminish slowly, so he loosened his grip before he killed him. Curiosity got the better of him; he just had to know why. He let go of him with a rough push and gathered together his composure again. It was rare for him to lose it, but it had been a rough day.

Antonio gulped huge lungfuls of air and held his throat, sounding a little like a seal.

Impatient for him to speak, Malleven grabbed a pitcher of water and slopped some messily into a glass. Then he handed it to Antonio for him to take. "Here … tell me the truth now, before I kill you."

Antonio shifted his head forward between his knees as if he was going to be sick. Then he drank the contents of the glass and looked up at Malleven. His eyes were bloodshot and watery and all pretence gone. "Yes, I helped her."

"You helped my wife go to Cesaré and the king?" Malleven said with disgust, raising his arm ready to hit him.

Antonio shook his head like a madman. "No, no, I promise you. She didn't go there. She hasn't gone to Ireland."

"Where … Where has she gone? And speak carefully, Antonio, or I swear I will kill you on the spot." Malleven bore down on him menacingly.

"California … she's gone back to her Protectors. She needed to get her head together, that's all. I swear it."

Malleven froze. The Human in the vision came to him. This could be as catastrophic as her going to Cesaré. *But weren't those bunch of lowlifes Atlantean?* It could be that all was not lost.

He grabbed Antonio by the hair and yanked him to him. "You did this out of jealousy." Then he put his mouth next to Antonio's ear. "If my wife bonds with anyone else, or completes her bond with Cesaré, *you* will answer for this," he spat and threw Antonio away from him.

Malleven began to pace the room.

Antonio tried to pull himself together and stop weeping, knowing that would enrage Malleven even more.

Malleven looked over to him and sneered with disgust. "Stop that snivelling. If you truly loved me, you wouldn't do such things."

Antonio dragged a shaking hand through his tears. "Not love you!" he said, his voice cracking. "I have followed you everywhere – even got myself disowned by my own family for you."

"To betray me like this?" Malleven shouted, his eyes wide and churning, spittle flying from his mouth.

Antonio recoiled at how angry he'd become. He was always so composed, even in his malice. Then the thought struck him as clear as day. He didn't know why he hadn't thought of it before. "Wasn't this the very thing you always worked for?"

Malleven stopped in his tracks and looked over at him in amazement.

"Back when you were with Isla," he rambled before Malleven had a chance to fly at him again. "I thought you went through all that deception to get a Siren YOU have bonded with into the king's court." Antonio averted his eyes when Malleven's expression didn't change.

When Malleven did nothing, he hazarded a look at him again.

Malleven frowned, thinking through what Antonio had said. "And to bond with Cesaré ..." His voice trailed off in thought. Then his face darkened. "And what if she loves someone else, not Cesaré ... Let us say for argument's sake, a Human?"

"Does it really matter?" Antonio said, his hopes rising that they were actually speaking without him trying to kill him. "A Human is weak. The king will expect her at court. Her power is already gone anyway. Then you have your original objective – a Siren you control, linked to the king and her sisters."

Malleven resumed pacing. Antonio was right; he'd gravely underestimated him. He had inadvertently solved the conundrum that had been bugging him for days – how to handle the situation with Lily going forward, with Cesaré holding her power.

If he could act the benevolent and forgiving husband, she would never want to hurt him. He knew her real innermost character and she was soft-hearted. In fact, he might even be able to get her to go out of her way to help him.

He turned slowly to look at Antonio, whose eyes were still on him fearfully. Then he beckoned him to him with his hands. "Come here, *amore mio* … I am sorry for hurting you."

Antonio ran into his arms immediately.

Malleven swayed with him gently while Antonio openly cried. "Shh," he said, over and over, until he eventually put him away from him and held Antonio's reddened face. "I would want to know before you try to help me in the future."

CHAPTER 51

The journey from California didn't take nearly as long as Lily thought it would. The tiny Marine Bug was a wonder of Murr technology and even navigated the Panama Canal without being seen.

The vessel was amazingly beautiful. The workings of it looked transparent, like a microscopic organism with lights pulsating all around it, and it was no louder than an electric razor. Its design made it possible to look out at the ocean without seeing anything inside except for the lights. It blew her mind that she was now part of an alien species this advanced.

Vionne and the other Murrs were polite hosts, but she didn't know them and found them a little strange. It was a relief when they finally arrived a little way off the west coast of Ireland.

It was still unclear why she was there, and she felt disloyal to Malleven, knowing how things were between him and the king. The only reason she had gone along with it was so she could have some more time to think and, if she were honest, the chance to spend longer with Lance.

The three Murrs swam with her for the last part to an underwater tunnel. At first, she thought it was a cave mouth, until she quickly realised it was a cylindrical horizontal corridor carved out of the rock with lighting every few feet. They followed it until it took a sharp upward turn.

Vionne took her hand. *The entrance to the castle is just up here.*

She nodded and followed him up until they came up into the centre of a beautiful black fountain in a cavernous black room.

They all climbed up and she stepped over the fountain wall. After efficiently evacuating her lungs, she turned around in amazement at the most beautiful, unusual room. Malleven had taken her to some fancy places, but never had she seen anywhere quite like this. It was like stepping into another world. She struggled to take everything in – the plush sofas, tables – everything arranged around a huge window as big as a cinema screen that appeared to look out at the sea.

A maid handed her a towel, just as a man's voice came from behind her.

"Welcome, my daughter ... welcome. I am Sebastian, your father, and this is my brother, Alfonzo. I am so pleased to meet you again, finally," he said with a very distinct Italian accent.

She stood woodenly, slightly stunned, while they kissed her on both cheeks. Then she looked around, hoping to find someone she might actually know.

"I am afraid you have arrived at a very inopportune time, my dear. The king is occupied with matters of state and your mother is attending to her grandchildren in Murrtaine, but will come to greet you as soon as she can. Also, your sister, the queen, is about to leave for Murrtaine herself. I promise there will be plenty of time for happy reunions," he said, smiling kindly.

There was only one reunion Lily was interested in, and her heart began to sink. *Something must have happened, or he'd had second thoughts.* She couldn't blame him; her baggage was a lot to take on. *Happy reunions? What a joke.* She had no interest in meeting the family who had abandoned her and left her husband to die.

Her resolve hardened. *Is there anyone here I know?* she asked. It had really been a bad idea to come here. Malleven would be pissed off with her already.

"Yes, yes … your mate, Cesaré, is here. We are so pleased you aligned yourself with him. He is a strong prince from a good branch of his family. We'll let you settle in and send him along to you shortly.

Great. Did they mean the same guy?

They led her along the dim corridors of the place she guessed was underground, and her mood got lower and lower. It had been a waste of time and she was feeling more and more guilty. Malleven would hate that she was there. *And Lance.* She wiped a small tear from her eye.

There was nothing to unpack, so she sat on the edge of her bed and tried to think what to do next.

A maid knocked and entered, bringing in a pile of clothes.

She bobbed a curtsey. "His Royal Highness thought you may need some clothes until you get sorted, miss."

Lily picked up a top and held it out in front of her. It was really quite nice.

"They belong to the queen, your sister," she said, smiling.

Great, hand-me-downs from a sister she didn't even know, and probably wouldn't like. She put it back on the pile with a sigh.

There was another knock at the door.

The maid beckoned someone in on her way out. Cesaré

put his head round the door and smiled. "Is it okay if I come in?"

She nodded. *Too late now,* she thought with a sigh.

When he came in a little unsure of himself, he actually looked really good – like the best she'd ever seen him. He still had that laid-back surfer style, but he brushed up pretty good. His hair looked great and his bright blue eyes twinkled. A neatly healing scar just above his right brow only added character to his handsome face.

She understood now why he was such a hit with the babes. He simply didn't look like the same guy. *You look better,* she projected.

He stood a few feet away from her and inclined his head. "Thanks to you."

She smiled wanly. *Oh yeah.*

"I never got a chance to thank you for what you did that day."

It's okay, she said. It didn't really hold much importance with her except that Malleven had hated it. She really didn't get what all the fuss was about. It wasn't like she was into him or anything.

"No, it's not okay. I was fucking awful to you and you saved my life … more than that, you gave me my whole life back."

My pleasure, she said with a wave of her hand. She didn't really know Cesaré or anything about his life. It was nice that he was better and appeared to be off the booze. There wasn't really anything left to say.

He wandered over and sat next to her on the bed.

She moved away from him a bit. *Lance said you nearly died the other night?*

"As did you," Cesaré said, looking meaningfully into her eyes.

She frowned. *No, he didn't mean to hurt me, Cesaré. And I'd managed to hide you up till then.*

Cesaré looked at her quizzically, as if she'd just said something of particular interest to him. "You have genuine feelings for Malleven?" he said, really surprised.

Of course ... he is my husband ... was my ... oh I dunno, I'm confused at the moment, she finished huffily.

Cesaré's look was one of bewilderment, then he shook his head as if he was dumbfounded. "What about Lance?"

With those simple words, she put her head in her hands.

"What is it? ... He is on his way. He'll be here in a while."

Her tears stopped immediately and she looked up. *He's coming?* Then she shrank back into her misery. *Oh, it's such a mess.*

"What is?"

You, me, Lance ... bloody hell, I'm married to Malleven. He hates it. He'll hate that I'm here with you ... and you hate me, she tacked on as if it was another thing to add to her list of miseries.

"Me?" he said, amazed. "Lily, you don't even know what you did for me, do you? Let me tell you, you gave me the biggest gift anyone could give an Atlantean royal. You not only bound me to you, but I was your first." He looked into her blank face as if she should understand something.

She just stared blankly at him.

"That means your power passed to me and I am now head of my family and part of the king's government. I will be eternally grateful to you for that." He reached for her hand, but she pulled it away and stood up.

It all made sense now, why Malleven was so utterly disappointed. *I didn't do it as a gift, though; I didn't know what I was doing.*

"Thank God," Cesaré said, shaking his head with relief.

"That small mistake could very well have helped save the kingdom."

Lily whirled around on him. *You don't know that,* she snapped.

Any humour dropped from his face. "Why did you leave him?" he asked curtly.

She frowned and resumed pacing. *I found out ... I found him ... I needed some space, okay?*

"Was it Antonio?" he said, more softly.

She stopped and faced him again. *Was it so obvious to everyone else but me?*

"Don't be too hard on yourself. I know Malleven very well. We are cousins who were brought up together as brothers." He looked away bitterly. "He and Antonio have been close for a long time."

She didn't want to feel sorry for Cesaré; it only complicated things. *We were fine before Antonio. He was the kindest, nicest person anyone has ever been to me. In fact, it was only when he found out about you ... what it must have meant to his plans ...*

Cesaré lost a little of his patience and came closer to her. "Please listen to me, Lily. I know Malleven better than anyone alive. It is your power and the crown he wants ... it's all he's ever wanted. It doesn't matter which Siren you are, only that you *are* a Siren." He laughed derisively. "Only this time you'd already given it away."

No! she said with horror. *It is more than that, I know it is.*

He sighed. "Look, just remember one thing if nothing else … he wants to win."

That's what you all want ... you're all the same.

Cesaré bobbed his head. "You're probably right, but he used your sister in the same way."

She betrayed him.

He shifted his feet and looked up in exasperation.

All she wanted to do was scream at him.

"He betrayed ME. He used her and me to get close to the crown. That was the truth of it. I have no reason to lie to you, Lily."

Tears were streaming down her cheeks now, and she was shaking her head. She turned to hide and waved her hand for him to leave her.

His hands softly touched her shoulders as he stood behind her. "I will ask nothing from you, Lily, but one thing; for the safety of the kingdom, yourself and your family, I beg you to complete the bond with me." He turned her around to face him.

He seemed so honest. *I don't want to hurt him.*

"I promise it will only hurt his pride. It will give you and me a strong mental link so we will be able to talk to each other even at a distance."

She was already shaking her head before he had a chance to finish, and pulled out of his grip. "I won't betray him like that. I won't be like my sister."

Cesaré sagged and then walked slowly back towards the door. He opened it and paused. "All but one of your sisters has pledged to the king. I'm not asking you to betray him like that. Just to complete what you started with me. Think about it, please."

The information he had given her was overwhelming. She wasn't sure what to believe, what not to believe. She was torn between Malleven, how she felt about Lance, and now Cesaré was laying this on her.

"There is just one last thing you should know; the bond is like a living thing that must be fed."

Lily frowned in confusion.

"You have to keep on doing it."

And if you don't?

"You will both get sick and eventually die."

He gave her a wan smile and left her with her head reeling.

EVERYTHING FELT strange and unwelcoming at Ballygowan Castle to Lily. With no one to greet her except for Cesaré, it was little wonder that she had a fitful night filled with vivid dreams. One dream was particularly realistic.

It took her by surprise at first. Malleven had been so forceful in the past when trying to speak to her telepathically or enter her mind. This time, she felt a gentle nudge, then he waited patiently for permission to enter her outer subconscious.

What is it, Malleven? she thought drowsily.

Then, suddenly, it was as though he was there with her in the room. The drowsiness left her and she felt wide awake. Her hand went to her mouth in shock at how devastated he looked. In fact, he looked ruined. It seemed impossible that such an impeccably dressed man should look so dishevelled.

Lily sat up.

He regarded her through his eyebrows with his hands on his hips as if he'd just finished some vigorous exercise. His white shirt was dirty, the neck open, and his tie was undone, hanging on either side of his chest. *You did that ... how could you, Lily?*

Her heart was beating wildly in fear. *Did what?*

Bound another to you. He shook his head as if he didn't quite believe it, and his eyes looked worn-out and bloodshot, flickering from their usual indigo to gold.

Lily's fear was making her almost hyperventilate; she was breathing so fast. *You took a lover too ... we hadn't even finished our honeymoon.*

That's what it's all about ... Antonio? he began to shout.

I do care about you, she said, trying to keep the fear out of her voice.

Malleven came closer and loomed over her as she sat up in the bed, but she didn't cower away like she was sure he was expecting her to do. She flinched when he reached out his hand, but he touched the side of her face. *We are bound completely, Lily. I feel everything – know everything. This one ... he is Human?*

Her eyes were wide and her blood pumped in her ears. She nodded.

Malleven swore and closed his eyes for a moment as if she'd physically struck him. *You went to the king's court ... did you go there to betray me?* he said, his voice cracked and weary.

No, I promise you. I was sent here for safety. I haven't even met the king. He is occupied with something to do with his wife. I will leave as soon as I can.

He narrowed his eyes and studied her for any duplicity. *If I give you this Human, are you still mine?*

It was the last thing she expected him to say. She was confused at first, unsure what he meant. *Are you asking for an open marriage – one of convenience?*

His eyes bore into hers and his face hardened, making her shrink. *I am talking about a true marriage based on affection, where we respect and understand our need for certain distractions.* He held up a finger sharply, making her jump. *Only one! Mine will be Antonio, yours is your Human. I give you this. Such is my regard for you.*

Lily was astonished at what he was proposing. It was the answer to what had been driving her mad since she had seen Lance again. With no divorce, he was offering her a way. Hope began to fill her. Just ten minutes ago, everything was hopeless for them all. *I accept ... thank you so much, Malleven.* Her heart swelled with gratitude.

There is just one thing I would ask that you swear to me, Lily.

She nodded enthusiastically. *I promise I will.*

Despite what they say to you, or promise you at the castle, that you remain true to me always.

It was a strange thing to promise when she would be with Lance, but how could she deny him such a request?

I am not talking about physical love, Lily; I'm talking about your allegiance. The king will try to convince you to side with him with that harlot of a sister who left me for dead.

Lily felt his anger and hurt. *I won't side with him; I'll leave here as soon as I can.*

Malleven leant down and brushed his lips against hers. Then he surprised her. *That is not necessary. As long as I can trust you, you can remain.*

But what will I do if he puts pressure on me?

Just keep the line of communication open. Don't shut me out, he said, tapping her temple gently.

I won't, she said enthusiastically. He was kinder than she deserved and understood everything. A lump appeared in her throat. *I am so lucky to have you as my husband, Malleven.*

He pinched her chin and held it so he could look into her eyes. *You may love this Human, but you are mine. I always give those who are loyal to me everything they want. Remember that.*

Real tears of love and gratitude were now running down her cheeks. Malleven kissed her deeply and she responded wholeheartedly. Then he began to fade in her arms as if he had never been.

She lay back down and cried at the loss until she drifted back into troubled sleep.

MALLEVEN WAS MENTALLY exhausted after his psychic conversation with Lily. He was bent over his knees on the edge of his bed in his New York apartment. Antonio was gently rubbing his back.

Malleven breathed hard as if he'd been running.

"What is it?" Antonio asked softly.

"She finally let me in to speak to her. It is as you suspected, she has been taken to the king's court."

"All is according to plan then," Antonio said, resuming massaging his back.

Malleven sighed. It was true, it was, but he was disturbed, and far more than he would admit to Antonio. "She has taken a lover," he said, looking sideways at Antonio.

Antonio frowned. "And you are allowing it?"

Malleven nodded and leaned down with his elbows on his knees. It did seem out of character. "For the time being … I felt a shift in the bond a few hours ago. It must be someone she has known for a while; she has bound him to her."

"So you can get to him through her," Antonio said, running his fingers through Malleven's hair.

Malleven nodded, still distracted by his thoughts. "Now is not the time. For the moment, he is perfect leverage."

"And then what?"

"When I have them all where I want them …" He turned and glared into Antonio's eyes. "I will crush him."

CHAPTER 52

The time had finally come for Tia to leave for Murrtaine. Dante had arranged for her to stay at the royal palace with the Lord Advocate, Darl, and his sons, Vionne, Dax and Caan. Her mother was there with their other two children, Xavier and Alexia, as it was where they went to school. And her sister, Isla and her mate, Darres, lived nearby with their children, so Tia would be surrounded by family.

Dante had also started the ball rolling in the search for a new medication for Jay. The problem of his connection to Tia was a thorn in his side he was determined to pluck once and for all.

Tia's sister, Lily, had already arrived, but he didn't want to delay sending Tia off with lengthy introductions, so he didn't tell her. She was to go in the small vessel that brought Lily first thing in the morning. Vionne waited nearby.

Lily woke before dawn with the remnants of the conversation she'd had with Malleven still in her head. It was with a prickle of excitement but tinged with fear. There was no telling whether Lance would accept such an arrangement.

Sleep was now impossible, so she got up. After a quick shower, she picked up the clothes her sister had given her. Holding out the top in front of her, she couldn't help wondering what her sister was like. If she were here in the castle, she would have thought she'd come to see her, to satisfy a curiosity if nothing else.

Well, it wasn't like she'd make a difference to her life, anyway. With a shrug, she quickly dressed and slipped out of her room, intending to explore a bit before the castle woke up.

Lily looked left and right in the long corridor outside. The smell of food was coming from one way, and the other, she was sure, was the way she came. She opted for that.

After a few minutes, she came out into the great hall. It was empty and silent but lit for nighttime – like the set of a fairy tale, with little lights twinkling in alcoves. She twirled, taking in its magnificence. Walking to the large window, she put her hands against it and peered out and marvelled at the blue grey of the sea. It was mesmerizing and she could watch it all day. Instead, she continued to investigate the room, wandering through the plush sofas and chairs dotted here and there around low tables.

At the furthest corner, there was a small stage. She guessed it was for parties where an orchestra or a band would set up. It just had a single cabinet on it that day. She stepped up to take a closer look and realized it held DJ decks – but not just any old ones; these were turntables for vinyl records.

Not able to resist, she flicked a switch and heard the thump and buzz as they came on and the speakers kicked into life. She ran her fingers over the knobs and buttons of the panel. Somehow she knew they belonged to one of her sisters, and wondered which one? She guessed they were the queen's.

Her foot kicked a silver box. She crouched down, undid the clip and opened the lid to reveal a box full of twelve-inch records. *Wow.* She eased them out, one by one, reading each song title and artist. Most of them she knew, and all of them were dance tunes.

Her sifting stopped at one particular record. *The Funky Drummer,* she read. *Oh my God!* She just had to play this. *This'll wake the bastards up.*

Lily placed it gently onto one of the decks, put the needle to the record and turned the fader up. She almost dissolved into the heavenly rhythm. *God must be a drummer,* she thought, and not for the first time.

Turning it up a few more notches, she closed her eyes, nodded her head, and lost herself in James Brown's vocals, punching in and out like a beat of its own.

Tia had just said a tearful goodbye to JJ and left him with the nanny. For some reason, Dante had arranged for her to leave at the crack of dawn. It was probably because he had a nightmare going on with Malleven and Cesaré.

She was walking back from the nanny's quarters at the far end of the underground level of the castle, lost in thought, when a noise brought her up sharp. It was music coming from the hall. *Who would be up at this hour?*

Whoever it was had picked one hell of a tune.

She was ruminating on what a wicked beat it was when she came out into the great hall and saw its source.

A girl was behind her decks.

Tia moved closer, completely drawn to her black curly hair and stripy face nodding in time. Her eyes were closed as if in ecstasy, letting the music flow right through her.

She knew that feeling; she got it herself every time she played. Except this girl was tuned into one instrument – the drums. The track was built for it. And the reason she knew was what she saw and what she felt just standing there watching. Just like the day she'd met Lacy, she was pulsing her power in time to the music. It was in short bursts of energy in quick succession, and she could see it like a flashing blue grey strobe.

It happened much quicker than it did for her and Lacy. Just like the drums were the foundation for a song, the girl's power beat like the rhythm of a heartbeat. It made her wonder what would happen if they all got together to play music. *That would be one hell of a party.*

It also dawned on her that her sister wasn't actually drumming – merely listening, and could still emit her power. Maybe that meant they all could do that. Perhaps it was the love of the music and not what they did exactly that held the power. It was just the channel they used. *Interesting.*

THE MUSIC FADED out and Lily stood for a few moments in the calmness that followed. It almost felt as good as when she played herself. It was the best therapy for a racing mind.

She took a deep breath, slowly opened her eyes and was shocked to see a girl standing watching her a few feet away. For a long moment, they just stared at each other.

Even if she could speak, she wouldn't have said a word. She instinctively knew she was the queen and she'd been watching her using her decks. And, by the expression on her face, she knew who she was, too.

She nodded once.

The queen did the same.

Lily stepped down from the stage and walked quickly back to her room.

. . .

TIA WAS STILL a little stunned at the encounter when Dante found her in the hall.

"Ready?" he said, taking her into his arms.

She gazed up into his face and wondered briefly whether her sister was the reason she was being packed off so early.

Dante smoothed back her hair, assuming her preoccupation was to do with going away. "Don't forget you'll get to see Xavier and Alexia," he said. It comforted her a little. There was so much going on she didn't want to miss, but she also knew that Dante wanted her away from Jay – particularly now she was pregnant.

So with a quick sweep of his emotions, and feeling only longing and love, she decided it wasn't worth bringing up her sister right then. *She could wait.* Instead, she smiled up at Dante and said honestly, "I'll miss you … please be careful."

His face broke into his beautiful smile and he kissed her. Then the two of them stepped over the wall of the fountain. She took a final look around, knowing she'd be away for months. Then nodded to say she was ready. Holding hands, they jumped into the deep hole in its centre and swam out of the tunnel. The small Marine Bug purred near the ocean floor a little way off.

The technology of the Murrs still astounded her, and that mankind knew nothing of its existence. Just before she entered the small hatch underneath, Tia hugged Dante to her. She hated leaving him and sensed the weight of his worry.

Be safe, he projected with a regretful smile.

And you, she said, touching his cheek. The sister she'd met briefly that morning wouldn't be as easy to get to know as the others. For a moment, she was afraid for him.

He took it as reluctance to leave, squeezing her harder, and she let him.

Stay as long as you need, but promise me you'll let me know as soon as the doctors confirm it. He put his hand on her stomach.

DANTE KNEW in his heart of hearts that she was pregnant and he already rejoiced. The more tightly this woman was bound to him, the better he liked it.

He kissed her one last time, and one of Vionne's lieutenants escorted her in through the hatch in the floor.

Vionne came forward and touched his shoulder. *Don't worry; she will be treated like a queen with me.*

Dante nodded and thanked him. *Please, look into Jay's medication urgently, Vionne?*

I will, without delay.

I want Jay free as soon as possible.

Understood.

Vionne entered the bug, and Dante stood back, reining in his emotions before he went back in to sort the latest clusterfuck in his life.

But for a few moments, he stood back and watched while the little Marine Bug gradually rose higher, turned, and eased away on a whirr.

CHAPTER 53

*L*ance's car pulled up right outside the castle doors. He was glad he had his brother Nathan and Shona with him. After what had happened with Lily, he wasn't sure of his reception.

The imposing grey fortress didn't help with his feeling of dread. Protector or not, he had overstepped the mark.

A servant showed them to the lift that took them down below ground. The lift doors opened and Lance watched his brother open his mouth, amazed by the great hall, while they slowly descended the marble staircase. "We're in the twilight zone, Bruh," Nathan said, taking it all in. "Shit!" he said, spinning around. Shona laughed.

Lance nodded. It was an Alien world he could never leave – especially not now he and Lily had sealed the deal.

The bond was a truly amazing thing. He could even feel her close now, and his body yearned for her. A few months ago, he never would have thought it possible to feel this deeply for a girl. After a few hours of meeting and, especially after getting it together, it was as though he was hooked on a drug. And where he was drawn to her before, he didn't have a hope in hell of keeping away now.

They didn't wait long. Cesaré came out of a corridor and greeted them. Kissing Shona, shaking both their hands, and clapping them on the back. "Come! The king wants to talk to you."

Lance and Nathan followed him to the far side of the great hall, to where the king sat sifting through papers next to the light of the aquarium-like window.

Dante looked up when he sensed them approaching. He stood, inclined his head to Shona, and shook both their hands.

"You know Shona. This is my brother, Nathan, also one of Lily's Protectors," Lance explained.

"Good," Dante said, and indicated for them all to sit in the chairs Cesaré brought nearer. "Drink?" he asked.

"No thanks." Lance was eager to find Lily. "Is she okay?" he said, looking around.

"She's fine," Dante said. "I wanted to speak to you and Ches before the two of you got together." He smiled. "She's been here a few hours. I haven't spoken to her yet. I was a bit preoccupied with my wife's departure to Murrtaine."

Lance noticed a flicker of worry cross the king's face.

"I didn't want to introduce them yet. If she knew Lily was here, she wouldn't have gone," he explained.

Lance smiled in understanding and willed him to just get on with it.

"You've been a bit of a puzzle to me, Lance," the king said, leaning back and tapping his chin.

Lance wasn't sure how to answer that and looked around him. In all honesty, he didn't care. He'd just come to see that Lily was okay.

Dante was still studying him. "Here's my problem: I've got

this Siren – Lily, sister to my wife, who's gone and bound two men to her – nothing new, I hear you say. But not just two men, both of them are princes, and from the same family. Both of them hate each other and neither of them is me."

"Three!" Lance said, before Dante could go on.

The king stopped what he was about to say and frowned at him. Lance didn't usually kiss and tell, but he guessed it was kind of important to speak up. "She did the breathing thing with me just before she came here."

Dante sat quietly in deep thought and then nodded. "Cesaré may not … Mmm – Malleven *will* know." He narrowed his eyes. "Yes … a puzzle of a Human."

"But isn't your wife …?" Lance trailed off. The king probably didn't need reminding about his best friend. The last thing he wanted to do was get involved in all that shit, and longed to get away.

"And that is some major fucking aggro, I can tell yer," Dante said, laughing in a single blast of air. "No, what intrigues me about you is that you weren't together previously?"

Lance shook his head.

"Then she goes off, marries a prince and has a full bond," the king said, thinking aloud.

"She bound Ches before that …" Lance added.

Dante pointed at him in thanks at the reminder. Then he shook his head. "That's not the puzzle."

Lance waited, not sure where he was going with this.

"It's why when she got herself free, she ran to you and not Cesaré."

Lance didn't get why the king was puzzled. It didn't seem complicated to him. After the time they spent together, they just realised how they felt. Cesaré had just been an accident. That was the way he saw it, anyway.

"Listen, I just want to meet her first, then you can see her, okay?" Dante finished with a smile. "I've got a hunch I want to look into."

Lance stood and went to walk away, figuring the meeting was over.

"There aren't many things stronger than the bond you know, Lance."

Lance nodded, confused, unsure what to say.

LILY WAS SHOWN BACK to the great hall where she'd had the encounter with her sister earlier. Lance was nearby; she could feel him. Her hopes rose that she was being taken to him. Instead, she was led to a strikingly good-looking man with wavy black hair to his shoulders and slate grey mischievous eyes.

The maid left them and he smiled. It changed his face from handsome to rakishly gorgeous. *Wow!*

He stood immediately, approached her and kissed her on both cheeks. Then he indicated with a hand for her to sit. "You must be Lily who I've heard so much about."

She smiled. His Irish accent pleasantly surprised her. It was as attractive as he was.

You can speak telepathically?

Yes, she projected, smiling a little.

He grinned that knock-out face transformation again.

I am the king and married to your sister. You can call me Dante. Then he bobbed his head. *Well, I'm married to three of your sisters, actually.* He finished with a laugh.

Lily found herself laughing with him in spite of herself. He surprised her. She wasn't expecting to like him.

He poured a glass of wine, passed it to her and topped up his own. "Well, aren't you a little spanner in the works," he said with a grin, sitting back in his chair.

The smile dropped from her face. *Because I'm married to Malleven?*

He bobbed his head in that very Italian way so many of them had. "Partly, but all my wives, except for Tia, have other husbands. It's that you bonded with Cesaré first."

She looked at her fingers. *Oh that. I just saved his life. I don't get it ... I mean, Malleven explained a few things.*

Dante raised an eyebrow as if to say, "he could imagine". "Let me lay it on the line for you, Lily. To rule effectively, a king needs the power of all five Sirens. At the moment, I have three. Cesaré has you but is allied with me."

It struck her then that there were four sisters she had never met – not that it really made a difference to her life. *That's okay then, isn't it?*

"Kind of ... The thing is, you have a full bond with Malleven, who has managed to make an enemy of just about everyone."

Lily instantly bristled. *My sister betrayed him,* she projected forcefully.

Dante studied her before speaking. "Your sister had become bound to someone else before she met Malleven – she was *never* bound to Malleven." He emphasised the word "never". "She loved her man."

None of it made sense. She was trying to process what he was saying to her, but the king interrupted her thoughts. "That wasn't the case with you ... what I don't understand is your attraction to Lance?"

She frowned. Lance had told her he wasn't the only Human, and she didn't want to get into the whys and wherefores of how she felt about Lance, and what she found attractive in one man over another. It simply was none of his business.

"A Human," the king continued, "who had no bond with you until recently?"

She scowled. "Can I see him? It's the only reason I agreed to come here."

The king nodded as if she had merely confirmed something in his mind. "He's in your room."

Her eyes went wide with surprise. She was expecting to have to fight to see him.

"There is no point in separating you. You'll go to him, whatever."

How did he know?

He smiled. "Go!"

She got up, more confused than when she first arrived. *What had really been discussed here?*

CESARÉ CAME from the shadows and stood next to Dante. "What do you think?"

"You must complete the bond immediately," Dante said, any hint of amusement now gone.

"And Lance?"

"I agree there is something amiss. I've got my man, Max, working on it, and I've sent a message to Murrtaine for what I need."

Cesaré nodded.

"We'll get you in the water with her, and hopefully we'll have some answers by then."

Both men stared after Lily in deep thought.

CHAPTER 54

*L*ance stood with his hands in the pockets of his jeans in Lily's room and everything felt out of whack. It had felt that way ever since he'd met Lily, but especially since they'd finally got it together. Used to spending his life in board shorts, teaching surfing and playing in his band, looking around him now, he just didn't belong.

At last, the door latch clicked, and she walked in. The object of his disquiet, as lovely as she ever was. "Tiger!" came out on a breath.

Lily stood still in the doorway, so relieved that he was actually there. He was standing awkwardly amongst the opulence of the place, even though his face softened when he saw her.

Not able to help herself, she ran and threw herself at him, knocking the air out of his chest with a huff. It felt so safe with his arms squeezing her and her nose buried in his chest. His distinctive smell swamped her senses. *You came,* she projected.

Lance nodded. "Said I would, didn't I?" He kissed her on the forehead.

She searched his face with a frown. This wasn't how she saw this reunion going. Her eyes strayed to the bed. *I haven't been able to get you out of my head since the other night.*

He smiled ruefully. "Same."

Lily touched his cheek. *It's okay, Lance.*

"Is it?" His smile was small and uncertain. Then he took a step back and put her away from him.

What's the matter, Lance? Panic started to rise in her as she felt him slipping away. *What did they say to you?*

His hands were back in his pockets. "Nothin'. The king wants to see me again before I go."

Go? ... but you just got here. Her psychic voice was small, like a little girl.

Lance was forced to look up at the rough edges of the rock ceiling rather than look at the disappointment in her eyes. It would have been so easy to roll around in the sheets with her. That part was like breathing. *But then what?* It was the rest of it that was impossible.

How could he tell her that every time he closed his eyes, he saw the blood – her blood. Over and over, all he saw was the two of them making out as if their souls were lost, bathing in the stuff.

He shook his head. "Look, I'm your Protector. It killed me that I couldn't bring you here myself, so I had to come ... ya know? ... to make sure you're okay."

The look of disappointment on her face gutted him, but he had to press on. "But the other night ..." He closed his eyes as the mental images of what they'd done tortured him again. The stirrings in his pants proved him a liar. "I was outta line, and I'm sorry. I should have been protecting you."

His eyes flashed at her and took in the look of horror

spreading over her face. "You'll go back to Malleven at some point, and he'll give you a hard time …" he persisted.

And you've worked this all out by yourself, have you? she said, suddenly losing patience with him.

But it was all good; it just got to the desired outcome more quickly.

For your information, I spoke to Malleven and he understands.

"He understands…" Lance repeated with his head hung low and his hands on his slim hips. "Trust me, Lily, no man understands."

No, that's not what I mean … he has Antonio, and I have you.

Lance laughed derisively and narrowed his eyes. "Am I hearing you right?"

She was nodding like a mad thing.

"He's allowing you to keep me like some pet?" He'd heard enough and walked towards the door.

Everything was spiralling out of Lily's control. It was obvious she'd been pushing a lot of stuff under the carpet where she didn't want to deal with it, but how she felt about Lance was the one thing in her life making sense at that moment. *So you're throwing what we had away … not even giving us a chance?*

He whirled around so fast he made her jump. "There is no *us*, Lily. There's never been any *us*."

Despite her best efforts, her face began to crumple. The last thing she wanted was to cry in front of him.

"I'm not some part-time guy you can pick up and drop. I can't be that way with you." His voice cracked at the end.

It was then he made sense. He was guarding his emotions and she couldn't blame him. It had to be all or nothing.

I understand, she thought.

"I'll help you in any way I can, but I can't be with you, okay?"

She gave him a small nod. It wasn't total rejection. She was convinced he wanted her, but he wanted all of her and that was impossible. *So you won't stay with me here?* she said, holding out an arm to indicate her room.

He shifted his feet impatiently. "I'll just be here to make sure everything's okay, and then I'll go back."

She swallowed hard and nodded. It was the best she was going to get.

WHEN THE DOOR KNOCKED AGAIN, Lily stupidly thought it was Lance having a change of heart, but it was Shona.

"Gee, thanks for the welcome," she said at her obvious disappointment and came and sat next to her on the bed. "You okay, darl?"

The kindness and familiarity of the first and only female she could count as a friend tipped her over the edge. Shona quickly threw her arms around her and Lily sobbed into her chest.

"What's that flamin' galah done now?"

Lily half laughed and half cried at the Australian slang, and that she knew she meant Lance without even projecting a word.

"He ain't still fart-assing around, is he?"

Lily nodded.

Shona pulled apart and held Lily's face between her hands. "Look, I've known that guy for gotta be going on ten years and, believe me, when I say he loves you. Christ, I've never seen him act the way he does around you, not never."

Lily gave her a wan smile. *I think it's coz I'm married and I can never be really free.*

"Is that what he said?"

She shrugged. *Pretty much.*

"Listen to me, right? Give him time … you know what I think? He's scared shitless of how he feels about you. For cryin' out loud, he's got ya stamped on his back, for fuck's sake."

Lily couldn't help laughing at Shona's delightful choice of words.

"Okay?"

Lily sniffed and nodded.

"If he don't, I'll have to knock some sense into him … Now, shove over."

Lily instantly moved to the opposite side of the bed. *Are you sleeping here?* she projected as Shona stripped down to her underwear.

Shona nodded, getting under the covers. "Yeah, this place gives me the creeps."

Lily instantly brightened and did the same. Then she clicked off the lamp and lay flat on her back. Shona fell asleep in under two minutes and, even though she was wide awake, she was grateful to have her there.

LANCE STORMED into the great hall. He needed to find someone – anyone – to tell them he needed to get the hell out of this madhouse.

Dante was standing in conversation with Cesaré and the two old guys at the foot of the marble staircase.

"Lance!" Dante said as soon as he saw him come out of the corridor to the bedrooms.

"I need to talk to you," Lance said, cutting him off. "I need to get out of here." He felt like a caged animal; hot and anxious to get away.

Alfonzo and Sebastian made their excuses and left him with Cesaré and Dante.

Dante was looking at him with that puzzled expression he seemed to reserve for him. "What's up?" he said.

"I'll leave you two ..." Cesaré went to turn.

Lance grabbed his arm. "No. It's okay ... Look." He began to pace manically in front of them. "It's impossible for me to be here. I thought I could, but I can't?"

Dante frowned at Cesaré. "Are you feeling okay, Lance? You don't look so good."

"I feel fine!" Lance snapped.

"You and Lily are arguing?"

"No!" Lance said, exasperated. "It's not that ... it's ... I can't ... Look, she's married ... she can't divorce even if she wanted to."

Dante nodded as if he started to understand. "Don't worry, Lance. If you could just bear with us for a couple more days, it will all come clear, I promise."

Lance stopped pacing, looked at the floor and let out a deep sigh. Then he ran a shaking hand over his forehead. *Why was it so fucking hot in here?*

Have you been given any Elixir, Lance?" Dante said, looking at Cesaré.

"I gave him some a few weeks back."

"I'll have your own room made up for you, and some Elixir sent. You'll feel better."

"I just need to get out, that's all." The feelings of claustrophobia were becoming unbearable.

Dante nodded after an exchange of looks and Cesaré went off somewhere. Then he put his arm around Lance's shoulders and guided him back to the bedroom corridor. "Listen, Lance, all this that you're feeling is normal. It's just your physical reaction to the bond. You'll feel better, I promise."

"What's going to happen ... why is she here?" Lance said, putting his hand to his chest, feeling his heart racing.

"She just has to complete the bond with Cesaré."

Lance looked into the king's eyes and he frowned again as if there was something about him that troubled him. He was sick of it – sick of him looking at him as if he was weird.

"It's just a simple ceremony where he has to do it back."

"Do it back?" Lance repeated with a frown. An image of him and Lily rolling around in the surf came back to him. "Cesaré has to get close to her like that?"

Again, that puzzled look. "It's just a ceremony. It won't last more than a few minutes, then she's all yours."

Lance almost choked. He thought he would combust with the heat and rage that surged through him. It felt so acute that he needed to kill something.

"You okay, man?" the king said, looking at him in that peculiar way again.

They'd come to a stop outside a door. *No, he wasn't fucking okay.* His heart was beating like a train.

Cesaré came jogging up to them and handed the king a vial.

Lance looked at him with such hatred that he recoiled in confusion. He frowned and smiled a little nervously. "Are you okay, Lance?"

Except the words sounded like an echo bouncing around in his head. The world began to spin. The king came up in his face. "Drink this," echoed like it was a long way off.

Lance saw the test tube-like bottle come towards him. His arms came up to protect himself and he fell against the door.

"What's wrong with him?" Cesaré said.

"Not sure … Lily, probably."

Lance was getting nearer and nearer to the floor.

"Because he's Human?"

Lance was spacing out. His eyelids were opening and closing in slow motion.

"Maybe, I've never seen anything like this."

"Is it Malleven?"

Dante had no time to speak as Lance lurched to his feet and pushed him hard in the chest. Before Lance knew what had happened, he was lifted off his feet at least a foot off the ground.

Lance tried to look down to see what had him, but there was nothing there.

Both Cesaré and the king were standing shoulder-to-shoulder, looking up at him. "Don't struggle," the king said calmly. "You're going to sleep for a while, just till we get enough of this stuff down you," he said, holding up the empty vial.

Lance's eyes slowly closed.

"What the fuck was that?"

"I don't know. Did you see how weird his eyes went?"

"Yes ... for just a moment."

Everything went numb.

CHAPTER 55

The next morning, Lily left Shona snoring and went to Dante's study after spending a restless night.

"Take a seat," Dante said.

He was seated behind his desk and Cesaré was in an armchair to his left.

Where's Lance? she projected, looking around the room. She knew he was still in the castle, she could feel him.

The king sighed. "He'll be up and about soon."

Lily's heart thumped. *What's wrong ... is he ill?*

"Not exactly ... he was behaving very erratically last night. I gave him some Elixir. He's just sleeping it off."

Oh no ... He seemed okay when she last saw him. *Can I see him?*

"There is something I need you to do quite urgently first, then you're free to do what you want."

She shifted uncomfortably. Cesaré hadn't said a word, but he hadn't taken his eyes off her.

"Just a simple and quick ceremony. You need to do the breathing thing again with Cesaré to top up the bond; he does it back, and it's all over."

I'm not some stupid little girl, you know. I'm married; I know what you are asking me to do.

Dante and Cesaré exchanged a look. "I never thought of you as that," Dante said. Then he studied her for a few moments as if he wasn't sure how to phrase his words. "I'll level with you, okay? Cesaré is your first pledge – your true mate – not your most compatible, granted."

Lily rolled her eyes.

"But you can't have that one-sided. It isn't safe for you or for him – and especially not for the kingdom. We live in dangerous times, Lily. It is my job to lead a nation that could implode any minute – and that's without the constant threat from the Humans."

Lily's mind was jumbled. If she were really honest, none of that interested her; all she could think about was Lance at that moment. *But what about Malleven,* she said, shaking her head. *I don't think he would like this.*

Dante and Cesaré exchanged another one of those looks. "Do you love Malleven?" Dante asked, a little more kindly.

She looked down at her hands in her lap. *I wouldn't want to see him hurt.*

"And yet you left him."

She frowned. It felt like he was twisting everything.

"You know there is someone out there who is your most compatible mate in the world, Lily; someone who could bring you indescribable joy."

Lily huffed, losing patience. The only thing on her mind right then was the night she'd spent with Lance and she couldn't imagine any feeling stronger than that. *That's of no interest to me,* she said, in all honesty.

"I'll lay it on the line for you, Lily. You have bound three men to you and the bond – even one-sided – is a living thing. You'll have to repeat it with all of them, and with Cesaré it has been a while. If you don't renew it, you'll begin to get tired, and eventually you will get sick. That goes for both parties."

It was hopeless. She let out a ragged breath. Saving Cesaré's life was one thing, but getting into the water and doing something as intimate as that on purpose was a whole other thing. *Can I have some time to think?*

Dante bobbed his head and looked at his watch. "We'll meet in the great hall at ten … I'll have the witnesses assembled by then."

LILY FELT SO TRAPPED at the castle. It seemed like everyone needed her for something – everyone that is, except Lance. He'd gone stone cold again.

There was only one thing she could do; she must attempt to reach out to Malleven. With only an hour until she was due to meet with the king and Cesaré, it didn't leave much time. Even though she'd been given time to think, a swimsuit left neatly on the bed meant there wasn't much room for a no.

She sat on the bed and crossed her legs. Her hands lay flat next to her, feeling the soft fibres of the comforter while her mind reached out.

At first, she felt silly, unsure if she was doing it right. Then she began to concentrate hard, sending out a call to Malleven.

What is it mio fiore? his clear, rumbly voice said. *Is everything okay for you? I feel your anxiety.*

No, Malleven, it is not. They want me to meet them in under an hour to complete the bond with Cesaré. I need to leave, Malleven. I don't think they will give me much choice.

Malleven was silent for a long moment. It went on so long she thought the psychic connection was lost. Then, when he finally spoke, a huge wave of affection came with it. *Are you okay, Malleven? I'm sorry it came to this.* She felt terrible that through her naivety, she'd brought him trouble.

Please, Lily, do not feel bad. It is unfortunate I was not first in your pledge, but all is not lost. Now I know I have your loyalty, it brings me joy and confidence in our future.

But I'm not sure how long I can hold out against them. He must have read her desperation, but something deep inside her told her to give Lance a bit longer before she ate humble pie and asked to go back.

Another wave of affection washed through the bond, making her feel even guiltier.

Has anything been said of forming a bond with the king?

No, just Cesaré.

Again silence.

Malleven?

I am still here ... can I ask how your relationship is with your Human? I feel your unhappiness, mio fiore. *I fear he is not giving you what you need.*

Emotion welled up in her that she could have treated Malleven so badly and he still be so compassionate – so caring. *Can I ask you a question first?*

Of course ... If it is in my power.

How deep are your feelings for Antonio?

Amusement came through the bond then.

Don't laugh at me, Malleven.

He laughed loudly then. *What can I say,* mio fiore. *I know Antonio well. I am comfortable with him. It is easy ... as it should be. As it should be with your lover.*

It was a heavy hint that he more or less guessed how things were. She stifled a sob. *It is not easy ... in fact, it is always so hard.*

Malleven was quiet for a beat. *It would help me to under-*

stand if I knew who it was, Lily. I sense a shift in the bond when you bind someone to you, but I do not recognise any of the neural pathways.

Lily really didn't understand the mechanics of the bond, but what he was asking made her feel uneasy. Malleven was so powerful; there was no telling what he was capable of and what he would do to Lance if he decided he didn't like it. She opted for honesty. *I am afraid to tell you.*

Have you learnt nothing about me yet, mio fiore? *You are the other half of me. We are one and the same. That can never be broken – except by death itself.*

It was a sobering thought. *He is one of my Protectors.*

One of the surfers?

Yes.

The Human?

It frightened her that he already knew that much. *Yes,* she thought warily.

Ah yes …

It alarmed her for a second as she felt him inside her mind. She wasn't aware that he could do that at a distance. He was searching just like he did on that first time, except this time she hardly knew he was doing it. That was until he reached an area he hadn't been before. She flinched with the pain. *Malleven, please!*

He withdrew. *Pardon … I merely found the place in your mind you reserve for him. I will leave you to your privacy.*

Lily relaxed with relief when she felt him retreat. The whole idea of him knowing stuff about Lance felt creepy and wrong somehow. *You still haven't told me what to do about Cesaré?*

Ah, yes, Cesaré, my hapless cousin.

I don't think I can get away, she thought, beginning to panic again.

Do it.

What? She wasn't sure she understood. *You want me to complete the bond?* She needed to be absolutely sure on this.

I will level with you, mio fiore, *I have no issue either way with your bonding with Cesaré. It will be good for the stability of the Florianna family. What I will be interested in is when your pledge is expected with the king.*

Lily was alarmed. No one had said anything about that so far.

This will be necessary for the link between you and your sisters, Malleven explained.

She frowned. She had mixed feelings about the whole thing. It did occur to her that, for something that was meant to be like some magical connection between mates, it was getting banded about a bit like a commodity, and she wasn't sure she liked that. Although she did feel a measure of relief that she could go ahead and complete the bond with Cesaré with Malleven's blessing.

She was apprehensive about getting that close with the king. He was at least as powerful as Malleven. Her heart sank.

What is it, mio fiore?

You have helped me so much. I feel so ungrateful that I still feel so confused. A sob rocked through her. How could she admit to Malleven how deeply she felt for another man?

There was a long silence again. She'd given herself away. It devastated her that it was the way things were, and she had to hurt Malleven, who had been nothing but kind to her.

His sadness compounded her feelings of wretchedness. *You do these things for me, with Cesaré and the king, and your Human will come to you, I promise. You are the most beautiful Atlantean I have ever met; a mere Human cannot resist that.*

With that last heart-wrenching comment, she felt him

leave her. She cried real, heartfelt sobs then. It was so self-sacrificing of him when she knew how he felt about her.

She wiped her tears away with her fingers. It seemed unlikely that he would be able to convince Lance to be with her. Lance wouldn't do anything he didn't want to do.

CHAPTER 56

*L*ily was still hoping to see a glimpse of Lance when she was waiting to go into the water with Cesaré. They stood together at the large fountain, she in her swimsuit and he in his board shorts.

There were huddles of people in the great hall. The king, her father and uncle, with some other older people she didn't recognise. A group of Murrs, easily spotted because of their height and weird stillness, and a group of Italians she guessed were Cesaré's family. All seemed exuberant and excited with what was about to happen.

It all felt fake and wrong to her. They were all pleased because she was mating with Cesaré, but there was no mention of her legal marriage to Malleven, which was much more authentic than this one. It was all about power; something she was finding more and more distasteful.

Cesaré picked up her hands. "Thank you for coming to this decision, Lily. I will forever be in your debt." His startling blue eyes bore into hers.

I am still married to Malleven, she reminded him.

He smiled warmly. "He is a lucky man, and I am never

one to stand in the path of true love." His eyes were kind but slightly mocking.

Before she could come back with some cutting remark, Lance entered the room, and her eyes were lured straight to him. He remained right at the back with his brother Nathan and Shona, who waved and gave her a thumbs-up.

"How are things with Lance?" Cesaré asked, as if to add salt to the wound.

Her eyes flashed to his angrily. She could no more hide her feelings from Cesaré than she could from Malleven. It would be even worse when the bond was complete. She was suffocating.

Lance's eyes were on her continually. Every time she looked over her shoulder, there he was – *if looks could kill.* Her heart hammered when he didn't look away. *If only he would come and speak to her.* But he didn't, and she was stuck there.

Cesaré leaned down to her ear. "It's time."

Lily took a last, agonising look at Lance, whose face was like thunder, and she stepped into the fountain.

The ceremony was quick, just like they promised. They trod water in front of the large window so all the witnesses were satisfied with the marriage.

Lily breathed somewhat clinically for Cesaré to renew the pledge. Although she had to admit he did look pretty magnificent, fully transformed in his stripes. Despite their differences, he was a beautiful man, with his shoulder-length hair framing his handsome face while he drifted in the afterglow of her essence.

The euphoria passed, and with his eyes still low, he beckoned her to him.

This was it. The part she was dreading. It couldn't be much different from Malleven, she told herself. There was no more stalling and she cautiously approached him.

Cesaré placed his hands gently on her shoulders and pulled her in close. He completely dwarfed her now, looking remarkably like a full-blooded Murr. Then he gazed into her eyes with kindness.

Her heart slammed against her chest. *Malleven!* she called frantically.

Don't be afraid, came back instantly. *I am here but silent. Never think you are alone.*

She swallowed and tried to relax as Cesaré slowly slanted his mouth over hers. *Where was Lance when she needed him – when she needed his reassurance?* She parted her mouth to receive the tingling breath. It travelled over her tongue and moved slowly down into her body, feeling every millimetre.

It surprised her how different it was – like a signature or different personality. She guessed that was exactly what it was – the very root of a person. Her thoughts continued to scramble as it made its journey, getting hotter and hotter while it wrapped itself around her heart and exploded.

White light robbed her of vision, then left her with a feeling of absolute bliss. It felt warm and cosy like the softest cotton wool. It was easy and safe, and not at all demanding or forceful, as she'd become accustomed to from Malleven.

I have your power, and I have purer blood than my cousin, Cesaré projected, unnerving her by answering an unspoken question. She was wrapped in his arms while his laughter rang out in her head. He reluctantly put her away from him. *You are incredibly desirable, Lily.* His face was mischievous.

He must have read the horror on her face because he added, *Remember, I am always here for you as a friend.*

Lily studied his face.

He winked.

She was beginning to think she was getting to know his real personality and smiled in spite of herself. Maybe this arrangement wouldn't work out too badly after all.

Come; let's go back inside. We need to sign some documents and then it will be over.

She nodded and held his hand and they swam together towards the castle.

THEY CLIMBED out of the fountain to a round of applause. How different it was from her marriage to Malleven. It made her a little sad for him.

After emptying their lungs, they were wrapped in towels and the king pulled both of them into his arms and kissed them.

It lightened Lily's heart. Suddenly, she felt the most optimistic she had in a long time. She searched the room for Lance.

"Lance!" the king called.

Lily followed his line of vision, and was shocked to see Lance, Shona and his brother climbing the staircase about to leave.

A guard barred his way and pointed back to the king. Thankfully, he was forced to go back down. Her heart sank at his obvious reluctance. He only obeyed because he had no choice.

The king was busy talking Italian to Cesaré, so she slipped through the crowd to intercept him and get him on his own. She was gobsmacked when he attempted to ignore her and slip past her. *Please, Lance,* she projected, grabbing his arm. *Did he want her to beg?*

He looked down at the hand that held him and reluctantly looked at her.

"Lighten up, mate," Shona said.

Nathan smiled at her apologetically. Even he couldn't understand him. He put up a hand and moved away to give them some privacy. Shona gave her a reassuring nod and did the same.

You were leaving? she said, still not believing he was acting like this.

He looked her dead in the eye, then, so long her heart rate went up. It was as though he hated her, and she had no idea what she had done. "I said I would make sure you got here safely." Then he looked over at Cesaré, laughing with the king and his family. "You have Cesaré to look after you now."

Was this jealousy? There seemed to be no other explanation for this cold shoulder. *You knew I would have to replenish the bond with Cesaré,* she said, almost crying.

He didn't answer, but looked down at the hand that still held his arm. She let go of it instantly. All he wanted to do was escape from her and nothing she could say would change it.

"Lance!" the king called again.

Lance used it as an excuse to move away from her and her hand flopped down by her side. She would have skulked away to lick her wounds if the king hadn't called her to him as well.

Shona came up behind her and put her arm around her. "Remember what I said," she whispered.

Lily wasn't sure how much longer she could kid herself that Lance cared about her. All he did was give her little crumbs of affection and she was so pathetic that she gobbled them up and hung on like some lovesick puppy.

Cesaré pulled her into the circle of well-wishers, kindly. Of course, he was reading her feelings. Lance's face was cold and angry, staring confrontationally straight at Cesaré. Cesaré was looking back at him, puzzled and amused. The king looked from one to the other, trying to read the situation, and guessed there may be trouble. He whistled to a guard and nodded his head towards Lance.

It was so weird, it felt like a bad dream. Lance was always so laid-back and Cesaré was always happier around women; the last person you would imagine getting macho and butting heads with anyone.

"Lance!" the king barked to break his fixation. "Hey! I thought you two were friends?"

So did I, Cesaré projected, still unable to speak, glancing quickly at the king. *Are we okay, Lance?*

"Sure … I was just leaving," Lance said, giving her a filthy look as he went to turn away.

Lily felt like she'd been slapped. His lids were low with contempt and his body was tense, like a powder keg about to go off.

"It was a marriage for the state, Lance," the king tried to explain.

Lance just switched his dark look to the king.

The king was mildly taken aback but amused.

Lily's heart thumped. Surely this can't be over her.

"I wish the happy couple well, but I'm outta here." He went to turn away again.

The king signalled to the guard, who put out a hand.

"One more night, Lance. Then you can go," the king said.

Lily held her breath.

Lance shifted his weight with impatience. "What for? You have everything you need."

"Humour me," the king said, no longer laughing. "I'll send my nurse to your room to take a blood sample – you too, Nathan. I'm just waiting for something from Murrtaine. It will be here in the morning. Then, if you still want to, I promise you can go."

"Why do you need my blood?" Lance said, narrowing his eyes.

"Just routine."

Lance swore under his breath and pushed through the crowd. Nathan smiled an apology again and followed.

Lily was left stunned. It was as though their night at the beach never happened. It obviously meant a whole lot more to her than it did to him.

Cesaré put an arm around her shoulders. *Don't worry. This is out of character for him. He'll be okay.*

The king and Cesaré swapped a meaningful look that she was too upset to decipher. It felt as though she'd been totally cast adrift. Malleven wanted her here and she thought she'd be here with Lance. She looked at Cesaré and the king with tears in her eyes. *Where do I go from here?*

"Let's meet tomorrow morning in my study. We'll know more then."

But where will I live? She wiped her eyes and looked in the direction Lance had gone.

Cesaré gave her a squeeze.

"Here, most likely," the king said. Just give it tonight and we'll see."

LILY GOT IN BED AND, after settling down, she let her mind wander. Her skin still felt feverish, even after a cold shower, since breathing with Cesaré. It was a powerful, emotional experience and one she wasn't expecting. He certainly wasn't the person she'd built him up in her mind to be.

That brought her mind back to Lance. Everything always came back to him. She bashed her pillows with annoyance and attempted to settle again. Life would have been so easy if it didn't.

She was supposedly virtually a full-blooded Atlantean married to two royals; there shouldn't be room for anyone else, if all accounts were true. But Lance had lured her in from the moment they met as if he had mystical powers of his own. Yes, it had started the minute she stepped into his van.

And so her mind drifted on until sometime later she'd managed to fall into a fitful sleep.

Her eyes flashed open.

Her heart was beating so hard she could hear it in her ears. Someone was inside her room. She froze and held her breath, straining to hear quiet footfalls on the floor.

Who is it? she projected. Even her psychic voice felt restricted and squeaky.

"It's me."

Her eyes were wide in the darkness, instantly recognising the voice. *Lance.*

"Scoot over."

She should have been angry, but she was too surprised. Instead, she moved over before thinking about it. The bed dipped and he got in next to her. Without speaking, he slipped an arm under her and pulled her tightly against him. In the weirdest turnaround of events, her head was on his bare chest, a leg over his and his arms around her. Her temperature immediately soared and was soothed the minute her body came into contact with his. It was the first time it had occurred to her that it was strange. Malleven had to take her into water or give her some potion to drink, but for some unfathomable reason, with Lance, she was comfortable. In fact, when she thought about it, he'd always had that effect on her.

Nonetheless, she wasn't going to let him smooth over his bad treatment of her by creeping into her bed in the middle of the night. Her brain shook off the soppy sentimental claptrap and she became angry. *What's going on with you, Lance? Why are you here? Weren't you trying to leave?* she projected but didn't pull away; she found that she couldn't.

Lance sighed deeply. "You've got every right to be mad at me, I'm all over the place. I can't explain it."

Lily leaned up on her elbow. Despite the darkness, she had good night vision and could clearly see the beautiful lines of his face. *I did warn you. I explained that it was for ever. You told me to do it.*

"I know," he said, stroking a finger down the side of her face.

A tingle of electricity shot through her straight to her core.

"I'm not talking about the bond – that was awesome, but it was happening even before that. Don't you see? You've been in my dreams over and over since I was a kid. It's like a madness that, since the bond, has got fuckin' worse."

With every word he spoke with anger and real passion, he was actually drawing her mouth closer to his. And even though she knew he hated himself for it, he closed his mouth over hers like some junkie. Then let loose with the most blistering of kisses – one so powerful she couldn't reject. Open-mouthed, she ate him up like she was starved. Stroking and twirling her tongue with his, she pushed her body tightly into him. She found herself moving rhythmically on his leg that had become nestled between hers.

The first spike in body heat immediately dissipated with his touch into a simmering warmth across her sensitive shoulders. The electrifying tingle that had set her alight and calmed her right from the beginning. He was cooling her and igniting her at the same time. Everywhere his body touched, he complemented, eased, and electrified. It made no sense. They shouldn't be able to be like this out of the water.

It was so overwhelming that she went to break away.

"Don't stop, Lily, please," he said with slow, sexy bites along her jawline and down her neck. Little spears of erotic heat shot to her heart and immediately cooled, but warmed into coiling desire in her lower abdomen. Instead of pushing him away, her hands found the loose waistband of his jeans. *Off!* she commanded.

He immediately obeyed, lifted his hips and wriggled them down. She helped him pull them off his feet, then pulled her sleepshirt over her head. He pushed her over onto her back, but instead of putting his weight straight down, he hovered over her, slowly letting himself down as if the sensation was as electrifying to him as it was to her. They both gasped at the point their skin made contact. It felt like everything between them was amplified – a total sensory overload.

Lance cupped her jaw with his hand and, even though it was dark, she knew he was staring into her eyes. She pushed back his silky hair and rubbed a thumb along his cheek.

The bond bubbled and pushed in her chest; determined to be heard. *I love you, Lance.*

His thumb went over her lips as if he was sensing it there. *Do you want my breath?*

There was no reply, but his mouth slowly covered hers, and he kissed her slowly and reverently. It was a sensual invitation and his hips began to circle into hers. His hardness pushed and nudged into her soft wetness, teasing and tempting. He was deliberately driving her mad. *It will only bind you tighter to me,* she tried, before she lost her half-hearted control. It was her last-ditch attempt at a warning.

CHAPTER 57

Lance nuzzled into the curve of her neck, his heavy erection still pressed to the softest part of her. He seemed to want her to snap, to take control and the decision away from him. He lingered over the ticking pulse at her neck, licking and nipping until she quivered with need. He continued his way, kissing down the column of her neck until he found and circled her hard, waiting nipple. She gasped and writhed beneath him. He smiled against her skin – the sod knew precisely what he was doing. A blast of raw sexual pleasure washed over her. Her hands gripped the smooth skin of his shoulders. He continued to torment her by blowing and drawing her nipple into his mouth.

You bastard! she projected in a needy whisper.

His mouth teased and nipped his way back to her mouth and she felt the smile playing on his lips.

Before she allowed herself to let go, she just had to know: *Are you here just because of Cesaré? Are you just staking some macho claim?* Even though she risked ruining the moment, she just had to know. Nothing was making sense with him.

He paused, breathing heavily. "No, I am not."

What's going on with you, Lance? You pull me in and cast me off so fast I don't know what's happening. You're angry with me, angry with Cesaré, and he's one of your best friends. Please ... I need to understand.

Then, just as she feared, the fire between them went out and Lance pushed off her. She reached over and switched on the bedside lamp. He was sitting with his elbows on his knees. And when he looked over his shoulder at her, she was shocked. His eyes were hollow, dark and ruined. He looked like a man in agony, with the life sucked out of him.

The wind totally went out of her sails. She wanted to be angry with him, but it simply evaporated when she saw the state of him. He always looked so healthy.

Instead, she crawled towards him and put her arms around his neck. He pulled her into his lap. *My God, Lance, what's the matter ... is it me?*

He nuzzled into her shoulder and just breathed her in. "The truth ..." he said with a sigh. "I don't know what the hell's wrong with me." He pulled apart slightly and ran his fingers through his hair. "Ever since I met you, it's been like I'm outta control. Like I'm fighting something – heading towards some disaster – and there isn't a damn thing I can do about it." He looked at her as if he were totally defeated. "Love shouldn't hurt this bad, should it?"

Lily looked into his eyes, amazed. She should be upset about being called a disaster, but it was rare for him to mention love. She found herself cradling him in her arms, whispering *Shh,* and gently rocking him.

Her hand stroked his hair and trailed over his feverish back. *I'm so sorry, Lance.* She couldn't think of what else to say. He'd have been so much happier if he'd never met her. But the truth was, that just the same as him, her damned vulnerable heart had been his from day one and she simply had no defence against him. And she wasn't sure she wanted one.

Lance remained silent in her arms for a while, until he began to feel cooler and calmer. Lily continued to play with his long strands of hair and run her hand over the tattoo on his back. The very symbol that bound them together from the beginning – and way before she'd breathed with him. *Maybe there is more to it?* she thought absently.

He pulled out of her arms to look at her with bleary, bloodshot eyes. "Like what?"

Maybe we were meant to be together ... did you ever think of that? Did you ever wonder that maybe you shouldn't fight it ... that there are some things in this world that are stronger than we are?

His eyes seemed to glaze over while he thought about it. "But you're married ... to two men, Lily," he said eventually, as if dismissing it.

She stiffened in his arms. *I was kind of pushed into it both times, you know.*

He continued to search her face until the corners of his mouth began to curl into a small, flirting smile. *How did he manage to do that?*

Annoying laughter bubbled up in her. It bugged her that he broke through her defences when she wanted to hang on to her anger a bit longer. She sobered suddenly. *I never would have gone to Malleven that night if ... well, you know.*

He nodded thoughtfully, his eyes already straying to her mouth. It made her smile and she wriggled around in his lap so she could face him and clamp her legs around his back.

His eyes stayed riveted to hers the whole time. She brushed her lips against his. *Open ...*

He relaxed under her hands with complete acceptance and parted his lips.

She could feel the surge in his blood as his heart rate

jacked. He was already closing his eyes. *Don't!... Stay with me.* With that, his eyes held hers.

Her breath came out steadily in a long, constant flow and his brow furrowed in a blessed torture. But he stayed there, right with her the whole time.

With their eyes locked, Lily could see every wave of pleasure cross his face. This one moment made all the anguish between them worthwhile, because instead of pushing her away, his arms came around her backside and pulled her onto his hard erection in his lap, sparking a near-painful need. His mouth began to move over hers, changing the intake of breath into a demanding kiss. His tongue pushed into her mouth with a feral ferocity that made her gasp. This incendiary need in him wasn't just coaxing her into giving him everything; it was leaving her without a choice. She was being outwitted – outmanoeuvred.

It felt like her words had finally made sense to him and he was no longer fighting her. It wasn't just acceptance, he was welcoming it – welcoming her.

With every movement of his hips and every touch of his cooling hands, it ran liquid to the rippling tissues at her core. They moved together, her blowing intermittently until it nestled in his heart. There it took root and he could no longer hold eye contact and threw his head back and groaned loudly. His eyes rolled up into his head in ecstasy and all he could do was let go.

Lily held him as he fell backwards onto the bed, where he shuddered and convulsed with endless waves of pleasure. His body was gorgeous, ripped and corded, writhing in bliss – his length hard and straining for her. He was irresistible in the soft orange glow of the lamp, gasping in pleasure – the most beautiful thing she'd ever seen.

Without further thought, she gripped him and placed him to her, and sank slowly onto him. Then she began to move on him torturously slowly. His eyes were barely open and his lips parted enough to let out a contented sigh. The sensation and the sight of him were so intense that everything clenched in her lower body. Her heart soared when he arched his back instinctively. She never imagined sex could be like this.

He began to be able to coordinate himself again and his hands gripped her hips to help her tired legs. She hitched a breath in surprise when he adeptly pushed her over onto her back and was on her again in a flash. He spread her thighs, moving slowly, deliberately, stroking her delicate muscles over and over. He turned her body to liquid with his deep, measured strokes – His hardness sinking home time and time again into her possessive heat. His pace began to build, ramming and pushing her into the bed. She realised how much he must have held back the other night. His thickness pounded over and over, building to such ferocity that she felt herself scatter, body and mind, as they literally came to pieces in each other's arms.

Exhausted, Lance flopped down and their bodies slid together with sweat as they tangled in a heap of limbs and sheets.

Both of them were breathing heavily and didn't speak for a long while. Lily was so satisfied, she couldn't think of a single thing to say. She loved him and he must surely know it from her essence. She only wished he could do it back, to stop the doubts before they crept in. For now, it was enough to feel him close and contented before he tried to run from her again. If only they could stay like this for ever, the way she was sure it was meant to be between them.

After the franticness of the first time, they found their bodies began to move towards each other again – slower, tenderly exploring. They spent the rest of the night as lovers, completely lost in each other.

. . .

Lily woke up smiling in the morning and her heart fluttered. Lance was lying half on top of her, breathing softly into her hair. He hadn't run away – not that he could. She was sure she had exhausted him completely. In the meantime, she revelled in the completely comfortable buzz she felt, despite all the bruises, aches, and pains he'd given her. And he didn't make her too hot, which still amazed her about him. If she had vocal cords, she would have purred.

Nothing was making sense, but right now, she was going to enjoy and languish in the tingly warm feeling Lance always gave her.

"What are you grinning at?" he said, with a lovely croaky morning voice.

She moved her head slightly to look at him, but his eyes were still closed. *How did you know I was smiling?*

"I know it all now – remember?"

She sighed and nestled back into him and supposed he did. She kissed his shoulder open-mouthed, tasting his skin. She nudged him reluctantly. *I think we'd better get up, Lance. I got the impression the king was serious about seeing you this morning.*

Lance sighed deeply and tried to get up slowly as if he were hungover. He threw his legs over the side of the bed, rested on his knees and ran his fingers through his sundried hair.

Lily watched him carefully. This was the part she always dreaded; the nice time they'd spent together was coming to an end, to be followed by the inevitable let-down. *Don't run away,* she whispered in his head.

He let his hand drop and looked over his shoulder at her. "I need to know one thing, Lily, and you have to be honest with me?"

Okay, she thought, holding her breath.

"How do you feel about Malleven? ... Because, man ... I don't get it."

It was a fair question, one he deserved an answer to. He could now feel her, and her emotions were a mess. *Well, when I originally went to him, it had a lot to do with thinking I had nothing to lose. He was nice to me and promised me everything.*

Her heart thumped as she watched him frown.

"And now?"

I won't lie to you, Lance; I do have genuine affection for him.

Lance nodded and looked down at the floor, as if it was what he expected.

I haven't finished, Lance.

His eyes were flat and dead when he looked back at her, as if the light had gone out of them. He was shutting down again and she wouldn't allow it. She crawled towards him over the bed and gripped his arm to stop him bolting. *Listen to me, okay? But I know I don't love him ... At first, I was bowled over by all the attention and grand gestures, and the way he swept me off my feet. But then I found out about Antonio, and then you and me finally became close for the first time ... and I just knew. It has always been you ... nothing will ever come close.*

They looked into each other's eyes for a long moment. She wanted to convey how much she meant her words so he could gauge her sincerity. *Can't you feel me in you now, Lance ... can't you feel me?*

After a few agonising moments, he nodded.

Please give us a chance – at least stay to hear what the king has to say.

A blast of air left him in a mirthless laugh and he shook his head as if she baffled him.

. . .

THE TWO OF them presented themselves in the king's study as soon as they'd showered and dressed. Nathan and Shona had joined them and they were ushered inside the room.

"Ah, there you are!" the king said with a warm smile.

Lily looked around at all the faces in the room.

There was Cesaré, sitting to the king's right, the big Murr, Vionne, leaning against the wall to his left, her uncle and father, and a small, older gentleman she hadn't met, sitting with them on a sofa.

"Take a seat," Dante said, indicating to the three chairs arranged opposite him. Shona was given a chair at the back of the room.

Lily looked sideways at Lance, who was gazing around as wary as she was. She wondered how all this had anything to do with Nathan. It wasn't as if he and Lance were blood relatives, but she was comforted a bit by his presence. To her, he was one of her Protectors, just the same as Shona. Lily checked over her shoulder, and Shona raised her eyebrows to say she was as mystified as she was.

"Right!" the king said. "We'll get straight down to business. The blood test results are back ... no surprises there, really. You, Nathan, are quite a mixture, but you have a lot of Dubonnetti in you. Welcome to the family," he said with a grin. "And you, Lance ... are completely Human of Northern European descent.

Lance looked bored and shrugged. "We already knew that."

"Well, you see, you were a bit of a puzzle," the king said, relaxing back in his chair. "There were a few things Cesaré said, and I saw myself in your behaviour around Lily, and it got me thinking that maybe there was a bit more to you."

Lance looked at Cesaré to give him a clue.

"Humans don't act as you do around a Siren; it's just unheard of," Cesaré said.

"So I thought I'd get my man Max here ..."

Max nodded a greeting.

"To look into your history and anything about Humans in our old books."

Lily gripped Lance's hand but watched Dante intently. She almost crossed her fingers that there was something tangible to tie her to Lance. They needed something.

"Tell 'em what you found, Max."

The old gentleman stood up with his bundle of papers and coughed to clear his throat. "It was really rather fascinating when I sifted through the mysterious circumstances of your adoption and what it might mean in relation to the ancient tomes of Atlantis. Some interesting facts came to light.

"You see, back in Atlantis before it was destroyed, its inhabitants had many religions, but the one that thrived at the time was the Order of the Five Moons. (The five moons are of significance because they represented the ones that orbited their former planet, Atlas) But this is where it gets interesting. As with most things in Atlasian culture, it was the women who took precedence and, in this case, not only was it an order of priestesses, but an order of Human women – five, to be exact. The rights of each priestess could only be passed down to their female offspring. Each one represented the ancient elements of Atlas, that is: Electricity, Water, Ice, Wind and the Sun."

Lily watched Cesaré mouth the words of each one. *What happened to all the boys?* she asked, not sure she wanted to know the answer. She gripped Lance's hand tightly.

"Good question," Max said, inclining his head towards her. "There were no boys born. I checked and rechecked – everything was documented, you see. That is, unless Sirens were on the earth. It was treated as the loudhailer to begin the search."

"Unfortunately, after the destruction of Atlantis, the importance of the sect was realised by everyone, and so it was forced to go into seclusion. Human agents would destroy them, and Atlantean royals wanted the upper hand over the other families."

Lance began to fidget and Lily sensed they had about two minutes before his attention span went completely. *Where does Lance fit in?*

Those very rare male offspring were known through history as the Incarnates and were believed to be the reincarnation of the very first boy born to the order in Atlantis. It is my belief that you, Lance, are the very last of these."

Lily squeezed his hand, but he remained motionless, facing Max.

"I discovered that the last-known surviving priestess served the goddess of the wind and, when the last temple was burnt to the ground in the early nineties, she had already arranged for a respectable Atlantean family to care for you." Max paused and smiled at Nathan.

Nathan nodded. "He came when he was around three years old."

Lance looked at him and frowned.

"It seems that your incarnation always awaited your corresponding goddess of the wind … Lily."

Lily sagged. It all sounded ridiculous. *Come on, how do you know that?*

Max looked at her as if it were obvious. "Because you are the Siren of the wind, Lily."

She looked at the king, who looked thoughtful and then began to smile. "Lillian Gale – Wind!" he said with a blast of laughter, turning to Cesaré.

"Isla Snow – Ice!" Cesaré said, testing the theory.

"Lacy Rain – Water!" they said together.

"And Tia Storm – Electricity," the king said, smiling

ruefully. "Figures." He shook his head. "Right under our noses all the time … But this means something more, Max."

"I agree," Max said, nodding. "There must be a greater significance to those elements being related to each Siren, but I haven't got to the bottom of that yet."

"That still doesn't explain why Lance reacts the way he does to Lily," Cesaré said.

"Quite right … I had to delve deeper … The Siren legend says that each Siren is the reincarnation of one of the original daughters taken from each family when Atlantis was punished and destroyed. It seems that every time they emerge on the earth, a boy is born to the Wind Priestess."

"Now it would appear that the very first Siren fell in love with this firstborn boy ... The legend gets a bit hazy after that, but the gist of it is that they fall in love at every incarnation. They find each other only to be ripped apart before they can get together. It seems he is always cut down by one of the princes seeking to marry her. It's a story of star-crossed love told around the campfire for centuries, always doomed to fail as she would always outlive him."

The king was nodding. "We live long lives," he said thoughtfully.

Like, how long? Lily said, pulling Lance's hand into her lap.

"Up to around three hundred years or so to a life-span."

Max was looking uncomfortable.

What? Lily said, her throat already constricting.

"All the ancient texts say that the boy never lives much beyond young adulthood … Aquilo, as he is known, always dies protecting his Siren. He always dies young."

Lily sat stunned. In fact, the whole room did the same.

No... I can't believe it. It's a load of old wives' tales.

When she glanced at Lance, he was running his finger over the underside of his wrist. He had many small tattoos as well as the large piece of her on his back. There, in ancient font, were six letters spelling the name Aquilo. Stamped like irrefutable proof of what they were saying. It was so small and insignificant; she'd never taken any notice of it.

Lance's eyes went to hers with a look of bewilderment. "It means the north wind," he said. "It was important that it meant that … I can remember …" his voice trailed off like he was lost.

She gripped his hand. The whole thing was astonishing. But she had to admit she loved the idea of the romance behind the story. It was the kind of love she'd only ever dreamt of, and far too foolish to admit to anyone in real life.

He continued to look into her eyes as if he could find the answers there. Her heart caught in her chest. To think that they hadn't just fallen for each other in this life, but in many lifetimes before. *Why not … why couldn't this be true,* she thought more for her own benefit than anyone else's. *Everything else in her life was seriously weird; why not this? Why couldn't she have an extraordinary love?*

Lily had been so lost in thought and Lance's eyes that the king coughed to get their attention. "I almost forgot."

Lance broke the stare and they both looked over at the king. Vionne was passing Dante a dark blue velvet bag. He emptied the contents into the palm of his hand. There were two rings, similar but not identical to each other, both pearl white. The king had one on his hand, except his was turquoise.

Cesaré nodded and smiled, as if he got what Dante was going to do.

Lance continued to look bewildered.

Dante turned to Cesaré and held one out to him. "I thought it was time you wore one under happier circumstances … I noticed your finger was empty. He pointed at Cesaré's left hand and smiled with real warmth.

Cesaré appeared slightly overcome with emotion and

shook his head. He exhaled a small blast of laughter. "I threw mine in the sea."

"Well?" Dante said, with his eyebrows raised.

Cesaré took the ring and nodded. He held it and pushed what looked like a clip on the side, and a spike, almost an inch long, shot out from the band.

Lily watched in horror as Cesaré put it partway onto the middle finger of his left hand, held his breath, and pushed it hard all the way. It pierced the delicate skin between his knuckles and blood immediately ran between his fingers.

She looked around the room in shock at all the rapt expressions watching his hand intently. *Was she the only one thinking it was barbaric?*

When no one else looked away, curiosity got the better of her and she became glued to the spectacle again. Smoke began to swirl around the opaque white stone, gradually changing to blood red. Then smoke appeared again and it changed to the same turquoise colour of the king's, and settled at that. In fact, when she glanced at all the men wearing rings, they were all exactly the same colour.

Dante laughed. "Welcome back, my friend."

Sebastian, Alfonzo and Vionne all clapped. It was baffling.

Then the room fell silent again when the king's attention turned back to Lance. He sat forward and held out the other ring. "Your turn."

Lance looked sideways to Nathan, who shrugged, and then to her. *You don't have to,* she projected. It looked like some silly macho right of passage and really painful.

"Humour me," Dante said.

Lance stood, reached over and took the ring from the king's hand.

After a quick inspection, he found the catch and released the spike. Then he glanced at Dante for confirmation that he wanted him to copy what Cesaré did.

"Just make sure it breaks the skin. It needs your blood to work," the king said. Then he raised his eyebrows at Cesaré as if to say, "This will be interesting."

With a last look at her, Lance inhaled a deep breath and pushed it onto his finger, blinking hard with the obvious pain.

The blood trickled and the smoke swirled the same as it did before.

"It hasn't burnt him yet," Cesaré said.

Lily looked over at him, alarmed.

"Humans can't normally bear the metal against their skin," the king explained.

Her eyes fell on it again as it reached the blood-red phase.

"Wait for it," the king said, clearly delighted.

Then it swirled and settled on the most beautiful shade of purple.

CHAPTER 58

*D*ante clapped his hands, laughing loudly. "There it is … I knew it," he said, pointing his finger.

Cesaré and Vionne looked really shocked. Sebastian was smiling benignly and Alfonzo was taking notes.

What the hell is going on?

"I don't get it?" Cesaré said.

"There it is, man … the Wildcard Prophecy, right there," the king said, still laughing. "I had a hunch … tell 'em Max."

Max was smiling broadly as well when he took a single page out of his notes. "The original Siren Prophecy states there should be five Sirens destined for five sons from each of the royal families."

Cesaré wasn't getting it and neither was she.

"The Sirens are from the Bonaci family," Max continued, "In some generations, one has come from a distant branch of the Sirens' family, but to guard against too close a family connection, there is a wildcard. They could be from any one of the families, or, it seems in this case, someone from the Human world – an Incarnate."

"It's perfect," the king said, shaking his head in disbelief.

"To take someone already connected to our race, but from the host species of this planet. What better representation for the council: a prince from each family and one Human."

"Yes, but that would be six, and what of the Bonaci?" Cesaré said. "There is no one on the council for them."

Dante tipped his head to acknowledge the good point. "I think we'll have to see how it plays out with the last Siren."

Would someone mind explaining it to me? Lily said, still completely confused. *What does the purple ring mean?*

"Your man here is your destined mate … the most compatible mate for you," Dante explained. Then he grinned mischievously at Lance. "Welcome to the race."

AFTER THE MONUMENTAL meeting that still left Lily in a dazed state of shock, she finally got to spend some time alone with Lance in her room. He seemed completely numb following the revelations.

When she thought about it, it all made such complete sense. The way they had always felt such a strong recognition for each other. The way he could soothe her high temperature with just a mere touch.

Lance was sitting on the edge of the bed, still staring at the name inked on the inside of his wrist. "Can it be true?" he said.

Can it be anything else? she threw back, linking her arms around his neck. She kind of liked the idea that they were always meant to be together.

"But what now?" he said, looking up with hopelessness in his eyes. "Nothing's changed. There's still Malleven … and what I see every time I sleep … when I touch you."

Tell me about it. What do you see?

"I used to think they were dreams, but now I'm not so sure."

What do you think they are?

"I think they are past times we've been together."

Like past lives? she said, sitting up and looking at him.

He nodded.

What is it?

He smiled a little. "They're always off the chart hot … me and you always doing the deed," he said with a sad smile. "But then it morphs into something. There's blood … a lot of it. It looks like … I kill you." He pulled out of her arms and stood up. The caged Lance was returning like he couldn't wait to get away from her.

The morning's surprises had been bewildering. Lily felt a mixture of confusion and exasperation with him. When she ran through what she'd learnt and what Lance had just told her, she could only come up with one conclusion. She wouldn't let him run away this time.

Lily stood behind him and gently touched his arms. *But it's not me that dies, is it, Lance. I don't think the blood you see is mine … I think it's yours.*

EPILOGUE

The very first of the king's council meetings was in session and there was just one empty seat. Dante smiled as Lance took his.

The prophesied wildcard – it still amazed him.

He would carry the Human vote, as proven by divining ring. Cesaré would represent the Florianna as first pledged to the same Siren – as he held her power. Even though it should have been him, Dante wasn't too disappointed at the outcome.

His eyes travelled around the circular table reminiscent of King Arthur's. Darres, the huge and brooding Murr, had made the trip to represent the Borge, and Sebastian and Alfonzo continued to represent the Bonaci. It seemed the right thing to do as they had steered the nation all these years – at least until another representative from their family appeared – or not, as the case may be.

And lastly, Keenan, now able to leave Lacy after she had made a full recovery. Dante kept him sweating over the debacle that happened in his house with Tia – although, secretly, he didn't hold him responsible.

It felt good when he brought the meeting to order and held the first Atlantean council meeting for a thousand years. He felt kind of choked up when he welcomed them all.

They quickly worked through the agenda. Lance was officially introduced, various topics were discussed, and it was decided that they would meet quarterly.

After it was brought to a close, Lance approached him and thanked him for the trust he was putting in him.

"Don't mention it," Dante said. "It was the fates who spoke loudly. I just listened." He smiled broadly. "How are things with Lily?"

Lance nodded. "Good … we seem to be doing okay."

Dante touched him affectionately on the shoulder. Things were really starting to come together. He had three Sirens directly pledged to him and a fourth pledged to someone he could trust at his right hand.

"Just one left," Lance said, as if reading his mind,

Dante nodded. "Very true … it's just a matter of time."

"Won't you want them all pledged to you … if I understand right?"

Dante paused at the comment, just for a beat, and tipped his head in agreement.

Lance smiled and left Dante watching him a while after he went.

He felt Cesaré next to him. "Problem?"

Dante frowned. "I'm not sure." He was getting another of those gut feelings. Princes didn't usually take well to him bonding with their wives.

He shrugged the thoughts away. Lance wasn't Atlantean. *Still, it was odd. And he could have sworn the guy's eyes had gone weird again. Like he had glitter in them for a moment.*

He shook his head and put his arm around Cesaré's shoulders. "Where do you think the next one will turn up?"

* * *

Click here to: https://books2read.com/u/49qezJ to read book 5, Night Goddess, right away!

CONTACT T

To receive your two, 21st Century Sirens Novellas, and be the first to know anything relating to T's books, leave your details here: tstedmannovellas
And please don't forget to leave a review wherever you bought your book, I really appreciate the feedback.
Much love
T
www.tstedman.com
Facebook
X
TikTok

ACKNOWLEDGMENTS

A special thank you to the surfing community of Twitter –
Jay and Jack Morrissey and the RealSurfinChef, for all their
advice on essential films, art, language, and what it really is
to live the Endless Summer. My readers for being patient
through a turbulent year of house moves and heart-
wrenching new starts, and not forgetting Diane Burke and
Stephen Maden for casting a critical eye.

GLOSSARY

Characters in family groups
Bonaci
Alfonzo Bonaci – Head of the Bonaci royal family and uncle to the Sirens
Sebastian Bonaci – Brother to Alfonzo and father to the Sirens
Luca Bonaci – Half-brother to the Sirens
Dino Bonaci – Full brother to Luca and half brother to the Sirens
Tia Storm – Siren – First wife and most compatible to Dante – queen – bonded to Jay
Lacy Rain – Siren – Mated and most compatible to Keenan Santalini – second wife to Dante
Isla Snow – Siren – Mated to Darres Borge, third wife to Dante. Most compatible to Malleven
Lilian Gale – Siren – Mated and most compatible to Lance McCabe – bonded to Cesaré Florianna by First Breath and therefore the only Siren not married to Dante

Royal Children

Xavier – Son of Dante and Tia
Alexia – Daughter of Dante and Tia
JJ – Son of Jay and Tia

Borge
Darl – Lord Advocate of Murrtaine and father to Vionne,
Dax, Caan, Axyl and Darres
Vionne Borge – Murr and eldest son and successor to Darl
Dax Borge – Son of Darl, brother to Vionne
Caan Borge – Son of Darl, brother to Vionne
Axyl Borge – Son of Darl, brother to Vionne, Dax, Caan,
twin of Darres and ruler of Murrla
Darres Borge – Son of Darl, twin of Axyl, brother to Vionne,
Dax and Caan – Mate to Isla Snow
Naomi – Wife to Sabastian Bonaci – Mother to Sirens

Royal children

Keefa – Son of Darres and Isla Snow
Dannon – Son of Darres and Isla Snow

Dubonnetti
Dante Dubonnetti – King and most compatible mate and
married to Tia Storm and Lacy Rain
Duke Ormond Deliss – Biological father to Dante and
Ambassador for the Atlanteans in Washington DC
Christian Dubonnetti – Stepfather to Dante and head of the
Dubonnetti royal family
Marco Dubonnetti – Half Brother to Dante
Paulo Dubonnetti – Half Brother to Dante
Antonio Dubonnetti – Half Brother to Dante – Lover to
Malleven Mancini
Stephan Dubonnetti – Youngest – Half Brother to Dante

Florianna
Cesaré Florianna – One of the five sons of the Florianna and cousin to Malleven Mancini
Sandro Florianna – Eldest brother to Cesaré
David, Roberto and Mario – Brothers to Cesaré
Malleven Mancini – Cousin to Cesaré – most compatible with Isla – Married to Lilian Gale
Ronaldo Florianna – Cesaré's Father
Rodrigo Mancini – Uncle and benefactor to Malleven

Santalini
Andreas – Elder of the Florianna royal family and uncle to Keenan Santalini
Keenan Santalini – Most compatible and mated to Lacy Rain
Ruby Santalini – Sister to Keenan
Marius Santalini – Eldest brother to Keenan
Adriano, Drago and Louis – Brothers to Keenan
Reeve Santalini – Fellow guard and cousin to the brothers

The Humans
Lance McCabe – Most compatible mate to Lilian Gale – Reincarnated from the male heir of the sect of the Five Moons (Incarnates)
Jay Gardiner – Protector/Lover bonded to Tia Storm – Best friend to Dante
Max Brunswick – Advisor to Dante for Atlantean history and language.
Nasr – High Priest of the Magi

Those filling council seats and whom they represent
Dante Dubonnetti – King and head of council representing the Dubonnetti
Cesaré Florianna – King's right hand and representing the Florianna

Keenan Santalini – Representing the Santalini
Darres Borge – Representing the Borge/Murrs
Lance McCabe – Representing the Human population
Sebastian and Alfonzo Bonaci – Representing the Bonaci in
the absence of a Bonaci mate.

Protectors (Appearing in this book)
Nathan – Surfer & Lance McCabe's brother
Shona Mathews– Surfer

Terms particular to the Atlanteans

Divining ring – worn by all princes and forged particularly
for them. Can only have one wearer. Forged from the Orb
itself. Determines whether a Siren is nearby and the wearer's
status to her by its color
Opaque white – default resting color
Turquoise/green – a Siren is nearby
Purple – the Siren nearby is the wearer's most compatible
mate

Elixir – Potion taken by princes and those humans in
contact with a Siren to prevent an extreme reaction or even
death in the event of breathing her essence.

First Breath – The breath passed from a Siren for the very
first time. Her power passes to the recipient only on the very
first exchange. Usually reserved for the king.

The Magi – an ancient order of magicians and alchemists of
which Malleven belongs. Mainly Human in origin, but have
worked alongside the Atlantean nation since the beginning
of their colonization.

The Orb – the ancient power source of Atlanteans. Believed to rest beneath Murrtaine and came with their ancestors from Atlas.

485

ALSO BY T STEDMAN

21st Century Sirens Series

Soul Breather

Blood Sister

Shield Maiden

Tiger Lily

Night Goddess

Darkly Begotten

The Dark Valentines Collection

Diablo

The Watchers

Star Child

Non-Fiction

My Migraine Story